STRENGTH FROM LOYALTY (LOST KINGS MC #3)

AUTUMN JONES LAKE

COPYRIGHT

STRENGTH FROM LOYALTY

LOST KINGS MC #3

AUTUMN JONES LAKE

Edited by: Cassie McGowan at Gathering Leaves Editing
Edited by: Marti Lynch
2018 Cover Designed by: Letitia Hasser, RBA Designs
Photography: Wander Aguiar Photography
Model: Kaz

Strength From Loyalty (Lost Kings MC, Book 3) / Autumn Jones Lake

This is an original work of fiction by Autumn Jones Lake. Published by Ahead of the Pack, LLC.

AutumnJLake@gmail.com

2nd Edition

STRENGTH FROM LOYALTY ⚜ LOST KINGS MC #3 ⚜ ROCK & HOPE ⚜ BY AUTUMN JONES LAKE

As a dark cloud descends over Hope and Rock's already precarious future, will a long-hidden secret push them both past the point of no return?

Struggling attorney Hope Kendall loves her outlaw biker boyfriend Rochlan "Rock" North with all her heart, but the questionable activities his motorcycle club is involved in threaten her legal career.

But does she even want this career anymore?

As a near-death situation makes their professional differences seem insignificant, a cloud descends over their personal relationship's already unsteady future.

Even though Hope seems to have finally found her niche in the club as Rock's ol' lady, can she mingle in politics with neighboring clubs as well? A trip to the Lost Kings MC downstate charter will put her to the test.

While Rock works hard to give Hope the honesty she craves without betraying his loyalty to his brothers, tension from outside forces threatens to push him to the brink. But it's the one secret *Hope* has hidden all along that may finally drive them apart for good.

ACKNOWLEDGMENTS

I know some people prefer to put these at the end. But I feel it's important to thank the people who made Strength from Loyalty possible up front. So here goes:

My faithful critique partners, Cara Connelly, Kari W. Cole and Virginia Frost. You've entertained some very filthy questions from me with this book. Thank you for not kicking me out of the group! I'm sorry to say the next one won't be any cleaner.

KA Mitchell, who has been as excited about my success as I am. Thank you so much for always taking the time to help me work through problematic scenes.

Angi J., Brandy, Chris, Clarisse, Elizabeth, Iveta, Katie, Krystal, Shauna, and Shelly. Thank you from the bottom of my heart for sticking with me. Thank you for your wonderful advice, suggestions and sharing your stories with me.

Shauna, thanks for listening to my crazy on an almost daily basis.

LJ, thank you for your patience and another beautiful cover!

Thank you, Cassie for taking me on at the last minute.

Marti, thanks for sticking with me and being so enthusiastic about my work.

Elizabeth, Terra, Jorja, Navene, and Grace, thank you for the time you spend promoting my books.

Not Another Damn Blog and Jordan Marie thanks for inviting me to my first author take overs. I always have a blast.

Readers who have taken the time to reach out to me in one way or another—thank you so much!

There are so many other people I'd like to thank, but I'm afraid I'll forget someone.

Last and never least, my husband, who works so hard so that I can spend time playing with my imaginary friends—thank you. None of this would be possible without you. I'm tickled by how much you love the Lost Kings.

LOST KINGS MC SERIES READING ORDER

Slow Burn (Lost Kings MC #1)
Corrupting Cinderella (Lost Kings MC #2)
Three Kings, One Night (Lost Kings MC #2.5)
Strength From Loyalty (Lost Kings MC #3)
Tattered on My Sleeve (Lost Kings MC #4)
White Heat (Lost Kings MC #5)
Between Embers (Lost Kings MC #5.5)
More Than Miles (Lost Kings MC #6)
White Knuckles (Lost Kings MC #7)
Beyond Reckless (Lost Kings MC #8)
Beyond Reason (Lost Kings MC #9)
One Empire Night (Lost Kings MC #9.5)
After Burn (Lost Kings MC #10)
Zero Tolerance (Lost Kings MC #11)
White Lies (Lost Kings MC #12)

STAND ALONES SET IN THE LOST KINGS MC WORLD
Bullets & Bonfires
Teller and Murphy appear here.

Warnings & Wildfires
Wrath and Murphy appear here.
Matches & Misfires

DEDICATION

For those who have struggled with depression and loss.

CHAPTER ONE

ROCK

THE THOUGHT OF HOPE WEARING MY PROPERTY PATCH GETS ME HARDER than a motherfucker.

It's time for me to announce my intent at church. Technically, I don't *need* the club's approval. I can claim whoever I want. But if I'm going to give her the Lost Kings property patch, I need the votes of my officers. Even though she doesn't yet realize it, being my old lady gives Hope a lot of power. She knows, or will learn, shit law enforcement would love to know. Giving her this patch is more than decorative. It's more than my caveman need for everyone to know she belongs to me. It means not only am I taking one hundred percent responsibility for Hope, but so are my brothers. I trust her completely, and my brothers know I don't trust lightly.

The clubhouse is quiet. All our guests from last night have departed.

Wrath looks downright exhausted as he hobbles in on his crutches and drops into the chair on my right.

"You feelin' all right?"

For once, he's not smirking. "Yeah. Fuckin' cast is bullshit."

"Slowin' your game?" Z asks helpfully from my left.

"Brother's got no game. Trinity's been carrying his balls around in her back pocket for weeks," Dex snarks. Everyone chuckles, even Wrath.

Instead of some pissed-off retort, my friend *laughs* and shakes his head.

Interesting.

The rest of the guys seem to be having some sort of contest to see who can get their ass in their chair the slowest. Sparky is naturally the last one in. He's jittery from being away from his plants for more than five seconds.

We go through regular club business and get it out of the way. Teller reports to us that earnings are good. All club accounts are flush and balanced. He reads the numbers off a sheet of paper, passes it around for everyone to review, then shreds it.

Sparky reports a fresh crop is almost ready. We have an increased demand from Green Street Crew, but we'll be able to meet it along with the new pipeline I lined up. Sparky is excited about his newest strain. Stash asks for extra help with packaging.

Z and Dex report Crystal Ball is doing well and they've secured a few new feature dancers to replace the void left by Inga.

Wrath informs everyone he's decided on a trainer to teach his classes at the gym. He asks the brothers to help him keep an eye on things while he's laid up, and we work out a schedule.

Murphy brings up a run that's been scheduled for months. With Wrath unable to ride, someone needs to take his place. We still have a little time to deal with that, so I table it for later discussion.

Wrath offers to turn in his cut since he can't ride. His offer is voted down with a "fuck no" from all members.

"There's an exception in the bylaws for injuries, you fuckhead, so stop offering," Z grouches at Wrath. Wrath flips him off, and that discussion is over.

Once general club business is out of the way, I excuse everyone except my officers: Wrath, Z, Teller, and Murphy.

Expectation is written all over each face.

No reason for a speech. "I want to give Hope a property patch."

It shouldn't really be a surprise, but they act like I dropped a fucking live nuke in the middle of the table.

After a few beats, Z asks, "You asking for our votes, prez?"

"Yes."

Z nods slowly. I meet every one of their gazes head on, settling on my enforcer last.

"You lay it out for her?" he asks.

"Yes."

"Everything?" Wrath pushes.

Through clenched teeth, I spit out, "Not quite."

Wrath's eyes widen in a "what the fuck you waitin' for" face that I want to punch.

"She knows enough. I trust her. You heard her the night of the party. It ain't gonna rattle her."

Wrath nods slowly and turns to the rest of the guys.

Teller is the first one to raise his hand. "She's been real good to Heidi. Trinity too. She's got love for the club. Prez is happy. She gets my vote."

Wrath's shrewd gaze focuses on Teller as he takes that all in. *That's fuckin' right, brother. She jumped in to help one of us out.*

Murphy raises his hand next. "She's a classy girl. Doesn't give anyone grief. She was ready to rip those cops' heads off after Heidi's party. Abso-fucking-lutely."

Yeah, my girl got herself pretty worked up that night. The memory of her standing in my front yard, hands on her hips, giving those pigs hell still makes me smile.

Z has been good to my girl. He's taken on more of a friendly, brotherly role to counteract Wrath's dickishness. He's enthusiastic with his praise. "She keeps her shit locked down. Took that bullshit the club girls heaped on her with class. Treats Trinity with respect. Never cops an attitude in public, even though I know she gives prez hell when they're alone. Fuck yes."

His little endorsement makes me chuckle, because even when she's pissed at me, I still want to stick my dick in her so bad I ache.

Wrath can make or break this. He's been my best friend for a long damn time, but I also know he's got a lot of reservations about Hope's innocence when it comes to the MC. The club comes first, but if he kills this for me, I'm gonna have a hard time looking at his face for a while.

He levels his cool enforcer stare on me. "You trust her?"

"You know I do."

"You trust her with your life? Our lives?" He points to everyone at the table.

"Yes, she'd never spill club business."

Wrath nods, and my tension level ratchets down a notch. "How much club business you gonna let her in on?" he asks.

"She understands but said she doesn't want details in case she ever ends up having to represent one of us in court."

Wrath seems surprised by my answer. "Okay. You got my yes."

Thank fuck.

I point to Z. "Order it up."

HOPE

I've just stepped out of the shower when I hear a *thump-thump* on my front door. Dripping water and muttering a bunch of curses, I grab my robe and scurry down the hallway. By the sound of the fist against my door, it can only be Rock. My mouth turns up and my belly flutters with excitement, imagining him on the other side.

Flinging open the door, I greet him with, "Why haven't I just given you a key?"

The hardened expression he's wearing breaks with a smile. "'Cause we're never here, Baby Doll."

Wrapping his arms around me, he picks me up and plants a hungry kiss on my lips. I take in his crisp outdoor scent and savor the sensation of our bodies pressed together, his arms holding me tight. Every time we touch, I swear it's as exciting as the first time.

As he sets me down, his gaze skims over me, from wet hair to bare feet. His grip on my hips tightens. "Do you realize when I see you fresh from the shower, it makes me want to get you all filthy again?"

His words, combined with the lascivious gleam in his smoky eyes, cause my breath to catch. I wish I were wearing something sexier than my ratty old terrycloth robe.

Not that he seems to mind.

Before I can come up with an appropriate response, he pounces, picking me up and scanning the area. By some silent agreement, we've never really ventured into my bedroom together. Like Rock said, we're rarely here. And there's a whole lot of other surfaces he enjoys defiling.

At the moment, he's eying my dining room table with less-than-noble plans. Since I usually eat alone when I'm here, the only thing my dining room table is doing right now is supporting a pile of mail I've yet to go through and a basket of laundry I was planning to sort after my shower.

I never know how long Rock will be when he has "church," and I never ask what the club discusses at the table. I trust if he wants me to know, he'll tell me.

Let's face it. I probably don't want to know.

He kicks out one of the chairs and sits down, setting me on my feet. His hands immediately go to my robe, working the knot loose in no time. A shiver works through me when the material parts. His hands cup my hips, his thumbs stroking my belly. He nudges me in small increments until my butt is resting against the edge of the table.

"I'm starving, baby."

I open my mouth to answer, to tell him I'll make him something for dinner. But the white-hot scrutiny of his gaze tells me he's not talking about food. His hands travel up, smoothing my robe off my shoulders. He flicks the material over the table and stands. Tipping my head back, his serious face comes into view, storm-gray eyes darting from my lips to my breasts and lower. My heart thuds in my chest as he leans in, his lips finding mine.

No matter how many times we kiss, each time is electrifying. Full, firm lips press hard against mine. One of my hands dives into his thick hair, pulling him closer. He responds by tugging me against him tighter. A lick against my bottom lip, and I respond with one of my own. Rock groans, and the sound sends shivers through me. I'm very aware of my nakedness and the fact that he's still fully dressed. My beaded nipples rubbing against the soft fabric of his shirt sets me on fire.

Big, rough hands skate up my sides, cupping my breasts, thumbs rubbing my nipples. My hips shoot forward, grinding against him, and I gasp for breath, breaking our kiss.

"Lie back for me," he commands, voice low and rumbling with need.

My mouth opens to protest, but I decide I'd rather see what he has in mind first.

Because I know whatever it is, it'll be *good*.

Before I do what he asked, my hand reaches out and brushes against him. He's hard, erection straining against his jeans.

I can't fucking wait.

He helps me lie back on the table, pushing mail and stuff out of his way. I flinch at the soft flapping of fabric and envelopes hitting the floor, and he presses a finger to my lips.

"Stop. We'll take care of it later."

I nod. Who can think about mail when a man like Rock wants to do all sorts of delicious things to you?

He slides one finger down the length of my body as he walks to the end of the table and sits back down. One of his hands wraps around one of my ankles and lifts my foot to the table. Feeling much too exposed, I hesitate when he goes to lift the other one.

"Hope," he warns.

"Rock, don't," I plead. I haven't been to the waxer or anything in too long.

He sighs. "When will you learn?" Then he picks up my other foot, placing my heel on the edge of the table.

My knees slam together, and he traces a hand down my calf, his mouth following the same path. "Open," he murmurs against my skin.

I can't resist. His voice, his touch, his hot breath tickling over me. My legs part, but he doesn't dive right for me. His hands slide up the inside of my thighs—hard enough not to tickle, soft enough to send pleasurable tingles through me. My legs part a little more.

"That's better."

I can't speak, so I respond with, "Mmm."

His thumbs rub over my quivering outer lips, massaging and kneading my warm flesh. The first touch of his fingertip over my clit makes me hiss and bump up my hips.

"So sensitive and ready for me."

I nod my head but can't get out any words as I fall into the sensation. His thumb teases over the tip of my clit again. My back arches with ripples of pleasure, offering myself to him. He lets out a satisfied grunt and pushes closer. Suddenly, his tongue laps at me, and my hips shoot off the table.

"Easy, baby."

But, oh, that feels good. Hot caresses with his tongue subtly pressing down. Wave after wave of heat crashes through me as he keeps applying soft pressure, stroking in a steady pattern. So close. My body is so close. I strain, needing a little more. The lapping stops. Sealing his mouth over my clit, he sucks, and I scream out.

He keeps going, growling as I squirm and wriggle, pushing my pussy harder against his face. His hands hold my hips where he wants them as he keeps kissing and licking me. Hooking his arms under my legs, he hoists me higher, burying his face, sucking and licking at me harder.

"Shit!"

I can't. The sensations are too much. I'm climbing higher and higher, about to shatter. Sweet pleasure unfurls from my core through my body. I'm still yelling and thrashing around, but he keeps me where he wants me. Over and over, his tongue sweeps over my pussy.

Gently, he eases me back onto the table. Slipping two fingers inside me, he curls them against that special spot while flattening his hand on my belly and pressing me into the table.

"Rock, what—" I try to lift my head, but his mouth latches onto my clit again. His fingers keep rubbing and stroking, slow at first, then more insistent. My legs are trembling so hard they fall to the sides.

Briefly, he lifts his head from between my thighs. "Come for me."

"I did. I don't think…"

He growls against me, sending shocking vibrations through my core.

I'm done. Shattered. Flying through time and space.

I barely have a chance to come down when Rock slides me off the table, grips my hips, and flips me over. My legs are like jelly, so I curl my fingers over the edge of the table and hang on.

An excited tingle races through me at the clink of his belt. The lazy ticking sound of his zipper lowering. The reaction in me is automatic—I rise on tiptoes, arching my back, offering myself.

And he takes me.

Rough hands cup my hips, holding me in place while he pounds into me from behind. My breasts are squished, trapped between me and the table. Planting my elbows, I lift up and push myself back.

"Don't stop," I chant breathlessly, over and over. I'll die if he stops.

"No chance," he grunts out, barely out of breath. "You comin' for me again, doll?"

I open my mouth to answer, but pleasure grabs me and I let out a wailing moan instead. His furious thrusting doesn't let up as I scream through my orgasm.

"That's it, Baby Doll. Give me everything."

He lets out a deep, satisfied groan and warm wetness sizzles over my back. I turn my head and quirk up my mouth at him. It takes him a second to come back to himself. When he does, he meets my gaze, a flicker of worry passing over his face.

"You mad?"

I hold down my grin as long as possible. "No, I'm not mad."

I get a playful slap on my ass. "Stay there. I'll be right back."

When he's done cleaning me up, I get soft kisses along my neck and shoulder.

"Come on, my sticky little girl, let's go wash you up," Rock says as he hoists me into his arms.

Looping my arms around his neck, I burrow my face against his shoulder, running my mouth over his skin. I love the salty taste of my man.

He growls, moving us faster to the bathroom. Inside, he sets me down gently next to the tub and gets the shower going. Feeling suddenly overwhelmed, I trace my finger down his arm. He turns and gives me a questioning look.

"Did you… Have you always done that?"

I don't have to be more specific. Another flicker of concern. "No, baby. I don't know why." His dark-gray stare roams over my face. "I've never done that before. Before you. Does it bother you?"

A smile tugs at the corners of my mouth. "No."

A relieved smile spreads across his face. "Go on. Get in."

As soon as he steps in behind me, I turn and wrap my arms around his waist. I don't know why, but I'm suddenly overwhelmed with emotion and the need to be close. It's on the tip of my tongue to ask him to spend the night here—something we haven't done yet.

I open my mouth, but a strangled sob comes out instead.

"What's wrong?" Rock asks, leaning over to swipe my bangs out of my eyes.

I force up the corners of my mouth. "Nothing, baby. You just overwhelm me."

"Did I hurt you? Before?" he asks, his face darkening.

"No. Not at all. I love everything we do. Always."

He still doesn't look convinced.

"I think I just missed you a lot today."

His face softens, and he runs his hands over my arms. "Missed you too. Thought about you all day," he says with a secret smile.

After we're squeaky clean and wrapped in towels, Rock turns to me. "Mind if I shave?"

"Not at all. Although, I'm kind of digging the scruff on you."

He gives me a lopsided grin.

Reaching up, I run my fingers through his hair. "I like that you're wearing your hair a little longer, too."

His eyelids close briefly. Almost as if he's embarrassed. "Haven't had time to get it cut."

I've never thought of Rock doing something so mundane. It's difficult to picture him sitting still in a barber's chair for a simple haircut.

An easier scenario to imagine is Trinity sitting all the guys down once a month and sheering them like reluctant sheep. It's an amusing image.

"Hang on. I'll grab you a razor. There's none in here anymore."

When I return, Rock's facing the door, patiently waiting.

"I'm sorry. All I have are girly pink ones."

"Babe, I'm more than man enough to shave with a pink razor," he says while holding out his hand.

13

"Well, manly man, the only shaving cream I have is also pink and strawberry-scented."

He chuckles, then eyes me up and down. Suddenly, I'm self-conscious about how I've been running around the house in such a skimpy towel.

"What?"

Rock rubs his hand over his chin and down his neck while his gaze roams over my body. "I was just thinkin' maybe my scruff can wait." He picks up the razor, twirling it between his fingers. "Instead, maybe I should use this pretty pink razor to shave *my* pussy, so next time I want it, you're not pulling away from me."

I'm struck dumb by his words. "Excuse me?"

"You heard me," he says, setting down the razor. His strong arms band around me, lifting me in the air so he can kiss my forehead. "That pussy is mine, baby. I don't like you hesitating when I want to see it."

My skin is so hot and tight. I'm sure I'm blushing like crazy. "You're so dirty."

"You just realized this now?"

Soft smacks rain down over my ass, and I squeal and wriggle out of his hold. "Aren't you satisfied yet, caveman?"

He grins and plants another kiss on the top of my head. "I can't ever get enough of you, baby."

"Shave. Worry about my bush later."

With a smirk, Rock ducks back into the bathroom, and I run down the hall to get dressed.

While waiting for him to finish shaving, I bend over to pick up the mail and other things we tossed on the floor earlier.

One envelope stops me cold. Unfolding myself from the floor, I turn it over in my hands. The New York State Attorney Grievance Committee. Mailed over a week ago. Of course, I haven't been home much to check the mail, so it's probably been sitting here like a career-ending bomb. My heart drops to my stomach. My fingers tremble so hard I can barely rip open the seal and get the letter out.

I've never been in trouble in my life. In fact, I've always been teased for being the "good girl." The oath I took to become a lawyer is important to me. I take it seriously. Mentally running through all the cases I've handled in my career, I can't think of anything I've ever done that could be construed as malpractice. Hell, I've only had two clients in the last year and a half.

Both connected to Rock.

Both cases he practically forced on me.

Dammit!

Since complaints cannot be made anonymously, I see it's Winter's ex who filed the grievance. He's claiming, first, it was a conflict of interest for me to represent Winter when I had previously represented her boyfriend. That one is bullshit, and I'm surprised the committee is even investigating it.

It's the next one that makes my chest constrict and my fingers go numb.

He claims I am involved in a criminal enterprise. That my representation of members of the Lost Kings, a known criminal organization, is personal, and I'm bending the law to cover up their crimes.

This is why they're investigating me.

From what I understand about the process, normally I would be given an opportunity to submit a response in writing. But they're actually calling me in for a face-to-face interview.

"Hope, what's wrong?"

Freshly shaved and too handsome for my sanity, Rock strolls into the dining room with nothing but a towel wrapped around his hips. With a shaky hand, I pass the letter to him.

"What's this?"

"I'm being investigated by the disciplinary committee for ethics violations."

"What the fuck for?"

My jaw tightens. "Winter's ex. The case you forced me to take."

As soon as I drop the words in the air, I have a twinge of regret. But I thrust up my chin and glare at him.

"Babe, I'll take care of this. That motherfuck—"

My rage boils over. He doesn't *get* it. "Don't you fucking dare! If anything happens to him, it will be so much worse for me. It will look like everything in his complaint is true!"

He moves to put his arms around me, and I flinch.

"Don't touch me."

"Hope—"

"No. I'm so fucking mad at you right now. You pushed me into taking that case when I wasn't ready. Do you know what this kind of thing will do to my career?" The years I spent in law school, suffering through the bar exam, all the struggling I did to stay afloat before Clay died—all of it for nothing now if I lose my license to practice law.

"None of it is true."

"It doesn't matter! They're actually calling me in before the committee. So someone thinks it's got merit. Most complaints go unfounded, and the attorney never even knows about them. They should have given me a chance to answer it in writing. You don't understand how bad this is, Rock." This is so humiliating. How will I ever explain this to my friends? If I get disbarred, it will be made public. Even if I manage to skate out of this with a suspension or warning, it still gets published. Everyone will know.

Rock runs a hand through his hair.

"Hope, let me fix this. The club—"

I can't believe he still isn't getting it. His "fixing it" will make things worse. Without thinking through my words, I explode. "Fuck the fucking club! You and your stupid club are what got me in trouble!"

Oh no.

I want to yank back the words the second they leave my lips. The shock and anger they bring to Rock's face is a gut punch I can't handle.

His eyes go cold, and he storms down the hall. When he comes back, he's fully dressed. He tosses the letter on the counter.

I'm frantically trying to wipe tears off my cheeks. I'm humiliated enough. I don't need him to see me crying too.

But he barely throws a glance at me as he marches out the door.

CHAPTER TWO

ROCK

FUCK THE FUCKING CLUB.

Those words keep banging around inside my skull. The day I get her voted into *the fucking club*.

I've never been a fan of irony.

When I finally hit the highway, I can breathe again.

I don't even know where I'm going. The clubhouse is out. There's no way I could look my brothers in the eye right now.

Fuck the fucking club.

I should have seen this coming. No matter how many fucking talks I have with her, she's never going to *get it.* Our relationship was bound to go to shit eventually.

For miles and miles, I drive like a bull out the gate. The memory of Hope's furious face chases me down the road.

Even after I've put a good chunk of highway behind me, I still can't stop picturing her face. And there's something else there I can't quite put my finger on.

Embarrassment. Hurt.

Fuck.

From the day we met, I've known how insecure and sensitive my girl is. Since I find everything about her fucking perfect, I'd forgotten about her self-esteem issues.

A seed of doubt weasels its way into my concrete block of self-righteousness. I'd been so infuriated when she rejected my offer to help her I didn't consider her feelings at all. No. All I thought about was how to fix it. Along with the doubt, I'm pissed because she's right. I pushed her into doing that case and now she's going to have a whole lot of bullshit to deal with because of my heavy-handedness.

Slowing down, I take in my surroundings. I've managed to put a good ninety miles between us.

Impressive.

Finding a motel to crash in is easy. Our downstate charter would take me in, no questions asked, and find a spot for me. I'm tempted because their clubhouse isn't far, but I really need to be alone.

What's not easy is checking my phone and finding no calls or texts from Hope. Not that I expected an apology. But I'd rather have her bitching me out some more than nothing at all.

The ride back the next morning seems to take forever.

I stop at Hope's house first, but she's not there.

It's probably for the best, because I can't fight with her again. Even with all my realizations last night, that *fuck the club* thing is still messing with my head.

Z meets up with me in my office, a stupid jolly grin on his face.

A simple, "Hey," is all I manage before he starts letting me in on why he's so excited.

"Kiss my ass now, fucker. Hope's cut should be ready later this week. Patches and everything."

Fuck me.

"You want to have a party or give it to her in private?" He waggles his eyebrows at me.

"Uh, she's going through some stuff. I may wait on it a little bit." Christ, *wait on it* might be putting it mildly.

His face falls. "Seriously?"

I pull him into the conference room and, just my fucking luck, Wrath spots us before I get the door closed.

"Where you been, dick? I'm fucking bored." He hobbles in and drops his ass in the first chair he sees.

Z's watching me with an intense expression. "What's going on with your girl?"

Wrath perks up at that.

"That fucking ex of Winter's reported Hope to the attorney whatever board. It's bad. She has to go in and explain herself. It's all bullshit, but she's pretty upset." I leave out our argument.

"Me and Bricks will go take care of the little fuck," Z says, already pulling out his cell phone.

I hold up a hand between us. Hope was right to reject my offer to take care of it. That became clear to me on my little run downstate.

"No. One of the things he's accusing her of is covering up ongoing criminal activity for us. Something happens to him, she's toast."

I can feel the anger radiating off Wrath, so I turn and face him.

"It's all bullshit. He's taking a stab in the dark to get even for losing his case."

"Don't get pissed, but what's our exposure here?" Wrath asks.

His meaning is clear, and it does piss me the fuck off. "Nothing, you fuck. That's not what it's about. It's not the fucking cops she has to talk to. It's a bunch of stuffed shirts who are going to decide if she gets to keep her license or not."

Wrath's immune to my outburst. He nods but doesn't say anything.

Z taps my shoulder. "Uh, we have another issue. What the fuck has Bricks told Winter, and did she blab any of it to her baby daddy?"

Fuck. In all my fury, I didn't even consider that possibility.

"Last I knew, she was pretty clueless. He's met Bricks, though. He saw me at the hearing. I had words with him outside when he attacked Hope. I owe him a fucking beatdown for laying his hands on her." I seethe with rage at the memory. "I'm sure he took notice of the cuts and decided to make up a story to fuck with Hope. Bricks is fucking solid. You know that."

"Since we can't kill this fucker right now, how's Hope doing? Anything we can do for her?" Wrath offers.

Trying not to show my surprise at his concern, I shake my head.

"Uh, she's a little pissed at me. I kinda pushed her into taking the case when she wasn't really feeling it…"

Z shakes his head. "That fucking sucks. I'm sorry, brother. You gonna work it out?"

"I think so."

Wrath's still watching me with his shrewd enforcer expression. "When's the hearing?" he finally asks.

I sigh and try to recall what the letter said. "Tomorrow."

"You gonna go?"

"Fuck no. That'll just make it worse."

Wrath looks at me like I'm nuts. "You're gonna let your woman walk into that shit storm alone?" His tone makes it clear he thinks I'm being a douche.

Z makes a *duh* face at me. "Just don't wear your cut, asshole."

HOPE

Adam scratches his head and slips into that maddening lawyer mode he does so well. "Hope, you know as well as I do that the most ethics complaints come from family or mat law cases. That's why I do T&E. All the people I owe a duty to are dead. Can't report me if I fuck up."

Leave it to Adam to see it that way. I came here for some guidance because jumping off a bridge seemed like too much work. Now I'm reconsidering. "I didn't fuck up," I grumble at him.

"I know you didn't."

I jab my finger at the stupid letter. "The one about me representing her current boyfriend I can knock out. That one's not the problem. I just couldn't represent either one of them in the future against each other. The other thing he's accusing me of—ongoing criminal activity based on my association with Rock's club—that's a problem."

He makes a frowny, twisty-lipped face that doesn't look encouraging. "Hope, from what I remember—and you know I prefer to spend the ethics portion of CLEs napping—you've got to have a damn good reasonable basis before you can disclose client confidences to anyone. You represented your man for what? Some weed? And you're supposed to extrapolate *what* from that? That he's going to smoke weed in the future? Who gives a flying fuck?"

He's right, except I have an inkling the Lost Kings are into other things. Okay, more than an inkling. The illegal underground fighting and betting for one. Crap, I was a spectator at Wrath's fight, so that makes me an accessory or something. I'm pretty sure Rock and Z murdered or at least attempted to murder the guys who ran us off the road. Although it's probably a gray area, I don't think I'm *obligated* to disclose those things to anyone. Rock told me about those guys after he'd already taken care of it, so I couldn't report that to anyone.

I feel a little more optimistic about my chances.

"Thanks, buddy. It helped to talk this out."

A sharp stabbing pain rushes through my side. *Ouch.* Just what I need. Cramps and my period tomorrow when I have to deal with this interview. My cycle has been weird since getting on the birth control shot.

Heat curls in my belly at the thought of Rock. Shame for how I lashed out at him isn't far behind.

"You okay, Hope?"

"Yeah."

"You're welcome to hang out here if you want and do some research to prepare."

Actually, I want to pop four Advil and crawl into bed with my heating pad, but he's right. I need to prepare myself.

I take my time gathering enough cases and information to draft a brief but—in my opinion—eloquent statement.

When I get home, I collapse into tears. Rock hasn't called. He hasn't even sent me a text. I'm terrified that I fucked things up beyond repair. And for what? A career I'm pretty sure I don't even want anymore.

CHAPTER THREE

HOPE

I RECOGNIZE ONE OF THE THREE OLD WHITE MEN WHO MAKE UP THE grievance committee. He's a judge I've been in front of numerous times, and he smiles at me as I take my seat. Smoothing my skirt over my thighs, I curse the room for being so hot.

A bead of sweat rolls down my spine, and I shift. I'm so nervous my abdomen won't stop cramping, and I'm barely able to keep my breakfast down.

"Ms. Kendall, we realize it's unusual to call you in first, but since the allegations were so abnormal, we thought we should just get to it," old white man number one says.

One after another, they pepper me with questions. Trying to trip me up. I want to throw the statement I prepared yesterday at them and say, "There, read that!" but I maintain my composure and answer their questions the best I can.

In the end, I know nothing, so that's what I tell them. I represented Elias Serrano in a custody matter. Rochlan North in a misdemeanor possession charge. And Winter Curtis before the support magistrate. Mr. North runs a motorcycle club, but I don't know a lot about it. Mr.

Serrano works for Mr. North. And Ms. Curtis and Mr. Serrano are dating. Anything other than that is privileged information that I won't disclose. As for ongoing criminal cover-up, I work my best innocent you-can't-be-serious expression.

When I'm done, my bangs are plastered to my sweaty forehead. Great. All this sweating probably spells guilty to them.

Judge Gibson smiles at me warmly and turns to old white man numbers one and two. "I think we can agree this complaint is nonsense. There really is no reason to investigate this further."

Surprisingly, they agree.

I'm free.

As I step into the hallway, I dig my cell phone out of my purse and send Rock a text.

I'm sorry.

Simple, direct, and honest.

While I'm waiting for the elevator, I wobble a bit. The whole time I was in the meeting, I couldn't stop sweating. Now I'm freezing but still sweaty.

I sway as I step into the elevator and press C for concourse. The motion of the creaky old box rocks my stomach. A few deep, cleansing breaths later, I burst out of the elevator.

Rock is standing directly across on the other side of the metal detectors everyone has to go through before they go upstairs. His head is down while he checks his cell phone. From here, I see a smile cross his face. The ding of the elevator catches his attention, and he tips up his head.

His happy expression morphs into panic as he strides over. "Hope, are you okay?"

I'm too embarrassed to tell him it's a combination of nerves and my period, so I fake a smile. "What are you doing here?"

"I didn't want you going through this alone." He jerks his thumb over his shoulder at the security guard. "They wouldn't let me upstairs."

My breathing falters. My vision swims.

"Baby, you don't look very good." He takes me into his arms. "Honey, you're awfully cold."

24

Blinding agony burns through my left side, and I'm suddenly painfully uncomfortable *down there*.

A veil of red blurs my vision.

Blackness swirls over my eyes.

Then, I'm lost.

ROCK

The second I see Hope, I know something's wrong. Her normally pale, creamy skin is almost waxy. Rushing to her, I see she's sweat-soaked.

What did those assholes do to her up there?

I know she must have been scared, but her reaction seems awfully extreme. Even for her.

"Hope, are you okay?"

Her lips tremble. "What are you doing here?"

"I didn't want you going through this alone."

The whole time we're talking, all I can think about is how much I fucking love her. Her sweet, simple "I'm sorry" text really got to me. I was about to send her one of my own when she appeared looking like death warmed over.

"Baby, you don't look very good." She seems close to hitting the floor, so I wrap my arms around her. Touching her cheek scares the shit out of me. "Honey, you're freezing."

Next thing I know, she collapses in my arms.

The pudgy security guard who gave me shit when I tried to go upstairs rushes over. "Sir, what happened?"

"I don't know. She fainted."

I'm crouching on the floor, holding her in my arms. She's breathing, but it's shallow. I tap her cheek. "Hope?"

Nothing.

A state trooper comes over to help just as I realize something wet is seeping into my jeans.

Jesus Christ. She's bleeding!

What the fuck?

"Call an ambulance!" I roar.

The trooper kneels down and checks her pulse. He sees the blood on my hands and shifts into action. "Sir, an ambulance will take forever. Empire Medical is right up the road. I'll drive you, lights and sirens. We'll get there much faster."

I stand, keeping her body cradled against me as he leads the way out. I don't see anything except the officer's back as I follow him.

At the car, he tries to take Hope from me, and I snap at him. "I've got her."

Getting us both in the backseat isn't easy, but I tuck her up against me. Brushing her hair off her cheek, I press a kiss to her forehead. "Baby, please wake up. You're scaring the shit out of me."

"Sir, is she breathing?"

"Yes. But it's shallow. Her pulse is weak."

I hold her, speaking nonsense to her the whole way, dangerously close to losing my shit by the time we pull up to the emergency room doors.

"Stay here, sir. I'll get them to bring out a gurney."

It takes way too fucking long for the medical team to rush out. Hope's taken from my arms. When the staff sees the blood on me, they start barking questions. Somewhere in the middle of answering their endless interrogation, I'm aware of the officer handing me Hope's purse and a nurse pushing me inside while she drums more information out of me.

I stumble and lean against the admissions desk.

The little pit bull of a nurse is right in my face. "Is she pregnant?"

"What? No. I don't know. I don't think so."

"Are you her husband?"

"Boyfriend." Fuck, I hate that useless word.

"Is she on birth control?"

"I think so."

Her lip curls with disdain, and I'm swamped with regret. I'm always in such a hurry to stick my damn dick in her. I never asked her what the—

"Sir, does she have any family we can call?"

I'm her fucking family.

"Uh, her mother," I answer stupidly.

She ushers me into a private waiting room. I don't know what the fuck to do. I want to throw shit and rip the fucking place apart.

Instead, I sit my ass in a flimsy plastic chair and tap out a message to Z.

At Empire Med with Hope. Bad

My phone pings back almost immediately.

Be there in 20.

Z and Wrath are there in fifteen.

"Brother, what the fuck?" Z asks when he sees me.

"I don't know. They haven't fucking told me anything yet."

Wrath sits next to me and puts his hand on my back. "What happened?"

I tell him about meeting up with her, how sick she looked, and her fainting.

"Uh, we thought she like got shot or something," Z points out.

I turn my hands over, seeing the blood. "No."

"Aw fuck, man," Z says.

There's a sink in the corner of the room, and I stumble over to clean my hands the best I can.

"Mr. North?"

I whip around. "Is she okay?"

Not liking the grave expression on her face, I storm over. "Is she okay?" I ask a lot louder this time.

She glances at Wrath and Z, then pulls me into the corner. "We think it's an ectopic pregnancy. She's bleeding heavily, indicating her tube has ruptured. We're prepping her for emergency surgery now."

My throat constricts. "She's pregnant?" I manage to choke out.

She puts a hand on my shoulder and gives me a sad look. "I'm sorry. A tubal ectopic pregnancy like this *never* survives."

"Emergency surgery? Is she...?" I can't even say it.

"It's a life-saving operation. I'll come back when I have more information for you."

I fall heavily into the chair next to Wrath. What the fuck did I do to her? I remember back to the morning in Sophie's shower when Hope told me she had trouble taking the pill. Then the night of my birthday when she said we could skip the condoms. I never thought about it again.

Selfish fucking asshole.

A baby. She's pregnant. Hope carrying my child.

No, *was* pregnant. Was it…? I can't. I can't even think about it. I just need my girl to make it through this.

Wrath puts his hand on my shoulder. "She's a little spitfire. She'll be back to busting your balls in no time, brother."

After that, my brothers are quiet, but they stay with me while I wait.

Trinity comes in an hour later. After a quiet hug, she pushes a clean pair of jeans and a T-shirt into my hands. Shuffling into the bathroom, I change quick, stuffing my stained clothes in the garbage. I hurry out, but no one has come to give me an update. I should call her mother. Digging out her cell phone, I scroll through her contacts until I find one labeled Mother. The phone rings twice before someone picks up.

"Um, Mrs.—"

Fuck, I don't know what her mother's married name is.

"This is Rochlan. I'm a friend of your daughter's, Mrs. Kendall."

"Knight," she corrects.

What-the-fuck-ever. "Listen, Hope's in the hospital. She's having emergency surgery."

I give her the scant details I know and feel like an absolute fucking asshole the entire time. When I tell her we're at Empire Med, she makes a clucking sound. "Okay. Well, call me back tomorrow and let me know how she's doing."

"Ma'am? You're not going to come down and see her?"

"What for? You said she's in surgery. It's an hour drive."

I swallow down my rage and hang up.

Looking at my brothers, I shake my head. I can't speak. I'm dangerously close to tears. What kind of mother doesn't care if her daughter is in the hospital and might die? I know how shitty I am with words. Did I not explain it right?

The nurse returns, and I jump up. "Is she okay?"

"There were some complications. Sir, do you know if she has a health care proxy?"

"What?"

She explains what that is, and my entire body numbs. "She's a lawyer, so probably. I don't know," I manage to mumble.

"See if you can find out. I'll be back in a bit."

Swiping at my damp cheeks, I realize I'm fucking crying.

Scrolling through her phone again, I find Sophie's number.

"What's up, buttercup?" she answers.

"Sophie, it's Rock."

"Oh. Hi. What's wrong? Is Hope okay?"

"No. She's in the hospital. They're asking me if she has a health care proxy, Sophie. I don't know. I thought you might."

She lets out a string of curses. "Yes. We all did them after law school. I have no idea if she updated it after Clay died. I was the second person, though. Fuck. I'm down in fucking Delaware, Rock. It's going to take me a little while to get there. Call Adam. He might know. I'm going to check out of my hotel and drive straight there. I'm leaving right now."

We say our good-byes. No matter my irritation with Sophie, I'm so grateful Hope has at least one other person who cares about her. I manage to get ahold of Adam, but he's not much help. He's got no idea about the health care proxy but says he'll be at the hospital right after court.

While I'm holding Hope's phone, her text chain to Sophie pops on the screen. Remembering the awful fight we had about me messing with her phone, I hesitate. But I can't stop scrolling through their messages because they're full of Hope's snarky wit that I love so fucking much. Under the circumstances, I think Hope will forgive the intrusion. Right now, I need to feel close to my girl in some small way.

Looks as if they go back and forth all day. Sophie's lewd as a devil. Hope's comments are more reserved, but she definitely pays me a few compliments here and there that make me smile.

Please let my girl be okay

One text catches my attention. From yesterday morning.

I fucked up so bad, Sophie.

???

I said something horrible to R I didn't mean.

A good fuck fixes everything

I snort at that, not surprised that's Sophie's solution to everything. *Not this time.*

They must have talked right after, because there's only one more message. It's from Sophie this morning.

Good luck. Give that committee a kick in the balls from me.

Wrath props up his cast and sprawls out as much as his big body and the tiny hospital waiting room chairs allow.

An hour later, Lilly shows up. Z snaps to attention when he sees her, but she doesn't notice him at first. She places one hand on my shoulder. "Any news?"

"No, she's still in surgery."

She nods and sits to wait with us. Trinity brings me coffee. She and Lilly talk softly to each other. Z watches both of them like a hawk. I'd laugh my ass off if I wasn't so torn up. I can't wait to tell Hope about this little soap opera.

Please let me be able to tell her this.

A couple hours later, Sophie rushes into the room. She glances at the guys and approaches me slowly. Her touch is light on my shoulder as she gives me a gentle squeeze. "Any news?"

"Not in a while."

Wrath's busy glaring at her so hard I don't bother introducing them. Never should have confided in him about Sophie's drunken attempt to get me in the sack. After I fill her in, she wanders over to talk to Lilly and Trinity.

"Mr. North?"

It's a doctor this time, and I steel myself before getting up.

"She's doing well," he says right away.

All the air I'd been holding in comes rushing out of my lungs.

Sophie joins me, explaining to the doctor that she's Hope's health care proxy. He nods.

"She came through surgery okay. We had to—" He looks around the room and lowers his voice. "Her fallopian tube ruptured. We had to remove part of it along with the pregnancy." Next to me, Sophie gasps. "It was done laparoscopically so her recovery time won't be as long."

"Thank you," I manage.

"Did she complain of any pain, or did you notice anything unusual?" the doctor asks.

I shake my head. I don't want to discuss the fight we had in front of Sophie.

The doctor shrugs. "She would have been feeling bad for a couple days. Probably in a lot of pain today," he explains, making me feel a thousand times worse. Thinking my girl was suffering while I was off taking a joyride and whining like a little bitch because she insulted my club? That shit is hard to handle.

The doctor's gaze darts between Sophie and me, finally landing on me. "Will you be helping her once she's released?"

I don't even have to think about that. "Yes, she'll come home with me. I'll take care of her."

He nods. "We'll discuss care instructions when she's awake. She's still out now, but one of you can go in and see her if you want."

"You go," Sophie urges.

I follow him to her room and want to cry when I see her. Rushing to her side, I'm shocked at how small and fragile she looks surrounded by all the medical stuff.

"Baby doll," I choke out. I glance up at the doctor. "Can I hold her hand?" I'm so afraid I'll do something else to hurt her.

His mouth turns up slightly. "Yes."

I barely notice the door snick shut.

Taking her hand between mine, I bring it to my lips. "I'm so sorry, sweetheart. So fucking sorry for storming out the other night and not calling you. I'm so sorry this happened, because I know it's my fault. Please be okay, Baby Doll. I haven't had nearly enough time to love you yet."

A nurse comes in, watching me for a minute. "Sir, she's going to be out for a few more hours. You can go home and get some rest."

Nailing him with the hardest biker stare I can muster, I inform him in no uncertain terms, "No. I need to be here when she wakes up."

CHAPTER FOUR

HOPE

PAIN SHAKES ME FROM SLEEP. THE MOTHER OF ALL CRAMPS IS RAISING HELL in my uterus. My head throbs. The overpowering scent of antiseptic makes my nose twitch.

What the hell?

Snapping my eyes open, I find Rock sprawled out in a chair next to me, his hand wrapped tight around mine even in sleep.

It takes me a minute to remember what happened. *How long have I been out?* Uncomfortable, I shift, startling Rock awake.

The elation on his face is clear. Whatever happened was bad.

"What happened?"

"Baby—"

The door swishes open, and a nurse charges through. "Hey, chickie. Good to see you awake." She's friendly and checks me over with respectful efficiency. "Let me grab the doctor."

My throat tightens and suddenly I'm flooded with tears. Rocks stands and awkwardly pulls me to his chest. "It's okay."

The doctor explains about the pregnancy and the rupture. My mind is spinning. How did this happen?

"Can I still have children—after something like this?"

He's the kind of doctor who's chosen efficiency over a coddling bedside manner, so he doesn't sugarcoat a thing. "There's a good chance you may not be able to get pregnant again, and even if you do, your chances of this happening again are higher."

Rock is stoic as he holds my hand and rubs my back the entire time.

Then the doctor mentions I shouldn't try to conceive again for at least three or four months.

"Wait a second. Doctor, I wasn't trying to get pregnant. I'm on the shot."

The doctor falters. "How long ago?"

I glance at Rock and heat stings my cheeks. "Maybe eight weeks? They told me it was good for twelve."

"Well, that changes things a little. Statistically..." He trails off. "Well, it's very unusual. Get some rest. We'll probably discharge you in the morning."

As soon as he leaves, I burst into tears again. Rock's right there soothing me. "Hush, baby, it's going to be fine."

"I may not be able to have children, Rock. I mean, I don't even know if I want them, but having the option yanked away?"

"Hope, just worry about getting better. I'm so sorry. If I hadn't been such a selfish fuck, this wouldn't have happened."

With his head bowed and lips pressed against the back of my hand, he looks so sorrowful. I burst into tears again.

"You don't have to stay."

The stern expression on his face quiets me. "I'm not going anywhere."

The chipper nurse is back. "Honey, you've got a waiting room full of people out there. You feel like some visitors?"

My gaze bounces to Rock, and he squeezes my hand.

"Sure."

Wrath swings in on his crutches first, bumping Rock out of the way to drop a kiss on my forehead, then throws himself down in the chair next to my bed. "Sugar, you gave us all some scare," he grumbles at me.

I'm so touched I start weeping again. Rock glares at Wrath.

Z comes in with a scowl in place. "What the hell did you say to her, jerk?" he barks at Wrath.

The distressed look on Wrath's face makes me cry even harder. Darting his gaze between Rock and Z, he spreads his hands out palm up.

"It's not you." I sniffle.

Sophie pokes her head in and rushes to my side. "You scared the fuck out of me, buttercup!"

"What are you doing here?"

She shoots a glance at Rock. "Honey, I drove up from Delaware the second he called me."

"Thanks, Sophie."

"Lilly was here too, but she had to run. She wanted you to have this, though." Sophie sets a petite vase of tulips on the table next to me.

"I'm gonna let you get some rest, sweetie." She turns to Rock. "Call me if you need something?"

He nods, and she takes off.

"Thanks for staying with Rock, you guys," I choke out.

Wrath and Z share a look.

"Trin will be back a little later," Rock says.

On the verge of tears again, I gulp in big lungfuls of air.

"Breathe, Baby Doll," Rock reminds me.

He glares down at Wrath, who's made himself comfortable in the stiff hospital recliner and shows no sign of moving. "What?"

"Asshole," Rock grumbles.

Wrath's impish grin when Rock storms to the other side of the room to pull over a chair makes me laugh. Then he winks, and I really lose it.

"Prez, you need me to do anything?" Z asks from his corner.

"No—aw, fuck. Her car and my bike are probably still downtown."

Z seems relieved to have something to do. "I'll take care of it. Keys?"

After he leaves, the three of us fall silent. Well, Wrath starts snoring. Rock shakes his head.

"Has he been here all night?" I whisper.

Rock nods. "Yeah."

"Why?"

"You're family now, babe," Wrath mumbles without opening his eyes.

ROCK

Trinity finally returns with pizza for everyone, which the nurse promises to ignore. Teller, Murphy, and Heidi join us. Still nauseous from the pain meds, my girl is only able to nibble on some crackers.

After we eat, Hope gets a round of kisses, and everyone takes off. Trinity even manages to get Wrath to leave Hope's side and go home with her.

Hope is still pale, and I'm relieved when she finally drops off to sleep.

Early the next morning, the doctor comes in to check on her. After he's finished, she falls back into sleep, and he pulls me into the hallway.

"We're going to keep her one more day."

A crack of fear splinters through me. "Why? Is something wrong?"

"She's doing well. But she lost a lot of blood, and I'm not comfortable releasing her so soon."

I blow out a breath, relieved they're not just gonna toss her out. Honestly, I haven't a clue if she even has health insurance.

The rough way I handled my girl the other night has been banging around in my skull. I can't stop thinking somehow I did something to cause this.

"Doc..." Shit, I have no idea how to frame what I want to say without sounding like an abusive dickwad. "We... I didn't know she was pregnant. Could, ah, could I have somehow caused what happened?"

He cocks his head at me, clearly not getting my meaning. Jesus fuck, I'm gonna have to spell it out for him. Even as I'm running my hands through my hair, I don't break eye contact with the man. "A couple nights ago, we had sex. Pretty intense—"

He stops me with a hand on my arm. "No, Mr. North. In a normal pregnancy, the fertilized egg would have moved into her uterus. With this, the egg stayed in the fallopian tube, so no, vigorous sex wouldn't cause this. Did she complain of any pain?"

I mentally run over that night, trying to remember anything I missed.

"No."

He nods once. "You didn't cause it, so put it out of your head. Ectopic pregnancies only happen maybe one in every fifty pregnancies, but the fact that she was on a reliable method of birth control is concerning. I've conferred with her gynecologist."

I don't really care about that end of things. All I'm thinking of is taking care of my girl. Getting her back to the clubhouse and smothering the fuck out of her.

"You should really go home and get some rest." He doesn't say it with much authority. Probably because the look on my face makes it clear I'm not going anywhere.

"I can't leave her."

He nods once before leaving. "I'll be back to check on her later."

After he leaves, I lean against the wall, tipping my head back and closing my eyes. The doc was telling me the odds of this happening are apparently zilch. It hits me that a lot of bad shit has happened to my girl since I came into her life. I've done so many awful things in my thirty-eight years on this planet; I figure my karmic debt is huge. But Hope? I can't imagine she's ever willingly hurt another living creature. She's such a loving, caring soul. It seems awfully unfair for karma to fuck with her for the shit I've done.

HOPE

Rock's grave expression when he enters the room tightens the knot in my chest.

Even rumpled from sleeping in the chair, he's so handsome.

Somehow we made a baby. I had his child inside me. This perfect man who loves me and would protect me with his life. And I lost it. I didn't even know, but the loss echoes through me.

Is this my fault? I've been so indecisive about having children. I probably don't deserve to be a mother.

The thought that I could lose Rock because I'm defective in some way terrifies me. He's the picture of male virility. A hard man in his prime. Men like him want to reproduce, don't they? It's a miracle he doesn't already have a bunch of kids running around by now.

The way he protects everyone he loves, I know he'd be an amazing father.

I can't stop thinking I failed him somehow, and I hate it.

ROCK

The next morning I find myself in the hallway with the doctor again. "She's going to be sore for the next two to three days, so she needs as much rest as possible."

"Okay."

The doc eyes me skeptically. I gotta say I'm happy we're leaving. The suspicious looks I get every time he pays Hope a visit are getting old. The fact that he's answered all my questions and seems to be taking good care of my girl are the only things keeping all his teeth intact.

"In about two to three weeks, she should be fully recovered. At least physically," he clarifies.

"She's been crying at everything, doc. That normal?"

"Yes. Her body is going to be flooded with hormones. She may cry in spurts for up to six weeks. Keep an eye on her. If it seems worse, take her to her regular doctor. Does she have any history of depression?"

Although I suspect she does, I don't have anything concrete. "She lost her husband a while ago, and from what her friends described, she had a rough time."

For the first time since I've been dealing with this guy, his professional doctor mask slips. "Well, keep an eye on her. It will be normal for her to be sad and fatigued, but if it goes on for too long, she needs to talk to someone."

"Okay."

He sighs. "I'd limit her interactions with people for at least a few days. Let her grieve and process. Don't let her get overwhelmed. Her friends might mean well, but unless she asks, I'd screen her calls and visits."

Shit. That's a tough one. I'd been planning to care for her up at the clubhouse, but there's not a lot of privacy there.

"I can do that," I assure him.

He nods and pushes his way inside. Hope's awake but clearly still out of it.

"Okay, Ms. Kendall. We're going to discharge you today. It will take a little while to get the paperwork done. The nurse will bring you your written instructions and the prescriptions."

I listen to every word because I'm going to make damn sure I take the best care of my girl.

The doctor stops and levels a stern look at me. "No sexual intercourse for at *least* two weeks."

We're back to this.

Next to me, I feel Hope twitch, and I imagine she's red with embarrassment, but I don't turn away from the doctor. He seems to be challenging me. I'm not a fucking animal.

"Since the shot failed, you must use a barrier method for at least the next three to four months." He raises an eyebrow at me. As if I don't feel shitty enough. "You said you weren't trying to get pregnant, so you should discuss what other options are available with your regular OB/GYN when you're ready. They'll probably suggest some sort of oral contraceptive in addition to a barrier method."

Hope sort of wrinkles her nose, which makes me want to laugh. Instead, I rub my hand over her back.

He rattles off more instructions, some of which frankly are more than I ever needed to know. I pray like fuck someone is going to hand us this shit in writing.

After the doctor leaves, Hope seems to be a little more with it. She gets up and sorts through the clothes Trinity brought her last night. Holding up a pair of jeans, she winces. "No fucking way," she says, pointing to her belly.

Lifting up her hospital gown, she angles and turns in front of the bathroom mirror. "God, I look disgusting."

"Don't talk about my girl that way."

I get a small smirk out of her.

After a lot of indecision, she finally settles on a loose pair of sweatpants that I help her into. She still yelps when the material touches her tummy.

"Sorry, baby," I mutter.

"Hey," she says, placing a hand on my arm. "Thank you so much."

Entwining my fingers with hers, I bring her hand up and run my lips over her knuckles. "What are you thanking me for?"

"For staying with me."

I have to take a deep breath. Here she is thanking me when it's my fucking fault this happened in the first place. "Baby doll, you don't ever have to thank me for that. I love you."

She presses a soft kiss against my lips, then turns to finish getting ready.

The nurse stops in and confidentially informs me to pick up some Gas-X on the way home.

Jesus Christ.

Z meets us at the curb with my SUV. The orderly helps me get Hope out of her wheelchair. Once she's up, I swing her into my arms and settle in the backseat with her.

Z reaches back and gives her hand a squeeze. "Let's get you outta here, girl."

CHAPTER FIVE

HOPE

"Z, drop us off at my place," Rock directs.

"No problem."

I'm excited to be out of the hospital, but I'm also exhausted. It's possible I doze for the few minutes it takes to get to Rock's house.

Rock wants to carry me inside, but I brush off his hands.

"The doctor said I needed to walk a little," I remind him. I'm embarrassed to be hobbling around like an arthritic bird in front of Z, but he doesn't say anything.

"You hungry, doll?" Rock asks as soon as we're inside.

I think about it for a second. All I am is tired. "No."

I don't get to protest this time as Rock gently lifts me into his arms. "Wait here," he tells Z. He carries me upstairs and settles me in the bedroom. "I'll ask Z to run out for some things. Anything you feel like having?"

"Toast and butter?"

"That's it?"

My stomach rolls at the thought of eating anything else. "Yeah."

Rock brushes my hair off my face. "Rest. You need anything, call me," he says, setting my phone on the nightstand.

"You're going out?"

"No. Hell no. I'll be downstairs working on some stuff. I just don't want you havin' to yell or risk not hearing you."

"Okay." I can't keep my eyes open another minute. As I drift off, I'm vaguely aware of Rock moving around the room.

It's almost dark when I wake up. I don't feel rested, but I get up and run to the bathroom. The house is quiet. A quick glance out the window shows me nothing. Crawling back under the covers, I contemplate calling Rock. I don't *need* anything so I hate to bug him.

This is stupid. Snatching up the phone, I send him a quick text.

I'm awake

Rock's filling the doorway not three minutes later.

"What do you need, Baby Doll?"

"Nothing. I'm sorry. Were you busy?" He walks into the room, and I get a better look at him. Grease-stained jeans and hands. "Were you working on something?"

"Yeah. Give me a second to clean up."

"Okay."

He strips off his T-shirt as he strides into the bathroom.

"You can do that out here," I call after him.

He pokes his head out. "What?"

"You can get undressed out here, where I can watch," I say with a small smile.

He flashes a grin at me and ducks back into the bathroom.

"I wasn't joking," I grumble.

"What?" he calls out over the sound of the shower starting up.

"Nothing!" I shout back.

He emerges damp and sexy, towel wrapped around his lean hips. And gets dressed.

"Okay. All yours."

Feeling uncertain, I just stare at him until he comes closer. Then I throw back the covers and pat the bed.

The corners of his mouth lift as he slides in next to me and gathers me in his arms. A breath I didn't realize I'd been holding rushes out of me.

Rock's big hand strokes over my head and down my back. "Got your meds downstairs. Ready to eat something so you can take 'em?"

My arm wraps around his middle and I cling to him for a while. Enjoying the thump of his heart under my ear. He runs one hand over my back and one up and down the arm I have wrapped around him.

"You wanna talk, Baby Doll?" he asks after a few minutes.

I do. But I don't know what to say. Overwhelming grief and guilt consume me, but I don't know how to express it to him. There's also a part of me that's afraid of what he'll say.

"Hope?" he prompts.

The lump in my throat makes it impossible to force out any words. Finally, I manage to whisper, "I'm sorry."

"'Bout what?"

I don't know how to phrase what I want to say. "You remember… I'm not… I wasn't sure I ever wanted children." Now that I got part of it out, I'm determined to push out the rest. "But your… our baby. Even though I didn't know, it still hurts. I would have wanted—"

His arms pull me against him, his touch easing the ache in my chest. "Hope, honey, stop please. You're the only woman I've ever thought about having kids with. But you know, when you were in surgery, they explained to me the way it happened. The baby couldn't survive. I was so fuckin' scared I was gonna lose you."

I'm not sure what he means. Does he think I'm making too big a deal out of this loss? "If… if it hadn't. If…" Oh my God, I know what I want to ask, but I just can't form the question. "Would you have been happy? If things had been different? Would you have wanted—"

"Jesus Christ, Hope. Of course I would have been happy." The sound of his voice breaking destroys me. "I would have wanted our baby, Hope. Don't ever doubt that."

ROCK

I'm not sure what the right words are to tell Hope how much I love her and none of this is her fault. A part of me is crushed she doesn't realize how much she means to me. I don't want to make what she's feeling seem insignificant. In a way, I've had longer to process the loss. When they told me in the hospital the baby couldn't have ever survived, I put it out of my head and focused all my energy on my girl surviving.

Now her questions bring me right back to that place. Another person to be responsible for. To protect and take care of. Christ, could I handle a daughter who ended up being a smart mouth like her mom? I sort of half chuckle at the thought, and Hope peers up at me with wide, wet eyes.

I press a kiss to her forehead. "I want you to rest and heal. When we're ready, we'll figure it out, Baby Doll."

"Thank you," she whispers.

"I'm here. Whatever you need."

I don't think she hears me, though, as she seems to have drifted back to sleep. It's a fight not to wake her up, because I'm worried she hasn't eaten yet. But at least she doesn't seem to be in any physical pain.

Time passes, and I just listen to her breathe, thankful she's in my arms. After a while, she shifts and whimpers. More movement and she drops out of my hold and rolls over on her side. Settling the covers over us, I carefully pull her against my chest and doze with her.

"Rock," she whispers, startling me out of sleep.

"Yeah, baby," I rasp out.

"I hurt."

Instantly, I'm awake. "What's wrong?"

"I think I just need the pain meds. I feel shaky too."

Fuck, she hasn't eaten all damn day. What the fuck was I thinkin'?

"You gotta eat something, baby."

"Okay," she answers softly.

"I'll be right back."

Fuckin' pissed with myself, I struggle not to slam shit around in the kitchen. I don't want her any more upset. Toast. That's what she said she wanted before. I get that and her pills together, then grab a yogurt from the fridge and a bottle of water. I don't keep shit like trays in my house, so I stick the water in my pocket, grab a spoon out of one of the drawers, and head back upstairs.

"Babe?" I call out when I step into the bedroom and find the bed empty.

"In here."

The bathroom door opens, and I'm not liking how pale she looks at all.

"Come on, back in bed," I order as I set everything on the nightstand next to her.

She sits back and quietly munches on her toast, then spoons down half her yogurt before swallowing down her medication.

"Good girl," I tell her as she hands the bottle of water back to me.

I get a narrow-eyed expression in response that makes my heart jump because it means she's feelin' more like herself.

"Better?"

She places a hand on her belly, then winces. "Yeah, I guess. I need to take a shower, though. I feel disgusting."

"Later."

"Okay." She closes her eyes and rests against the headboard.

"You want to go back to sleep?"

"No," she answers without opening her eyes. But after a while, she drifts back to sleep. I try to settle her so she's more comfortable, then run downstairs to check the instructions the hospital gave us, afraid I missed something.

The slam of a car door outside pulls me out of my reading. A few seconds later, someone raps on the back door before opening.

"Hey," Z calls out.

"Come on in. Just keep it down. She's sleeping."

"Sure."

Wrath and Trinity follow in behind him. I raise an eyebrow at the trio. "What's up?"

"Nothing. Wanted to see if you needed anything," Wrath answers.

Trinity sets a couple bags on the table. "I brought some of her stuff that was in your room and a few books for her."

"Thanks, Trin. Appreciate it."

"You got enough food and stuff?" Z asks.

The corner of my mouth turns up at his concern. "Yeah, we're good. I need a few days. You guys can handle things?"

"Of course," Wrath answers.

Z glances at Trinity. "We just gotta figure out that thing by the weekend."

Trinity gets all twitchy. "I can go wait—"

Wrath puts his arm out to stop her.

"It's fine," I tell her.

Turning to Z, I address his concern. "I'll be there for church. We'll get it sorted out."

Wrath snakes his arm around Trinity's shoulders. "We'll get going."

"Tell Hope to call me," Trinity offers. "You know, if she wants to—"

"I will, hon, thanks."

After they leave, I lock up and shut everything off, then head upstairs.

Hope's still sound asleep. When I slide into bed, she turns and curls herself against me.

"I'm here, doll," I whisper against the top of her head.

HOPE

The next day I feel a little more normal. Around noon, I decide to venture downstairs. Rock's been working out in the garage since early this morning, and since he's been taking such good care of me, I want to return the favor.

I jump at the thud of footsteps behind me. My back faces the doorway, but before I can turn to greet Rock, he places both hands on the counter next to me, locking me in place. His head lowers so our cheeks are touching, and my eyes close. Carefully, he eases the knife out of my hand, setting it down.

"You're supposed to be resting." His voice is low, vibrating against my ear, stealing my voice.

I can't respond because he pushes my hair aside, exposing my neck, and nuzzles my ear, placing soft kisses below it all the way to my shoulder.

"How's my girl?"

His warm lips meet my thundering pulse, so all I'm able to say is a breathless, "Okay."

My head drops back against his chest as I continue to breathe him in. "I wanted to make you lunch."

He doesn't answer because he's still busy assaulting my neck, sending warm tingles scattering over my skin. Arousal tugs at me, so I squirm until I'm facing him, throwing my arms around his neck and holding him close. His warm mouth covers mine. Big hands come up to angle and cup my face. He presses one more kiss to my lips and steps back.

"Sorry, I shouldn't have gotten—"

I try to pull him back, but it's not easy to move Rock if he doesn't want to be moved. "I'm fine." I'm not fine, though. I'm desperate to know he still wants me.

His big hands circle my arms, pulling them off his shoulders until we're holding hands. "What are you making?"

"Nothing fancy. Sandwiches? I think you're out of mayo, though."

He gives my hands a quick squeeze and releases them. "I'll run down to the store. You need anything else?"

I need a lot of things. None of them will be found in the grocery store.

"Seltzer? Limes?"

He grins. "If you think of anything else, text me."

"Okay."

I watch him walk out. Something inside me wants to call him back. I should have offered to go with him or something. Except I'm still in my pajamas.

Rock hasn't been gone very long when someone pulls into the driveway. A skittering of fear runs through me. But one look out the window, and I break into a smile. Hurrying out to the mudroom, I throw on one of Rock's sweatshirts and open the back door.

"Hey, Bricks!"

He strolls up the driveway with a smile on his face. I wrap my arms around him for a quick hug and invite him inside.

"Prez here? He said he needed some help today," he says while jerking his thumb at the garage.

"He ran out to get a few things but should be back soon."

He seems uneasy but follows me inside.

"Do you want something to drink?"

"Sure, water's fine. How are you feeling? We were all so worried about you."

My cheeks heat up. For some reason, I'm sort of embarrassed that every one of Rock's brothers knows what happened.

"Better."

I set his water on the counter as he settles himself on one of the stools.

"Winter and I stopped in to see you, but you were out cold."

"Oh, geez. I'm sorry."

He cocks his head at me but doesn't say anything at first. "You doin' okay?" he finally asks.

"Tired, but yeah, I'm okay."

We're interrupted by Rock returning. His hands are loaded down with bags, and Bricks rushes over to help him, setting everything on the counter.

They go over some stuff, and Rock leads him out to the garage while I work on emptying the bags.

The sweet scent of roses hits my nose, and I turn.

"Rock! What—"

He's standing there with a big plastic-wrapped bouquet of red roses. An uncertain smile plays over his mouth. "I should have brought you some before this." He glances down. "They're just grocery store—"

Plucking the flowers out of his hand, I stick my nose in them and inhale. "They're lovely," I murmur.

Rock's gaze darts around the room. "Shit, you know, I didn't think about it. I don't even have a vase." He turns and takes out a pair of heavy beer mugs.

"I don't want to ruin your—"

"Hope, it's fine."

Leaning over, he presses a kiss to my forehead. "I gotta go get Bricks set up. You okay?"

"Yup. I'll bring lunch out in a few minutes."

"Just call me. I'll come in and take care of it."

"Okay."

I set about putting the roses in water, smiling and sniffing them the whole time. Then I finish putting lunch together. But as I step outside with a plate in each hand, white-hot, searing pain slashes through my side, and the plates crash to the pavement.

Rock tears out of the garage. "Hope, what's wrong?"

"Cramp." Tears sting my eyes. Besides the pain, I'm so damn embarrassed to be so weak in front of him. "I'm sorry."

He growls and lifts me up. "Told you to rest, Baby Doll. Should we go back to the hospital?"

"No. I'll lie down, take the pain meds, and if I still feel bad, you can take me."

He stares at my face but nods.

Once I'm settled upstairs, Rock stays with me while I fall asleep.

After that scare, I spend the rest of the day napping. Rock checks in on me frequently.

"Taking some vacation time," he tells me when I question how he can be away from the club for so long.

"Do bikers get vacation?" I tease.

"This one does," he answers with a smirk. His thumb caresses my chin. "I do need to be up there this weekend. Think you'll be ready for a drive Friday?"

"Sure. We can go whenever you want. I'm getting a little claustrophobic."

He chuckles and shakes his head at me.

The next morning is incident free. I wake up with my roses in my line of vision.

Rock's pressed tight against my back. "How do you feel?"

"Better. Thanks for bringing those upstairs," I say, gesturing to the flowers.

"You're welcome, baby."

After a quick run to the bathroom, I'm ready to crawl back into bed with my man, but he's up and getting dressed.

"What are you doing?" I ask, trying to keep the pout out of my voice.

"Taking you to the doc."

I cross my arms over my chest and glare at him.

"Glare all you want, Baby Doll. You scared the shit out of me yesterday. I called and they said they'd see you at ten."

"I feel fine today."

"Good, then you won't mind getting your hot little ass dressed and in the car."

Now what am I supposed to say to that?

"Fine," I grumble.

"This is a waste of time," I mutter as Rock holds the hospital door open for me.

"I know. Humor me."

We wind our way through the massive medical complex until we find my surgeon's office. The nurse rushes me into an exam room right away. An overwhelming vulnerability steals my breath. After closing my eyes for a second, I stare up at the nurse. "Can you please bring my boyfriend back?"

"Sure, hon."

Poor Rock is clearly uncomfortable in the tiny exam room, but he squeezes my hand and gives me a reassuring smile when he enters.

ROCK

If looks could kill, I'd definitely be nursing a gut punch right about now.

Hope's giving me every pissed-off face she can come up with. Unfortunately for her, I'm not intimidated one bit. They're cute as fuck.

I'm also trying to ignore the highly personal questions the nurse keeps asking.

Hope's red in the face and squirming as she answers. "Not much heavier than a regular period. But bad cramping yesterday, even with the painkillers."

"What about today?"

"No cramps."

"Bleeding?" the nurse prompts.

"Yes," Hope grinds out, and if it wasn't so serious, I'd laugh at how pissed-off embarrassed she is.

"We'll do a quick test, but I think it's a good sign that your hCG levels are dropping rapidly."

"Is the doctor going to see her?" I ask.

Now it's the nurse's turn to give me a dirty look. "Yes, he'll be in after we run the test."

"This is mortifying," Hope grumbles after she returns from the bathroom and hands the nurse a sample cup.

My teeth sink into my tongue so I don't say anything to make it worse for her.

The doctor is a different one than the one who treated Hope. But he's aware of her case and seems to be thorough.

"You're doing fine, Ms. Kendall. Incisions look good. HCG is falling. How are you feeling otherwise?"

"Still tired."

"That's to be expected."

Hope flicks her gaze at me. "Still weepy."

"Also understandable. Anything gets worse or the bleeding persists past, say, another five days, come back in."

"Okay."

The doctor shakes my hand on his way out, and I help Hope get dressed.

"Happy now?" she asks.

"Yes, actually. I'm relieved. Aren't you?"

Oh, I can tell it's killing her to agree with me, but I try to keep my gloating to a minimum.

"Yes," she answers.

On the way home, she asks if we can stop for ice cream.

As if I can say no to her.

CHAPTER SIX

HOPE

COMING TO THE CLUBHOUSE WAS ALMOST WORSE THAN STAYING AT ROCK'S house. After a few days, I'm dangerously close to strangling someone. After my forced trip to the doctor, we packed up and arrived in the afternoon. Worn out and still in pain, I slept a good portion of the first twenty-four hours away. But I've been lucid since.

Rock is driving me nuts.

You'd think the doctor telling us I'm healing and things are fine would alleviate Rock's concern, but it seemed to have the opposite effect. His constant hovering stopped being sweet yesterday. If I want to go downstairs, he insists on carrying me. If I need something, he jumps up to get it.

I had to draw the line at him following me into the bathroom.

Trinity giggles at my frustration. She's never seen Rock act this way and finds it adorable.

Okay, I kind of do, too.

I still want to throttle him.

Just a teeny-tiny bit.

At least with him constantly buzzing around me, I don't have time to dwell on all the dark thoughts that followed me home from the hospital.

So when he returns to our room after a club meeting, looking uncertain, raking his fingers through his hair, Trinity escapes with a brief wave. Whether her hasty departure is from Rock's serious expression or because she knows Wrath is free and waiting for her downstairs, I don't know.

"How do you feel, Baby Doll?"

I grit my teeth. He asks me this about five hundred times a day.

"Fine," I answer because I know he's just worried about me.

He leans over to kiss my forehead, and I inhale his wonderful scent. Leather, musk, man. My tummy flips. I tip my head up for a real kiss but only get a peck.

Sitting next to me on the bed, he takes my hand. "Baby doll, I have to go on a run. You know I would never leave you after... if it wasn't important. It's been scheduled for a bit now. Wrath was supposed to do it, but he can't. Murph and Z will be going with me."

Yippie! Oh, I mean, "Okay. Where?"

"You're not upset? After everything that happened, I should really be here with you. I feel like shit for taking off already."

I wipe the eager look off my face and smooth on something a little more concerned. "Of course I'm not happy about it. But I understand. Club business?"

"Yeah."

"How long?"

"Should take a week."

Okay, that's a little long. Since I can already sense how torn he is, I don't want to make things harder on him. "I know you wouldn't go if you didn't have to. You've taken such good care of me, Rock. I'll be fine."

"You'll stay up here while I'm gone?"

Although he phrases it as a question, I don't think it's up for debate. "Of course."

He nods once. "Good. Wrath and Trinity will be here to look after you if you need anything."

I quirk an eyebrow at that, and he smirks in return.

With the backs of his fingers, he sweeps aside my bangs. Running his hand down the side of my face, he cups my cheek. "You're so beautiful."

My cheeks heat up under his intensity. I point to my belly, which has yet to fully deflate from the surgery.

"Hopefully *this* will be gone when you get back."

One corner of his mouth kicks up. "I don't know what you're talking about."

Yeah, right.

I sit up on my knees and steady myself on his shoulders. Leaning against him, I whisper in his ear. *"I'll* be ready for you when you get back."

This pained look stretches across his face, and the urge to throttle him returns. Even though physically I'm still dealing with some gross side effects, mentally I'm ready to jump his bones. I miss the physical closeness. We spent days at his house, talking and just being with each other. But since we've come back up to the clubhouse—even though we've slept side by side every night—there's a strange emotional wall between us, and I can't figure out how to scale it.

I rake my nails through his hair, which I know he loves, and he closes his eyes. "Maybe a long ride will help you clear your head?"

"Hope—"

"Shhh." He's silent, but after a while, I have to ruin the moment. "Rochlan?"

"Yes, Baby Doll," he answers in a dreamy tone since I'm still running my nails over his scalp.

"You're not mad at me about the fight we had. You know, before?"

His eyes snap open, flashing with fire. "Fuck no. If you have to ask, then I'm doing something wrong, baby."

"I don't know why I overreacted like that when I'm not even sure I still want to even be a lawyer anymore."

"Baby, you worked hard to get where you are. No one likes being accused of doing something they didn't do."

"I just… I know this sounds like an excuse, but I think… my temper… I got so upset, I think, because—"

"Stop. Please, Hope. I almost *lost* you. Some little fight isn't even on my give-a-fuck radar after that. We were good before. I got your sweet little text and was about to send you the same thing. We're solid."

"Okay," I answer, even though I'm still uncertain.

ROCK

Hope's still asleep when I slide out of bed the next morning. Part of me wants to stay right where I am so I can watch her wake up, but I've got some things to do before I can leave.

Wandering downstairs, I find Wrath in the dining room, sipping coffee by himself.

"Can I talk to you for a sec?"

With his good leg, he kicks a chair at me in response.

"You all right?"

He grunts back. "I'm just pissed I can't go on the run. You shouldn't have to do it. Shouldn't be leavin' your girl after everything you two just went through."

My lip twitches as I try not to smile. "Something tells me she'd like some space."

He stares at me, then nods. "Yeah, you've been overdoing it a little, playin' nurse."

"Listen, this is stupid, but if anything happens—"

"No way. Shut that shit down right now, prez."

"Wyatt, I'm serious. Come on. You never know. She fell apart after her husband died. You gotta promise me if something happens—on the run, next year, ten years from now—promise me you'll take care of her."

"Fuck, why you gotta do this to me? Of course I'll take care of her. The club will take care of her. Now, knock it the fuck off. You're drawing bad mojo your way."

I snort because hearing the word mojo come out of Wrath's mouth is pretty damn funny.

I've been debating all morning whether I should mention this to him or not. "One last thing—and I swear to fuck if you make a joke about this, I'm going to break your other leg."

Wrath snorts. "This should be good."

Christ. "She's still hormonal and stuff, so could you please try not to give her shit. She's liable to either rip your head off or cry. And if you make her cry, I'm going to kick your fuckin' ass."

For once, he loses his silly smirk. "I'm not completely stupid. Poor girl almost died. I'll behave myself."

"Do your best."

He opens his mouth to say something but pauses as he looks over my shoulder. "Fuck you," he says, pasting his silly smirk back in place.

Soft arms snake over my shoulders, and Hope's scent wraps around me. She plants a kiss on my neck that makes my dick want to punch through my fucking jeans. Maybe this run will be good for me after all.

"Morning, baby," she says all soft and husky.

Wrath clears his throat. "You sure you want to get him all horned up, then send him on his way, Hope?"

The gentle pressure of her lips against my neck disappears. "What's that supposed to mean?" she snaps.

Encircling one of her arms with my hand, I pull her around and into my lap. "Ignore him, Baby Doll."

She touches her forehead to mine and rubs my nose with hers. "I'm going to miss you."

Running my hands through her hair, I tug on the ends a little. "Me too."

"Let's get on the roaaad!" Z shouts from somewhere behind me. Sighing, I pull back from Hope. She places a hand over my heart. "I'll go grab you something to eat and coffee."

Z straddles the chair next to me. "Will you feed me too, Hope?"

I growl out, "No," as Hope slides off my lap. She pats Wrath's shoulder as she passes him. Dammit. Even in the loose pajama pants she's been wearing, the sway of her hips is noticeable enough that I want to follow her into the kitchen and bend her over the counter—

"Prez, you okay?" Z snaps his fingers in front of my face.

Slapping his hand away, I grunt at him.

Wrath leans forward. "Prez is so backed up, cum's gonna shoot out his ears if he doesn't get some pussy soon."

My fist slams into his shoulder.

"Ow! What the fuck you do that for?"

I level an are-you-kidding-me stare at him. "Stop being a disgusting asshole."

"You're just pissed 'cause it's true."

Z leans in. "Plenty of pussy where we're—"

"I will motherfucking gut you if you finish that sentence," I growl at him.

Fuck me. I don't know why Hope's so worried about having kids. I already have two delinquents right here.

"Where's Trinny?" Z asks instead.

Wise choice, fucker.

"Sleeping," Wrath answers.

"Wear her out again?"

I smack Z on the back of the head. "God, you're a nosy dick."

Hope bustles out of the kitchen, and we fall silent. She casts a suspicious glance at each of us. "Talking about pussy, guys?"

Wrath snorts. "Tryin' to. Your man keeps slapping us."

She giggles and bumps him with her hip.

Suddenly, I'm not too happy leaving her here alone with him.

She sets two mugs down and pours coffee for all three of us.

"What did I say about bringing him anything?" I ask her and get an eye-roll in return before she saunters back to the kitchen.

Wrath's gaze focuses on something behind me, and by the look in his eyes, I assume Trinity is awake.

She sneaks up behind us and wraps her arms around Z and me, giving each of us a peck on the cheek. "You guys be careful."

I pat her hand. "Hope's in the kitchen."

"Okay, I'll shoo her out."

As she walks by Wrath, his arm shoots out to hook his fingers in her back pocket. She giggles as he pulls her back, then cups his cheek, her thumb rubbing over his lips. "I already said good morning to you."

Z and I pick our jaws up off the floor.

"Care to share?" I ask once the kitchen door closes.

"Nope."

"She and Hope seem tight lately," Z tosses out.

Wrath eyes him warily.

"I bet they share a lot of girl talk." Z continues poking the bear.

At that, Wrath smirks and casts his sneaky gaze my way. "Yeah, they do."

"Fuck you both," I mutter.

Hope storms out of the kitchen. "Did you make Trin kick me out?"

"Get over here," I call.

She stomps over, face screwed into one of her sexy-as-fuck pouts.

I pat my lap and she settles against me with minimal squawking. "I want to spend time with you before I leave, Baby Doll," I whisper against her ear.

My words sink in and she goes all soft against me. Exactly the response I was after.

Trinity sets plates in front of us. Hope playfully feeds me bits of toast. Even with my brothers making gagging noises next to us, I love every second of it.

HOPE

When Rock runs upstairs to grab a few more things before they take off, I'm able to get Z alone.

"Can we talk?"

"Yeah, babe, what's up?"

"You remember that talk we had about Rock's need to protect the people he cares about?"

"Of course."

"You'll watch out for him, right?"

"Always."

"I couldn't... You know I lost my husband. And I think you understand how I feel about Rock... I couldn't stand to lose someone else I love."

Z lets out a long sigh. "There's no guarantees in life. You know that better than anyone probably. But I'd protect him with my own life, babe. I can promise you that."

"Okay."

"Fuck. I shouldn't say anything." He ducks his head and rubs his hand over the back of his neck. "Look, this run? It's not dangerous. I mean, it shouldn't be. All friendly territory. Okay? So try not to worry."

Stunned barely covers it. That's a lot for Z to share with me about club business, and I'm extremely grateful.

"Now look who's dragging ass," Rock says, coming up behind me.

Z's mouth curves into a wide grin. He quirks an eyebrow at me as if to ask if I'm satisfied with his answer, so I nod.

Rock's arms slip around my ribcage and pull me tight against him. His lips tease against my earlobe. "Next run I have to go on, I want you with me," he says so low my knees turn to jelly.

I squirm around until I'm facing him and throw my arms around his neck. "Is that allowed?"

"Fuck yeah. If I say so, it is."

"Okay. I think I'd like that."

His lips curve into a soft, sexy smile, and suddenly, I don't think I can survive five minutes without him.

"You gonna be a good girl for me while I'm gone?"

Good girl. Hmmm... maybe he can't go soon enough.

The frown on my face makes him chuckle. "I want you to rest up and take care of yourself. Have Trinity or one of the guys drive you anywhere you want to go."

I open my mouth to protest, but Rock silences me with a kiss. "Please? I'll worry about you otherwise, baby. I already feel like shit for leaving you so soon after you got out of the hospital."

My throat clogs, and it takes a second to remember how to breathe. "Okay. I can do that."

"Thank you, baby."

CHAPTER SEVEN

HOPE

I SHOULDN'T HAVE BEEN SO EAGER FOR ROCK TO GO, BECAUSE NOW I'M miserable and miss him like crazy. Even though Wrath and Trinity are downstairs, the house seems quiet, giving me plenty of time for my thoughts to turn dark.

Lucky for me, Heidi calls and shakes me out of my melancholy.

She's the reason two days later, I find myself driving us to Planned Parenthood. Sneaking past my two watchdogs was easy enough. Wrath and Trinity tend to disappear right after breakfast.

How I got nominated for *this* job, I'm not sure. I understand not wanting to talk about birth control with her grandmother. Heidi says she can't tell Trinity because she will tattle to her brother, and she doesn't want Axel to get his ass kicked.

I sigh. "Honey, if you're worried, maybe it's a sign you're not ready."

She makes this exaggerated, eye-rolling *duh* face at me. "Well, I'm not *yet*. I just want to be prepared. You know. In case."

Can't argue with that logic.

"I didn't even tell Axel 'cause I didn't want him to think I was giving him the green light or something."

Good girl.

Heidi's quiet for a while, twisting her hands in her lap.

"Are you having second thoughts?"

"No. I just—will you promise not to laugh?"

"I'll do my best."

She groans out a very dramatic, teenage girl noise, and I almost lose it.

"Well, I always thought, you know, Blake would be my first. Is that stupid?"

Reaching over, I put my hand over one of hers and give her a gentle squeeze. "No, that's not stupid, honey. First loves are very powerful."

"Ugh, I'm not in love with him."

Seriously—I'm going to bite my tongue off I'm trying so hard not to laugh.

"I love Axel. He's super sweet and always listens to me. *Murphy* has turned into a big manwhore like my brother." She fake shivers. "They are *so* disgusting."

Yeah, I'd really like to steer this conversation... elsewhere. "Okay. Listen to your gut, though. Don't let *anyone* talk you into doing something you're not ready to do."

"Hope, I needed a ride, not a mom lecture."

"Listen up, kid. You asked for my help, so that means you get my advice too. And I am not old enough to be your mother." Well, maybe biologically I am, but good grief. "I say it as your friend. I'd say the same thing to my best friend Sophie if she started dating someone new."

"You would?"

"Yes." Sophie would tell me to fuck off, but still.

"Oh my God, you're not gonna tell Uncle Rock are you?"

I have to stop myself from giggling at the panic in her voice. "This just occurred to you *now*?" We pull into the clinic lot and I shut off the car. "I won't say anything as long as you promise to think about what I said."

She glances at the building. "Does it hurt?"

"It's uncomfortable, but no, it doesn't hurt."

Given what I just went through, I can't say I'm excited to be inside Planned Parenthood. But this trip also brings back memories of me at Heidi's age. I didn't have anyone to go with me, and I'm glad I can be here for her now.

When she's finally done, Heidi doesn't look as enthusiastic as when we arrived. I hang on to my completely inappropriate chuckle by a thread.

In the car, she whips out a brown paper bag. "They gave me a bunch of condoms too," she says with a look of disgust.

"Better to use two methods and be safe than sorry." What I said hits me, and I almost burst into tears.

Dammit.

"Ugh, yeah, they said the same thing." She glances at me. "You, uh, haven't seen Axel with any girls at the clubhouse, have you?"

I honestly haven't and I tell her so. "He's usually outside working on stuff when I see him."

"Okay. I mean, I trust him, but I know how bikers are too."

Interesting.

"Honey, it's not just bikers who cheat."

"Yeah, duh, I know. But..." She shakes her head. "Nothing."

It's stupid, but suddenly I'm wondering what Rock is up to— wherever he is.

"Hope?" she asks, breaking me out of my thoughts.

"Yes?"

"Um, do you think I should wait? I mean, all my friends have already... But I don't—"

"If you're not ready, you're not ready. Don't let your friends talk you into something because they want to feel better about their own decisions."

She sucks in a deep breath. "Oh, wow. I never thought of it like that."

Finally, I've managed to impart some useful wisdom here.

"Um, if I tell you something, promise you won't tell anyone else? You're a lawyer, right? So you have to keep this between us if I ask you to."

I groan because that's a dirty trick. "It depends. If it's something I think is dangerous to you, then no, I don't."

"No, nothing dangerous. But, um. Blake and I kissed."

"What?" I'm trying to drive, but I don't think I can have this conversation and concentrate on the road at the same time. There's a McDonald's right before the entrance to the thruway, so I pull into their parking lot.

"Are you hungry?" I ask.

"No. Are you mad? Please don't tell Uncle Rock. I don't want my brother to find out. He'll be pissed, and they've been best friends forever."

Her concern for the other people in this situation startles me. She's so young, but she's also wiser than her age in some ways. Closing my eyes and sighing, I ask, "When?"

She waves her hand in the air. "Last Christmas, and then the night of my birthday party."

Dammit. I suspected more than an innocent ride went on the night the cops brought the two of them back to Rock's house.

"Is that it?"

"Yeah. I mean, I wanted… but he said no."

I can't help snorting at that image. Poor Murphy. "And?"

"He's pretty much been avoiding me since."

Good.

"Hope, please don't say anything. I don't want Axel to find out. He already knows there's some weirdness there. And I don't want you thinking… If it wasn't Blake, I'd never do that behind Axel's back. I'm not some slut."

Turning in my seat so I can see her better, I take her hand in mine. "Heidi, I would never think that about you."

"Well, I've heard my whole life what a slut my mother was, and I've tried really hard not to be like her."

That grandmother of Heidi's really pisses me off. Saying things like that to a kid about her mother. For Heidi's sake, I keep a lid on my anger.

"That's a rotten word, and I'm sorry you've had to hear that about your mom. I would never think that about you, Heidi. It's okay to be a little confused and have all these feelings. Just be careful." Crap. I have no fucking clue what I'm saying or if I'm saying the right thing. What do I know? "Honey, you've got so much to worry about the next few months. You've got graduation coming up. Try to focus on that stuff. You can sort the relationship stuff out later."

She shakes her head, a cloud of sorrow settling around her. "You know when I was a freshman, I made Blake promise to take me to prom, and now Axel expects to take me."

I don't want to laugh, because I can see this is bothering her, but I highly doubt Murphy is expecting to be held to that promise.

"It's okay, Heidi. I'm sure Murphy will understand."

She huffs out a long sigh and wrinkles her nose. "I gotta find a stupid dress."

Okay, I've been holding in my laughter all day. "I can help you with that."

"Yeah?" She looks so hopeful my heart breaks for her. "Sweet! Thanks."

"Anything else you need to unload on me before we head back to your house?"

She rolls her eyes at me. "No. But can I get a milkshake?"

Putting the car gear, I glance over at her. "You got it."

Teller is in the front yard when I pull up to the grandmother's house. He jogs over to greet us, and I roll down my window.

"Hey, I didn't realize she was out with you, Hope. I've been going nuts."

Out of the corner of my eye, I see a red-faced Heidi shoving her Planned Parenthood swag bag in her purse.

"Sorry." I'm not really sure what else to say.

Heidi is quicker at thinking—or lying—on her feet. "She took me shopping for a prom dress," she says as she steps out of my car.

He looks at her and then inside my car. "Yeah, where is it?"

"I didn't find any I liked. Thanks, Hope!" Heidi slams the door and runs inside.

Teller leans on my car. "You didn't have to do that, Hope."

I shrug nervously. I like Teller, so lying to him bugs me. "She's a fun kid."

He snorts. "Yeah, fun. She's a fucking handful."

"Nah, she's a sweet girl. I like spending time with her."

"Well, I appreciate it." He cocks his head at me. "How'd you manage to get out of the house, anyway? I thought Rock didn't want you out by yourself?"

My cheeks heat up, but I shrug it off. "I was getting cabin fever."

Teller shakes his head. "Rock's gonna kick all our asses."

"Well, then don't tell him," I joke back.

He grins at me. "Drive back safe, Hope."

Alone in the car, I'm assaulted with a hundred different images and feelings from my childhood. Especially after my father died.

Loneliness. Desperation. Fear.

I haven't been to my house since before the hospital, so I want to stop there before going back to the clubhouse.

After pulling in the driveway, I just sit and stare at the house for a while.

It didn't escape my notice that Rock called my mother when I was in the hospital. From my phone, I'm able to see the call lasted long enough that they must have had some sort of chat about my condition. Yet she's never tried to get in touch with me to see if I'm okay.

I'm not at all surprised, but it still hurts.

I wander through my house, staring at my stuff, thinking of what I can get rid of and what I'd keep. In the bedroom, I stop and stare at Clay's side. I managed to get rid of his clothes finally, but his other things are still here.

Grabbing a few boxes, I set about packing up more stuff. I should call Lynn and see if she wants any of it, but the thought of speaking to her makes me ill.

Actually, maybe it's not Lynn making me feel bad. I've probably done way more than I should have today.

Leaving the boxes on the bed, I stare at my bookshelf. Three photo albums are lined up on the bottom. One has the only pictures remaining of my dad. One is filled with friends I haven't seen since high school, and the last is my wedding album.

I pull out the green leather one that has the old family photos and the white-and-gold wedding album before plopping down on the floor. It's been so long, sometimes I just have memories and impressions of Dad more than a clear picture of him in my mind. To me, he was the biggest, strongest man in the world, and I always felt safest around him.

My favorite picture is in the front of the album. Christmas morning, my dad helping me ride my first tricycle. It was shiny purple with white flowers, and I rode that thing until my knees hit the handlebars two years later.

In my pocket, my phone buzzes against my hip, startling me out of my reverie.

It's Wrath. *Uh-oh*, my escape has been discovered. Thankfully, it's just a text.

Where the fuck are you?

Nice.

On my way back.

Grabbing the two albums, I search my closet for a bag to put them in and then toss in some extra clothes on top.

I don't get any more texts from Wrath, but he's waiting for me when I return.

"Where the fuck did you go?" he snarls at me as I walk in the door.

"I, uh, took Heidi out."

"You didn't think to tell me? Rock's gonna have my ass."

"I didn't want to bother you." My gaze flicks around the room, seeking Trinity, but she's not here. "I figured I'd be back before you noticed I was gone."

He shakes his head at me. "Teller called me."

"That little fucker," I grumble.

Wrath laughs. "Agreed. But still, not cool, Hope. You took so long getting here from his house you had me worried."

My eyes sting seeing that he's sincere. "I'm sorry. I stopped by my house to grab a few things."

"Okay. You need to go anywhere else, though, just tell me." Yeah, right—he would've *loved* to tag along with Heidi and me today.

"I think I'm done. I'm exhausted." I'm not lying either. I'm thinking of sprawling out on the couch because I don't have the energy to crawl upstairs.

"Go get some rest, Cinderella."

ROCK

"Move along, sweetie," I growl at this bitch for the second damn time.

Z's sitting beside me, quivering with laughter. *Asshole.*

Murphy's off balls deep in some bitch who tagged him the minute we got here.

The ride did its job and cleared my head.

Only to have it fucked with when we stepped inside the Devil's Demons clubhouse. I haven't set foot in this place in probably seven or eight years. Back when the Demons and I had a mutual enemy that needed to be put to ground. We've maintained a friendly relationship between our clubs, but since Wrath or Z usually took the runs that sent them through Demon territory, there'd been no need for me to come out.

After blowing off sweet butts all night, I have to say I haven't missed this place at all.

Their president, the aptly named Stump, settles on the stool next to me. "Nothin'?"

"Naw, man, prez here is all wifed up now," Z chirps.

"So fucking what?" Stump grumbles.

"Been there, done that. This one's a keeper," I tell him, hoping it will shut him up.

"Yeah, found himself a real smart, classy girl," Z adds.

It's a nice thing to say, and I appreciate Z feels that way about Hope. But I'm not sure if I want Z talking about Hope's charms to a guy like Stump. The less he knows about my personal life, the better.

A sharp bark of laughter erupts from Stump. "What's that like?"

"It's good," I answer with a straight face.

Stump studies me for a minute. "Never thought I'd see that. Good for you."

Surprised, I thank him.

"How you been? Besides the wife thing?" Stump asks.

Wife. Fuck, I wish. That needs to fucking happen soon.

"Good. Business is good." Demons are into way harder stuff than we are. Always have been, and that's fine. They can keep their H, coke, and weapons running. I really don't give two fucks if they think I've gone "soft." None of the brothers in *my* charter are serving life sentences. The average life expectancy of a King is much higher than a Demon too. Those are the things I take pride in.

"Sucked about that thing awhile back. We got short notice about that wedding. Didn't realize how close that park was to your area."

I wave my hand in the air. "Not a problem."

He jerks his chin at Z. "Well, at least we got to chat. I hear you've got a line of good shit coming up."

I give Z the signal and he strolls outside.

"That we do."

Z returns and drops a package of our new strain on the bar.

"Since when you run weed?" I ask.

Stump takes a long drag of his cigarette before answering. "People ain't buying the heavy shit around here no more. Everyone wants the fucking green these days. Got no regular suppliers around here. Just punks."

"I can get you a steady stream. I can't guarantee we'll be able to run it all the way out here every time."

"My guys can meet you halfway. Outside Syracuse?"

"That would work."

We hammer out a few more details. I gotta add a hefty surcharge because of the travel involved and the fact that Stump is stuck and can't buy good, reliable shit anywhere else.

I also need to make sure this deal stays off the radar of the GSC.

"How's Trinity doin'? She still with your club?"

My jaw clenches. "Yup. Still a big help to us."

"That's good. I remember she was a nice kid. Nothing like her whore mother."

I make a noise that sounds something like agreement.

"How's Wrath?"

"Laid up with a broken leg."

"No shit. Didn't think anything could take that big fucker out."

"Yeah, he's plenty pissed about it too."

We end up talking business for a while. When we exhaust that topic, we catch up on some other things. Around midnight, my phone goes off. Thinking it might be Hope, I step outside to answer it.

"Rocky?" comes the tentative voice over the line.

"Who's this?"

"It's me, Inga."

Fuck. "What do you want?"

"Don't hang up, please."

I don't know what the fuck is wrong with me. I should hit *end.* There's no reason for us to talk, but I feel a little shitty for the way things ended between us. "I'm here."

"I just wanted to tell you I'm sorry."

Aw, Christ. "Okay."

"I, uh, you surprised me with Hope."

"Inga—"

"No, no. I just want to explain."

In the background, there's suddenly a lot of noise.

"Where are you?"

"Back in California." As soon as she says it, I realize I never actually knew where she lived when she wasn't traveling. It kind of makes me feel like a dick.

"Well, not home, though. I'm in rehab."

Fuck, I don't know what to say to that. "That going okay?"

"Yeah. Yeah, it is. I'm leaving the film industry and dancing."

Shit. "Sounds like that's for the best."

"Yeah, it is. I thought I could handle everything, but, well, I couldn't. Obviously." Her soft, nervous laughter comes through the line, surprising me. I can't remember ever hearing Inga less than one hundred percent confident. It's why I always thought our arrangement worked so well.

I swear I'm not so fucking full of myself that I think I'm the reason for her troubles, but I gotta ask anyway. "Inga, I'm sorry if I ever—"

"No, Rock. You were always straight with me. I think I just had it in my head that when I retired from dancing and films, maybe we could be together for real, but—"

"Shit, Ing, I'm sorry if I led you on."

"You didn't. You were always honest. You treated me well, trust me. Maybe that's why I just figured there could be more between us. I don't know."

Nothing she's saying is making me feel like any less of a shithead.

As if she hears my thoughts, she continues. "Ah, I'm not trying to make you feel bad or blaming you for my problems. That's not why I called. I've had this habit a long time. I just always hid it well, but it finally caught up with me."

Now I'm pissed I never noticed she had a drug problem and wonder how many other girls at CB are hooked on shit.

"Anyway, I kinda freaked out when I saw how serious you were with Hope. She doesn't seem like your type. I mean, she's awfully sweet. I feel terrible..."

"Inga, it's fine. Just worry about getting yourself together."

"Thanks. Will you tell Hope I'm sorry?"

"Yeah, sure." Like fuck am I telling Hope about this phone call. She doesn't need the stress.

"I, uh, already called Dex and apologized to him."

"That's good."

"Okay. I'll let you go. Thanks for listening."

I don't know how to respond. I want to end in a nice way so she can do her program with a clear head, but I don't want to encourage any more phone calls either. "Get yourself well, Inga. Don't worry about anything here. We're good. Okay?"

I'd like to offer her some nice platitude like, "Your job is here when you're ready," or "Feel free to call me if you need something," but they're both lies, so I bite my motherfucking tongue.

"Thanks, Rock."

We say our good-byes and hang up.

We're going to be able to head home earlier than planned. So the day before we leave, I decide to do some sightseeing, which is a joke—there's nothing of note for miles—and make a special stop.

Z's all for it, until I hand over what I want to the artist.

"Prez, you fucking serious?"

"As a heart attack."

He flicks his hand against the paper. "You're the first one always telling us *not* to do this."

I flick his shoulder in retaliation for touching the drawing. "Yeah, saved you some trouble once or twice too, didn't it?"

Z shakes his head and gives me a comical eye-roll worthy of the most dramatic club girl. "Fine, let me see it again."

Reluctantly, I hand over the drawing.

Since I guess he's over the shock, he gives it a more critical review this time. "You have Bricks do it?"

"Yeah."

"I guess it looks good. Pretty sappy, though."

"Fuck you."

Z smirks. "Where?"

"Her favorite spot."

Z gags. "I don't think Bronze wants to see your dick."

Bronze chuckles. "I've tatted worse, dude. Trust me."

I knock Z back with a slap and point to the spot I want the ink to go. Christ, just thinking about the way she likes to kiss and nuzzle my hip gets me hard

"Not my dick, fuck face."

I settle into the chair and let Bronze do his thing. He gets carried away and wants to add some color and shading to my pirate ship.

"'Nother time. Why'd you have to set up shop so far away?" Back in the day, he was the only one I would let near me with a needle.

He chuckles softly, his eyes and hands never wavering. "Kings need an official tattoo guy? I'll move back."

I snort at that. "You'll have to do more than that to earn your keep, man. Besides, I thought you were tight with Stump's crew?"

"I am. It's boring as fuck out here, though."

"Empire ain't exactly jumpin'," Z says.

Bronze grunts and keeps working. "The talent out here is lacking."

I don't want to disturb him, so I hold in my laughter.

After a while, the buzzing and pain lulls me into a meditative state. The whole time, I'm imagining the look on Hope's face when she finds this surprise.

HOPE

My adventure with Heidi wore me out more than I realized. After sleeping in the next morning, I wander downstairs to find Wrath taking up residence on the couch.

"Hey."

He looks up with a faint smile on his face.

Jerking my chin toward his cast, I ask, "How's the leg?"

"Okay."

"You eat breakfast yet?"

A small smirk, so I guess he's forgiven me for sneaking out yesterday. "I'm fine. Thanks."

No one's in the kitchen. Not even Trinity. I scarf down some cereal and return to the living room. "Where's Trin?"

Wrath's jaw ticks. "Out."

Oh dear. I'm not touching that.

I throw myself into the corner of the other couch that sits at a ninety-degree angle with the one Wrath's on. He glances over at me, taking in my sweatshirt, flannel pants, and wool socks.

"You cold?"

"I'm okay."

He grunts and returns his attention to the television. I don't think we've ever sat this close to each other when I wasn't distracted by Rock or Wrath wasn't trying to scare the crap out of me. The sleeveless shirt he's wearing shows off his ink. Like a doof, I sit and stare, trying to make out the different images in the full-sleeve tattoo. The one on his upper bicep intrigues me the most.

"Is that Thor's hammer?"

His lip quirks before he swings his gaze to me. Thrusting out his arm so I can see the intricate Celtic design better, he answers, "Yeah. You got any ink, Hope?"

I shake my head.

"Didn't think so."

If he's trying to be insulting, it's lost on me. When I don't take the bait, he falls back against the couch, studying me.

I guess I look a little stiff.

"You still in pain?" he asks, his voice laced with surprising concern.

"A bit. I stopped taking the pain pills 'cause they made me loopy."

Leaning over, he opens a drawer I never noticed in the coffee table and pulls out a long, slim box.

"You smoke?"

"No."

He raises an eyebrow at me. "Never?"

"You mean weed?"

A snort. "Yeah."

"I tried it in high school a few times."

He nods in an approving manner. "Well, well. You do have a little bit of bad girl in you after all. Come on, *Fight Club* is even better stoned."

We pass the joint between us, and in no time, I'm out of my mind high.

"Feel better?"

Giggling too hard to answer, I nod my head. "Feeling no pain." I gasp.

He gives me a blissed-out, serene smile.

"Why're you being so nice to me, Wrath?"

Exhaling a stream of smoke, he flicks his bloodshot eyes my way. "I been mean to you, sugar?"

More giggles. "Uh, duh. Yeah."

He passes the joint to me again, and I inhale like a pro now.

"You proved yourself. You got enough love for Rock to accept all this shit," he says, waving his hand in the air. I'm not exactly sure what he means, but I don't interrupt him. "Known Rock more than twenty years. Went through lotta bad shit together. Never seen him cry once until that day in the hospital when he thought he might lose you."

Maybe it's the pot, or maybe it's lingering hormones, but my eyes well up.

He wags a finger at my face. "Don't you cry. Can't handle females cryin'."

"You think I'm too soft for Rock's life. For the club, I know."

He cocks his head to the side and studies me for a minute. "Yeah, sugar. I ain't gonna lie. You're soft. Took me some time to get it, but that's what Rock likes about you so much. Your softness. Our world is hard most of the time, so I guess he needs that. You give him something he can't find anywhere else."

Wow. Pot seems to bring out Wrath's romantic side. And he's not finished. "Besides..." He continues. "You're a good girl. You've been tough when it counted." He stops, and before I can absorb all of that, he pins me with a hard but not unkind stare. "You realize I worry about your safety? You ever got picked up by one of our enemies... I can't even think about it."

Rock has told me bits and pieces, but the grave tone Wrath uses makes the threat of their rivals seem much more real. "Shit, Wrath."

"Hope, we've worked damn fuckin' hard to strike a balance and keep our alliances tight." He shakes his head and gives me a level stare. "But this life ain't easy on women."

"What about Trinity?"

His face hardens. "She's been through enough."

"You love her, don't you?" I must be high or I'd never go there.

Wrath doesn't answer my question. Not really anyway.

He snorts. "That girl's made me work harder than anything in my life."

We're silent after that. I don't know what to think. I sniffle and swipe under my eyes. "I miss him."

"Yeah. I know. I'm sorry, sugar. Shoulda been me on that run."

"What is this 'run' anyway? Rock never said."

He rolls his eyes at me. "Club business."

"Ohhhhh." I let out a snicker. "Top secret, big, bad biker stuff. I get it."

"You are soooo fucked up right now," he teases.

Suddenly, he whips out his cell phone. One look at the screen and a slow smile spreads over his face. "Yo." His gaze slides over to me.

"Yeah, she's right here." Pause. "Living room." Another pause. "Gettin' her high."

Loud yelling comes out of his phone.

"Is that Rock?" I shriek, then throw out my hand for the phone. "Gimmie."

He slips the phone into my palm with a chuckle.

"Hey, baby," I chirp into the phone.

"Hope, what the fuck are you doing?" he yells back.

Ignoring the question, I blurt out the only thing on my mind. "I miss you so bad."

His heavy sigh comes through loud and clear. "I miss you too, Baby Doll. We're wrapping things up early, so I'll be back soon." In a lower voice, he adds, "You gonna be ready for me?"

"So, so ready."

"Not sure how I feel about you hanging out with Wrath in your impaired condition."

"Pfft."

"Yeah. Is he behaving himself?"

"Yes, he's been a perfect gentleman."

Wrath shakes his head as if I'm ruining his street cred, and it makes me laugh.

Rock's exasperated groan has me giggling even harder. "I am so gonna spank your ass when I get back."

"Not if I spank yours first."

Wrath gags.

Rock and I spend considerable time saying our good-byes with a lot of love yous and miss yous. Wrath points a finger-gun at his head. I flip him off. When Rock and I finally hang up, I pass the phone back to Wrath.

"He threatened to kick my ass, you know."

I snort at that. "I don't ever want to see you two trade punches."

"He can hold his own," Wrath assures me.

"I don't doubt it."

We go back to smoking quietly.

Fight Club has never interested me, high or not. Flipping chunks of my hair through my fingers, I notice a lot of split ends. "I need to get my hair trimmed."

Wrath's eyebrows draw down in a why-are-you-telling-me-this face. "You and Trin should go out tomorrow. Do some sort of girly salon day thing."

"Does she...? She's not really the girly type."

The door slams. We both look up and find Trinity.

"Jesus, it fucking reeks in here." She comes closer, studying the both of us. "Goddammit, Wyatt. Did you get her high? Rock's gonna kill you."

"Yeah, he already chewed me out." He holds out his hands to her.

Ignoring the offer to sit in his lap, she plunks down next to me and plucks the joint from my fingers.

"Hey!" I yelp.

"Trin, Hope wants to go get her hair cut. Can you take her tomorrow?" He flicks his hand at my hair while he's asking.

Exhaling, she nods. "Sure. Girl I know owns that pin-up salon downtown. She always fits me in. I'll text her later."

I know the place she's talking about. "I'm not too nerdy for that place?"

She quirks her lips up. "No."

Wrath chuckles at both of us and lights a fresh joint.

Trinity's friend has two spots open. Before we leave for the salon, I catch Wrath slipping a bundle of cash into her hand. She shakes her head, and he leans down to whisper something in her ear.

Because I'm so boring, I get a regular wash, trim, and blowout. Trinity has her friend dye the ends of her bright-blond hair beautiful shades of blue and turquoise. It looks amazing, and I'm insanely jealous.

As we're checking out, I discover the cash Wrath shoved at her was to pay for our little excursion. I must say I'm touched.

The salon has a lingerie store attached to it that naturally specializes in pin-up style pieces. Trinity yanks me in there next.

"You need something sexy for your man when he gets back."

I never thought I'd find myself shopping for fuckwear with a friend,

but Trinity makes it fun instead of icky. After a lot of indecision, I settle on an emerald-green halter bra covered in black polka dots and lace accents with a matching ruffle-trimmed garter skirt. The high-waist style hides the small scars left from the surgery, which is the reason I finally decide on it. I also grab several pairs of stockings and this sheer spandex and lace open-back panty contraption that ties in the back with a big bow.

If I'm indecisive, Trinity is outright reluctant, even though she's the one who insisted on dragging us in here. I finally manage to shove her in the dressing room with a similar bra and garter skirt set in sapphire blue. After some furious muttering and cursing, she waves me in to help her with one of the hooks.

"Geez, girl, it's like that thing was made for you," I say, only an itty-bit jealous. "It looks gorgeous with your new hair. Wrath's going to flip."

Now, this is the first time I've acknowledged what anyone with two eyes and a brain can see. She blushes and offers a weak denial.

"Sorry," I say. Although I'm not.

After our awkward moment, I have to talk her into getting the set. She finally relents and takes forever to get dressed again.

We go out for burritos before we head home.

Yes, somewhere along the way, I started thinking of the clubhouse as home.

As she pulls the car around the back of the building, I'm bummed to see Rock's bike still isn't here. When he said he'd be back sooner than he thought, I'd been hopeful that meant today.

Wrath eyes the bags in our hands right away.

"Get anything good?" he asks with a restless smile.

Making a run for the stairs, I shout, "Nothing but some sex-wear."

A growl, a squeal, and a door slamming are all I hear from Wrath and Trinity for the rest of the night.

CHAPTER EIGHT

HOPE

THE NEXT MORNING, WRATH'S ALL TWITCHY WHILE I'M CURLED UP ON THE couch, trying to read. He keeps checking his phone and shooting weird faces in my direction.

"What?" I ask for the tenth time.

"Nothing," he answers for the tenth time.

The rumble of bikes can be heard outside, and I swear my panties are soaked the minute my brain registers what it means.

"You're evil! Why didn't you tell me?"

Wrath grins. "Go greet your man."

I'm already off the couch and halfway to the door before he gets the sentence out. Flinging the front door wide open—there he is. My belly flips. I fly into his arms, almost knocking him down. Effortlessly, he lifts me, my legs wrapping around his waist, our lips fusing together.

Time stops while our tongues twine together. Every soft, teasing stroke tells how much he missed me.

We must have stayed like that for a long time. Eventually, Z clears his throat and we break our kiss. Rock's face makes it clear how much he didn't appreciate the interruption.

"Don't kill me, but you're blocking the door, and I'd really like to get inside and take a fucking shower," Z says in a rush.

A peal of giggles comes out of me. "Sorry."

Rock tightens his grip on my ass as he takes us inside. I nuzzle my face against his neck, breathing him in.

As my man takes us up the stairs, I hear Wrath and Z greeting each other. I hear Murphy thumping some bags on the floor, and then I lose track of everything except us.

Inside our room, he sets me down gently. My chest tightens as I take him in. I can't believe this sexy man is all mine. Taking another look at him, I can't believe how hungry he is. *For me.* My insides melt seeing how much he still wants me.

He slips off his cut, still not taking his eyes off me. My jaw clenches as I remember the outfit I'd wanted to surprise him with. Dammit.

My face must reveal a hint of annoyance.

"Are you okay, Baby Doll?"

Oh no. I don't want him to think for a second that I'm not ready. I'm so damn ready I think I'll explode from just the sight of him without his shirt.

Pressing my body against him, I shamelessly run my palm over the thick, heavy bulge behind his fly. His stormy-gray eyes watch my face, but I see I'm getting to him.

My tongue darts out to wet my bottom lip.

"I need you badly, Rochlan," I whisper.

"You've got me."

He strips out of the rest of his clothing. I hesitate because I'm still a little insecure about some of the remaining marks from the surgery.

He seems to understand as he tugs me over to the side of the bed. Keeping hold of my hand, he reaches into the nightstand and scatters a bunch of condoms on top. My teeth sink into my lower lip. "I'm sor—"

He's on me instantly. "Don't. You. Dare."

Both hands cup the sides of my face and he tips me up for a kiss. At first, his touch is light, using his heat and a hint of pressure to invite me to open to him. The tip of his tongue touches mine, sending a shudder from my head to my toes. With a cherishing slowness, he tugs off my clothes, steps back, and inhales sharply.

"Hope," he breathes out. "I've missed you so much." The sound of his voice, throbbing with so much emotion, makes my eyes sting.

He tumbles into the bed, stretching out on his back. Reaching for me, he takes my hand and guides me onto the mattress.

On my knees next to him, I wait while he gazes up and down my body. Then, ever so slowly, his fingers trace the same path.

"Tell me how you need it," he commands.

"Slow and easy."

He reaches over and grabs one of the condoms, carefully rolling it on while he watches my face for any reaction. He sits up and tugs me into his lap. "Just a precaution, we don't have to do anything you're not ready for yet," he says while stroking my hair and kissing down my neck. The tips of my breasts rub against him, sending a rush of pleasure through my body. He groans, and I can feel the restraint radiating through him.

His mouth finds my nipple, lips sucking, tongue lashing, wet and greedy. Possessive hands knead and plump both breasts.

"Please," I sob. I need him inside me. I need to be certain he's still mine.

"Take me, Baby Doll. Take me the way you need to. I'm right here."

I shiver and ache, needing to feel him inside me. Lifting and settling myself, I place his pulsing erection at my opening, sliding down so carefully.

"Oh, oh," I moan at the familiar and dearly missed pleasure.

His lips roam over my jaw and neck. "Good girl. Fuck, you feel so good. I've missed this, baby."

I rock up, then back. My hips move, my thighs clench, and I focus all my energy on reuniting with my man. My sudden orgasm takes me by surprise. Swift and brutal. It's almost too much.

When I open my eyes, Rock grins at me. His hand cups my face, his thumbs gently rubbing over my cheek. "My girl needed that, huh?"

Blushing, I look away. He falls back against the pillows, and I follow him down, covering him with my body while he pins me tightly to him. My lips press and nip at his skin as my hips keep restlessly working him. It's a very different but no less intense sensation from this angle.

Pressing his palm over my ass, he slows my movement. "Stretch your legs out," he whispers against my hair.

I do as he asks, extending my legs straight between his spread thighs, while angling my hips to keep him where I need him. Holding me tightly to keep me still on top of him, he thrusts up into me over and over. From this angle, the penetration isn't deep, but the friction sends me spiraling into another orgasm, my nails digging into his shoulders.

Our sweat-slicked skin slips and slides against each other. Shuddering, Rock tightens his arms and buries his face against my throat. "I love you so much, Hope," he murmurs.

"I love you too," I whisper back.

We snuggle and cuddle for a while after. Rock taps my hip. "Babe, you wanna say hello to your favorite spot?"

I prop my chin on his chest and squint at him. "Is that your subtle way of asking for a blowjob?"

His chest rumbles and shakes with laughter. "No. Maybe later."

Curious now, I sit up. He's lying back with one arm tucked behind his head. I swear he's so sexy I want to take a million pictures of him just like that. His lips twitch, and as my eyes roam over his body, I remember I'm supposed to be investigating—

Oh. *Oh!* My gaze shoots to his face.

I crawl over to his left side. "Can I touch it?"

"Of course."

Tentatively, I reach out and touch his smooth, hard muscles, running my fingers down to the sexy V of his hip. "It's still new. Did I hurt you before?"

He snorts. "No, babe."

I trace my fingers over the golden-and-blue anchor. Wait. On closer inspection, I notice the ribbon wrapped around the anchor with three clearly inked words.

Hope Anchors Me

Stunned, I look up at him.

"I thought you said you'd never get a woman's name on your body?"

He holds out his hands to me. "Come here."

Tugging me down on top of him, he wraps his hand behind my neck, pulling me close for a kiss. "You're not just any woman."

"You anchor me too, you know. I felt completely adrift while you were gone."

"That why you got high with Wrath?" he says in a teasing way, then slaps me on the ass.

I groan and bite his shoulder.

"My baby likes that, huh?"

We keep teasing and tickling, and before I know it, we're wrapped together snugglefucking, and it is fucking *fantastic*.

ROCK

I've died and gone to heaven. Maybe that's corny, but I don't give a fuck. It's how I feel as I explode into Hope. Not that I'd even been tempted, but I'm so fucking thankful I turned down every tart who approached me on the run. Somehow my girl has gotten ten times more gorgeous in the five days we've been apart. Keeping my cock confined from the time she met me at the door until we made it into the bedroom tested all my will. The minute I got her naked, my instincts screamed to take her hard and raw.

One look at her soft, quivering body, and I knew she needed it sweet and slow.

So that's what I gave her. Or rather, what she took from me.

And it was better than anything ever.

If it's even possible, the second time blows the first time away.

She's spent, curled against me, holding on to me like her life depends on it, even in sleep. Running my hand over her hair, I kiss her reddened lips one more time. Sliding out of bed so I don't wake her, I head straight for the shower. Road dust still coats my skin, and I feel a little guilty that I just rubbed myself all over my sparkling girl. I glance down at my new tattoo and grin. Best ink ever.

Once I'm clean, I throw on a pair of loose track pants. My girl is still out cold, so I head downstairs. I plan to have a surprise ready for her when she wakes up.

Shockingly, downstairs is deserted. Not sure where everyone scattered to, but I don't really care at the moment. I know they'll all be back later for a party. We always have a party when brothers return from a run.

This party, Hope will be wearing my property patch.

I find Z and Dex going over some paperwork in the war room. Z glances up and gives me a dirty smirk. "Reunite with your girl?"

"Fuck you."

He turns to Dex. "Can you believe this fuckbutt got his girl's name inked on him?"

Dex raises an eyebrow. "Holy hell. You been bitchin' at us *not* to do that for fuckin' ever."

"Advising, asshat," I growl. "I'm a little concerned about Z's obsession with my anatomy."

Z's not done gossiping about me, though. He jabs a finger in my direction. "You should have seen this fucker turning down wild pussy left and right."

Dex chuckles and shakes his head. "You're an asshole. I'd rather fuck one good girl, like Hope, who actually gave a shit about me, than ten fuckin' skanks."

I cross my arms over my chest and try to close my mouth. Never heard D spout off like that. "You all right, bro?"

He nods briefly. "Yeah, just statin' facts. That woman fuckin' adores you. Looks at you like you're the only man in the world. Don't fuck that up. Way more valuable than nailing skanks who spread for anyone with a dick."

Z gives him the side-eye before continuing. "Whatever. You're both fucked in the head. Never seen so many unhappy whores. Hope's vagina must be lined in gold."

"Actually, it's lined in platinum," comes a soft voice from the doorway.

The shock on Z's face amuses me so much I forget that I want to break his neck for talking about my woman that way.

He mumbles out an apology.

I take a good look at my girl. She's wearing one of my T-shirts. It almost reaches her knees, but I'm pretty sure she's not wearing a damn thing else. Her hair is all mussed, and she's so gorgeous I can't stand my brothers stealing an ounce of her beauty with their hungry gazes.

"Eyes elsewhere, assholes," I grumble at them before turning to Hope. "Baby doll, what are you doing down here?"

I bite back the "dressed like that" part, but I think she senses it because she twists her fingers into the hem of the T-shirt, which doesn't exactly improve the situation.

"I got up, and you were gone," she says simply.

"I needed to grab something," I explain.

Eyes sparkling with amusement, she leans against the door frame, crosses her arms over her chest, and lifts her chin at Z. "So wild pussy, huh? Did you take up Rock's slack?"

The asshole actually turns red, and I lose it, laughing so hard my gut aches. When I finally catch my breath, Z's glaring at me. By the twitch at the corner of his mouth, I know he's more amused than pissed. I return to what I originally came down here to do, but not before I catch a sly grin spread over Z's face.

"Actually, Hope, I did *not* partake. You can feel free to pass that along to your friend."

Hope's gaze skitters to me for confirmation, and I shrug. "I don't keep track of who garages his dick, babe."

She wants to be outraged, but her lip twitches, giving her away. "You're awful."

"Now Murphy, on the other hand. Bro collected mouth hugs like fucking quarters," Z adds.

Hope shakes her head. "That's a mental image I could have done without."

Unlocking my personal cabinet, I tug out the plain brown box. Thank fuck, when her cut arrived, after I examined it to make sure they got the patches right, I put it back in the box. It's safe, secure, and ready for my girl. Grabbing the box, I salute Z with my middle finger.

Wrapping an arm around Hope's waist, I pull her out of the room with me.

"Bye, guys." She waves over her shoulder.

Determining she's wearing underwear by running my hand over her ass, I ask her to hold the package and swing her up into my arms.

"What's in it?"

"Nothing. Don't open it."

Her lips part to protest, I'm sure.

"I mean it, Hope."

She bristles but settles down.

Voices come out of Murphy's room, one definitely whiny, and I wonder which club girl is up here so early.

When we get inside my room, I set Hope down and turn on the light.

"Sit down. I want to show you something."

Her face twitches and she hops from foot to foot. "Can I run to the bathroom first?"

"Yeah, yeah."

While she's gone, I arrange things the way I want them.

And then lose my motherfuckin' mind when she opens the bathroom door.

HOPE

The awed expression on Rock's face is even better than I'd

imagined. Propping my arm up over my head in the doorway, I cock my hip in what I hope is a more seductive than awkward pose.

"Uh, whatcha wearing, doll?"

Running my hands over the bra cups, I stop to plump my breasts. A strangled groan is all I hear from Rock's side of the room, and I smother a smile. I slide my hands down to my hips, smoothing them over the satin garter skirt. My fingers skip down to adjust the garters holding up my sheer black stockings. Then I twist to check the ones in the back.

"Turn around, babe."

Holding on to the door frame, I do a little spin, arching my back and running my hand over the skirt that doesn't really do much to cover my ass.

"I thought it came with panties, but I guess it didn't," I tease.

"Looks fine to me. Now quit messing around and get the fuck over here."

The sky-high black platform pumps I borrowed from Trinity click softly over the floor as I make my way to him.

His arm encircles my waist when I reach him, sliding around my back so his hand curls over my hip. He tugs me down to the trunk at the end of the bed so we're sitting, legs touching from hip to knee. Pressing a kiss to my cheek, he murmurs, "When did you get this?"

"Yesterday."

"I like. In fact, I think it goes very well with this." From behind his back, he pulls out a black leather vest.

The sight of it makes my stomach churn. My hands tremble. Longing so intense hits, surprising me.

"Hey, you look so serious."

He spreads the vest out on his lap so I can see the patches on the back.

Property of Rock
Lost Kings MC

SOMEWHERE INSIDE ME, I wonder if I should be insulted. A voice taunts me, saying I shouldn't want to be branded like cattle. It's archaic and *wrong*. But a calmer voice overrides my inner sarcasm, cherishing the feeling of belonging to someone. This is a symbol of how much I'm wanted, protected, *loved* by this wonderful man.

With cautious fingers, I reach out to trace the embroidered words. "I didn't think you still wanted me to have it." What I mean is I'm not sure I deserve something of this magnitude.

His rough fingers brush down my face, chasing away some of my anxiety. "Baby doll, there is no one else who could ever wear this. You're the only woman I've ever offered my patch."

My heart squeezes.

He flips it over to show me the patch that reads "First Lady" on the left side.

Four smaller symbols along the bottom right catch my attention. Tracing my fingers over them, I seek his eyes. "What are these?"

His mouth curves into a soft smile. "Your seal of approval from the other officers."

"What?"

He points to the green four-leaf clover. "That's Murphy's. The dollar sign is Teller's. The Z is... Well, you can figure that out because he's not very creative."

Rock tips his head up, a smirk playing over his lips.

"This last one." He points to a blue-and-black nautical star. "That's Wrath's."

Thinking about it, I remember he has a bigger one of these on his own cut and at least two of them tattooed on him. "He voted me in too?"

"Yeah, doll. That means they've always got your back."

"Wait, where's yours?"

He cocks his head and points to the crown over the First Lady patch. "Right there, babe."

I'm not sure what to say, so I lean over, wrap my hand around the back of his neck, and pull him to me for a long, drugging kiss. Barely breaking contact, he stands us up and holds the vest for me to slip into. There are several slim buckles on each side, and he works to fit the vest to my shape.

Once he arranges it the way he wants, he twirls his finger in the air, asking me to spin for him.

"That's perfect, Baby Doll." He turns his head. "Go stand in front of the dresser and take a look."

With the heels giving me the extra height, I can see the entire outfit, including a hint of my bits peeking from beneath the flounce of the tiny garter skirt.

Our eyes meet in the mirror as he slowly approaches me.

He stops behind me, just watching. Then he slips something over my head, dangling it in front of me. A necklace.

"What's that?" I ask, reaching out to touch the simple gold anchor pendant suspended sideways between a delicate gold chain.

"For you. Didn't think you'd be ready for some ink, so I got you this instead."

My throat constricts and tears fill my eyes. I'm stunned. Bewildered. Between his tattoo, the vest, and the pendant, it seems the entire time he'd been away, I'd never been far from his mind.

ROCK

I'm so motherfuckin' turned on.

My girl wearing my patch and some of the sexiest scraps of lace I've ever seen has me ready to blow. As she lets me drape the necklace over her head, a calmer feeling settles over me. The gold chain glitters over her pale skin, highlighting the beautiful angles of her collarbones.

Meeting her gaze in the mirror, I can sense her uncertainty. I reach out and mold myself to her body, cupping her hips and pulling her against me. Sliding my hands down, I knead the flesh of her plump little ass.

Her hair is all twisted up in this sexy, messy little knot, and I grab it, angling her head so her neck is exposed for my tongue. Very slowly, I make my way to her ear, gently licking. She lets out a mewl and her hips shoot back, bumping my cock.

"Put your hands on the dresser," I whisper in her ear.

This tiny fucking skirt thing is killing me. I'm so damn turned on knowing while I was away, she went out and bought this skimpy thing to surprise me when I returned.

As I run my finger under one of the garter straps, she exhales sharply. "That tickles," she moans.

I love my girl like this, all breathy and needy. "Stay like that."

Keeping my eyes trained on her, I walk backward to my nightstand and grab a condom. My cock's in my hand and I'm rolling down the latex before I get back to her.

Once again, I squeeze and stroke her ass cheeks, pushing and spreading. "Arch your back."

My hand slips lower to her satiny pussy. Little shudders work through her body as I push into her from behind. My hands smooth up and down her thighs. "Are you okay?"

"Yes. Just be gentle."

"Always."

My thighs coil with tension, wanting desperately to slam into her. *Slow.* I give it to her slow, until my cock fucking throbs with every stroke. She quivers and gasps. I flatten my chest against her back, finding her clit and rubbing until she yelps, short, sharp little cries of pleasure. I'm rocking into her so hard the dresser thumps against the wall, but I can't pull back. Her pussy keeps squeezing me so fucking tight. She bucks wildly against me, and I lose it. I come with a burst of violent intensity.

"Fuuuuck!"

She's whimpering in my arms and still grinding backward on my half-hard cock.

"Baby, stop." I grip her hips, trying to still her restless movements. Her skin's covered in a fine sheen of sweat. We both are, actually. I kick my pants the rest of the way off, then unzip her vest and set it on top of the dresser.

"Shoes off, babe." She gingerly steps out of them, and I lead her to the bed, where I drop the condom in the wastebasket.

I love her sexy little outfit, but I also want to feel all of her soft skin against me. Once I figure out the top half, I seat her on the edge of the mattress, unhook the garter, and work the stockings down her legs. "Scoot."

She hasn't said a word, and her silence worries me. Once I get her in my arms, I stroke her hair. "Did I hurt you?"

"No. It was... amazing."

She's right.

I've never been the type of guy to kick a girl out of bed. I never exactly encouraged any to stay either. But snuggling and cuddling with them afterward?

Fuck no.

A slap on the ass and something along the lines of "thanks for a good time" were as cuddly as I got.

That was before Hope.

Now I can't wait to snuggle down with her.

Every. Single. Fucking. Time.

"Tell me what you did while I was gone, Baby Doll," I ask while running my hand over her hair.

She props her chin up on my chest, arm banding around my waist. "You mean besides miss you like crazy?"

"Yeah."

She lets out a, "Hmmm," and rolls over to her back. "Went out with Trinity yesterday. Got my hair trimmed. We went and bought the outfits."

"Wait, what?"

"Oh. Oops."

I turn and face her. "I'm not sure how I feel about the two of you trying on sexy outfits together."

She snorts. "You've watched too many pornos. It wasn't like that at all."

I chuckle because she's probably right.

"What's their deal, anyway?" I cock an eyebrow at her, and she rolls her eyes at me. "Wrath and Trinity."

Now I roll my eyes. I'd need a year and a lot of scotch to tell that story. "Christ. They have a long, fucked-up history, Hope. Some of it is my fault. They seem to finally be working their shit out. Leave it at that."

She makes a noise that tells me she's not satisfied with my answer, so I decide to change the subject.

"I heard you took Heidi shopping for a prom dress. That was sweet of you."

"You heard about that?"

She tenses up, and I can't figure out why. Then something occurs to me.

"Hope—"

"Please don't."

Fuck.

"Tell me she's not knocked up. Tell me I don't have to murder Axel."

She lets out a long sigh. "No. Not at all."

My racing heart calms. "So it really was just prom dresses?"

That tension again. "Please don't ask me. I promised her."

"Promised what?"

"Club comes first, right? So if I tell you, you'll tell her brother, and it will cause a big fucking mess. But I don't want to lie to you either, so please just drop it."

I turn her words over. Club comes first. *Yes.* Hope is going to be my wife. She also comes first. Not everyone in my world would agree with that, but my way of thinking is I can keep her secrets if sharing them would be bad for the club. Presidential discretion and all that.

After I work it out in my head, I explain this to her.

"You promise?"

I grit my teeth. "Yes."

"She wanted me to take her to the clinic for birth control."

My anger ignites at my girl having to endure that. "Aw, fuck. Baby, after everything you just went through? Jesus Christ."

"She didn't know. Look, she's not *there* yet with Axel. She just wanted to be prepared in case."

I shake my head. Why the fuck do I need to know these things? And why is my woman the sweetest damn person I've ever known? How did I get so lucky?

I kind of want to shake Heidi hard next time I see her. Then I remember her as a kid. I've known the little troublemaker since she was in fuckin' pigtails. "I'm going to have to keep that fuckin' prospect real busy," I mutter.

"Oh, please. Like you weren't doing the same at seventeen."

Never mind what I was doing. The thought of some horny teenage dickwad putting his hands all over my sweet, innocent Hope pisses me off. "Were you?" I shoot back.

"Yes. And I didn't have anyone to go with me to the doctor, so I'm glad I was there with her."

I roll over and cup her jaw, running my finger over her cheek. "You're the sweetest. Thank you."

"You're not mad?"

"No. Honestly, it's none of my business what she does with her body. He's not that much older than her. It's not fucking illegal. As long as he doesn't hurt her, I'd rather not know about it."

"Well, I had the 'don't let anyone talk you into things you're not ready for' chat with her."

I snort, imagining that conversation must have been a load of fun for both of them.

"She wanted to know if I've seen Axel with girls up here."

"And?"

"I haven't, so I told her so. She said she knows how bikers are. Pretty fucked up for a kid, no?"

"Not really. Her grandmother has strong opinions about us. Heidi's mom spent time as a club whore before she took off and left her with the grandmother."

"Here?"

"No." I think about the wisdom of Heidi asking Hope questions about her man. "Uh, babe. Part of being an ol' lady now. You can't be starting trouble. She asks you a question like that again and you know different, you need to just lie."

She jackknifes into a sitting position. "What are you talking about? If I see him cheat on her, I'm not supposed to say anything?"

"Correct."

"That's the code around here? So if you had availed yourself of some 'wild pussy' on your trip, no one would have told me?"

"No," I say simply.

"If you nailed someone here, no one would tell me either, would they?"

"I'm not nailing anyone but you, so drop it."

I should know better by now. Telling my mouthy lawyer woman to drop something is about the same as waving a red flag in front of a bull.

"No. That's bullshit. If someone's in an open relationship, she should at least know about it. Otherwise, what's the point?"

"*You* are *not* in an open relationship. No one else's relationship is our business."

Her voice takes on a deadly soft tone. "So that means if *I* fuck someone else, no one would tell you either?"

"No. That's *not* what it means. You better fucking believe if you so much as ever *look* at another man, I'll be the first one to know about it."

She glares at me.

I glare right back.

"Why are we even talking about this, Hope? No one else here even has a committed relationship, so why are we talking about these ridiculous what ifs? And no, two horny teenagers do not count as a committed relationship."

A heavy sigh escapes her. "Fine. But know this: if I catch Wrath with someone, I'll tell Trinity."

Jesus Christ, she's a pain in my ass.

"Yeah, and what if you catch Trin in a Teller/Murphy sandwich? You gonna go tell him that too?"

First, she wrinkles her nose. Then I see the gears turning in her head. She sucks in a deep breath, eyes going all owl-wide. "Oh my. Lucky girl."

"You." I lunge and tackle her to the bed, pinning her wrists above her head with one hand. I seal my mouth over hers. Her tongue slides over mine, soft and inviting. I slip my mouth from hers, kissing her cheek, then down her neck. Tasting and sucking her soft skin all the way.

"Rochlan," she sighs so sweetly. Fucking music to my ears, hearing my full name on her lips. I can never stay mad at this woman.

"Rochlan," she says a little clearer. "You ever cheat on me, and I'll kill you."

I grin against her throat. "I know, Baby Doll."

CHAPTER NINE

HOPE

When we make it downstairs a little later, we're greeted with a round of applause. I assume it's because I'm wearing the vest Rock gave me—this time paired with jeans.

"Hey, porn stars," Wrath calls out.

"I take it she liked the patch, bro?" Z jokes.

Whipping my head around, I nail Rock with a glare. He throws his hands up like he has no idea what they're yammering about.

"About time you gave it to her good. Never heard noises like that come out of your room before," Z adds.

I try to laugh it off, but hot tears sting my eyes and my cheeks flare with heat. Turning to head back upstairs, Rock catches me.

"I'm going to gut you," he growls at Z.

"Aw, shit, Hope. I'm just messing with you."

"Yeah, and I was trapped down here, so I couldn't hear a thing," Wrath adds in his helpful manner.

Rock's hand smooths up and down my back. "Honey, Z's not used to girls who don't need an audience to get off. He thought he was paying you a compliment."

Okay, that's so stupid it makes me laugh. I'm a little embarrassed for overreacting. "I'm fine," I say, pushing away from Rock.

Keeping a safe distance from him, Z tugs on my hand. "Come here, Hope. Let me see how it looks." Leading me over to the couch, he drops down and pulls me with him so I'm sandwiched between him and Wrath.

Wrath traces the star patch on my side. "Did your man explain these?"

"Yes," I whisper.

He stretches one arm around my shoulders and gives me a squeeze. "Good."

"*You* really voted me in?"

His lips curve into a genuine smile. "Yeah, sugar."

"Could you tell which one was mine?" Z asks, making me giggle.

"Uh, the four-leaf clover?" I answer in a fake airhead voice.

A glance up at Rock shows he's still giving Z murder eyes.

Z notices it too. "Gotta go. Hope, I'll see you at the party later."

He gives my hand a quick squeeze and takes off around the other side of the coffee table. Shaking his head, Rock sits next to me. He gives Wrath a hard stare, then slaps his arm off my shoulders. "You're both looking for it today."

I can't stand him being cross with his friends because of me. "Stop —I think it's the hormones still running through me."

Wrath looks queasy, and I suppress a giggle as I watch him shift his body away from us, into the corner of the couch.

Rock pulls me against him, nuzzling my hair, kissing the tip of my ear. "Remind me in the future, the dresser may not be the best item to fuck you against."

A warm, happy buzz settles over me. He always knows how to make me feel safe and accepted. I turn my body into him, pressing tight. Tilting my head back, he takes my mouth, kissing away the rest of my sadness.

He breaks our kiss and stares at me for a moment. "Are you still in pain?"

I shrug. "A little. That's why Wrath offered to get me high," I explain with a small smirk.

Wrath chuckles. "See, I told you I'd take good care of her."

Rock grunts at him before kissing my neck again. "Tell me where you hurt, Baby Doll."

I flick my gaze to Wrath, sure he really doesn't want to hear all these details. His eyes are focused elsewhere, though, as if he's trying to give us privacy.

Throwing back my arm, I point at the spot on my shoulder that's been bothering me the most.

Rock brushes my hair to the side and kneads his strong fingers into the muscles of my neck and shoulders.

"There?"

"Mm-hmm. The doctor said it was probably leftover bubbles from the gas they used in my tummy for the surgery or something like that."

Behind me, Rock hums an affirmative sound and keeps rubbing the spot in question. My head drops forward, and I fall into the pleasurable feelings.

"Hey, boss, I could use your help," someone asks, breaking into the floating sensation. Looking up, I see one of the guys whose name I can't remember. From what I know, he's always in the basement. He seems nice enough, if not a little weird.

"Let me take care of this, Baby Doll. I'll be right back." He gives me a quick peck on the cheek and gets up.

"What is it, Sparky?"

Sparky, that's it.

After they leave, I turn to Wrath.

"Enjoy Trinity's new outfit?" I ask.

A long, slow grin spreads over his face. "I sure did. Heard you got one just like it. That what got prez so worked up?"

I tap his side with my fist. "Jerk."

"You started it. I'm not sure if you noticed, but no one's sex life is a secret here."

My nose wrinkles. "I'm a bit of a prude, aren't I?"

He chuckles. "We'll work it out of you. Oh, and I gotta tell you, the idea of you and Trin trying that shit on together is going straight into my spank bank."

"Oh my gosh! It wasn't like that. And ew."

Wrath's grin fades a little as he traces a finger over my vest. The contact is brief but odd for him. I can't quite describe the expression that comes over his face. "I'm sure it had more to do with this. He's been itching to give it to you for a while now."

"Really?"

"Yeah, he got our votes right before you went in the hospital."

A sick feeling twists my gut. We had that awful fight right before that. No wonder he was so furious with me. I need to tell him again how sorry I am.

Wrath sits up and turns to face me. "You know you're family now, and we all bust each other's balls. If Z picks on you, it's 'cause you're one of us. That and I think you guys woke him up."

Dammit! I feel the tears welling in my eyes again. How much longer did the doctor say this bullshit would last?

I sniffle and force out a laugh. "And here you said I'd never be one of you."

The smile on his face fades to a somber expression. "I'm not afraid to admit when I've been wrong. Besides, if I gave you shit, I was just worried about him getting hurt."

"Seriously?"

"Yeah. He's the closest I've ever had to a brother."

He says it so naturally it tugs at my heart. I don't know much about Wrath's childhood, except he was living on the streets by the age of sixteen. And I know Rock's was no picnic. Even though it was before my time, I'm grateful they managed to find each other. Rock explained it's Wrath's job to protect him and protect the club, but it's clear by Wrath's face and the sound of his voice he doesn't only look out for Rock because it's his duty.

A soft sigh escapes me. "If anyone's going to get hurt, it would be me."

He reaches over and pats my hand. "Yeah, you got it bad for my boy, don't ya?"

Lifting my gaze to his, I see he's teasing me again, but I answer him honestly. "I do. I really do."

We sit in silence for a while. Wrath glances over at me. "You know, some exercise might help with the pain if it's trapped gas bubbles."

Startled by the advice, I'm not sure how to respond.

Wrath shrugs. "You should get up and work out with Trinity in the mornings."

"Are you calling me fat?" I tease.

He runs his gaze over my body before answering. "Fuck no. Just thought it might help."

I think I might have actually hurt his feelings. "Thank you. You sure she'd want me bothering her?"

"Yeah, she'd probably like the company. Gotta catch her early, though. Five a.m. usually."

"Geez. How does she do everything?"

He shakes his head. "Girl never sleeps." The serious way he says it is enough for me to know how much he worries about her.

"You should do a better job wearing her out."

He chokes out sharp laughter and grins at me. "Don't think I haven't been tryin'."

I'm happy I seem to have cheered him up, but I'm also getting anxious. *What the heck is Rock doing downstairs?*

"Wrath?"

"Yes, sugar."

"What's downstairs?"

"*The* club business," he answers with a chuckle. When I don't laugh, he eyes me more seriously. "Rock still hasn't told you?"

"Geez, don't tell me it's more strippers," I grumble.

My attempt at a joke doesn't make him laugh this time. "No strippers."

"Porn studio?"

"No, sugar. Nothing like that," he says, still watching me intently.

Rock finally emerges, and Wrath gives him a hard stare. "Can I have a word with you, brother?"

Rock waves him off. "Not now. We've got a problem."

"Why don't you take Hope on a tour of downstairs?"

Rock's jaw sets in a hard line. "Not now."

This situation is getting out of control. "Wrath, it's fine. I don't—"

Wrath cuts me off. "What the fuck you waiting for? You patched her."

Rock's gaze skips to me. "Fine. You want to see what's downstairs, Baby Doll?"

I'm not really sure. "If you want me to."

"Christ, it's not that big a deal at this point." Wrath sighs.

"Shut up. Remember, you started this," Rock growls.

The door up here is a dummy door. Decorative. The real door is right below it. Steel. Rock needs to punch a code in and it makes a funny air sealing noise. The smell on the other side is moist, humid, *skunky*. The first room has nothing but tables covered in packing supplies and empty wooden crates. To the left, it looks like a two-bedroom with an adjoining bathroom setup. *Huh. No wonder Sparky doesn't venture upstairs often.*

Sparky hustles out of a room to our right. "What up, boss?" When he sees me, he grins broad and happy. "Hey, Hope. I been waiting on prez to give you the tour. Come on."

Rock looks up at the ceiling, muttering to himself. Ignoring him, I follow behind Sparky. I kind of have it figured out. They've got a grow house down here. I'm amazed at how extensive their little pot farm is. I shouldn't be, though, because the center itself is massive.

The first room holds the largest plants. "These are almost ready for harvest. Demons in two weeks, right, boss?"

"Shut it, Sparky."

I pretend I didn't hear anything. Some of the plants look a little different. In fact, each row seems to have distinct characteristics. "Are these all different strains?"

Sparky's grin is fast and relieved. "Yes! It's so awesome you get that right away." He starts explaining the different strains he's developed.

Rock huffs behind me. I guess he's heard the sales pitch before. But I think it's interesting all the different ways Sparky is able to manipulate his plants.

In the next room, the plants are a little smaller.

"Now this line is experimental. It's called 'deepest gray' 'cause it's gonna get you super high—into like hallucinating shit kinda high."

I chuckle. "How do you do it? Develop the strains?"

He launches into a lecture worthy of a college-level science course, and I'm lost. But I nod and ask questions, which seems to make Sparky happy.

His demeanor changes as soon as we enter the last room. "This is my latest project, Green Machine. It was for our regular—"

Rock cuts him off. "That's enough, Sparky."

"Okay, yeah. I need it ready to harvest in about six weeks, but they're sick."

Behind me, Rock sighs. I guess he didn't want me to know what he'll be up to six weeks from now.

Suddenly, I'm a little pissed he's been hiding all this from me. A long time ago, he promised me truth. Yet he's been hiding a major part of his life from me this entire time. Setting aside that thought, I bend down and look at Sparky's "sick" crop.

"What's wrong? How can you tell they're sick?"

He pulls me closer to the plants and we lean over. "See the brown spots on the tips?"

I do indeed see little brown speckles on some of the leaves.

"Is it treatable?"

"I tried giving them copper and then another supplement, and—"

"Wait. Maybe you should let them rest between treatments. See if one works before trying another."

"I'm so careful with the soil, though. I mix everything just so." He looks at Rock as if disappointing him is the worst thing in the world. I understand the feeling all too well.

"I'm sure you're very careful with them." Taking a deep breath, I continue. "They're like your babies, right?"

His eyes light up. "Yes! Thank you, Hope."

"So you said this is a new strain. Maybe it's just more susceptible to certain deficiencies. I bet you'll figure it out."

We have this entire conversation as we're leaning over the affected plants. I can practically feel Rock's eyes boring into me.

When we wind up the tour, I ask Sparky if he's coming upstairs for the party. He looks at me like I'm nuts. That's right. He has sick babies to attend to. I'm not sure what it is—he's definitely spent too much time cooped up with his plants—but there's something really sweet that I like about Sparky. It's clear he enjoys what he does and he's good at it. He tells me he designed and built the entire system downstairs. Rock nods encouragingly. I'm really impressed.

"Well, New York is closer to legalizing it for medical use. Maybe when it finally happens, you can start building mini grow houses for people or something."

Rock narrows his eyes at me, and I guess that was the wrong thing to say.

Oops.

Sparky seems enthusiastic about my idea, though, so whatever. I give him a quick hug and head upstairs, Rock close behind. When I stop to talk to Wrath, Rock keeps going straight upstairs.

"Rock?"

Wrath frowns, watching Rock's back. "What did you think?" he asks me.

"Pretty cool."

Wrath's mouth curves into a surprised grin. "You're very unpredictable, Hope."

I race up the stairs and find Rock almost at the bedroom. Sprinting to catch up, I grab him at the door. "What's wrong?"

"Nothing." He shoves inside, and I follow right behind him.

"Why didn't you just tell me sooner? I hate that you're still hiding stuff from me." Actually, the more I think about it, the more pissed I get. "Why did you bother giving me this if you don't trust me?" I say, jabbing a finger at the vest.

"Not now, Hope. Just go."

Go? "What?"

"I wanna grab a shower and get the smell off me. We'll talk later."

Since when does he take a shower without inviting me in?

He closes the bathroom door, and I fight the urge to smack it back open with my foot. Throwing the vest on the dresser, I grab my purse and fish out my keys. Then I snatch my cell phone from the nightstand and take off.

Wrath calls to me as I fly down the stairs. "Hope! What's wrong?"

People are starting to fill the club, and I want to get to my car before I'm blocked in. A few of the remaining catty bitches who enjoy reminding me they've fucked Rock are also here, and I don't want to give them the satisfaction of knowing Rock and I are having problems.

Cast or not, Wrath is still an athlete, and he catches up to me at the door. "Hope. Stop. What's wrong?"

"He told me to go. So I'm going. He doesn't fucking trust me, and I'm tired of being lied to."

"Fuck, this is all my fault. Don't leave like this."

I just keep shaking my head, tears clouding my vision.

He tries to grab me, but I slip out of his grasp and down to my car. One of the prospects approaches, but I gun the engine and he moves.

When I get to my house, everything is dark. Not one outside light illuminates my lonely yard. The motion sensors must have burned out or something, because nothing comes on when I step out of the garage.

With the stupid app Rock installed on my phone, I know he'll track me down eventually. Until then, I need some fucking space.

I flip on the hall light to make sure the power isn't out. I'm momentarily blinded, so I shut it off. I throw my phone, keys, and purse on the kitchen counter and make my way to the bedroom.

Crap.

I forgot I'd been in the middle of packing up boxes of Clay's stuff the last time I was here. I set the boxes on the floor, strip down, and crawl under the covers. My cell phone rings and vibrates, the sound traveling all the way down the hall. So I pull the covers up over my head to drown out the noise.

ROCK

"Rock! Open the fucking door."

What the fuck is Wrath doing up here? How the hell did he manage all the stairs on those crutches?

Rushing into the bedroom with only a towel around my waist, I fling open the door. He's standing there breathless and sweaty.

"What the fuck did you say to her?"

"Who?"

"Hope, you asshole. She just took off in fucking tears."

A glance at the dresser, and I see she left her vest. *Oh, that's not good.* I spin and see her phone and purse are also gone. *Fuck.*

"She's not going to run to the cops, if that's what you're worried about. She thought Sparky and his setup were adorable."

Wrath's voice is full of menace. "I know that, fucker. I'm more concerned she's going to wrap herself around a tree when she can't see where she's going because she's crying her eyes out! I can't drive or I would have gone after her instead of killing myself hopping up here after your sorry ass."

"What did she say?"

He pins me with a hard stare. "She said you told her to go."

"I meant downstairs, not leave the house."

"And that you don't trust her and she's sick of being lied to. Rock, fix this, man. Stop fucking lying to her."

"I didn't lie to her."

"No, you just didn't tell her, and that ain't right. Fuck—we ever got raided, they'd scoop her up right along with the rest of us—"

Cold twists my gut at the thought. "She's got nothing to do with it."

"Still take time to sort out, you dick. Tank her career. You got her practically living here. She's your ol' lady now. She has a right to know."

"There's nothing left. She knows everything now."

"Does she?"

Okay, I can name a few things she still doesn't know.

"Get out of here so I can get dressed." I fucking hate that he's right about something that pertains to my girl.

After muttering a few more curses at me, he hops next door to his room.

I know I'm to blame for this, and I'm not sure why I reacted the way I did. Maybe because seeing how at ease Hope was with Sparky and the whole operation made me realize I'd been an asshole for hiding shit from her for so long. I don't give her enough credit. I keep thinking she's all good girl, when in reality, she has many different facets to her. She's not a black-and-white kind of person. She lives very much in the gray area right alongside me. We think a lot alike.

Protective and loyal to the people we care about. Willing to accept things outside her comfort zone.

On the way to her house, all these thoughts flood my brain as I worry about how to fix this.

Beyond our relationship, I'm stressed the fuck out because Green Street Crew has been pressing me for larger and larger orders. With Sparky's sick crop, we won't be able to meet the demand of both GSC and the new thing I put in place with the Demons. Lost Kings have a reputation of being reliable and having quality product. We can't afford to fuck that up.

Revealing our setup to Hope came at the worst fuckin' time.

It's creepy dark when I turn onto her road. Her car isn't in the driveway, so I almost leave. But I know my girl. She's sneaky. Glancing at my phone, I call up the app that will show me where she is—provided she didn't stop to chuck her phone in a lake.

Nope. Pink blinking heart shows she's here. I shut off my bike, although she would have heard me coming. I dial her number. Sure enough, I hear my ringtone go off in the kitchen.

Fuck, we've never gotten around to exchanging keys or anything. We're almost always *together*. But it's not as if I don't know how to pick a lock. And it's not like I haven't been bitching about the shitty security at Hope's house since the first time I ever paid her a visit.

Takes me fifteen seconds to get inside. Another ten to figure out she's in the bedroom. The bed is lumpy, but there's no sound. Is she holding her breath? Trying to hide from me like a little kid? The thought makes me smile. I fuckin' love my girl—even when she's being a pain in my ass.

I shuck my jacket and hang it on the doorknob, then kick off my shoes.

"Hope?"

A ragged sniffle drifts out from under the covers.

"Baby, what are you doing?"

"Choreographing a tap dance."

A sharp crack of laughter leaves me. *Okay, she's seriously pissed.* "Can I put the light on?"

"No," she answers in a cranky baby voice that makes my dick hard and my hand itch to spank her fuckin' ass.

That's fine. Can't find the fucking switch anyway. Besides, my eyes have adjusted enough that I can just make out the top of her head.

I yank my jeans down, kick them off, and drop my shirt on top of them. This is uncharted territory. We've never been in her bed together.

"What do you think you're doing?" she asks.

I freeze, unsure if she's asking because she's mad at me for earlier or because I'm about to crawl into her bed. I choose to use a bit of humor to lighten things up. "You want insects and road grime in your bed?"

"Ew, no."

Leaning down, I attempt to throw back the covers, but she wraps herself tighter and rolls away from me.

"What are you doing? Get over here."

"I'm not having sex with you. I'm mad at you."

"Who said anything about sex? I don't want to have sex with you either." That's a total fucking lie. I'm so hard I could pound nails, but it's not my fault. If I'm within ten inches of Hope, my dick is hard. That's just the way it is. I'm in a permanent state of arousal around her.

Using the heel of my hand, I push down my erection, not wanting to jab her with it—yet. "I'll leave my undies on."

That gets the response I'm looking for—a soft giggle. "Undies," she snorts. "Some big, bad biker you are."

I grin into the darkness.

"Hope?" I tug on the comforter. "Baby, I'm chilly. Won't you share?" I know she can't resist my soft, pleading tone.

She wriggles and struggles to unwrap herself. The entire time, I'm biting my lip so I don't laugh.

"Here," she fumes, throwing half the cover at me.

Once I arrange it over myself, I dive at her, grappling her squirmy body into my arms. "Shhhh."

I hold her to me, tucking her head under my chin, stroking down her arm, trying to soothe her. "I'm sorry you think I don't trust you. I do, honey. Remember when I told you I didn't want the ugliness from my life bleeding into yours? That's why I've been holding back. Not because I don't trust you."

"It's a stupid grow house. The way you were acting, I thought you had like a little human sweatshop down there or something."

I huff out a laugh. "Please, Sparky takes enough care and feeding."

"He's sweet. I'm guessing he's very familiar with his products?" She chuckles.

I snort at her comment. "Yeah. He's been a godsend, though. We were neck deep in a lot of shit when he came up with that idea."

"So that's how the club makes its money?"

"Yes."

"Is there a lot of money in that?"

I'm not sure why she's asking, but I answer as truthfully as possible. "Not as much as the shit we used to be into, but it's a lot safer. Most of the time."

She's silent. Thinking about what that means, I guess. "I don't care, you know. I don't even understand why pot's illegal but alcohol is okay."

"I know, babe. I'm starting to get that about you."

"Tell me something else I don't know, Rock."

Fuck. Fuck. Fuck.

Her fingers drift over my arm. "I'm not asking for details about club business. I understand why you can't share some of that with me."

Relief crashes into me. She *gets it* and that makes it easier to spill the secrets I've been keeping.

All right. *Here goes.* "Can you promise to hear me out before you get mad?"

She stiffens, but I feel her nod, her silky hair sliding along my shoulder.

"I told you when we met I was fucking nuts about you, right?"

She snorts like she still thinks I'm full of shit. "Yes."

Fuck, this is embarrassing.

"After that kiss in my office, I found out where you lived. I couldn't stop myself. I used to just sit at the end of the street and watch your driveway, hoping to catch a glimpse of you."

"Rock..." She kisses along my jaw, and the tightening in my chest relents a bit. She's not mad. She doesn't think I'm a whack-job stalker.

"I did this... a lot. Remember how I told you about our rival, the Vipers?"

"Yes."

I take a deep breath before going into this next part. "On one of my 'stakeouts,' two of them drove down your street, paying close attention to your house. I knew there was no other reason they were here. Somehow, they'd put together your connection to the club."

"Didn't they see you sitting there on your bike?"

"I... uh, was using the SUV by this point, so no. I don't know if they used court records to find our connection or if one of the fucks followed me to your house. Either way, I knew your life was in danger. These two—they weren't normal. We... Fuck, Hope, I don't want to drag you into this shit any further."

"Just finish the story."

"Fine. I figured if we cut ties in a very public way, it would end their interest in you. Obviously, if you weren't our lawyer, there was no reason to come after you. And if I was willing to humiliate you in public, I must not have any romantic interest in you."

"Okay," she whispers.

"You'll never know how much I hated doing that," I whisper against her hair. I press a kiss to her forehead and hold her tighter for the next part. "Even though I thought that resolved the immediate problem, the fact that these two knew about you at all didn't sit well with me. We took a vote to put them down."

"Because of me?"

"Yes."

"No wonder Wrath hated me."

"He never hated you." I pause and think of how best to explain preemptive murder. "You weren't the only woman they targeted. And even though we're outlaws... that's not how we operate. MCs go to war all the time. They don't target innocent people who have no idea what they're into. That's mafia, cartel behavior. They had other people in mind too."

"Glassman?"

"Yes. Although, to this day, he thinks it was just a random mugging. And I'd like to keep it that way."

"Uh, it's not like we're lawyers who lunch."

For now, I ignore the bit of self-deprecating humor I detect in her comment. "We had to tighten our alliance with our other rival I've told you about."

"Wolf Kings?"

"Wolf *Knights*. We're the only Kings, babe."

Another soft chuckle. I love that laugh so much.

"They're a rival, but we've always had a decent relationship with them. We've got a similar mindset about certain things, and we share certain business interests. They were more than happy to cooperate." I pause, remembering my meeting with Ulfric, the anguish in his eyes as he told me about what the Vipers did to his sister-in-law. "I didn't learn why they were so motivated until later, but that's not important. We also received the support of some of the Vipers. Most of them— although I disagree with the shit they're into—follow our code. These other fucks that came in and took over, not so much. We helped them cut out the bad shit."

I stop, remembering what it took to get what I needed out of those fuckers. I'm uncomfortable with the memories when my girl's so close to me. "It took me a long time to get the information about you that I needed from them."

I'm silent, thinking about what I want to tell her next, when she captures my hand and kisses my fingertips.

Maybe she didn't understand what I'm confessing here. "Hope, do you understand what I'm telling you?"

She's silent for a minute before answering. "Yes."

"Can you live with the things I've done, Baby Doll?"

"You did all that for me?"

"Yes. Remember, I explained you fuck with one of us, you fuck with all of us? If someone hurts you, baby, I'll handle it. I figured that would go against everything you believe in. But I'm not sorry. Those evil fucks posed a threat to you, and I dealt with it in the most efficient way. Going to the police wouldn't have helped. I had nothing but a gut feeling to go on. You would have ended up dead or worse. I did what I had to do to keep you from harm. I protect what's mine, Hope. And whether you knew it or not, you were mine."

Something hot and wet rolls over my chest. "Baby, don't cry. I'm so sorry I ever put you in danger."

She sniffles. "It's not that. No one has ever cared about me that way before. You barely even knew me at the time, but you were willing to start a war with these nutjobs to keep me safe? I can't even comprehend that."

"You were worth it, babe. I felt so fucking guilty that my obsession with you put you in danger."

"Jesus, do you know what it does to me to hear you tell me all of this?" More sniffles.

Then silence.

"I'm sorry I'm not a good man, Hope."

She sucks in a deep breath. "Don't *ever* say that. You're good to me. Your brothers. To your club. That's all that matters."

Shit, I'm so fucking stunned I don't know what to say.

After a few seconds, she says, "I know you called my mother when I was in the hospital."

The shift in conversation jolts me. I stiffen. This isn't something I want to talk about right now because I know it will hurt her. "Yeah."

She sucks in a deep, shuddering breath, but her voice is clear when she asks her next question. "She never came down to see me or called back to check if I was okay, did she?"

Now *I'm* fucking close to crying. "No, honey."

"You stayed. You never left my side the entire time, did you?"

"Only when you were in surgery."

"Every one of your brothers came too. Even if it was just to support you, they were there."

"They were there for you too."

She lets out a heavy sigh. "I've never belonged or felt a part of a family like that before. I don't know if I've ever told you this, but Clay came from a fucked-up situation too. He and his sister mostly grew up in foster care. And, well, you see what my mother's like." She pauses, and I feel her shaking her head against me. "He and I formed our own little insular world together. I mean, you know my few close friends, but otherwise, it was just the two of us. We only really depended on each other."

I'm not sure what to say to that because it sounds lonely. But in a way, it makes me understand her so much better. "I'm happy you two found each other, sweetheart, and I'm so sorry you lost him so young."

"I know."

"You've got a family now, full of overprotective, pain-in-the-ass big brothers."

"And sisters?"

"Yeah. Trin's got her own issues, but she likes you. You two are good for each other. And I'm sure Teller wouldn't mind some help with Heidi here and there."

"Heh." Then she turns a little more serious. "What else should I know?"

Here's where I should tell her what happened with Sophie when I escorted Hope to Judge Oak's fundraiser. How the woman who is supposed to be Hope's best friend drunkenly hit on me outside the men's room. But after admitting what a callous bitch her mother was, I don't want to hurt Hope with yet another person she loves failing her. Instead, I decide to tell her something else. A good thing about Sophie.

Hope elbows me in the ribs. "Anything else you're hiding?"

"One last thing."

Her body ripples with laughter. I guess after admitting I've killed people to keep her safe, anything else is tame in comparison.

"That first night when I ran into you at Hamilton's... Sophie set that up."

She squeals and thumps my chest, struggling to sit up. "I knew it! I always wondered what the hell you and Z were doing there."

At least she's not mad.

"How?"

"She was worried about you. Maybe eight months after the funeral, she came into Crystal Ball with Jonny on one of my nights."

"Ugh! I wondered how you and Jonny knew each other." She giggles, and I'm happy I was able to take her mind off her rotten mother.

"I don't know. I must have been real obvious that first time we met, 'cause she honed in on me right away."

"I told her about us."

I chuckle at the memory of Sophie's fierce expression that night. "Yeah, I got that loud and clear." Picking up her hand, I press her fingers against my lips, then hold her tight. "Everything after that was all you. I would have taken you home that night if you asked me to. I didn't have any other plans besides worming myself into your life. Making you my woman."

She kisses my chin. "So now I know everything?"

I actually stop and think before answering her because I want to be honest. "I think so."

"Nothing from your run?"

"Are you asking if I fucked anyone?"

"No. I think it's clear your mind was on me the whole time you were gone." As she says that, her hand drifts across my hip and over the spot where her tattoo is. I'm very conscious of and grateful for the trust Hope has in me.

Reaching out in the dark, I trace along her collarbone, seeking her necklace. "At least you didn't take this off. Although, I'm going to paddle your ass for leaving your vest."

"I'm sorry."

I sigh, long and deep, debating whether or not to tell Hope about Inga's phone call. "Ah, there's one thing from the run."

Next to me, she stiffens, and I automatically tug her closer. "Inga called me."

The breath she lets out drifts over my chest. "Oh. How did that go?"

I'm amazed at how calm my girl is, all things considered. "Uh, fine. She wanted to apologize. I guess she's in rehab back home. She's quitting porn and dancing."

"That's good. I mean, if she had a problem with it. Hopefully, she'll figure it out."

Holy fuck, my woman is something else.

"You're not mad?"

She pulls back and, in the dark, it's hard to gauge her reaction. "No.

Why would I be mad? I mean, as long as weekly chats with her aren't going to become a regular thing—no, I'm not mad."

"Thanks."

"What's wrong, Rock?"

It's almost unnerving how well she knows me. Christ, she won't want to hear this. I push the words out in a rush. "I feel like a scumbag for never noticing she had a problem."

"You realize this is awkward for me, right?" she says with a laugh. When I *hmm* at her, she continues. "I didn't get the impression your *relationship* was one where you spent a lot of time together when you weren't, uh, *occupied*, so why would you have noticed?"

Her delicate phrasing pulls a dark chuckle from me. "Yeah, I think that's also why I'm feeling like shit. I thought I was always clear, but she had this idea, I guess…"

"Uh, I can't speak for Inga, but I don't think most women can separate sex and emotion, even if they tell themselves they can."

"That doesn't make me feel any better."

She shrugs. "Too bad."

Yeah, I've definitely beat this conversation into the ground. But it felt good to get it off my chest. It's not really something I would discuss with any of the guys. I lean over and kiss her forehead. "Thanks for listening to that, baby. I'm sure it's the last thing you felt like hearing."

She pats my chest in response. I can't believe how kindhearted my girl is. Every other woman I've ever known would have used that conversation as an excuse to tear Inga down or bitch me out. Not Hope. I'm a lucky fuck.

Incessant buzzing reaches me from the floor. "My phone, babe."

"Go ahead."

Crawling out of the bed, I dig around 'til I find my jeans and dump my cell phone into my hand. "It's Wrath. He was worried about you," I explain.

"What?" I snap into the phone as I settle back into the bed. I hold the phone away from my ear so Hope can hear him.

"Where are you, dick?"

"At Hope's."

He blows out a relieved breath. "She okay?"

"Yes."

"Are you guys okay?"

Next to me, Hope sighs, "Awww."

I run my hand over her hair. "Yeah, we're good."

"Are you coming back up tonight?"

I glance at Hope and quirk my eyebrow. I'm leaving it up to her.

"Yeah, we'll be up in a little while," she answers.

"Oh, for fuck's sake, are you going to turn into one of those annoying couples who answers every phone call together?" Wrath bitches.

"Bye, Wrath."

Hope grabs my phone and ends the call for me.

Eventually, she rolls over and clicks on a light. Blinking from the glare, I don't see the room right away. But when things finally come into focus, I'm shocked.

"You've been packing?"

A nervous smile flickers over her lips. "Well, we talked about moving in together… and I just thought it was time to get rid of some things. It's harder than I thought, though."

Her hands flutter in the air as she's talking. Even flustered and rumpled, she's effortlessly beautiful. My eyes zero in on her slender fingers and notice how naked her ring finger looks.

CHAPTER TEN

ROCK

EXQUISITE BAUBLES ISN'T USED TO HAVING BIKERS IN THEIR DELICATE, prissy store. The unease rolling off the sales guy doesn't concern me, though.

I'm here to get my girl an engagement ring. This place is supposed to have the best jewelry designer in the area. My girl's getting nothing less than the best.

So I put up with the attitude.

For now.

Unfolding the drawing Bricks sketched out for me, I lay it out on the crystal-clear glass counter. "Can you do it or not?"

The sales guy's eyes bug out. "Let me get Arthur."

Arthur reminds me a bit of Sparky. Not that he's high, but he clearly doesn't like being taken away from his precious stones and metals.

He picks up the drawing and studies it. "The top here, this is the engagement ring?"

Ah, he gets it. "Yes."

"Clever. Very fitting for a queen."

Right. Essentially, Hope's my queen, and I want something that reflects that without being gaudy or obnoxious.

Arthur doesn't care about the patches on my cut, my inked skin, my grease-stained jeans, or anything else. He swings the counter door open and beckons me inside. "Come."

I follow him into a small room where he starts tapping information into a computer. He scans in the drawing, does some more tapping, and then hands me a printout.

He's made a few changes, but since they only enhance the design, I nod.

"It's intricate work, so it will take me some time."

That's not what I want to hear. "I need it as soon as possible."

Arthur studies me for a moment. "How long have you known her?"

"Almost three years."

"When did you know she was the one?"

"The day I met her. It's been a long, hard, twisted road to get here."

Arthur nods. He scribbles down a number on the top of the page. "Leave a fifty percent deposit with Kenny up front. I'll start working on it today, but it could be a couple weeks. I must order a few things to complete it, and I have no control over my suppliers."

I certainly understand that.

"Leave a number where I can reach you."

The amount isn't as high as I expected, so I'm prepared to pay in full today. I count out the bills for Kenny, whose eyes are big and much more pleasant than earlier. Arthur wanders back out to see how we're doing. He nods at the pile of cash.

"I need it soon. But it needs to be perfect. You feel me, Arthur?"

"Yes, sir."

"Good." We quickly shake on the deal, and I head out.

As soon as I get back to the clubhouse, I tuck the drawing and receipt into my locked cabinet in the war room. Not that I think Hope has ever snooped through my stuff upstairs. But it would be the worst possible timing if she decided to get curious now and ruin my surprise.

Since I gave her the property patch, I don't think she expects anything else. Everyone has explained that in our world, it's as good as a ring. Even though I swore I would never get married again, that was before I knew Hope. Although it's a big fucking deal to me, the property patch isn't enough. I need to own her in every single way available. It doesn't escape my notice how I never offered my first wife a property patch. She got the ring, nothing more.

Hope will have everything.

It's going to be torture waitin' for that ring to be done. While I'm waiting, there's other things I need to get in place. I think I know the exact way I want to propose to her.

I want it to be perfect.

Didn't give it a lot of thought the first time, but I am now.

I'm not sure why I'm dwelling on my failed marriage. It was a lifetime ago. I was a kid who had no fucking clue. What if I'd met Hope back then? She would have been eighteen, right before she met Clay. Would stupid twenty-three-year-old me have recognized what a treasure she was? Would she have had the strength back then to stand by me when I went to prison? Would we have survived all the bullshit the club went through when Wrath, Z, and I took over?

I don't know the answers to any of these pointless questions. All I do know is we're right where we should be.

The rest is irrelevant.

HOPE

"Hey, feel like going for a hike in the woods?" Rock asks out of the blue one afternoon.

We've been spending more time up at the clubhouse lately. Well, actually for a week or so, we were *snowed* in. Since the courts never seem to close—even for piles of snow—I had to ask Adam to cover the few cases I had. That certainly set me back a bit, but it doesn't bother me like it might have a couple months ago. Maybe there's something wrong with me, but I'm very content right where I am. I can't say it wasn't amusing to watch Z and Hoot try to keep up with all the snow we got pummeled with either.

Since the big nor'easter, it's been cold but sunny, melting away a lot of the snow.

Glancing up, I crane my neck to see out the window and shiver. "No. It's freakin' cold out," I finally answer Rock's question.

"Babe, it's supposed to be in the forties today."

"Yeah. Cold." Taking a closer look at Rock, I can tell he's frustrated. "Okay. I didn't bring any hiking boots up with me, though."

His mouth pops into a grin as he strides over to his closet. When he comes out, he's carrying a large box, which he sets at the end of my lounge chair.

My eyes skip from the box to his face. "You bought me hiking boots?"

"Yup."

Odd, but sweet. Even stranger, he presents me with a thick pair of woolly socks.

Sensing he's up to something, I keep an eye on him while I get ready.

Once we're properly bundled up, we trudge through the light layer of snow that's more crunchy than powdery this late in the winter.

Rock stops near a scattering of pine trees that looks very familiar.

"It's a little cold for sex in the woods, Rock."

He snorts, and we tread a bit farther before he stops again. I'm not sure what I'm supposed to be seeing, but a large area has been marked off with pink surveyor tape.

A very large area.

"What do you think?"

"What am I looking at?"

"Building site. *Our* building site. I want to build us a house here."

I suck in a deep breath and immediately start choking on the cold air.

Rock chuckles and pats my back. "Careful, Baby Doll."

"I love it," I finally manage.

Some of the tension he'd been carrying on the way up here drains out of him. "Good. We've got a few months before we can begin, so there's plenty of time to figure out what we want."

"Okay."

"We'll have to spend more time at the clubhouse until it's finished."

I cock my head to the side, inviting him to explain.

"I'm thinking of renting my house to Bricks and Winter. Give them a chance to save up and buy it in a couple years. Got the fenced-in yard and enough bedrooms for their kids. Plus, it's in the same school district Bricks's kids are in, so it should make things easier on him."

Inside, I melt at how much thought Rock's put into this. "Where are you going to work on your bikes?"

"The club owns that vacant piece of property next to Crystal Ball. I'm thinkin' of opening a shop there eventually. But for now, I'll keep doing it out of my garage. Gonna have Bricks help with the more elaborate paint jobs."

"That sounds great."

"So do you like this spot? We can pick out another one if you want. Got more than enough land."

Taking in the view, I picture what it would be like to live out here. It's peaceful, and if I ever get bored, the clubhouse is a short—

Next to me, Rock is suddenly on one knee.

And my hand is in his hand.

"Rock?"

"Hope, I waited a long time for you. I fall more in love with your beauty, kindness, loyalty, and courage every day. When we spend our first night in the house we're going to build here, I want you to be my wife."

Holy shit. When he explained the property patch meant wife status in his world, I figured that was his way of telling me he didn't want to get married again. Yet here he is—*holy shit!*

"Rock—"

"Babe, the only word I want to hear is yes."

"Yes! Of course, yes!"

He drops his gaze to the ground and lets out a barely audible sigh. I can't stop the tears rolling down my cheeks as he places the most beautiful ring on my finger. I've never seen anything quite like it. The intricate setting looks like a small crown, showcased by a diamond-encrusted interwoven band. The stones sparkle and dance in the sunlight streaming through the trees as I hold out my hand and wiggle my fingers.

Lifting himself from the ground, he sweeps me into his arms and seals his mouth over mine for a burning kiss. When we part, I'm dizzy, and one thought dominates. "Rock, please let me say something."

His eyes narrow, but he nods.

"You remember the doctor told me I might not be able to have children. If I can't give you a family, are you going to end up hating me?"

Confusion that morphs into anger settles over his face. "Hope, listen carefully to me. If my sole goal in life was to reproduce, I could have done it a hundred times over by now."

"That's not as romantic as you think."

He shakes off my attempt at a joke. "I love *you*. All I need is you. We are perfect together. We'll figure this out like we've figured out everything else. Together. You want kids, we'll figure it out. I hear science is pretty amazing these days. You don't want kids, I'm perfectly content with it just being the two of us for the rest of our lives. *You* are more important to me than any potential future children." He gestures back the way we came, toward the clubhouse. "Besides, we already have a houseful of kids to look after."

A very unladylike sound erupts from me, somewhere between a snort and a sob. In my wildest fantasies, I never could have come up with a man like Rock. The thought and care he put into proposing astounds me. His words. The beautiful ring that he undoubtedly had specially designed. Every detail. I can't even—

His fingers settle under my chin, tipping up my head, interrupting my thoughts. "Are we clear on this?"

Sinking my teeth into my bottom lip, I nod my head. How did I get so lucky?

"Don't make that face at me, Hope. Even though it's so cold my balls have crawled back up inside my body, I could pin you to that tree and fuck you senseless right about now."

"That is some lovely imagery, Rochlan," I manage before falling into a fit of giggles.

We're engaged.

ROCK

The hike back to the clubhouse is really more of a sprint. Hope wasn't kidding when she said it was too cold for sex in the woods. The thought of it shrivels my dick. But the thought of getting her alone in our room and stripping her down 'til she's wearing nothing but my ring keeps my feet moving over the rough ground.

Her excited *yes* plays over and over in my head.

Breathless, we tumble into the parking area around the clubhouse. Hope's giggles twist my own mouth up. Snagging her around the waist, I tug her against me for a kiss.

Breaking away, she runs her hands through my hair, staring up at me. The smile's gone, but there's a gleam of mischief in her eyes that's hard to miss.

"When do you want to get married?" she asks.

Right this second.

"Whenever you want," I answer.

"Where?"

That one's easier, because as long as Hope's at the end of the aisle, I don't give two fucks where we do it.

"Anywhere you want."

Her fingers lace behind my neck, but her gaze drifts around the woods behind us. "How about here? I like the idea of getting married outside, close to nature," she says with a dreamy tilt to her lips.

That's fine with me. I even know the perfect spot on the property. But as seamlessly as my girl has accepted everything about me and my world, I wonder if she knows what she's asking.

"Babe, you sure you want your family and friends at a white-trash biker-hillbilly wedding in the woods?"

Pain slashes across her face, and too late, I realize what an awful thing that was to say to her. Her arms tighten around my neck, forcing me down to her level. "You are my family." She jerks her head toward the clubhouse. "You and your club of delinquent, *loyal* biker brothers are my family. Anyone who doesn't like it isn't invited."

My heart is racing so hard. I want to drop down on my knees and ask her to marry me all over again. "I love you."

Her fierce face softens. "I love you, too."

"Aww, hey, lovebirds, where ya been?" Trinity calls out from somewhere behind us.

Hope spins out of my embrace, dropping me like a hot muffler, and races over the gravel. "We're engaged," she shouts, flashing her hand in the air.

Trinity bounces on her toes and claps her hands. When Hope reaches her, the two of them hug, and my chest tightens seeing how close they've gotten.

"Lemme see!" Trinity gasps.

I watch them ooh and ah over the ring. Even from here, I can see Trinity going into party-planning mode. I give them a few minutes of giggling together before I head their way.

Trinity glances up as I approach. Taking in her glossy eyes, I hesitate. She gives Hope's hand a quick squeeze, then throws her arms around me. "I'm so happy for you, Rock-n-Roll."

Chuckling into her hair, I return the hug. "Thanks, sweetheart."

"What's going on out here?" Wrath questions from the doorway. My gaze flicks to his placid expression, and for a number of reasons, I wonder how he'll take it.

I can see Trinity's dying to spill our news, but she waits.

Hope flashes her hand at my brother. "We're getting married."

"Holy fuck." He glances at the snow-covered ground separating us from him then down at his cast. "Get the fuck over here," he says with an irritated wave of his hand.

She runs up the stairs while Trinity and I hang back for a second. Wrath surprises the fuck out of me by taking her hand and checking out the ring while Hope excitedly chatters away. Then he outright floors me by kissing her forehead and whispering something in her ear that makes her grin.

"And that's enough of that," I grumble.

Beside me, Trinity breaks into laughter.

HOPE

The first thing I do when we get inside is send a text to Sophie, Lilly, and Mara, sharing my good news.

My phone vibrates in my hand instantly.

Lilly.

It's hard to understand her through all the screaming. "You did *not* just tell me you're engaged via a group text!" she shouts.

"I did."

My phone beeps.

Mara.

"I'm so happy for you, sweetheart," she says softly. "We need to get together Friday so you can celebrate with your girls. And I need to see Rock's rock." She giggles into the phone. "Hamilton's?"

The place where Sophie orchestrated Rock and me getting together? Yeah, that seems appropriate to celebrate our engagement.

I don't hear back from Sophie until later in the evening. "Hope! I'm sorry. I've been crazy all day. Congratulations! I'm really happy for you guys."

I recount to her in detail how Rock proposed.

"That's so sweet, Hope. Who knew such a scary guy could be so romantic?" she teases. At least I think she's teasing. It's hard to tell over the phone.

The memory of Rock admitting to me how Sophie arranged our first night together still astounds me.

"Hey, Sophie, Rock told me."

Over the line, her sharp intake of breath is clear. "What are you talking about?"

Her tone makes me laugh. "How you set us up to meet at Hamilton's." Warmth spreads through my chest as I think how important that night turned out to be. "I don't know how I can ever thank you enough," I say quietly.

"You're welcome, buttercup. I'm happy for you. You deserve good things, Hope."

"Thanks, Sophie."

We make our plans for Friday night and hang up.

Trinity is surprisingly excited when I ask her to join us Friday night. We take her Jeep into Empire, even though Rock mentions something about picking us up later.

After I shrug off my wool coat, the girls all giggle.

I quirk an eyebrow at the trio, inviting them to explain what's so funny.

"You look like a slutty Hello Kitty," Lilly says with a snicker.

Running my hands over the material of my dress and looking down, I shrug. "What? I think it's cute."

"Oh, it's adorable," Sophie chimes in. "Lilly's just jealous because her boobs would never fit in it."

"True story." Lilly giggles.

"I like it too," Mara says, reaching over to give me a quick hug.

I love this dress. Yes, it's a little close to the bubblegum end of the pink spectrum, but it's got long sleeves and a cute fit and flare skirt. I paired it with thick, wooly gray tights and gray patent leather Mary Janes. Rock made growly noises when I modeled it for him, something Trinity witnessed. And by the wink she gives me, I know she's about to spill to my friends.

"Her man almost didn't let her out of the house when he saw her tonight. You're lucky I got her down here."

Lilly and Sophie, of course, laugh it up.

"Seems like a good time to hand you this, then," Mara says, picking up a shiny pink gift bag from the floor.

Pinning each of them with a look, I joke, "I'm scared to open it."

My apprehension was justified. "Oh my God!" Inside are three books—one his and one hers *Guide to Going Down* and *365 Sexual Positions to Try with Your Man Tonight* complete with graphic descriptions and illustrations.

I'm laughing too much to maintain my stern expression. "Really? Have I given any of you the impression we need help in that department?"

Trinity laughs so hard she almost falls out of her chair. It's nice to see her a little more lighthearted, so I'm not insulted.

"There's more," Mara says as she flails her hands in the air with excitement.

One by one, I pull increasingly kinky items out of the innocent pink bag—candles, massage oil, warming lube, a tiny pink butterfly vibrator, a coil of pink silk rope... and a paddle.

"What the...?" I glance up, my gaze roaming over each of the girls, finally landing on Mara.

More laughter and a few snorts escape from Trinity.

Mara apparently doesn't possess an ounce of shame. She shrugs. "You never know."

"God, you're a horny bunch of bitches." I sigh and set the bag down next to me.

It's something so out of character for me to say that they all laugh. So loud we get stares from everyone in the bar.

"Calm down. Jeez, we haven't even had any alcohol yet," I scold in my best courtroom voice.

That's all the prodding Lilly needs to jump up and stride over to the bar. We watch her flirt for a while and take bets on whether she'll go home with one of the cute bartenders.

Sophie grabs my attention. "Are you going to take your time planning this one?" She waves her hand in the air, almost smacking Lilly, who has returned with a smug smile. "You and your mother threw the last one together so quick, we all thought you were pregnant."

I suck in air, gasping as the pain hits me right in the chest. Lilly, Mara, and Trinity all gape at Sophie. "Fuck, honey. I'm so sorry. I didn't mean... I forgot. Shit, it just happened, and wow, I'm sorry."

She didn't know. She didn't know.

Not wanting to hurt her feelings, I take a few rapid, cleansing breaths to push away the tears and paste on a fake smile. "It's fine. We did plan it quick. But we'd been together forever by then. It was time."

Everyone relaxes, except Trinity, who's still giving Sophie some serious stink eye.

"So have you had any ideas about the wedding yet?" Sophie finally asks.

"I don't know. Something informal and fun. Outdoors."

Sophie nods. "That makes sense since the last one was so over-the-top."

What the hell has gotten into Sophie?

Lilly and Mara also seem surprised.

Trinity glances at Lilly. "So, Lilly, are those knockers real?"

Well, that's certainly one way to take the focus off me.

Lilly's a good sport. And used to this question. She flashes a sexy smile at Trinity. "Yes. I expect in another couple years, they'll be hanging out by my belly button."

Wrong time to sip my water. I cough and sputter while Mara pats me on the back.

"Lilly stripped her way through college and grad school," Sophie adds.

Trinity nods as if she's not surprised, which makes Lilly narrow her eyes.

"Nothing wrong with that."

"Your MC owns a strip club. Why don't you dance, Trinity?" Lilly asks.

Trinity toys with her drink. "I'm getting a little old for that. Besides, Rock's never liked the two things mixing."

We're approaching awkward territory again. Thankfully, we're interrupted by Adam and Ross coming in the front door. Since our table is to the immediate right, they spot us before they're even inside.

I scoot out of my chair, and Adam scoops me into a hug, lifting me off the ground a little. "You bitch. Why didn't you tell me? I had to find out from these nuts?"

My shoulders twitch. "I didn't think about it. It's all been a little crazy. I'm sorry."

He shakes his head at me and goes to the bar.

Ross squeezes me next. "Let me see it."

Holding out my hand, I wiggle my fingers and enjoy how the light bounces and sparkles off the beautiful ring. I'm still stunned by all the effort Rock put into everything. He doesn't do anything half-assed.

"Wow. I've never seen anything like it. Very regal." Ross gushes. "Uh, not that I spend lots of time shopping for engagement rings."

The corners of my mouth twitch. "Of course not."

He gives me a playful shove, and I sit back down.

The guys drag chairs over to join us. Pitchers of margaritas show up, and we make quick work of them before more pitchers of margaritas show up. Our conversation turns loud and filthy. Around ten, the bar is packed.

The front door swings open and cool air sweeps over my flushed cheeks.

Rock steps in. I drag my gaze up, sort of in slow motion, taking in all of him. Boots to jeans to gloves and leather jacket. His serious expression undergoes a complete transformation as our gazes collide. I shove out of my chair so fast it almost tips over. Because I'm hammered and have been sitting for so long, I trip. Oh hell, let's face it. The man still makes me swoon. But Rock's right there to catch me.

"Careful, Baby Doll," he warns in his low voice.

Throwing my arms around his neck, I bury my nose in his jacket, absorbing the brisk, wintery scent he brought in with him. "What are you doing here?" I murmur against his neck.

His arms wrap around me tighter. "Missed my girl. Told you I'd come by."

Behind us, my friends whip out some wild catcalls and other assorted noises that make Rock rumble with laughter. After another squeeze, he releases me. Keeping an arm around my waist, he leads me back to my chair.

I'd been so caught up in my man I didn't realize Z had walked right in behind Rock. He winks at me when I finally spot him. "Hey, sugar." He's standing by Trinity and gives her a quick poke in the shoulder. "Your roommate's waitin' outside."

Trinity rolls her eyes but doesn't get up.

Adam and Ross both stand and shake Rock's hand, congratulating him—well, us—on our engagement.

After a few minutes of small talk, I glance up in time to observe Lilly and Z staring each other down. Since she's kind of in the middle, Trinity jumps up and gives Z her seat. Her face twists into a gaggy eye roll, which makes me snort with laughter. More chairs are pulled over to the table, and Trinity drags one next to me.

"Wait, is Wrath waiting outside?" I finally ask.

Z shrugs. "He's not comin' in here."

"Damon's on his way to pick me up," Mara says as she glances up from her phone.

"Okay."

Rock plants a kiss on the top of my head. "Be right back."

I turn so my gaze can follow Rock as he strides up to the bar. Something so simple still turns me on. Every move he makes is confident and sexy. All mine.

"Damn, girl, calm down," Ross teases, breaking my attention.

Shaking myself, I turn to him. "What?"

"Jesus, I'm horny just from watching the two of you," he jokes.

Mara bursts out laughing. "You're such a pervert."

Ross waggles his eyebrows at her.

Z laughs. "Try living in a room next to the two of them. Non-fucking-stop."

Ross nods knowingly. "Nonstop fucking, I get it."

My cheeks explode with heat. "We do not."

"Sure. Whatever you say, sugar." Z flashes a quick smirk at me before turning his attention back to Lilly.

Rock returns, standing behind me, settling his hands on my shoulders. I tip up my head, bumping him in the groin. "Sorry," I mumble.

He smiles down at me, absently rubbing my shoulders.

My head drops forward, and Rock's body ripples with laughter. "How much did she have to drink?" he asks.

I open my eyes and watch Mara pinch her thumb and index finger together. "Lil' bit," she answers.

Ross vacates his chair and motions for Rock to take it. After pulling the chair closer to me, he drops into it and curls his arm over my shoulder. My body automatically leans into him. "Tired, Baby Doll?" he asks.

"No."

"Don't forget to show Rock your presents, Hope," Sophie says.

I straighten up, and Rock's arm slides down my back, where he rests his hand against my hip.

"Shut up."

Mara breaks into giggles.

My lips twist into a pout, and I turn to find Rock staring at me with curiosity.

"What?" he asks.

"You don't want to know."

Mara, ever so helpful, snatches the bag off the floor and passes it to Rock behind my back.

My hand shoots out, reaching for the bag, but my balance is off and I miss.

Glowering at Mara and Sophie, I slump back and fold my arms across my chest. There's a moment or two where I'm floating, and I realize I've closed my eyes again.

From the end of the table, I hear Z and Lilly chuckle.

Rock's sharp laughter fills the air. "Nice." More paper rustling. Some hummy noises of approval. "Hope doesn't need any help in this department," he remarks.

"Thanks, baby," I say, opening one eye to find him staring at me.

He raises an eyebrow and pulls out the paddle. "Now what am I supposed to do with *this*?"

"Bend over?" I suggest helpfully, which gets a laugh from everyone at the table, even Rock.

"Aw, Christ, I'm gonna need to buy earplugs, aren't I?" Z moans.

Rock reaches over and gives him a friendly punch. Turning to the girls, Rock's lips curl into a smile. "Thanks, ladies. I'll put everything to good use."

"Jeez," I mutter.

Rock turns my way. "You ready to go, doll, or do you want to stay?"

Taking in my drunk friends, I shake my head. It's barely eleven o'clock. When did we get so old? "We can go. Damon's on his way to pick up Mara."

He nods at Mara. "We'll wait with you."

Sophie jumps up. "I gotta grab the bill."

Rock shakes his head but doesn't look at her. "All taken care of."

"Thank you, Rock," Lilly coos.

His mouth turns up. "Anytime."

Rock steadies me as I stand and helps me into my coat. Trinity grabs her jacket and pushes out the door first. Rock, Mara, and I follow.

Wrath's leaning on Trinity's Jeep, facing the bar. I assumed he'd be annoyed with waiting outside, but he gives Trinity a broad smile as she approaches.

"You could have joined us," I call out to him.

His head snaps up. "Nah, I'm good, Cinderella."

Mara giggles at the nickname.

"Oh, Mara, this is… Wrath. Wrath, Mara."

Wow, this is weird.

He nods at her, and she sort of finger waves back. "I've heard lots about you."

Wrath grins at me. "I bet."

"None of it good," she clarifies with a chuckle. That only makes his devilish smile bigger.

"Jerk," I grumble.

Trinity loops her arm through mine and chuckles. Wrath's eyebrows lift, but she ignores him.

I could get whiplash from these two.

Adam and Ross step out of the bar and join us on the sidewalk.

"What the hell are Sophie and Lilly doing?" Mara snaps at them.

Ross snickers. "Trying to figure out who's giving who a ride." He turns to Rock. "I think they're gonna fight over your boy."

Rock snorts and shakes his head. Against me, Trinity shakes with laughter.

"Great," I mutter. I'm sure Sophie is enjoying being the third wheel there.

Adam and Rock step away to talk.

"Goddamn," Ross whispers near my ear when he finally notices Wrath. "Please tell me *this* one is gay?"

Trinity doubles over so fast she almost knocks me over. She's laughing so hard she starts coughing.

Wrath narrows his eyes at me. "How much did *she* have to drink?"

I shrug. "Nothing that I saw," I say, pretending I don't know why she's having a hysterical fit. I'm not sure how he'll receive Ross's "compliment."

Ross leans over. "That's a no, isn't it?"

"Yes."

He shakes his head. "What a shame."

We're saved from this by Z, Lilly, and an irritated Sophie joining us on the sidewalk.

Wrath tips his chin up at Z. "What up, brother?"

"Gonna drive the girls home." Lilly opens her mouth to protest, and Z glares at her. "Neither of you are in any shape to drive."

Can't argue with that.

Damon pulls into a spot across the street from us. He waves as he gets out. It takes a minute as he pulls baby Cora out of her car seat and carries her across the street to us. Mara immediately runs to them. Damon pulls her close for a kiss, and Cora lets out a happy squeal when she sees her mom.

My breath catches as I watch them interact. Heart hammering, I turn away for a second. Then Rock's arms wrap around me, solid and comforting, holding me against him. He doesn't say anything, just rests his chin atop my head.

Mara grins at us.

Keeping one arm around me, Rock extends his hand to Damon. Damon takes everyone in, and I'm too out of it to make any introductions.

With the force of a whip crack, I realize how awkward this whole situation is.

Lawyers, one judge, and a few outlaw bikers all just mingling on the sidewalk together like it's no big deal.

This is what our wedding will be like... but worse.

ROCK

Hope's unease is obvious to me right away. In my own clumsy way, I tried to explain this to her when I proposed.

133

As president, it's my job to be the public face of the MC when I need to be. So I'm used to mixing with lots of different members of society, whether I enjoy it or not.

Wrath, on the other hand, doesn't have a lot of use for people not associated with our club or with fighting. I can see him twitching from here. It probably doesn't help that Trinity's been refusing to acknowledge him since we stepped outside.

Z's only concern is burying his face in Lilly's tits as soon as possible. That much is clear.

My only concern is getting to the clubhouse, taking Hope upstairs, and using the gifts the girls gave her.

Then I take a better look at my girl. Her gaze is fixed on Mara holding her baby and talking to her softly. Glassy eyes signal she's about to cry. I hug her to me tighter and kiss her cheek.

"Love you, doll," I whisper in her ear.

She twists away from Mara, wrapping her arms around my waist, and sniffles softly. Yeah, definitely time to get her home.

"Good seeing you again, Damon."

I shake hands with Ross and Adam, say our good-byes, and push Hope into my car. Turning around, I catch sight of Wrath snagging Trinity into his hold, and I shake my head.

"Trin," I call out, and both their heads turn my way. "You okay to drive?"

"Yeah, I only had water."

Z's already halfway down the street with Lilly and Sophie. Buddha help the poor bastard.

With the women, brothers, and vehicles accounted for, I get into the car with Hope. "Did you have fun?"

"Yeah," she answers softly.

I can tell something's bothering her. "That's good. You hadn't seen the girls in a while."

"True."

Firing up the engine, I shift into drive and point us toward the highway.

Even though I know she's tipsy, I want her to keep talking to me. I hate how down she seems. After a night out with her friends, I expected her to be bubbling over with stories for me.

An unpleasant thought occurs to me. "Did Sophie behave?" I ask in a teasing way.

Her head snaps up. "I don't know what was up with her. She was a little weird tonight."

That's not good. "Sorry."

"Poor Z's going to have his hands full with the both of them," she says with a snort.

"I'm sure he'll manage."

She's quiet after that. I realize she's drifted to sleep and click the radio on low. Kind of reminds me of the first time she spent the night at the clubhouse. I glance over at her and smile with satisfaction at the way my ring looks on her finger.

She doesn't stir when I park the car or when I open her door. Shaking my head, I extract her from the seatbelt and gather her into my arms. Trinity and Wrath pull up just as I'm realizing I can't juggle Hope and get the front door open.

Wrath snickers. "It's sad that you gotta keep druggin' your girl to get her up here."

"Fuck you." But I'm laughing as I say it. "Grab her stuff for me?" I ask, nodding at my car.

Trinity gets the door for me and they follow me inside. "Nice pink bag," she teases Wrath, who grins.

"What the hell's in it? It's heavy."

Trinity starts giggling. "Books and sex toys."

Wrath looks at me and raises an eyebrow. "Her friends' idea of an engagement present," I explain.

Of course, he digs through it and starts laughing his ass off.

"Give me that," Trinity says, snatching Hope's things out of his hands. "I'll go drop this in front of your door, prez." Wrath watches her run up the stairs.

Hope stirs and blinks up at me. "Where are we?"

Home. "Clubhouse, doll. Can I set you down?"

She tosses her head side to side like she just realized she's midair and giggles. "Yeah."

"Have a nice nap?" Wrath asks.

"I guess."

Wrath's got that expression on his face that I know means trouble. "So a paddle—that for you or him?" he asks, nodding at me.

Her cheeks turn pink. "Neither! Mara's idea of a joke."

"Sure, whatever you say, Cinderella."

"There's a guy's guide for going down on his girl. *You* can have that since Rock doesn't need it."

Yeah, Hope's definitely drunk.

Wrath throws his head back, laughing. "Trust me, neither do I," he manages. Trinity appears at the top of the stairs, and Wrath calls up to her, "Right, babe?"

She waits until she's downstairs with us before answering. "What am I agreeing to?"

"All right, doll, time for bed," I say, curling my arm around Hope's waist.

She follows but calls out to Trinity. "I offered him the guide to going down."

Trinity giggles. "No. He doesn't need it."

Jesus Christ.

"Leave it for Murphy. Brother needs all the help he can get," Wrath calls out as I drag Hope up the stairs while she yells, "Ewwww!" all the way.

"No more liquor for you, lightweight," I tease as I guide her inside my bedroom.

HOPE

A sensual tingling down below pulls me from sleep. My arms stretch over my head as a shudder works over my body.

Rough hands skim under my tank top, palming my breasts, thumbs brushing over my nipples. My lips part, and I moan. Blinking my eyes open, I find Rock's face inches from mine.

"Morning, Baby Doll," he greets in his sexy rasp.

I can't stop myself from reaching out to trace my fingers over his cheek, prickly with morning stubble. He turns and presses kisses to my fingertips. "Morning."

His hands continue pushing up my tank top until my only choice is to sit up and fling it on the floor. "Ready to come for me?"

"How long have you been up?"

He glances down the length of our bodies, and my eyes are immediately drawn to his thick erection. "Long time," he answers with a filthy grin.

"Oh yeah?"

He lowers himself over me. "Mm-hmm." His lips find mine, soft at first, then insistent, until I open for him. All his pent-up need comes through in each kiss, lick, and stroke of his tongue against mine.

He nips his way down my neck, leaving a wet trail. Dipping his head lower, he takes one of my nipples into his mouth, and I gasp. Always thorough, Rock pays equal attention to both breasts. Soft, sucking pressure zings straight to my clit.

"Please," I beg. I'm not even sure what I'm asking for.

"What do you need?"

"You."

"Good. Been thinking about your little bag of presents all night."

"Oh, geez." I roll to the side, but he catches me around the middle, pinning me where he wants me. Rock is multitalented. He manages to hold me down while working my shorts off. Of course, I offer assistance and kick them off my legs.

"Much better," he murmurs.

Wriggling my hands free, I run them all over his back and shoulders. "I love how you feel," I whisper.

Against my face, Rock grins. "Feeling's mutual." He touches his forehead to mine. "I need inside you so bad. I've been half hard all night."

"You're never half anything," I tease. "You should have woken me up," I add.

He shifts, and it's difficult to describe how excruciatingly perfect he feels against me. Skin on skin, the firm weight of his big body pressing into mine. A delicious shiver of anticipation flutters over my skin. His lips press against my cheek, trailing against my neck, and I sigh.

His body shifts again, but I'm too excited to bother to see what he's doing. I assume he's searching for a condom.

Instead, he reaches between us, caressing, then flicking his fingers over my clit, massaging, rubbing—driving me nuts.

"Rock, that's not... I'm ready," I beg.

He sort of chuckles against my hair, and I'm still not smart enough to figure out he's up to something.

The sharp tingling between my legs intensifies. "What the—"

More chuckling. "Warming lube," he answers.

"You, ahhhh, you better fuck me—now."

He has the nerve to laugh harder and take his time reaching for a condom. Underneath him, I struggle and wriggle, trying to get some sort of relief. He pauses to stroke my hair, which would be sweet if I didn't need him to stroke somewhere else instead. Preferably with his cock. My heels dig into the mattress, legs spreading wider, hips arching, anything to get what I need.

"Fuck, you're pretty when you're desperate," he whispers as he sinks into me.

The insistent throbbing between my legs isn't satisfied, though. "Rock," I plead.

"Hold on."

I arch, grinding up against him in time to his furious thrusts. The drag and friction of his cock sends shooting sparks of pleasure up my spine. I roll my hips, but after a while, his movements turn wild and unhinged. His forearms planted beside my head hold him up, keeping me caged in. His thumbs stroke over my cheeks. Then his mouth captures mine in a kiss that's almost tender despite the intensity of his thrusting.

Heat shivers over my chest, down my legs. Finally, I'm ready to tip over that glorious edge I've been seeking. My back arches, my hard nipples pressing against him. A sharp moan tears from my throat. My body jerks in violent waves of pleasure. I'm panting, trying to catch my breath, when Rock's arms scoop underneath me, twisting us until I'm on top.

"I love watching you come more than anything."

My skin blazes at his words. "Yeah?"

He rubs his thumb over my cheek. "You're always so shy, reserved, and in your own head. I like seeing you let go. Knowing I made you do it."

I plant my hands on his chest and sit up a little. My hips circle and I grind myself down hard. "We're not done, are we?"

"Fuck, no," he groans as I slowly keep working myself up and down.

His bottom lip rolls inward and he bites down. Sexiest face ever. That storm-gray gaze clings to mine while I ride him. He lets me tease him and please myself. Lets me think I'm in control while I'm on top. After another orgasm burns through me, he shows me who's actually in charge.

Strong fingers dig into my hips, holding me in place, while his hips snap up. I lean back, bracing my hands on his thighs. Beneath me, he tenses and lets out a deep, grunting shout of pleasure.

I'm done. I give him a second, then drape myself over him, kissing his neck and shoulder while he groans into my hair. His hands lift my hips, setting me next to him gently. Chest still heaving, he rolls to the side for a second, then returns, tucking me tight against him.

My hands drift down against the hard bricks of his abs, stopping to tickle his hip where the anchor tattoo with my name rests.

His breathing slows, and he presses a kiss to my cheek. "Wanna go back to sleep, baby?"

"No. This is nice."

His hand roams up and down my back, stopping to squeeze my ass every now and then.

As far as I'm concerned, nothing outside this room matters.

ROCK

Finally asking Hope to be my wife has lifted a weight off my shoulders. She still flashes me a dazed smile every time she glances at her ring.

I'm pretty thunderstruck myself, although I'm making an effort to keep it under wraps. My brothers, of course, see right through my bullshit act.

"Pick out your flower arrangements yet?" Wrath asks with a wiseass smile.

"Aw, now don't be jealous, dickhead. I'm sure Hope will ask you to be a bridesmaid."

On my other side, Z snickers like an ass.

Wrath brushes off my joke with a twisted grin.

After waking Hope in my special way, she ended up falling back asleep. Once I refuel, I plan to go back upstairs and wake her up with my face between her legs.

"I'll be surprised if she asks Sophie to be a bridesmaid after last night," Trinity comments, pulling me out of my filthy thoughts.

"What?"

Wrath glares at Trinity, but she ignores him. Z quirks an eyebrow.

Trinity lifts her chin at Z. "Your girl Lilly tell you what crawled up Sophie's ass last night?"

"No."

"Didn't she sneak out of here at sunrise?" Wrath asks with a dickish grin.

"Yeah, but we weren't talking about chick shit all night," Z grumbles.

Trinity sighs next to me. Normally, I'd laugh, but I want to hear more about what kind of bullshit came out of Sophie's mouth last night.

"Hope said Sophie acted weird," I prompt.

"Yeah, she just made this really bad joke about how Hope planned her first wedding so fast they thought she was pregnant. Hope looked like she'd been punched in the gut."

Godfuckingdammit. This doesn't sound like the same woman who came into my strip club, begging me to do something to help Hope out of her depression last year. *What the fuck is wrong with Sophie lately?*

But Sophie isn't my problem. Hope is.

"That it?" I ask Trinity.

She sort of shrugs, which isn't comforting. "Yeah, I distracted them by asking about Lilly's tits." She glances at Z. "Your girl's a good sport."

Z breaks out laughing. "Yeah, but she ain't *my* girl."

By the expression on his face, Wrath is clearly finished with this conversation. "Downstate called. Sway wants you to come pay a visit."

Now I understand why he's so annoyed. "Fuck. What for?"

Z bristles. "Fuck that. I ain't in the mood for that place."

Wrath flicks his gaze at Z, then back my way. "He said ol' ladies were invited. It's not a bad idea for you to bring Hope. Have her meet Tawny..." He lets the idea hang in the air.

Tawny is a hardcore ol' lady. Her man is president of our downstate charter. I get why Wrath thinks it's a good idea for Hope to hang out with Tawny for a weekend, but I won't lie and say there's no chance Tawny won't send Hope screaming for the hills.

"What's this, your last-ditch effort to scare Hope away?" I ask without a trace of humor.

He cracks up. "Yeah, man. If Tawny don't scare your girl away, nothing will."

"Don't subject Hope to that bitch on wheels," Z pleads with a headshake.

"What exactly did he want?" I ask Wrath.

"Something about national."

Inwardly, I groan. For bikers who claim to love living on the deviant fringe of society, the Lost Kings have turned into a complicated maze of political bullshit. I prefer to stay out of the political aspects and focus on my own charter.

Unfortunately, there are some responsibilities that can't be avoided. I can't deny that when I've needed Sway's help in the past, he or one of his guys has always been there. As much as it annoys me, it looks like I'll be planning a trip downstate.

Wrath can't go because he's still got his cast. Turning to Z, I lift an eyebrow.

"I'd rather not," he answers my unspoken question.

"Take Murphy and Axel," Wrath suggests.

"Really, Axel? He's a fuckin' kid. Barely been wearing that prospect rocker a month. Bad enough we broke the rule about allowing him up here before his year was up." I don't even bother mentioning the bad blood already brewing between Murphy and Axel over Heidi.

"It'll do Murph some good. Keep his cocky Irish ass in check. Plus, might as well see if Axel can hang now rather than later."

"That's fine. Hope likes both of them, and I know they'll look out for her."

Wrath seems insulted, which is amusing considering how much he enjoys tormenting my girl.

"Prez, I'll go if you're worried about Hope," Z offers.

"Nah, it'll be fine."

"Man, she thinks this place is the gateway to hell. Wait 'til she sees Sway's setup," Wrath says with a little too much glee in his voice.

"Dick," I mutter 'cause I know he's right.

CHAPTER ELEVEN

HOPE

WHEN ROCK FIRST ASKED ME IF I WANTED TO TAKE A TRIP, I WAS EXCITED. But I had something a little different in mind than what he presents me with.

A trip to visit the downstate charter of the Lost Kings. At first, it's news to me that there's another group of Lost Kings somewhere in the state. But then I remember him telling me he'd called some of them in to help out during their dispute with the Vipers. I just didn't understand what it meant at the time.

Who am I kidding? I still have no idea.

Nor do I understand why Wrath seems so amused and Z so concerned about this trip.

We're sitting around having breakfast when a bit of a discussion breaks out.

"Prez, I changed my mind. Think I'm gonna ride along," Z announces.

Rock gives him a sideways glance. Murphy quirks an eyebrow, and Wrath's mouth twists into a grin.

Trinity's watching all of this but hasn't commented yet. "I can go too," she offers quietly.

This earns her a glare from Wrath.

Rock hasn't said anything, but there's an awful lot of tension at the table all of a sudden.

"This is a friendly visit to our brother charter. Z, you want to come, I don't give a fuck. Trinity, I need you here. Murphy, you're with me. Teller's busy with Heidi, so I'm not even bothering him with this. Axel and Hoot will take the van. Dex, Bricks, Ravage, Stash, and Birch, I need here. And I don't think it needs to be said that Sparky's not leaving the basement." He gives Wrath a pointed look.

Rock's word is final. No one so much as utters a single syllable. He grunts and pushes away from the table.

"Hope." He jerks his head at me.

Between his gruff tone and the way he kind of ordered me to follow him like a dog, I'm miffed. My chair almost falls over I shove up out of it so fast.

"What's wrong?" I snap when I catch up to him in the hallway.

Rock's mouth curves into a soft smile, and for the first time, I notice the lines etched around his eyes. Something about this trip is stressing him out. He holds out his arm, beckoning me closer, and tucks me tight to his side. "Nothing, babe. Just a lot of things to get done before Friday."

Tipping up my head so I can kiss his chin, I ask, "Anything I can do to help?"

"Nah. Just rest up. I gotta take care of some things. You okay?"

"Yeah."

A couple days later, Trinity sits on the chaise in our bedroom, watching as I rifle through my closet.

"Have you been there?" I ask her.

She snorts as if it's a silly question. "Long time ago."

"I suppose it will be a bunch of half-naked chicks running around?" I call out.

"Pretty much."

"How many of them are going to tell me they fucked my fiancé?"

At that, she chokes with laughter. "None of them if they want to keep breathing. Sway's ol' lady runs a tight ship. None of those bitches should backtalk you."

It dawns on insensitive me that this might be a weird conversation for Trinity to be part of because she's not an ol' lady—yet. Technically, she's one of those girls I'm complaining about. Except I don't see her that way. I don't know what her arrangement with Wrath or any of the other guys is. And really, it's not my business what consenting adults do with their bodies.

What I *do* know is Trinity has been kind to me since day one, and I like to think we're friends. So I don't want to inadvertently hurt her feelings.

Stepping out of the closet, I take in her guarded expression.

"I wish you guys were coming with us," I say softly. Then thinking it over, I correct myself. "Well, I wish *you* were coming with us."

She chuckles and flicks at an invisible piece of lint on her jeans. "Hopefully, Wyatt's cast comes off next week."

"That's good. Maybe he'll be less cranky." My attempt at a joke falls flat. "What's wrong, Trinity?" I ask, tossing some clothes on the bed and heading toward the chaise.

She finally glances up as I sit next to her. "Nothing. I don't know. I'm not sure what happens... next."

I assume she's talking about what happens when Wrath's cast comes off and he no longer has a reason to stay downstairs in her room, but I wait for her to explain.

Trinity is a tough nut to crack, though.

"He wants... Never mind. It's stupid."

The suspense is killing me. I want to grab her and shake really hard. But I'm afraid if I push her, she'll clam up for good.

"You're going to have enough to worry about this weekend. Make sure you call or text me if anything comes up. Even if it's some stupid club question that Rock's not around to answer." Trinity is good at deflecting.

"Why wouldn't he be around?"

She turns so she's fully facing me. "I guarantee you this visit is more than a social call, Hope. Don't be surprised or hurt if you end up spending most of the trip hanging out with Tawny."

Wow. I don't know what to make of that. "Okay."

"Tawny is... more old school. She's going to be assessing you. Judging you. Rumors spreading through the organization that Rock's ol' lady is weak could hurt his position."

I blink a few times, swallowing all of that down. "Here?"

Her face brightens. "No, the guys here accept you. They know you're good for Rock."

After a minute, she shakes her head. "You know what? Forget I said a word. Rock will be pissed at me for saying anything. Just watch your back with Tawny. Don't volunteer too much information. Pretend you're in awe of her greatness, and you'll be fine."

Yeah, sure. That should be easy enough.

Hugging Rock tight as he sped down the thruway was fun for the first half of the trip. By the second hour, I'm shivering from the cold air whipping around us. It was a bright, sunny early spring day when we left the clubhouse. Since then, the sun disappeared behind gray clouds, so we're cutting through nothing but chilly air.

I'm also horny as hell. This annoys me because I doubt I'll be able to do anything about it anytime soon.

Beneath me, the bike shifts and slows. I flick up my eyes and see Rock signaling to the other guys that we're getting off at one of the rest stops. Interesting. I was under the impression the guys didn't take many breaks, and I hope Rock isn't doing this for my benefit. The last thing I want is for the brothers to start bitching about how having a girl on the ride slows them down.

Rock pulls up right in front of the convenience store portion of the station. Z and Murphy glide to a stop beside us. Hoot pulls the van into a spot ahead of us.

After removing his helmet, Rock reaches back and pats my thigh. I take it as my signal to dismount.

"Everything okay, prez?" Z asks as he walks around to my side.

"Yeah, just wanted to warm up a sec."

Murphy wanders over to the van. To harass Axel some more, I suppose.

Rock takes my hand and leads me inside. We walk straight through the store and into the main portion where the fast food kiosks and bathrooms are. Tugging me out of the flow of traffic, Rock settles his hands on my shoulders.

"You okay?"

"Yeah, why?"

The corner of his mouth turns up in a soft smile, and he traces a finger over my cheek. "You're shivering, Baby Doll."

Oh. I guess I am. My gaze sweeps over the hoodie Rock's wearing under his cut. My vest is too tight to fit much of anything underneath. I did layer a couple thin long-sleeved shirts, but I guess it's not enough.

"Sorry, I didn't expect it to get colder as we traveled south," he says while unzipping his hoodie and shrugging off his cut.

"What are you doing?" I ask as he hands me his vest to hold. He pulls the hoodie off and we trade. Subconsciously, I hug the sweatshirt to my chest, soaking in Rock's warmth.

"Come on." He wiggles his hand at me to hand over the sweatshirt so he can help me into it. My hands run over my vest. "I don't want to cover it up," I protest.

Sure, at first I felt strange riding down the thruway wearing this thing that proclaimed me "Property of," but a sense of pride also clung to me. A feeling of safety. I belong to Rock. He and the four guys with us would do anything to keep me safe on this trip, and my patch announces that to the world.

Covering it up seems wrong, no matter the reason.

Heat flares in Rock's eyes as my refusal sinks in. He drapes the sweatshirt over my shoulders and uses the material to tug me tight against his body.

It's instantly obvious I'm not the only one who's been aroused by this trip.

Rock presses his lips to my forehead. "How'd I get so lucky, baby?" he murmurs. With the sweatshirt sort of shielding us, I brush my hand over his crotch. He jumps as if he's touched a live wire. His wild gaze darts around.

"Come," he orders, tugging on my hand.

Yes, please.

ROCK

As the sun started to set, the shivers wracking Hope's body signaled it was time to pull over. She's squeezing me so tight, if she gets any closer, she'll be up inside me. We're only about forty-five minutes from our destination, but I don't think she can hang on much longer. Fuck, she's barely a month and a half out of the fucking hospital. I should have my head examined for taking her on this ride.

I'm thinking of sticking her in the van with the prospects for the rest of the trip.

First, I want to get her into my sweatshirt and warmed up. She actually protests because she doesn't want to cover up my patch.

It takes a minute for that to sink in.

Here I'd been thinking Hope was pretty pissed off when I told her to wear it all weekend.

Actually, because I understand it's all still a little weird to her, what I said was, "You *can* wear your patch all weekend," like it was some special treat for her.

I got a sarcastic smirk at the time.

But just now, she surprised the fuck outta me. She does that a lot.

I love it.

All I can think about is that unisex/family bathroom I know is stashed in the back corner. Pulling Hope along behind me, I shove through the door and lock it behind us.

"What are you doing?" she asks breathlessly.

"Fucking you."

She sucks in a breath, eyes going owl-wide, and presses her back against the door. Her nose wrinkles. "Here? Now?"

"Yes." I stalk toward her and throw my hands up on either side of her face. She continues staring up at me with her wide, innocent green eyes. I love that fucking expression, and I don't ever want to see her lose it. I don't want to be the cause of her losing a bit of her sweetness.

She tips up her head, and I seal my mouth over hers, taking her in a harsh kiss meant to express everything I'm feeling inside. Her soft moans flow right into me, confirming this was a good idea. Who knows when we'll have another chance this weekend?

Breaking our kiss, I drag my mouth down along her jaw, burying my face against her neck. She makes this sweet, contented sigh as if we have all the time in the world and aren't about to fuck in a rest stop bathroom.

"Babe, this is gonna be quick and dirty," I whisper into her ear. Against my cheek, I feel her face pull into a smile.

"Then let's get to it," she says.

Fuck. Yes.

Gripping her hips, I tug her away from the door and over to the sink. I don't even have to voice what I'm planning. She's already unbuttoning her jeans.

"Uh-uh," I *tsk* at her. "Put your hands on the sink."

She glances at me, and I catch a hint of a playful smile curving her lips as she does what I ask.

I take a minute to get myself ready. I'm pretty much carrying condoms in every goddamn pocket these days and giving serious consideration to getting snipped, because fuck if I'm going to risk Hope's life again.

The memory of taking her to the hospital stops me.

"Rochlan?"

Her soft, questioning voice pulls me from my dark thoughts. She wiggles her butt at me, which is damn cute. But in the mirror, I see the worry tightening her face.

"Please fuck me," she says so low I barely catch it.

Hope talkin' dirty without any prompting is a rare treat, and it revs me back up in no time. My hands find their way to her jeans and shove them down her thighs, leaving them around her knees.

"Tip that ass up, sweetheart," I whisper harshly against her ear. She arches her back, going up on tiptoes just a bit, and I slide home.

"Fuck, you're wet. Ride work you up?"

She sort of puffs out an answer, but mostly she's thrusting back against me. Her fingers are curled tight over the edge of the sink and she rocks back, harder and harder. Her head is tipped down, so all I can see in the reflection is the crown of her head.

"Look in the mirror, doll."

Shaking her hair out of her face, she glances up and our eyes lock.

Fuck, I wish she was naked.

Her lips part and her eyelids drop.

She's so fucking snug around my dick. "Babe, this isn't going to take long."

She groans, long and low, her pussy locking down on me. White heat streaks down my spine, tightening everything in me. It feels like I come for hours, although it's probably not even a minute.

Carefully, I pull out and clean up. Hope is still bent over, clinging to the side of the basin. I can't help but give her ass a little smack. She doesn't even jump, just sighs as a content little smile curves her lips.

Outside the bathroom, someone bangs on the door. Loud.

"In a minute," I shout.

Hope's so blissed out she doesn't even notice the audience we have waiting. Gotta say, that makes me real fucking happy and ready to fuck her all over again.

"Come on, Baby Doll," I encourage, slipping my hands around her waist to hike her jeans into place.

Finally, she straightens up and takes over. She turns and loops her hands around my neck.

"I love you," she says very softly.

Time sort of stands still. It's not the first time she's said it, but her words have a strong effect on me. Before I can answer, her cheeks flush pink and her gaze bounces around the bathroom.

"What's wrong?"

"I need to pee."

I shouldn't be so amused at her discomfort, but after what we just did, it's hard not to chuckle.

She punches me in the arm. "Turn around."

That makes me laugh even harder, but the banging at the door again stops me.

"Dammit," Hope mutters behind me.

When we finally open the door, there's a very pissed off family across the way. I tuck Hope into my side and pull her along before she freaks out.

When we get into the convenience store, she pulls away from me. She's completely pink from the neck up. It's really cute.

"You want some coffee or something to warm up, doll?"

She glares at me but nods, then wanders off. When she returns, she's holding a banana and a bottle of water, which sets me off laughing again.

"Where the fuck did you find a piece of fruit at a gas station?"

She gives me a disgusted snort and heads for the front.

Z's waiting near the register for us. "The fuck, prez? Been waiting forever."

His gaze skips to Hope, who turns even pinker. Z chuckles but wisely chooses not to comment.

Outside, we sip coffee, and Axel and Hoot join us.

"I'm gonna send Hope in the van with you two."

Hope whips her head around. "Why?"

"We got plenty of room, Hope. I'll even sit in the back," Hoot tells her.

Hope's got a look on her face that tells me she has a lot to say on the subject, which surprises me. I thought she'd be relieved. Throwing my arm around her shoulder, I tug her away from the guys.

"Why don't you want me with you?" she asks. I swear she sounds close to tears, and I'm suddenly feeling kinda stupid.

"Of course I want you with me. It's just getting cold, baby."

"Oh. How much longer is the trip?"

"Probably another forty-five minutes."

Her eyes skip to the van, then back to me. "I'll be okay." She holds out her hand. "Give me your sweatshirt."

I hold her gaze for a minute. "You sure? I don't want you to get sick this weekend."

"I'm okay. I warmed up. I'm feeling *rejuvenated*."

I snort at that. I'm feeling pretty rejuvenated myself at the moment. "All right, but tap me if it's too much. Don't worry about what the guys or anyone but me thinks."

"Okay."

I help her into the sweatshirt, and we turn back to the group.

"Let's go."

HOPE

The rest of the ride is uneventful. Just as I'm thinking of taking

Rock up on his offer to ride in the van, he signals that we're getting off the thruway.

Wrath has told me he used to make lots of runs to California, but I can't imagine being trapped on a bike for days at a time. This has been plenty.

Although it's not nestled deep in the woods like our clubhouse, the downstate charter does have a bit of privacy about it. The building looks like an old chain hotel that's been taken over by a band of rowdy bikers.

Which is exactly what it is.

"Used to be a Howard Johnson's," Z explains. "They even have a pool. You bring your bikini, Hope?" he teases.

Rock growls and nudges him away from me. "Stop trying to see my woman without her clothes, dick."

Z and I both laugh, which makes Rock smirk. With a more serious expression, Rock settles his hands on my shoulders and tilts his head at the guys to join us. "This is a brother charter, Hope. Everyone will be aware you're my girl. Even so, if you're not with one of the old ladies, I want you to stick close to me or one of our guys." He points at everyone.

A skittering of unease travels down my spine. Trinity has explained to me that most MCs are very different than ours. I've never been clear if that extends to the entire Lost Kings organization or just the upstate charter Rock is responsible for.

Leaning down, Rock touches his forehead to mine. "Sway is the president here. His ol' lady is Tawny. You'll probably hang with her for a bit." He pauses, and I get the sense he's about to say something he thinks will tick me off. But I'm so out of my element it would take a lot for me to get upset right now. "Try to, uh, just observe her, okay?"

If I hadn't already been warned ahead of time by Trinity, I wouldn't know what to make of that. I'll have to remember to text her a thank you later.

"Trinity explained she runs a tight ship here," I tell him.

His mouth quirks. "Yeah, that's one way to put it."

Rock hasn't said a lot about what this trip means. But thanks to Trinity, I have an inkling it's more than just a social visit. I'm determined not to do anything that will make him worry or embarrass him.

"Listen and learn?" I ask him gently.

A look of relief washes over his face. "Yeah. You got any questions or get upset about something you see, we'll talk it out when we're alone, okay?" he promises me.

I can do this.

"Yup." I give him a quick peck on the lips, then step back and shrug off his sweatshirt. Smoothing my hands over my vest and loosening my ponytail, I paste a smile on my face.

"Let's do it."

As we approach the building, two large men step out of the shadows. They seem to be guarding the entrance.

"Evening," one calls out.

As we get closer, I see they're both wearing black leather cuts but no visible patches on the front. The guy on the left eyes Rock. "Oh shit. Sway said to be lookin' out for you. Hey, Mr. North."

Poor guy seems confused about how he should address Rock. Next to me, Z bumps me with his elbow and smirks.

Rock threads his fingers through mine and leans down. "Brace yourself," he whispers.

I assume he's kidding until the two prospects open the doors. It's a fight not to clap my free hand over my mouth like some prude.

Any wave of courage I was riding in the parking lot washes away the moment we step inside. I remember my shock the first time I set foot in Rock's clubhouse during a Friday night party. That was nothing compared to this. No wonder they have guys guarding the front door.

I'm not sure where to look first, or rather, where to safely avert my gaze. Drugs—more than the weed that is always available at Rock's clubhouse—are being enjoyed by a number of guests. And I've certainly witnessed my fair share of public sex at Rock's club, but this is damn close to a full-on orgy.

At Rock's, I'm intrigued and mildly amused or curious. Here, I'm sort of grossed out.

A woman I can only describe as *hard* greets us at the door. I imagine she was quite beautiful twenty years, twenty thousand cigarettes, and two hundred thousand tanning bed hours ago. She's got an impressive helmet of hair shellacked into perfection around her heart-shaped face.

If I were a nastier, more judgmental person, the words trailer and trash might spring to mind. But I'm not, so I push away the thought before it can fully form.

"Well, if it isn't upstate come to grace us with your presence," she jokes in a raspy voice before pressing her long talons against Rock's cheeks and giving him a quick kiss. The rest of the guys get the same treatment, even Axel.

"Tawny, this is Hope," Rock introduces.

The woman turns and her scary eyes sweep over me from head to toe. "Rock's ol' lady. Never thought we'd see that." She holds out her hand. Instead of shaking, she tugs me away from the guys. "I'll take good care of her. Go find Sway. He's been waitin' on ya," she says with a wave.

I flash a nervous smile at Rock and, determined to nail this ol' lady role, let Tawny drag me away.

ROCK

Watching Tawny drag Hope away isn't easy. Let's face it; I don't like having her out of my sight even when we're home. But here?

No.

"Want me to keep an eye on 'em, prez?" Hoot asks.

"Yeah, just don't be obvious. Don't insult Sway."

"I'll play dumb prospect."

"Don't overthink it," Z cracks.

Hoot's hard to insult, so he just laughs and takes off.

Since Tawny's here, the number of club whores present should be a lot fewer than it seems to be. Not sure what that's about. Before we even make it to the bar, Murphy's dragged off by a slim blonde who looks vaguely familiar.

Turning, I check on Axel, who seems to be handling himself fine. He flashes a quick smile at me.

"When we find out where we're staying, bring Hope's stuff in, then mine."

"Yeah, no problem, prez."

Sway walks out of his office with a big grin in place. "Motherfucker! It's been too long, brother." He greets me with a solid slap on my back.

Z gets the same greeting.

"Come on, let's get you a drink and some shitty bar food."

After we're set up at the bar, Sway makes a big show of looking around the room. "Weren't you bringing your ol' lady?"

"Yeah, she's with Tawny."

"God help her. Sorry, man," he says, completely serious.

Glad to see nothing's changed here.

"You're out of your fuckin' mind to be takin' an ol' lady when you got all those fuckin' strippers beggin' for your cock."

Standing next to me, Z snorts and looks away.

Sway pokes a finger at Z. "You disagreein', fucker?"

"Yeah. When you meet her, you'll understand," he answers, slapping away Sway's hand.

I cock my head at Z. Startin' to wonder about him lately.

Sway is surprisingly impressed. "Got your officer's approval?"

"Fuckin' A."

Thankfully, we move on from talkin' about my love life.

"Where's your RC?"

"Already took off with one of your girls."

Sway nods knowingly. "Serena. Bitch has been pining for him since the last time he was here. I got half a mind to send her back with you fucks."

Just what we need.

HOPE

Tawny pulls me into a quieter lounge area. There are a number of other women surrounding us. Some she says hello and introduces me to, some she outright ignores.

Club whores.

Rock tried to explain this dynamic to me once. But it's one of those things that needs to be personally observed to be understood.

Tawny stops to introduce me to one of the women she seems to feel is worthy. "Angie, this here is Rock's girl."

Angie is a tiny little thing. She's got a softer face than Tawny, but something about her still sets my radar off.

She walks around me, checking out my patch. "Well, well. He's patched you in already." She glances down at the officer's patches on my side and sneers. "Got the guys to vote you in? You must really be something," she says as if she's not impressed.

"Ignore Angie. She's just pissed Bull keeps blocking her vote," Tawny says with a wave of her hand. But while she says to ignore Angie, she seems secretly pleased.

I don't like either of them.

Is this what Rock expects of me?

Will this be what I turn into twenty years from now?

Yikes. Obviously, I haven't given enough thought to our long-term future. My fingers automatically start twisting my engagement ring, which suddenly feels very tight.

Tawny pulls me over to a couch and sits us down. She snaps her fingers at one of the girls loitering around, and a few minutes later, two beers are set down on the table in front of us. I smile and nod my thanks, which makes Tawny chuckle.

"How on earth did *you* hook up with Rock? It must be some story."

I'm not really sure where to start. It's a long and complicated tale. I don't feel like explaining to this woman that I'm a lawyer, and I don't think it will be received very well.

"I hear you're a lawyer," she prods.

Well, there goes that plan.

One corner of my mouth twitches into something resembling a smile. "Yeah, I got assigned to represent him at an arraignment and things just kind of snowballed from there."

Geez, what an understatement.

Her eyes drop down to take in my ring, which I'm still nervously twisting round and round.

"A ring and a patch. Rock's really not fucking around this time," she observes.

"How long have you known him?"

She tips her head back as if she's counting up the years in her head. "Long time. Sway was a member upstate when Rock was prospecting."

"Oh, really? How long have you and... Sway been together?"

"Since high school. So twenty-eight years?"

Wow, okay, so that only puts her maybe mid-forties. Here I was thinking she was a lot older. I should probably keep that to myself. No woman wants to hear that.

One of the girls runs into the room, shrieking for Tawny.

"Excuse me, honey. Fucking drama with these bitches nonstop," she says as she takes off.

Not sure what to do with myself, I look around the room. None of the other girls will meet my eyes. Little pit bull Angie has disappeared.

No one told me I had to stay here, right?

As soon as I get up, I need to find a bathroom. It's an old hotel, and this is basically the reception/lounge area, so there's got to be a bathroom somewhere.

I find one out in the hallway. As I'm walking out, I run smack into a familiar face.

Cookie.

The last time I saw her, she called me an uppity cunt and Rock had her booted from the clubhouse.

You've got to be fucking kidding me.

"Hope! My God. I heard you were here." She scans me up and down.

"Cookie, right?" As if I could forget.

She blushes and looks at the floor. "I was hoping I'd run into you so I could apologize for how I acted when we met."

Waiting for the punch line, I cross my arms over my chest.

Her gaze lands on my face again, and I detect nothing but sincerity.

"That night, I was a little tipsy. You know Rock and I... Well, he'd been so distant from all the girls for so long, and then you kind of showed up out of nowhere and you're nothing like us, and it kind of hurt. I shouldn't have lashed out at you. I'm sorry."

Holy shitballs.

Not that I have any reason to, but I want to apologize to *her*. Instead, I reach out and squeeze her arm. "I understand."

Relief floods her face. "Thank you."

"So you ended up here?" I ask.

"Yeah." She turns and points to a guy who's a slightly smaller, less absurdly sexy version of Rock standing at the end of the hallway. He catches her eye and smiles. "I'm with Steer. He's the VP here."

Well, didn't she land on her feet? "That's good."

She nods. "I'm glad I saw you. I felt really awful, but I knew Rock would never let me back up there, even to apologize."

A thought pops into my head. "Hey, the two charters must mingle from time to time, right?"

"Oh yeah, especially in the summers."

"Cool, so I'm sure we'll see you guys up at our clubhouse."

She seems startled. But hell, if she's hooked up with the VP down here, I'm sure as heck not going to be the reason he can't bring his ol' lady to our clubhouse.

"That's sweet of you, Hope. Thanks."

We talk for a few more minutes, then go our separate ways.

ROCK

From where I'm sitting at the bar, I'm able to spot Hope as she comes out of the bathroom. I'd heard Cookie was down here but never thought she'd be here tonight. She best stay the fuck away from me.

Instead, she catches Hope in the hallway. For some unfathomable reason, Hope's by herself—Tawny's doing a stellar job lookin' out for my girl.

Everything in me wants to go to her and make sure she's okay. But with Sway sittin' so close, I can't let him think my girl's weak.

Thankfully, they seem to be getting along. Hope gives her what I recognize as her professional lawyer smile.

Sway follows my line of vision.

"Oh yeah, heard they didn't get along so well. Sorry if it's a problem that she's here tonight. Steer seems to have taken a shine to Cookie."

"Nah, no problem."

Hope's weaving her way through the crowd toward me, and I give her a chin lift so she knows it's okay to approach us. This gets a genuine smile from her, and I let out a breath I didn't realize I'd been holding.

When she's close enough, I pull her against me, tucking her between my knees. She perches on my thigh and curls her arm around my waist. Sway has turned away to speak to the girl behind the bar, so for the moment, I have Hope to myself.

Leaning down, in a low voice, I ask if she's okay.

I get a nod.

"I saw you speaking to Cookie. Sorry 'bout that."

She seems surprised. "It's all good. She apologized. I told her we're fine and that I hoped we'd see her when the clubs get together or whatever."

Well, isn't my girl full of surprises? "That was very kind, doll. Thank you."

She shrugs and takes a sip of my Scotch. The wrinkled-nose face she makes is pretty funny. I hand her a bottle of water and try to keep myself under control while she wraps her lips around it and takes a deep gulp.

"Everything okay?" she whispers when she's finished.

Before Sway turns his attention on us, I want to give Hope a heads-up. "Don't get mad, but you need to sit here and look pretty, okay? Don't volunteer more information than necessary."

Instead of anger, she responds with a soft smile and runs her hand over my cheek. "I'm good, Rochlan."

"You're the best," I murmur into her ear.

Her eyelids drop and she presses a kiss against my jaw.

This isn't the time or place to get carried away—not that it would matter with what's going on in this room around us. I don't want to stop her, but my exhibitionist days are over. Not with Hope. She's mine and mine alone. All of her. Still, I can't find it in me to stop her as she nuzzles and trails her soft lips against my neck.

Sway stops her for me. "So you must be Hope," he says with a lot of laughter behind the words.

Hope's body snaps straight, but she stays tight to me. A glance shows me her cheeks are flushed pink.

"Sway." He introduces himself, holding out his hand. Hope's gaze skips to me, and I nod before she accepts his hand. For some reason, I find it awfully fucking hot she sought out my permission before touching another man, even for something as simple as a handshake.

I need my fucking caveman brain examined.

"Thank you for inviting me down."

"Sure thing. My woman take care of you?"

"Ah, she did, but she got called away for something, so we didn't get a lot of time to talk."

"Sounds about right. Tomorrow, you gals can get acquainted while we handle business."

Hope sort of twitches against me, and I'd bet my bike she's holding back laughter at the over-the-top way he says that. Sway and I go way back, and I got a lotta respect for him. But the fucker talks like a cartoon biker sometimes.

Sway's gaze springs to the door. "Excuse me for a sec," he says as he slides off his stool.

Behind the bar, Sara hands me a basket of cheese sticks.

Hope twists around, and I nudge her so she's resting against my other leg, facing the bar. "You hungry?"

Her nose wrinkles. "Yes. But—"

"Not a lot of gourmet dishes here, doll," I say softly against her ear. The shiver that works over her body surprises me. Suddenly, I'm very aware no one has given us a room yet. I need to remedy that soon.

Picking up one of the chubby, greasy sticks, I lift it to Hope's mouth. "Open."

A frisky smile kicks up the corners of her mouth as she follows my order. I groan as she sits and waits patiently, lips parted, for me to bring the food to her. Something about the trust she displays while waiting for each bite sends heat streaking through me.

What started out being sort of silly and playful, a way to ease the tension I think we're both feeling on this adventure, ends up turning my crank in a spectacular manner. Feeding my girl from my hand, taking care of her that way, a rush of power goes straight to my head.

Christ, the things I want to do to her. Right this fucking second.

When she's finished, I press a kiss to her forehead, and she lets out a satisfied sigh. As I run the back of my knuckles over her cheek, she leans into my touch. In the middle of this wild clubhouse with all sorts of crazy shit going on around us, my girl and I are having this intense moment, and I wish we were anywhere else in the world.

"Sorry 'bout that," Sway says, sliding back into his seat.

Really. Anywhere else in the world right now would be great.

CHAPTER TWELVE

HOPE

I don't know what's gotten into Rock. Or me for that matter.

I seriously want to jump him.

That's nothing new. I pretty much always want to fuck his brains out. But something about tonight is different. There's a strange dynamic going on between us. Some sort of power shift happened on the ride down here. I'm not sure what to make of it.

The fact that it doesn't bother me bothers me.

I'm used to feeling out of place in Rock's world. But Sway's clubhouse brings a whole new level of discomfort to my usual confused state.

After hanging with Tawny and Sway, I appreciate Trinity and, I'll be honest, even Wrath a whole lot more. I have a whole new respect for the way Rock runs his club; that's for sure.

Rock has me sort of cocooned against him, as I'm sure he can feel my unease. I appreciate the shelter of his body and plan to take cover against him as long as I can.

A gentle tap on my shoulder shakes me out of my thoughts. "You doin' okay?" Z asks softly.

A smile tugs at my mouth, and I sit up. "Yeah. Where have you been hiding?"

"I been around," he answers with a smirk.

"Yeah, I bet." I giggle and give him a soft shove. Rock's arm tightens around my waist and laughter rumbles out of him.

"Well, I guess some things don't change," comes from a shrill voice behind me.

Rock's body jerks upright, tossing me forward into Z, who turns and steps in front of me protectively.

I wriggle around to see what has them so worked up and find a short, curvy woman in front of me. *Fan-fucking-tastic.* Is there nowhere I'm safe from running into Rock's past pieces of ass? Wasn't Cookie enough fun for one night?

"Carla," Rock says tightly.

"What the fuck are you doing here?" Z asks, still shielding me from the woman.

"My old man has business with the club. Never thought I'd run into you."

"You should go find him," Z suggests.

Maybe I was wrong and this is a former fling of his.

"Jesus, Rock. What's it been? Eleven, twelve years?"

Or not.

"Not long enough," he answers.

Angling her way past Z, she narrows her gaze at me, thrusting out her hand. "Hi, I'm Rock's ex-wife."

Oh, for fuck's sake.

I've heard plenty about this woman. But no one has ever uttered her name. Wrath and Z both have other choice words they use to refer to her. Rock almost never mentions her. I know she cheated on him and his two best friends hate her—that's about it.

Reaching past Z, I take her tiny hand. She eyes me up and down, finding me lacking, I'm sure. "Hope." I introduce myself.

She raises an eyebrow as if she expects me to elaborate. When I don't, she sweeps her nasty gaze over me again, this time lingering on my vest and then finally my left hand, which is currently resting on Rock's leg.

"His ol' lady," she finally concludes. "Wow, that's some rock you got from Rock," she says with a smirk. My, she's a sharp one. "So you're getting married again finally? I'm happy for you."

I want to laugh in her face. It's not like Rock's been some lonely bachelor all these years.

"Thanks," Rock answers, not sounding a bit thankful at all.

Sway returns, and Z relocates behind Rock's chair.

"Jesus Christ, who the fuck dragged your sorry ass in here, Carla?" Sway asks. With those words, I find myself liking him a whole lot more.

She actually rolls her eyes. Nervy bitch. "You know I'm here with Barry."

"Good, that means you're leaving soon," Sway answers without looking at her. "Rock, anyone set you and your lovely ol' lady up with a room yet?" he asks.

"No."

"Sorry, that's not cool. Give me a second." Sway pushes away from the bar and storms over to a room off to the side of the front entrance.

For some reason, Carla's still standing with our little group. Man, she can't take a hint. "So how'd you two meet? You don't look like the usual club whore," she says as if that's an acceptable way to start a conversation.

"It's a long story," I answer.

"Oh, I can imagine. Has Rock ever told you how we met?"

"Nope. I didn't even know your name until a few minutes ago."

Z lets out a loud cough, and Rock turns toward the bar.

Carla narrows her eyes at me but doesn't give any other response.

Thankfully, Sway returns, rescuing me from any more awkward conversation. He gives Carla a pointed look, and she finally walks away, but I'm sure it won't be the last we see of her this weekend.

After slapping a room key down on the bar, Sway points down the hall. "Down at the end, 'round the corner. It should be somewhat quiet."

"You got another one down that way?" Z asks.

Sway quirks an eyebrow. "Since when you want some quiet?"

Z shrugs.

"Yeah, I'll hook you up."

Z and Sway take off together. Rock picks up the key, turning it over in his hand for a second. "You okay?" he finally asks.

"Yes. Are you?"

A small smile tugs at one corner of his mouth. "Yeah, doll. I'm good. You ready for bed?"

"God, yes."

That tempts a bigger smile out of him. He pulls out his phone and taps out a message. A few minutes later, Hoot and Axel show up with our bags. Stepping away from Rock, I try to grab my stuff, but Axel pulls it away with a laugh.

"Knock it off, First Lady. I got it." He grins at me.

"Thank you, Axel."

Rock hands over the key to Hoot and points them in the direction of our room.

ROCK

Except for Hope's presence, this entire trip has sucked. The thought that Sway wants me to join his bid for national and have to do this on a regular basis gives me fucking hives.

Fuck that.

Carla. What a deep well of bad memories she stirred up. It's probably been closer to fifteen years since I last saw my ex. I could have happily gone the rest of my life never seeing her again. I certainly never wanted Hope to meet her. I can't even imagine what's going through her head right now.

My girl is quiet as she takes my hand and we follow the prospects down the hall. Axel sets her stuff down on a chair right inside the door and asks her if she needs anything.

I have to admit, the way this kid looks after my woman, he's kind of growing on me.

After they leave, Hope rifles through her bags. With her overflowing pouch of who knows what in one hand, she wraps the fingers of her other hand around mine and tugs me into the bathroom. "Come on. I know what you need."

Her certainty would get a smile out of me, except she's so serious. I'm curious what she thinks I need. Besides her.

Because, honestly, as long as I have her, I don't give a fuck about anything else.

Once we're in the bathroom, she turns and shuts the door. Her bright green eyes search my face for a second before she stretches up and loops her arms around my neck. Her soft lips find their way to my jaw, slowly working lower.

"Mmm, you're right. That's exactly what I need," I tease.

"I'm not finished," she answers in a low, husky voice.

This will be interesting. Hope doesn't often take the lead. The fact that she's so eager to now has me practically jumping out of my skin to see where she's going with this.

Her soft fingers find their way to the hem of my shirt, teasing underneath, then tugging it up. I give her a hand and toss it on the sink. Next, her hands start working my belt.

I definitely like where she's going.

"Not fair, doll. You're still fully dressed."

She stops and takes a step back, lifting her arms over her head. I get the hint and work her shirt up and off.

"Better?" she asks.

"Yup."

Now that we're both shirtless, she reaches out to touch me. Soft at first. Gentle strokes down my chest and shoulders. Hope's not just touching me, though; it's more like admiring, and it's a jolt of arousal through my system. My dick jumps to life under her touch and appreciative gaze.

After a few more gentle strokes, she gets back to work on my belt, loosening it, flicking open the button on my jeans, and working the zipper. Tugging down my jeans, she kneels in front of me to work off my boots. Something about my girl on her knees undressing me like this is beyond fucking hot. Especially when she stops to peek up at me from beneath her lashes.

Holy fucking hell.

When she's done, she stands and turns toward the shower. Very precisely, she digs through the bag she brought in here, pulls out a bunch of small, colorful bottles, and lines them up on the narrow shower stall shelf. When she has the water running, she strips out of the rest of her clothes and takes my hand again, pulling me in the stall with her. She positions me where she wants me, under the spray.

"Turn," she says.

Like I'm going to say no.

Turning, I place my hands on the back wall, spreading my legs to give my girl full access to wherever she wants to go. A groan lets loose from my chest the instant she puts her hands on me. After a soft click, a woodsy scent fills the air. She lathers and soaps me from neck to ankles. Her small hands slide over my shoulders, back, legs. After a while, her cleansing strokes turn seductive. Before she put her hands on me, I hadn't realized how stiff and sore I was from the ride down. All her squeezing and massaging down my back feels like heaven. Her touch releases most of the tension that gathered there during the day.

"Hope," I groan.

Behind me, she lets out a happy humming noise. "Turn, please."

Fuck yes.

This time I brace my arms on the shower wall and the door. Again, she lathers me up while my back takes the hot, pounding spray of water. I'm so frickin' big Hope's still mostly dry. I'll need to fix that in a minute, but right now, what she's doing feels too damn good. Her soft hands are everywhere, kneading and massaging me—turning a simple shower into some of the hottest foreplay ever.

She rubs and strokes every part of me. Except the part I *want* her to stroke the most. I'm a patient guy, though, and I don't think Hope has it in her to be cruel. Slowly, she works her way down my legs until she's kneeling on the shower floor. Reaching down, I run my fingers through her hair.

"You okay?" I ask.

Instead of answering, she wraps her fingers around my dick, slowly sliding up and down. The sensation steals all thoughts and words from my brain. Even as my hips buck to her rhythm, I keep my gaze on her. An excited flush stains her cheeks pink, probably the most beautiful thing I've ever seen, as she kneels up, pressing herself against my thighs. She's not done teasing me, though. She places soft, open-mouthed kisses up and down my dick, then flicks her tongue over the head. For a brief second, she glances up, her eyes locking with mine before she wraps her lips around my cock.

I almost lose it right then. The eye contact, her forward yet somehow submissive behavior, her hot, wet fucking mouth—it's a lot to handle. I manage to hold on to control somehow as she wrecks me. Moaning around my cock. Sliding her tongue everywhere. Licking and tasting me like nothing has ever tasted so good. Using her hands. Fuck, my girl is so into this there's no way I'm going to last long.

Another groan tears out of me as she struggles to take me all the way down. She's definitely on a mission.

"Hope," I warn.

She hums in response, the vibrations traveling up my dick. White lightning streaks down my spine, and before I even know what's happening, she's pulling me out of her mouth. Kneeling up straighter, setting her shoulders back, she keeps working her hands up and down my length until I'm shooting hot cum all over her perfect tits. Every part of me drowns in the intensity of the orgasm she's given me. My deep groan reverberates around the tiny shower stall as I cover my girl in my seed.

The smile that plays over her mouth is so fucking hot. She's not pissed. She doesn't think I'm a degenerate fuckwad. Hell, she's as into it as I am. When I manage to recover, I pull her up off the floor and into my arms.

"Was that your plan all along?" I ask in between planting kisses over her cheeks and forehead.

"Mm-hmm," she answers, sliding her hands around my waist and up and down my back. Turning her in my arms, I spin us so she's facing the shower and set about cleaning her up.

"I'm okay," she says, brushing my hands away from her nipples.

"You're more than okay, baby," I whisper in her ear while taking her lobe between my teeth and flicking my tongue over the soft skin.

"No, I mean this was about you. I'm just going to wash off and get out of the shower."

I don't know what to make of that. Is she worried I'm too tired to pleasure her? Because if so, I need to correct her right away.

Pulling her back tight to my chest, I take both her wrists in one hand and hold them against her chest. "You think I'm too tired to repay the favor, sweetheart?"

Her giggle turns to a gasp as I work my hand between her thighs. "Spread your legs for me now, Hope," I growl in her ear as she tries to resist me.

She finally gives in, and I stroke my fingers through her silky, hot folds. Barely touching her at first. When she starts moaning and thrusting her hips, chasing my hand, I know I've got her.

Leaning down a little more, I press kisses against her shoulder, then whisper in her ear, "You're all mine, Hope. You belong to me. This beautiful pussy, your hot little mouth, your perfect fuckin' body—all of it mine. And I take care of what's mine."

I mean every fucking word.

She whimpers and nods her head.

That's more like it.

"You're gonna come for me." I'm not asking. Just giving her the facts.

"I—"

"No talking. Relax. Close your eyes and let me take care of you."

She gasps, then cries out and jerks her hips as I find her clit.

Knowing how sensitive my girl is, I work her with soft, slow strokes until she's panting. Looking down at her face blows me away. Lips parted, lashes fluttering, cheeks flushed.

"You gonna be a good girl if I let your hands go?"

She doesn't really answer, but the noises she makes sound similar to a yes. As soon as I release her wrists, she loops her arms up over her head, around my neck.

"Fuck. Baby, you're so beautiful all stretched out for me."

"Rock…"

"I got you."

She works her hips in restless circles. Sliding my hand down over her belly, I can't quite get where I want from this angle. Hope whines as I release her.

Slapping the shower off, I rip open the door and scoop Hope into my arms.

Her eyes snap open. "What are you doing?"

"This ain't workin' for me, babe. I want my fuckin' face buried in your pussy."

"I'm soaking wet."

"Yeah, you are," I agree with a smirk.

She taps my chest. "No, we're going to get the bed all wet."

"If you're still worried about the sheets in the next two seconds, then I'm going to question my manhood."

With those words, I toss her on the bed, enjoying the way she bounces in the air a little. She squeals and tries to roll away, but I grab her ankle and pull her where I want her.

"Spread your legs right now, baby. I need that pussy, and I am *not* in the mood to fuck around."

Very shyly, she complies, and I descend on her like a starving man. Her hips shoot off the bed, grinding against me, and I growl. Can't fucking get enough of her. Hot, wet, slippery woman on my tongue. My fingers find their way to her entrance and I sink one inside while lapping at her clit. Curling my fingers and stroking, I find the spot that makes her squirm the way I like. Her hands dive into my hair, gripping it, and I smile, happy I've been keeping it longer so she's got something to hold on to while I work her into a juicy little puddle.

I'm fucking roaring with satisfaction from the way she screams. Knowing how shy my girl is, there's no way she'd be making this much noise if she remembered where we were. Pride that I caused her to lose herself so completely pushes me to work her harder. When her screams turn a little sharper and she's wrigglin' away from me, I pull back.

"Oh, Rock. I can't. No more."

Yeah, I can't get this smirk off my face. "Good, baby?"

"So good." She uncurls her fingers from my hair and sits up a little. "Thank you."

Crawling into bed with her, I drop a kiss on her forehead. "Thank *you*."

Yes, I feel the need to thank her. Sex has never been like this. Doesn't matter how colorful my past. Nothing blows me away the way Hope does. Probably because just the thought of her gets me hard, but

I think it's that I love her so fuckin' much and I know she loves me. I feel it in every inch of her, and I want to keep her love more than anything. The connection we have, being in love—making love is new to me, and I don't know how I lived so long without her.

A shiver works over her, but I don't think it's from me this time.

"You cold, Baby Doll?"

"Yeah."

As much as I love her sleeping naked, I'm glad she brought pajamas on this trip. Digging through her hastily packed bag, I pull out flannel pants and a long-sleeved shirt.

"I can get it, Rock."

"Stay there."

For once, she listens. I help her into the clothes, then tuck her under the blankets. After getting myself ready for bed, I find Hope watching me with a quiet intensity that quite frankly turns me the fuck on.

As usual.

"Need anything else, baby?"

"Um, socks. My feet are still cold."

After that's taken care of, I shut off all the lights, check my phone, and crawl into bed. My girl's a nice, warm armful and snuggles down tight next to me.

My mind is racing a hundred miles a minute.

"Rock?"

"Yeah, baby."

She's quiet for a beat, and I wonder what's on her mind.

"How long were you and Carla married?"

I groan. It's the last fuckin' thing I want to talk about. But I understand why she's curious. "Fuck, it's so long ago, I don't even know. Two years? We were together maybe a year before that."

"How'd you meet?"

I sigh, because this is going to be a long night.

HOPE

I don't know why I need to hear about Rock's ex. I guess she got to me with her question. How did they meet? Was it love at first sight?

Obviously, at some point, he thought she was the woman he wanted to spend his life with. Why was that?

Rock is silent for so long I start to worry he's mad at me for asking.

Finally, he takes a deep breath. "She was living with a guy who used to smack her around. And I don't know if you've noticed, but I have a thing for damsels in distress."

"No," I answer in a fake shocked voice and get a pinch on my butt for the trouble.

"So I helped her out of that situation, and we kinda fell into a relationship. I thought it was love and she thought she had it made. After a while, she moved in with me and Wrath."

"I remember he said he didn't stick around long after."

"Mmm, he was there for a while."

Something about the way he says that gives me pause. "What did she mean by some things never change?"

"How should I know what's going on in her messed-up mind?"

"Rock—"

"Fine. You sure you want to hear this?"

Rock shifts beneath me, pulling away. Concerned, I wrap my arm around his middle. "Tell me."

"You remember that day Wrath found us in the garage?"

My cheeks heat at the memory. "How could I forget?"

"We used to share everything when we were younger. Especially women."

Wow. *Whoa.* "What?"

"You need me to explain?"

"Did you two—"

"No! Fuck no. Jesus."

I can't deny that the image of being worked over by Rock and Wrath is now seared into my brain. "She's such a tiny thing. How'd she ever survive the two of you?"

Harsh, uncontrollable laughter rumbles out of him. *"That's* your question?"

"I'm trying to imagine—"

Abruptly, his laughter stops. "Don't go there, Hope. Those days are over. Anyway. I thought she understood when we got married, that stuff would stop. I made it clear, but apparently, she didn't agree. So she started coming on to Wrath anytime I wasn't around, until he finally moved out."

"He never took her up?"

"No," he answers without any hesitation.

"Is that something you and Z did too?" Because, honestly, now I'm flustered conjuring up *that* image.

"No. Not for lack of trying on her part. She started fucking around behind my back, but I had a lot of shit going on at the time and didn't see it. Shortly after was when I got arrested. She filed for divorce the day I got sentenced and went inside."

"That's cold."

"That's Carla. She sat in the courtroom with me, kissed me good-bye, then hauled her ass down the street to a divorce attorney. Got served before I even got a cell assigned to me."

I'm so hurt and angry on Rock's behalf. No wonder he seemed floored when I told him I wouldn't desert him.

"Tried to clean out the apartment too. Luckily, Wrath stopped her. She did, however, manage to sell my bike while I was inside."

I'm surprised she's alive.

"That's ballsy." I want to learn more about this time in his life, but my mind can't give up the threesome thing. "So when did you and Wrath start doing... you know?"

"Why are you asking?"

"I don't know. I'm just so inexperienced next to you. I don't... You're going to get bored with me eventually."

"Hope, that's not going to happen. *I'll* be the one to give you whatever experience you think you need."

An uncontrollable laugh spills out of me. "I don't know. I feel like I should at least have a few more partners or something."

"That's not even remotely funny, Hope." Neither of us speaks for a moment. "Is that what you want?" he finally asks.

It's dark so I can't see his face, but his grave tone sends shame spiraling through me.

"No, Rock. That's not what I want at all. I'm sorry—I didn't mean that."

His arms tighten, reassuring me he's not angry. "It's okay, baby. I'm used to you blurting out whatever pops in your head when you feel threatened."

"What? I do not."

His chuckle is softer this time, and his rough hand caresses the side of my face. "It's one of many things I love about you."

"You love that I'm a jackass who sticks her foot in her mouth all the time?"

"Yup."

"Sweet talker."

Our mouths meet in the dark. Soft kisses that intensify quickly.

Rock pulls away, nudging me onto my back and settling over me. More kisses rain down over my cheeks, on my neck. Hot breath rushes over my ear. "Gonna make love to my girl now."

"Make love, huh?" I tease because his seriousness is a little alarming.

Rough hands trace over my cheek. "Yeah, baby. *That's* something I've never done with anyone but you."

My lips part, but he cuts off my question before it even forms. "I didn't know. Until you. The difference. So, yeah, baby, you're the first."

CHAPTER THIRTEEN

HOPE

For once, I'm awake before Rock. I'm freezing. Easing out of bed, I find his flannel shirt from yesterday and slip into it, then pad into the bathroom. When I walk back into the bedroom, Rock's still curled on his side, sound asleep. He's so much more relaxed and so gorgeous my heart skips while I watch him. Knowing how little sleep he normally gets, I want him to rest as long as possible. I also want to have some coffee waiting for him when he does finally get up.

My jeans are draped over the recliner across from the bed, and I tug them on over my sleep pants. I jam my feet into my boots too because I'm just not comfortable walking around here in my socks.

Pocketing the room key, I glance at Rock one more time before venturing out into the quiet clubhouse.

I find Axel sprawled out on a couch in the lobby area. He tips his head up and flashes a brief smile. "Morning, Hope," he rasps.

"Morning. Did you sleep out here?"

"Yeah. Prospects don't get rooms," he says with a tired grin.

Ah, to be young and still think it's cool to sleep on some random couch.

"I need coffee," I hush-whisper at him.

His face scrunches into a frown, but before he can say anything, a large hand shackles my wrist.

Definitely not Rock.

"Hey, you're new. Come here," he says, tugging me back.

"Get off me."

"Mouthy little bitch," he growls, grabbing me harder.

"Hey!" Axel says as he flies off the couch.

"My old man is gonna kill you," I grind out through clenched teeth.

"You ain't got no patch."

Dammit. I didn't know I needed to wear it everywhere like some sort of fucking safety vest.

"What the fuck's going on here?"

I whip my head around to find a shirtless Murphy entering from the hallway with the blonde he was cozy with last night.

"Fuck off, upstate," my groper growls from behind me.

To me, Murphy has always seemed very sweet and non-threatening. Burly and easygoing. I've apparently only seen one side of him, and I shouldn't be surprised. He is, after all, part of Rock's MC, and as willfully ignorant as I try to be, I know violence is a large part of their culture.

Before my eyes, Murphy transforms into pure menace. "What the fuck you say to me?" he asks with deadly calm.

"Mind your own business. This bitch is fair game."

I finally manage to jerk out of his grasp. Just in time too, because Murphy crosses the room with lightning speed and wraps his hand around my tormentor's throat, shoving him into the wall.

"She's my president's ol' lady. You don't even fuckin' *look* at her without permission, you fucking inbred piece of shit. You sure as fuck don't touch her. What the fuck's your joke of a support club teaching its bitch-ass hang-arounds?"

The guy can't answer because Murphy still has his hand clutched around his throat. He does sputter.

Axel comes over and curls his arm around me. "You okay, Hope?"

Too stunned to speak, I nod, and Axel walks me to the couch.

A few more threats and a good shake later, Murphy lets the guy go, and he stumbles down the opposite hallway.

"Motherfucker," Murphy grumbles while walking toward me. "You okay, Hope?"

"Yeah."

He plants his hands on his hips and jerks his chin at me. "Where's Rock?"

"Sleeping."

"Where's your rag?"

"In our room. I just wanted… I didn't think I needed to wear it this early."

"I know, sweetheart. We shoulda explained things better."

Murphy's skinny blond friend returns, handing him a T-shirt and his cut. With all the commotion, I didn't get a chance to appreciate bare-chested Murphy. What I thought was huskiness is bulky muscle covered in an explosion of colorful tattoos. Murphy plants a kiss on the girl's cheek and slaps her ass. "Thanks, babe," he says, clearly dismissing her.

Flicking his gaze at Axel, a smirk curls his lips. "What's wrong, prospect? Couldn't pull any tail?"

Next to me, Axel tenses. I frown. I appreciate Murphy saving me, but I hate how he's constantly picking on Axel.

I'm frantically thinking of what to say when Axel beats me to it. "I got a girl at home. Don't need some random skank."

Murphy's eyes narrow. "Your girl is underage, so you best be keeping your little pencil dick in your pants."

"Why don't you worry about where you park your own diseased dick and leave me and my girl alone?"

"What the fuck did you say, little man?" Murphy says, advancing.

Axel jumps up, ready to defend himself.

I spring off the couch between them. "Stop, guys. Please? Murphy, I could use your help."

My pleading tone diffuses Murphy almost instantly. With one final glare, he turns away from Axel, dismissing him entirely. "What do you need, Hope?"

"I want to bring some coffee back for Rock. Where can I find it?"

Murphy slings his arm over my shoulders and pulls me toward the back of the room. "Serena should be able to help you out. But maybe I oughtta stick with you for now. I'll walk you back to your room. Make sure you stay out of trouble."

I bristle at his words, except he's right. "Thanks."

Two Styrofoam cups of coffee in one hand, Murphy leads me down the hall. He's checking his phone, texting, and looking stuff up as we walk, so conversation is limited. When we stop in front of my door. I tug out the key and push open the door. Murphy hands me my coffee cups.

"After prez has had his"—he smirks and winks at me—"morning coffee, tell him I need to speak to him."

Worried it's about Axel, I try to get a little more information out of him. "Any more to the message than that? Is it urgent?"

"Nah. Just a highway report for him."

"Highway? Are we leaving today?" I might sound a bit too eager.

"Probably not."

Damn. "I'll tell him."

Murphy nods and pats my shoulder. Apparently, he's not leaving until I'm safely inside.

"Thank you for taking care of me."

His face lights up. "Anytime, First Lady. Text me if you need anything. And no more wandering around here alone and unpatched, okay?"

"Trust me. I won't."

Enclosed in our room, it takes a second for my eyes to adjust. Rock's still sound asleep, which makes me happy. I set his coffee on the nightstand next to him, shuck my boots and jeans, grab my book, and take up residence in the chair across from him. Every now and then, I lift my head and enjoy watching him slumber.

After a while, I get lost in my reading, but I sense his breathing has changed, so I look up to find him watching me.

"How long you been up, Baby Doll?" he asks in his sexy morning-rough voice.

Closing my book and setting it aside, I give him my full attention. "A little while."

"Why didn't you wake me?"

"I thought you needed some rest."

A soft, bewildered smile curves his lips at my explanation. He tosses the covers aside and strides over to me. Settling his hand under my chin, he rubs his thumb over my cheek. "You okay?"

"Yeah." I'm not ready to tell him about the incident in the lobby yet. There'll be plenty of time later to ruin his morning. Right now, I want to enjoy some peace and quiet with my man before God knows what goes on today.

His hand drops to the collar of his shirt. "Were you cold, baby?"

My shoulders lift. "A little."

"I like you in my shirt." He plants a kiss on the top of my head and pads into the bathroom.

When he reemerges, he notices the coffee and frowns. "Did you leave the room?"

So much for peace and quiet.

"Yes." Rising from the chair, I meet him halfway and wrap my arms around his middle. "I wanted to bring you coffee."

"Thanks, sweetheart." He picks it up and takes a sip.

"Still warm?"

"Yeah. Anyone bother you?"

That didn't take long. "Well. Sort of. Some guy, I guess, thought—"

"What guy?"

"I don't know. Murphy said from a support club? He was pretty rude, but Murphy and Axel took care of it."

Rock all but slams the coffee cup back on the nightstand and curls his hands over my shoulders, turning me to face him. "Are you okay?"

I wave my hand in the air between us. "I'm fine."

"Were you wearing your patch?"

I thrust my chin up. "No."

"Hope, I thought I explained—"

My temper flares at his tone, even though I expected the mini lecture. "You said I 'could' wear it all weekend, not I 'must' wear it all weekend—"

"Don't fuckin' lawyer me, Hope."

That almost makes me laugh, but I'm still annoyed. "I didn't know

I was leaving myself open to being molested if I went to grab a cup of frickin' coffee."

"Whaddya mean molested?" Rock practically shouts while grabbing a pair of jeans and throwing himself into them.

"Rock. I'm fine. Please calm down."

At my pleading tone, Rock slows his movements. "I'm sorry, baby. That shit shouldn't happen."

"Can we please spend some quiet time together before we go out there and do whatever for the rest of the day?" I ask with a flick of my wrist toward the door.

Rock's whole demeanor changes with my request. "Of course, Baby Doll. Come here." He pulls me close and wraps me in his arms.

"Thank you," I murmur against his chest.

"Tell me what you need."

"Just you. Just us for a little while longer."

ROCK

I'm seething with rage, knowing there's a motherfucker in this clubhouse who dared put his hands on my woman. But I can't ignore her request. Not when she asks with her soft, pleading tone and wide, innocent eyes. So finding this fuck and breaking every bone in his hand will have to wait. Besides, if I know Murphy, he's busy taking care of the guy for me.

"Come here." Adjusting my hold on her, I walk her over to the recliner and sit, pulling her into my lap. Right away, she tucks her legs up and curls her body into me.

"Did you sleep okay?" she mumbles into my neck.

I did, actually. Strange because I sure as fuck ain't comfortable here. Exhaustion, I guess. "Yeah. Did you?"

She nods, her silky hair sliding over my shoulder.

Suddenly, her whole body convulses in a violent sneeze. "Crap. Sorry," she mutters.

Brushing her hair off her cheek, I look in her eyes. "You're not getting sick on me, are you?"

"I hope not. I think it's just dusty in here."

"Hmm." I'm not so sure. And I wish like fuck we could go home today.

She picks up her head again. "Murphy wants to talk to you. About a highway report?"

"He does, huh?" I chuckle at that, surprised my tight-lipped road captain would give Hope even that much info. "He rescued you out there?"

She bristles at the question. "Yes, I always thought he was so sweet and mild-mannered."

My blood quickly jumps to boil. It must have been bad if Murphy got that intense. I hum again, but Hope isn't fooled.

All in a rush, she speaks. "I'm sorry. We haven't even been here twenty-four hours, and I already screwed up, Rock. I'm trying so hard. I don't want to make this trip harder or embarrass you—"

"Doll, stop. Please. You could never embarrass me." If anything, I should apologize to her. This is partially my fault for not being clearer with her.

She lets out a soft chuckle. "Come on, Rock. The guys in *your* club barely accept me. I can't imagine what these guys must think."

Something about her words and her tone bothers me. She's been voted in. Obviously, she still doesn't understand how monu-fucking-mental that is.

"Baby, that's not true and you fucking know it."

I'm interrupted from a lengthier explanation by my phone going off.

Z: Sway wants us @ church in 2 hours. K?

An exasperated breath slips out of me. I need to get my head out of my ass and stay sharp.

I tap out a "yes" to Z, then hit up Murphy.

Stop by room

"Everything okay?" Hope asks.

I'm not sure, but I don't want to worry her.

"Yeah. Why don't you get dressed? Murphy's going to stop by in a minute. Then we'll go down to the kitchen and have breakfast. If I know Tawny, she'll have a big spread ready for everyone."

"Should I go help her?"

"No," I answer simply. I don't like her waiting on the guys at my clubhouse. She sure as fuck ain't doin' it here.

A soft thump on the door turns my attention away from Hope bent over, pawing through her bag.

"I'll be in there," she says, pointing at the bathroom.

"Thanks, doll."

One look at Murphy, and the lazy ease from the morning flows right out of me. "What up?" I ask, stepping aside so he can enter.

"Nothing. Z tell you about church?"

"Yeah."

"Where's Hope?"

I cock my head at him. "Getting dressed. Why?"

Murphy's wide shoulders lift. "Just making sure she's okay. She tell you about earlier?"

"Yeah, but you're gonna tell me after you give me your highway report."

"We're clear to roll out tomorrow morning. Langan's got from here to Catskill, and Klouse has up past twenty-four. We don't have to take back roads unless you want to."

Back roads could be just as risky, more places for surprise road traps, but they were usually small-town sheriff departments that were easier to handle than state troopers.

"Let's see how things go down today. Sway tell you why he wants us at church?"

"Nope."

Great. It wasn't unusual for a visiting brother charter to be included, but I still didn't like it.

"Okay, so who am I killing?"

Murphy's mouth flattens into a grim line. "Fucking nobody hangaround from their support club. Don't worry. We had a conversation after I dropped Hope off earlier."

I don't doubt it.

"She was runnin' around unpatched, prez." What he means is my girl was in the wrong, so besides the beatdown, there's not a lot more I can do about it.

"She told me. He receptive to your advice?"

Now he smirks. "Sure. I used reason"—he lifts his right fist in the air—"and wisdom to get my point across," he says, waving his left fist in front of him.

A snort of amused appreciation leaves me. "Nice. Thanks."

"You know I got her back."

"I know."

From behind me, the bathroom door squeaks open. "Everything okay?" Hope asks, which I recognize is her way of asking if she can join us.

Turning, I'm relieved to find her in a loose turtleneck sweater, jeans, boots, and a smile. She's covered from neck to toes—the way I want her around here. "Yeah, baby."

Three sharp pounds on the door can only be Z. "Let him in. I'm gonna get dressed." I drop a kiss on Hope's head on my way to the bathroom.

HOPE

The tension rolling off Rock as we enter the common room practically vibrates through me. He has his arm draped over my shoulders in what seems like a casual pose, but I doubt I could get away if I wanted to.

Not that I want to.

My attacker steps up to Rock, and I gasp at his face. His right eye is swollen almost shut. Lip split. He obviously had another "conversation" with Murphy.

"Uh, Rock, I gotta apologize for earlier. I didn't realize she was with you."

Rock smiles. But it's not the easy or fun smile I'm used to seeing. It's his hardened biker smile, and it's more frightening than friendly.

"Apologize to my woman, not me."

"Um, Hope, right? Sorry about earlier." It's hard to tell whether he's sincere or scared of another beating.

I nod and whisper, "Sure. I forgot about the patch. It's a little new to me."

Rock's hold on me tightens. "Doesn't fuckin' matter." He shoots a glare at the guy who I finally notice has a patch that reads "Peanut." What an awful road name. I wonder how he got stuck with that. "You might want to learn no means no, clubhouse or not. Patched or unpatched. We clear?"

"Yeah, man. Are we good now?"

Rock glances at me. "Are you okay?"

I just want this over with. Rock's pulsing with so much anger I'm afraid he's going to kill this guy. "Yeah, I'm good."

Rock lifts his chin at Peanut. "My RC do that to you?"

He flinches but answers, "Yeah."

Rock glares at him a little longer. "We're good. Keep away from her, though."

"Okay. Thanks, man." He flicks his gaze to me. "I really am sorry," he says before taking off.

"Motherfucker," Rock grumbles under his breath.

"Geez, I had no idea Murphy was so—"

"Violent?" Rock finishes for me.

"Yeah, I guess."

"It's a hard life. I told you, baby, any one of my brothers would kill to protect you."

"I know. So does that earn Murphy special brownie points with you?"

His eyebrows draw down as he considers my question. I was really teasing, but he seems to be contemplating how to answer. "That's not what it's about, Hope."

"I know. I was only kidding."

He nods once and pulls me toward the kitchen.

A long table takes up one end of the industrial-sized kitchen. Bikers line both sides of the table, but a section at the end seems to have been reserved for us.

Z stands up and greets us, even though we just saw him like ten minutes ago. "Prez. First lady." He pulls out a chair for me. Surprised, I take it.

Rock sits at the head of the table. Sway is at the other end. They nod to each other. I don't see Axel or Hoot anywhere, so I guess prospects don't get to eat breakfast either.

STRENGTH FROM LOYALTY (LOST KINGS MC #3)

Murphy sets a bottle of water in front of me, and I thank him while uncapping it. After another quick glance around the table, I realize no other women are sitting down yet. There's water on the table, but not much else.

Pushing my chair out, I attempt to stand. "I should go help Tawny."

Rock places his hand over mine, gently squeezing. "You don't have to."

"It's okay. We're guests. Let me at least offer."

He nods and releases me. Before leaving the table, I lean over and brush a kiss on his cheek. His hand curls over my hip, squeezing tight before letting go.

The girls are organized with military precision under Tawny's sharp orders. Everyone seems to have a task. As I approach her, she breaks into a wide smile and motions me closer.

"Is there anything I can do to help?"

She points at the counter. "Can you bring those jugs of OJ out and set them on the table?"

"Sure," I answer, happy to have something to do.

There's four of them so I grab two in each hand and set each one down at spaced intervals down the table.

Sway sort of grunts at me when I set the last one in front of him.

Am I supposed to pour it for them too?

I almost smack into Tawny as I turn back to the kitchen.

"Oh, thank God you at least have a brain in your head. Those dumb bitches would just plop all four of them at one end of the table." She pats my shoulder. "Go sit down. We're almost done. Thanks, honey."

Relieved I seemed to have passed some sort of orange juice intelligence test, I return to my seat.

Breakfast here is much like it is at our clubhouse. The guys are rowdy and demolish every last bite. They rib each other and bullshit about their bikes. The guys who haven't seen each other in a while trade stories and catch up.

I don't have anything to offer to the conversation, so I just enjoy the chatter around me.

"You okay?" Rock asks when I set down my fork.

I flash a smile at him. "Yup."

When everyone's finished, Sway declares it's time for church. "Rock, you and your boys joining us?" He phrases it like a question, but judging by the expression on his face, it's clearly not optional.

This makes me wonder, because as far as I can tell, Sway and Rock are in equal positions of power within the Lost Kings. Sway is older, so he's probably been a member longer. Maybe that gives him some... *sway* over Rock. I store that question in the back of my mind for another time.

Tawny supervises the girls who clean up breakfast and calls me over. "You gotta keep the bitches in line, Hope," she informs me. "As the president's ol' lady, that's going to be your most important job."

Huh. I'm not sure how I feel about her acting as if these girls are some sort of servants.

"We don't have as many girls as you do. Trinity seems to be the one doing most of the organizing."

Tawny makes a disgusted face at the mention of Trinity's name, which automatically raises my hackles. "She's always had way too much power for a club whore. Never understood why Rock allowed that shit."

I resent her talking about Trinity that way, but I don't know what to do about it. "I guess there were no old ladies."

"True. But you're there now, so make sure you put her in her place."

To borrow an expression from my man, *like fuck* is that happening. But I don't say that to Tawny. Her opinion doesn't really matter to me. The only opinion I care about is Rock's, and I know that's not how he'd like me to treat Trinity. Even if I had it in me, which I don't.

When she seems satisfied the girls can handle things, she takes me on a tour of their compound. "Sorry about Carla showing up here last night."

I shrug. "No biggie. At least I finally learned her name."

Tawny lets out a brash laugh. "I hope you said that to her."

I let out a snicker of my own. "Yeah, I kinda did."

"Good. She did Rock dirty. She shouldn't even show her face here, but the club has business with her old man, and unfortunately, she tags along a lot."

Remembering some of the advice Trinity has given me, I bite down any questions I have about the "club business."

"It's okay."

"Then Cookie, but since she's hooked up with our VP, there wasn't anything I could do about that."

"It's really okay, Tawny. I spoke to her briefly, and we're good."

She eyes me skeptically. "You're going to want to rein in that soft side you got going on there, Hope."

I laugh before I realize she's serious. "I know. Wrath's always giving me shit."

She throws back her head and laughs. "I can't say I miss that big, miserable bastard much."

Hmmm... I don't think I really like her speaking about him that way either, which surprises me.

"You got any kids, Hope?"

Wow, that's a sore subject for me right now. But Tawny doesn't know that. "Not yet. Do you?"

"Yup. Boy and girl."

"Oh, how old?"

"Twenty and twenty-two. She's graduating from college in the spring, and he wants to follow in his dad's footsteps in the club."

I don't want to insult her, but I'm genuinely curious. "How do you feel about that?"

"I'm proud of him. When he's old enough, he'll take over the club for his dad. He's out on a run right now, or I would have introduced you."

"Was it hard raising two kids in the middle of all this?"

She gives me the strangest look, and I wonder if I somehow insulted her. But she can't really think this is normal, right?

"Not at all. Had a big, extended family to help watch them when I needed it."

A family full of criminals. But I keep that to myself. I may have accepted Rock's life, but could I bring children into this? Knowing their father's luck might run out one day and he could end up in prison or worse? Knowing the dangerous people he does business with?

It's a chilling thought.

"Besides, I've never worked outside the club, so I was always around for my kids." Tawny continues. "Watched a lot of the other club kids over the years too."

"Does your daughter help out at the club a lot?"

I get another curious look, and once again, I'm afraid I jammed my foot in my mouth.

"No. Her dad don't let her hang around the club much. Too much shit for his baby girl, ya know?"

Uh, yeah. After what we walked into last night, I certainly understand his reasoning. My throat clogs as I think Rock would be the exact same way with a daughter.

If I can even give him children.

ROCK

The chapel at Sway's compound is a lot larger than our war room at home. Kings from all over are apparently in visiting for the weekend. It's good to catch up with brothers I haven't seen in a while. After an hour of bullshitting, Sway slams his gavel and we get to business.

Chairs have been added and people have been moved around—which I didn't ask for—so Z and I are seated near the head of the table. Murphy's over on one of the couches lining the back wall, and prospects are not invited to church here. Axel has been tasked with shadowing Hope, making sure she stays out of trouble.

Sway methodically goes through business that only pertains to his guys. I'm bored and wish I could have skipped this part. When they finish their chapter business, Sway finally gets around to the reason we were asked to sit in.

"Got a guy who stole a shipment from us, and we need to retrieve it —*tonight*."

Fuck.

While my charter got out of running guns and harder drugs, this isn't true of every Lost Kings chapter. Each one is free to decide for themselves how they earn. Sway has apparently decided the risks are worth the rewards.

"What are we talking?" I ask.

"Three shipping crates. High-end AR-15s."

"They're illegal in New York now, you know," I joke.

Sway smirks at me. "Don't worry. We'll get 'em registered all proper-like."

Why Sway needs me or my guys involved in this, I don't know. If either Murphy or Z ain't feeling it, I won't force them to tag along on this mission.

Sway has a good tip that his shipment is being stored in an old barn about twenty miles west of here. The guy who stole Sway's shit is either stupid or crazy to be holding it inside Kings' territory. I point this out to Sway, and he agrees.

He's still convinced it's where we need to go.

"It should be quick and easy. In and out."

If I had a dollar for every time I've heard that... well, I wouldn't need to be here doing this in the first place.

We hash out the plan a little longer, and it's almost nightfall by the time we finally break. Sway wants us back in the lobby area in thirty minutes, ready to roll out. Four of his guys will be on bikes, the rest of us in vans or trucks. With a nod of my head, I silently ask Z and Murphy to follow me to my room.

As my hand curls around the knob, I hesitate. I don't need Hope overhearing any of this shit.

"Where's your room, Z?"

The fucker gives me a dirty smirk. "Right next to yours, prez," he answers, pointing at the room to the left. I pin him with a hard stare, daring him to say what he's clearly dying to say.

He shakes his head. I've taken all the fun out of it for him.

When we're inside Z's room, we huddle over the small utilitarian table. I can't be sure Sway doesn't have bugs all over this place.

"Listen, if either of you are having second thoughts, I'm fine with you backing out."

"Hell fucking no, prez," Z says emphatically. "Someone needs to watch your back, and I'm sorry, but I don't trust anyone here to do it."

"Me too." Murphy agrees.

Christ.

"I'm not going to be pissed. What he's asking is risky, and we all know there's a slim chance it's going to go down as smoothly as he says it will."

"Sorry, prez, I'm in," Murphy says.

Z just nods.

"All right." Pointing at Murphy, I say, "Go suit up. Don't stop to fuck around with Serena. Get your vest, check your weapons, and get your head straight."

Z bursts out laughing. Murphy glares at me for a second before leaving the room.

When he's gone, Z turns to me. "You got a bad feelin' about this, don't you?"

"Yeah. I have a feeling we're jacking someone else's stash more than rescuing Sway's shipment."

"I got that feeling too. So what do you want to do?"

"Brother charter. We'll help him out. Just stay aware."

"Okay."

I slap my hand down on the table. "I need to get ready. You too."

"Yeah, I got it."

Entering our room, I'm surprised to find Hope curled up in the recliner, reading.

"How'd you escape Tawny's clutches?" I ask. I'm on edge, so the question comes out sharp instead of teasing.

Hope's face remains passive as she seems to study me. "She went to visit her daughter, and I didn't think I should intrude."

Taking her tablet out of her hand and setting it on the table, I pick her up and shift us so she's in my lap. She loops her arms around my neck and peppers the side of my face with kisses. "Missed you."

"Missed you too. 'Fraid I'll be heading back out in a few."

The corners of her mouth twitch down, but she doesn't protest. "Okay. I'll be fine."

"Hoot and Axel are staying behind, so if you need anything, ask them."

"Will do. Axel said he'd take me into town later to grab some stuff."

"We're probably taking the van, babe."

"Oh. No big deal. I'll be fine. I wanted to find a Wal-Mart or something to grab a swimsuit."

I groan at the thought of my girl prancing around in so little in front of anyone except me. "Make it a one-piece," I growl against her ear.

She giggles and pushes me away. "Duh. Believe me, I was going to look for a full-on wetsuit."

"Good."

With great reluctance, I nudge her off my lap. "I gotta get ready." I hesitate because my "getting ready" is going to cause her to ask a lot of questions I can't answer now.

She cocks her head and takes me in. "Do you want me to leave?" she asks with a timid tremor in her voice that pisses me off. Not at her, but at the situation.

"No, baby. Stay. No questions, though."

Her lips curve into a smile. "My lips are sealed."

And she's true to her word. She glances up at the ripping sound of the Velcro as I strap on my Kevlar vest, then goes back to her book. When I rack a bullet into the chamber of my 9mm Glock, she peeks at me again. After a while, I need to shut out her reactions and get my head on straight so I don't forget anything. Two pistols, extra magazines—fully loaded—knife, burner phone.

My phone vibrates to life in my pocket. Pulling it out, I see it's Murphy.

Placing a finger under Hope's chin, I tip up her face. "I gotta go. Don't know how late I'll be."

She braces herself on the arms of the chair and pulls into a standing position. The chair gives her the extra height she needs so we're at eye level. She wraps herself around me and squeezes, then plants a gentle kiss on my lips.

"Be careful."

HOPE

193

Of course I'm freaked out after Rock leaves. It was quite a feat for me to bite my tongue and not ask the thousand questions brewing in my mind. From the fierce expression on his face, something unpleasant was happening, and I didn't want to do anything to distract him.

Making sure my patch is nice and visible, I wander down the hall into the lobby. A few guys are sitting at the bar.

Axel turns and walks over as soon as I enter. "Need anything, Hope?"

"Dinner maybe? Think we can raid the kitchen?"

The corner of his mouth turns up in a lopsided grin. "I don't see why not."

"Do you know if Tawny's back?"

"Haven't seen her."

I'm restless and want to get out of here, but I'm not really sure what to do. In the kitchen, we find cold cuts and fix ourselves sandwiches. Axel tells me some stories about Heidi and her friends that make me laugh. He's obviously very enamored with her.

"Have you talked to her?"

"Nah, she knows not to call unless it's an emergency. We've texted a few times. Gonna take her to this movie she's been wanting to see if we get back early enough tomorrow and Rock doesn't need me for anything."

He's so sincere. I make a mental note to ask Rock to give Axel a night off.

"Still want to hit up Wal-Mart?" Axel asks when we're finished.

"Rock said they were taking the van."

"They ended up leaving it. Rock said it was okay if I took you."

He did, huh? Interesting. "Yeah, let me grab my purse."

The ride into civilization isn't as short as Tawny led me to believe. It seems like we're driving for hours when all of a sudden, the road ahead of us is lit by rows of gaudy big-box stores.

Inside the store, Axel follows me around, always on alert. What he's so worried about, I don't know. I assume he's afraid if I break a nail on his watch, Rock will beat the crap out of him.

For all I know, that's the truth.

I'm a little embarrassed to stop and paw through swimsuits in front of Axel, but he turns away and pretends to glance around the store as if he senses my hesitation.

"I'll be right back. I want to try this on."

The suit is nothing exciting, but the coverage is as good as I'm going to find tonight. I grab it, a pair of flip-flops, and a big fluffy beach towel as well. Just in case, we stop by the men's department and I pick out something for Rock. I'm sure it's a long shot, but I'd like to be prepared.

When we return to the clubhouse, Tawny's hanging out in the lobby—knitting of all things. Perfect, poofed-up, shellacked hair, full makeup, tight jeans, knee boots, glittering belt, and zebra-print fitted shirt… and she's knitting. She belongs in a magazine. Something like *Domestic Biker Queen*.

I don't laugh, though. I'm not completely stupid.

"Let me toss this in our room and I'll be right back, Tawny."

She glances up. "Sure."

Axel walks me to the room and waits while I pitch the bags on the bed and grab my vest. Once I have my patch on, Axel seems a little less anxious. He walks me back to the lobby.

"You okay here, Hope?" he asks.

"Yeah, I'll be fine."

He pats my shoulder. "I'll come check on you in a bit."

Another woman I don't recognize has joined Tawny. I find out her name is Grace, but I haven't really determined her position in the club. Since Tawny's actually speaking to her, I assume she's not a club girl.

We talk about knitting—of all things—and I learn this tough, hard, scary biker lady knits tiny little blankets for the local animal shelter.

Seriously.

"Since I can't smoke anymore, gives me something to do with my hands while I'm waitin' on Sway to get his ass home," she explains.

"They certainly don't keep conventional hours," I say with a nervous snort of laughter.

Tawny glances up and flashes a tight smile. "No. They don't."

We talk about knitting for a while, and she even shows me how to cast on and a few stitches. I'm terrible at it, though.

"I've never been able to pick it up either, Hope. Don't feel bad," Grace assures me.

As it gets later and later, I start to worry about the guys but doubt it's a good idea to ask any questions. Grace leaves, and I still never figure out her connection to the club.

The front door opens, blowing cold air over us. Both of us turn, and I'm expecting the guys to storm in, but it's an older man in a wool coat.

And Carla.

Goddammit.

He's carrying a black doctor bag, and Tawny jumps up immediately. "What's wrong, Barry?"

"Nothing. Here to check on the other two."

Tawny drops back down next to me. "Yeah, okay."

She glares at Carla but doesn't say anything. Barry whispers something in Carla's ear, but she shakes her head. He doesn't seem to need directions. Without speaking to any of us, he takes off around the corner.

Carla pulls a chair over next to me.

Why me?

"Hi—Hope, right?"

My mouth twitches up into a nervous smile and I nod.

"Sorry we didn't get to talk much last night."

As if I spent the day worrying about it. "No problem."

Tawny snorts. "Don't press your luck, Carla."

"So have you guys set a date yet?" she asks.

Jeez. Are we really doing this? "Not yet."

"You been married before?"

Pain pierces my heart and must show on my face. Tawny settles her hand on my leg.

"Yes. I was." Then I rush to amend. "I'm a widow. It's—"

Next to me, Tawny sucks in a deep breath. "Shit, Hope."

Carla hasn't said anything. She just continues watching, waiting for me to finish.

"It's been awhile. Well, not really, almost two years, but—" I babble like an idiot, completely uncomfortable revealing so much of myself to complete strangers.

"Was he an outlaw too?" Carla asks.

The tone she uses is neutral, but my skin still prickles. An image of Clay—neat, buttoned-down shirts and pressed khakis—flashes in my mind. "No, he was an engineer," I answer with a sad smile.

Carla sneers at me. "So how the hell did you and my ex-husband meet?"

The possessive way she talks about *my* man ticks me off so much I'm slow with a response. By the time I open my mouth to answer, Tawny beats me to it. "She's a lawyer and she represented him in court."

Carla has the nerve to roll her eyes. "Oh yeah. Let me guess—he got himself arrested."

My jaw clenches, but I'm not sure what to say to that. Because it's the truth.

Tawny jumps up and jabs her finger in Carla's direction. "You shut the fuck up. Don't you dare disrespect one of the brothers under my roof. You know damn well what you're in for when you marry into the club. You're supposed stand by your man, not stab him in the back."

Carla is a brave soul—or feels Barry has enough juice to protect her from Tawny. She stands and takes a step back but unfortunately doesn't keep her mouth shut. "I was twenty-two years old. He could have gone in forever. I was supposed to just sit around and pray he got out?" Then she turns to me. "Do you actually understand what you're in for?"

"I know I love Rock, and I wouldn't try to fuck his friends while he was going through a difficult time," I answer evenly.

Tawny settles her hand on my shoulder and gives me a gentle squeeze. I choose to interpret it as an "I'm proud of you" gesture.

Carla stares daggers at me. "Well, that's precious. You know he—"

"Don't say another fuckin' word to her, Carla," Tawny warns.

"She doesn't know, does she?" Carla asks with a smirk.

I assume she's talking about the three-ways with Wrath.

"How's his best friend?" she sneers.

Yup. Wrath.

"Wrath? He's laid up with a broken leg so he's a little crankier than usual," I answer calmly.

Carla's jaw drops a bit. "He doesn't share you, does he?"

"No. And before you decide to educate me, he already told me."

"Yeah, I'm sure he did."

Tawny takes another step toward Carla. "Don't you fucking dare. I can't count how many times I caught your whoring ass going after one of the guys. You were doing that shit well before Rock went inside."

"Carla," Barry calls from the hallway, "I could use your help."

Carla stares at me for a second before following him.

After she's gone, I shake my head and sit back down.

"Sorry, Hope," Tawny says, and she does actually seem sorry.

"Oh, I'm used to dealing with Rock's exes by now," I joke with a wave of my hand. I'm not really in a joking mood, so it sounds pitiful.

I don't want to deal with any of this. Their history is so ancient it should be buried and they should both move the fuck on. But Carla seems content playing victim.

Tawny twists her wrist to look at her watch. "I'll be right back, Hope."

She's gone for a while. I'm tired and want to go to bed, but I don't want to be rude either.

The blonde Murphy spent time with last night saunters into the lobby. She approaches me slowly. "Hope, right?" she asks.

She's a pretty girl. Like stunning pretty. Tall, willowy figure, long Barbie legs, thick, flowing blond hair, cute-as-a-button face. Why she spends her time servicing guys here instead of modeling in New York or something I can't fathom.

She points to the spot Tawny just vacated. "Do you mind if I sit?"

I don't, so I tell her to go ahead.

She turns and gestures at my phone, which I'm clutching in my hands. "Have you heard from any of the guys?"

"Not yet."

"Oh."

We're silent for a while before she braves another question. "Did Rock patch you recently?"

My mouth automatically curves into a smile, remembering the afternoon. "Yes."

"Was it a surprise?"

"Kind of. He explained it to me first. So I wouldn't be offended, I think," I add.

She tilts her head at me like she's trying to make sense of that.

"Why would you be offended?"

"I, uh, didn't know much about this—" I wave my hands in the air. "Before I met Rock."

She still seems confused, but she laughs. "If I could get one of the brothers to patch me, I'd never take it off."

This strikes me as really sad, especially because from what I've been able to gather, the more brothers you sleep with, the less likely it is one will make you his ol' lady. I keep this to myself, though, and end up smiling awkwardly instead.

"What do you do, Serena?"

"Um, I tend bar and I'm taking a few classes at the community college. I was thinking of transferring up to Hudson Valley..."

That's in our area. If she's trying to hint that I should put in a good word for her with Murphy, I'm afraid she's out of luck. "They have a lot of good programs." I nod.

"Um, does Murphy have any regular girls at your place?"

Well, at least she's smart enough to know subtlety won't work with me. "I honestly don't know, Serena. I don't really pay attention."

And it's true. I only know about Wrath and Trinity's... whatever the hell they're doing, because, well, how could I not? Z, I only know about because he's had some weird on-again, off-again thing with one of my friends. Sure, I've accidentally seen plenty of things that required a good dose of brain bleach, but I try not to dwell on any of it. I don't mention Heidi because she's a kid, and I don't know what the hell's going on there either. I had a perfect opportunity alone with Murphy this morning to say something, but I was so damn flustered I let it slip.

"I don't blame you," she says with a laugh.

"How long have you been hanging out here?"

"'Bout a year or two. I was trying to model down in the city, but it was too expensive to live on what I was making—"

My brain-to-mouth filter is obviously on the fritz, because I let out a snort. Her face turns down as if I insulted her, and I feel bad. Reaching out, I gently pat her leg. "Sorry. It's just when I first saw you, I thought you must be a model or actress or something."

That seems to cheer her up. She sits up a little straighter and grins at me. "Oh. Thanks. Yeah. I got a few commercials. But it's so competitive. And you have to live with like fifteen people in tiny little shitbox apartments to survive. I was seeing a guy down there in another club, came up here with him for a party, and just decided to stick around."

City living has never appealed to me for the exact reasons she just listed. "I can understand that."

"Are you really a lawyer?"

I chuckle before answering. "Yeah."

"Do you like it?"

"Not really."

She nods, and I'm surprised with myself for admitting it, especially to a stranger.

"Isn't there a lonely cock somewhere you should be servicing?" Tawny snaps when she returns to find Serena in her seat.

Poor Serena jumps up like she's been stung. "Bye, Hope. Nice talking to you." And she scurries off without another word.

Tawny shakes her head and makes a big show of dusting off the couch cushion Serena just vacated. "Sorry 'bout that."

"No problem. She seems like a sweet girl."

Tawny raises a thinly penciled-on eyebrow. "Yeah, sweet until you find her sucking your man's dick."

Well. Wow. I don't know what to say to that. "Your man?" Crap, why did I have to say *that*.

Tawny smirks. "Don't worry. I get mine."

Yuck. I've overheard the words loyalty and brotherhood multiple times this weekend, yet none of these guys seem to stay loyal to their wives.

Despite all the women from his past I've had to confront, I've never worried about Rock cheating on me. Does that make me gullible... or loyal?

ROCK

Z, Murphy, and I ride with Sway, so we're not able to talk much. They each gave me an affirmative nod before getting in the truck. We're an ominous caravan of bikes, two heavy-duty four-wheel-drive trucks, and one van. Seems like a lot for a job that's supposed to be so simple.

"Two of my guys are down because of these fucks. We see any of them, leave them to me."

I'm still not buying the story, but I give him the answer he's looking for anyway. "No problem."

At the end of a long dirt driveway, we all stop. The guys on bikes get off and hop in the back of our truck. Two guys stay behind, while the rest of us take the long, slow drive up to the barn.

There's no house that I can see. Just a massive old barn looming up ahead. Lots of trees. Too many fucking trees for my taste. Too many places for people to wait in ambush.

I'm really hating this shit.

Sway tucks the truck up tight against the barn. Personally, I would have parked it pointed toward the escape route, but that's just me.

At least the rest of the guys do a perimeter sweep of the trees and circle around the building. Sway's men aren't completely useless. After getting out and taking a look around, Sway takes a pair of bolt cutters to the heavy padlock on the front door.

Inside smells like the shit of a thousand horses, and I choke back a coughing fit. Z's got his nose buried in his shirt collar, and Murphy gags.

"Fuck me, that's disgusting," Sway says, also holding his shirt over his nose.

It's nothing but a dark abyss inside until guys start pulling out cell phones and flashlights. I pull out my own penlight, and we get to work.

Suddenly, it's very clear why we needed so many vehicles for this job.

There's not three crates of weapons. There's about thirty.

"Guess we're not the only ones they been jacking," Sway notes.

Great.

"Find our supply first. Then we'll split up everything else."

The air fills with the sound of metal on wood as crates are busted open.

Z shrugs and steps back to the door to keep watch. Murphy looks to me for direction, and I give him a chin lift to let him know he's fine where he is.

"What are we looking for, Sway?"

"Twenty-five LWRC IC-PDWs."

Christ, he wasn't kidding about high-end. Or highly illegal. Those types of ultra-compact personal defense weapons are most definitely banned in New York. Again, I wonder where the hell they got jacked.

"Also looking for crates of Ranier uppers."

"No lowers," I joke. What the fuck is he planning to build with uppers and nothing else?

"Not this drop."

Fucking hell. With a nod to Murphy, we join the others in busting open crates, searching through shit. Some of the weapons are in cases inside the crates; others are not.

On my fourth crate, I think I've got something. "Sway," I call.

He jogs over, and with one glance inside the box, his face breaks into a grin. "Fuckin' A, that's our shit." He slaps me on the back and runs over to confer with his sergeant-at-arms. Next, they're throwing open the big barn doors and backing his truck inside. We get the crate I found and three others loaded into Sway's truck and covered with a tarp.

"Take whatever else you can. Then let's burn this mother to the ground," Sway announces to the group.

Awesome—guess we're adding arson to tonight's list of felonies.

Murphy cracks open a crate of ammo, something that's also hard to come by in New York these days. "Grab that," I tell him.

Z motions me over to three cases. Inside each one is a foliage-green Noveske Johnny Rifle. "Wrath will shit himself." Z snickers.

"Grab 'em."

The grab-and-go party seems to be winding down. There's not another inch of available space in any of the vehicles.

"They don't got no surveillance on this place?" Z asks. Because that's his specialty, naturally he notices.

"We had it taken care of earlier," Sway answers.

Oh, how comforting.

The shot that rings out is *also* not comforting.

Pulling my piece, I crouch down. Don't even have to say a word—Murphy and Z have done the same.

"Prez, tha fuck?" Z whispers.

I shake my head, silencing him.

Sway crab-walks over to me and puts up two fingers. Whether he's telling me there's two shooters or he wants me to do something in two seconds I have no fuckin' clue.

The stench of gasoline is thick in the air.

There's a struggle and shouting from the side of the building.

"Prez! Clear!" one of Sway's guys shouts.

Still have a bad feeling about this. "Stay down," I mouth to Z.

Another shot blows through the night. Someone's window shatters.

Not so clear after all.

"Fuck!" Sway shouts from somewhere around the van.

"Keys?" I ask Murphy. He shrugs and points toward the direction Sway went.

Fuckin' great.

HOPE

Tawny's phone buzzes. She glances at me and leaves the room without a word.

That's not reassuring.

Then Carla returns.

Fantastic.

"Had to help Barry with one of his patients," she explains, as if I give a crap.

Except... wait, what?

My question must be written all over my face.

"He's the club's doctor."

"That must be awkward for you," I retort with a bit of snark.

She curls her lips into a nasty smirk. "At least I don't worry about him going to prison all the time."

"Yeah, because treating outlaws off the books is risk-free."

That shuts her up, but not long enough for my taste.

"So you don't mind all the strippers and club whores?" she asks.

I cock my head to the side and pin her with a fierce stare. "I trust Rock."

She snorts. "God help you."

"You realize it's been years since you two were together, right? You don't know anything about him anymore."

Her mouth opens and closes. "You're probably right," she finally says. Her eyes dart to the space behind me before she opens her mouth again. The confrontational bitch face she had on has softened. "I felt safe with him."

I'm intimately acquainted with that feeling.

"I never had that before. When he got arrested, I was terrified. Fucking Tawny and those other bitches... Well, I guess they're made of stronger stuff."

Her words are like a fist in my gut. I know damn well I'm not as tough as Tawny. But I also know I don't have it in me to do what Carla did. My gaze drops to my hands twisting together in my lap.

"I was happy he got out as quick as he did. But I knew I couldn't go back. Rock's not big on forgiveness."

I don't think I'd be real forgiving either.

"You got friends outside the club, Hope?"

"Of course."

"Hang on to them. You and Rock ever part ways, the club pretty much shuns you."

"You deserted your husband at one of the worst possible times. What did you think they were going to do for you, Carla? Hold your hand and bake you cookies?"

Before she answers, her husband interrupts. "I'm going to need your assistance. Something happened. They're bringing one of the guys back now."

I shoot up off the couch. "What? Who?"

Barry's startled gaze flicks over me.

"Hope," Tawny calls. "Rock's fine."

I didn't even notice her standing behind him.

Axel wanders in and raises an eyebrow at me.

Tawny nods. "Go on, honey. The guys should be back soon."

I'm exhausted. But also worried. Clearly, Tawny wanted me out of the way for some reason.

As soon as we're alone, I ask Axel what he knows.

"Nothing. They wouldn't tell me stuff like that."

Guilt prods me into another line of questioning. "Are you going to find a bed to sleep in tonight, Axel?"

He stops and turns to me, obviously shocked. "I wouldn't cheat on Heidi."

"That's not how I meant it, sorry."

"Oh, okay. I just don't want you thinking I'm like the rest of them. Heidi's special. I wouldn't screw that up."

I'm not sure what he means by "the rest of them," since none of the other guys have girlfriends that I know of. Unless he means sticking their dicks in anything with boobs and a pulse. Because, yeah, that seems to be the way a lot of the brothers operate.

"I know. You're a good guy, Axel."

He brightens at the compliment. "Thanks. Are you okay for the night? Need anything from the kitchen?"

"I'm all set. Thank you."

"Okay. I got my phone on, so if you need anything, just text me, okay?"

"Will do."

Inside our room, I find my cell phone and check it. Nothing from Rock. I do have a message from Trinity.

Everything good?

It's late, but I text her back anyway.

So far.

I get a smiley face back from her.

Now, where the hell is Rock?

ROCK

More shots ring out. This night sure went to shit fast. Shouts and gunfire echo around us, then die down. It's fucking dark, and I have no goddamn idea what the hell we followed Sway into.

"Prez?" Z whispers, and I turn his way.

Other than a few shouts and rustling, things seem to have calmed down—well, except for the fucker sneaking up behind Z. I don't have time to warn him. Don't even think about what I'm doing. My body snaps into autopilot in reaction to the threat against my brother. My gun is already in my hand. Everything happens in slow motion even though it's over fast. I aim, finger already touching the trigger, and squeeze.

Too late, though.

My bullet hits him in the chest and he goes down. From where I'm standing, I can't tell if he's down for good. But I'm close enough to see Z's been hit.

"Murph!" I point at the guy, and Murphy runs over to secure the threat.

"Z! Fuck, brother, you okay?" I reach him quick and take in his pain-twisted face.

"Fuuuck! Goddammit." He's holding his arm. "That fucking hurts," he growls as I approach.

Not the first time one of my brothers has taken a bullet in front of me. Doesn't make it any easier.

"Let me see," I say, grabbing his arm.

"Ow, watch it, ya fuck."

By the amount of bitching he's doing, I think he'll be fine.

"Grazed your arm. Still gonna need stitches."

Murphy hands over a strip of cloth, and we bandage Z's arm the best we can.

I nod at Murphy. "Go find Sway."

This fuckin' mess is gonna take forever to clean up, but I want Z taken care of right the fuck now.

"Shit, guys. You okay, man?" Sway calls out as he jogs over.

"It's nothing," Z answers.

"Probably needs stitches," I add.

Sway pulls out his phone and calls the clubhouse. "Babe, need you to keep Doc there…" Sway wanders off to finish his conversation.

I pull out my phone and send a message to Axel.

Headed back. Make sure Hope is in our room.

Although it's not a serious injury, I do *not* need Hope seeing this.

On it, Axel replies.

"Prez, I'm really fine," Z says, standing in front of me.

"I know."

"Let's finish up here. Then I'll see the doc."

"Yeah, okay."

Finishing up takes too long for my taste. Altogether, Sway's got four bodies to add to the barn that's about to go up in flames.

Even though we're in the middle of nowhere, the fire can be seen in the rearview for some distance.

"All volunteer fire departments out here. By the time someone sees it and calls it in, it's done," Sway explains on our way back.

"So much for 'quick and easy, in and out,' right, brother?" I say. Is that disrespectful? Probably. Do I give a fuck right now? No.

"Yeah, that was unexpected." Sway agrees. It's as close to an apology as I'll get from him.

I'm fuckin' furious by the time we get back to the clubhouse.

"Prez, really, I'm fine," Z assures me again.

I know I'm actin' like a pissy little bitch. And I know this is the risk we all take doing what we do. But still, knowing that a few inches here or there and we'd be having a different conversation—or no conversation at all—is getting to me. We lost a lot of our brothers in the early days. And since then, I've worked hard to keep my guys whole.

"You know Carla's husband is the club's doc, right, prez?" Z asks. "Be happy it's me gettin' treated, not you. She'd probably ask him to stitch your mouth shut."

My brother, who just had a bullet go through him, is trying to cheer me up. Fucking wonderful.

"Keep it up and *I'll* ask him to sew your mouth shut," I snap back.

He grins at my retort and slaps me on the back. "Go make sure Hope's okay."

"Yeah. Call me if you need something."

"I will."

"I'll stay with him, prez," Murphy assures me.

On my way to our room, I check in with Hoot and Axel. Satisfied they've managed to stay out of trouble, I head for our room. I pray like fuck Hope's already asleep. I need a shower. I fuckin' reek. Plus, my head's still messed up from this entire shit show of a night.

I need to see my girl, though. If nothing else, I need to wrap myself around something pure and good.

HOPE

I'm freaking out by the time Rock finally returns to our room. At first, he steps inside with caution, but once he sees I'm awake, his steps become firmer.

"Hey," he tosses out.

"Hi. I've been worried about you." *Whoops.* I was trying to keep myself from saying that, not wanting to add to his stress.

He gives me a hard look but doesn't say anything. After kicking off his boots, he strides into the bathroom. A few seconds later, I hear the shower squeak to life. I want to go to him, but I'm not in the mood for sexy shower games, and something tells me Rock wants to be alone. So I stay in bed and wait.

He steps out in just a towel wrapped around his lean hips. It's a struggle not to stare at every glorious inch available to my gaze. For once, he seems indecisive as he stands there. Finally, he takes out some clothes and slips into them. The bed dips low as he sits next to me, rolling my body forward.

"You okay?" he asks.

"Ye—"

He cuts me off before I even get a word out. "Besides being worried. Anyone bother you tonight?"

"No."

"Good."

He reaches over and snaps off the light, plunging us into darkness.

"Scoot," he says, giving me a gentle shove. Blowing out an exasperated breath, I move, and he cuddles me close.

"Cold?" he asks.

"Yeah."

Safe in his arms, I allow my body to relax against him. He buries his nose in my hair, his lips kissing the top of my head. "Missed my girl."

"Missed you too."

A million thoughts and questions run through my mind, but I don't give voice to any of them.

Rock seems to sense it anyway. "Tell me what you did today."

"Talked with Tawny. A lot." My eye roll is lost in the dark.

He chuckles softly. "How was that?"

Paranoid of being overheard, I turn in his arms. Our foreheads touch. "She's complex. She was nice to me, but she's so... hard," I whisper. "Is that what you want me to turn into? Is that what I'm going to be in ten, fifteen years?"

He hugs me tighter. "No, baby. That's not what I want at all." One hand runs over my hair and down my back. "I deal with enough shit. I'm hard enough for both of us. Tawny thrives on drama and the power trip of being the prez's ol' lady. I don't have the patience for that type of woman. Never have. Don't get me wrong. She's good for Sway. Makes her a fine ol' lady here. But I've never wanted that."

His words are soft but earnest, and my heart beats wildly as I continue to listen. "At the end of the day, I want to shut all that bad shit out. Just be myself with my girl. Like this. Like we are right now."

Oh. My. God. I think that's one of the deepest things Rock's ever admitted to me, and I squirm to get closer to him.

Rock isn't finished, though. "You love me for *me*, Hope. You're not with me to be queen of an MC. You're with me for *me*."

He speaks the words so low I almost don't hear him. It's on the tip of my tongue to crack a joke. You know, like I never knew what an MC was before I met Rock, so how could I aspire to be queen of something I didn't know existed? But I hang on to the stupid comment. Instead, I tell him something I think he needs to hear.

"That's true," I say, running my hand over his cheek. "I *like* you too, you know. Always have. And I'd want to be with you no matter what you did."

He kisses my forehead. "I know, Baby Doll."

"What happened tonight, Rock?"

"Nothin' I want to talk about right now."

Nothing he *wants* to talk about. Not can't. It's a subtle difference, but I feel the power of it. I snuggle closer, tucking my head under his chin, listening to his heart thump.

"Carla didn't show up again, did she?" Rock asks after a while.

"Yes, she came with Barry. I guess he acts as a doctor for the club?"

He nods against me. "She bother you?"

I'm not sure how to answer. Nothing she said *bothered* me. "At first, she was claws out. Tawny set her straight. She has some strong opinions about the way Carla treated you," I tell him.

He snorts. "I'm sure she does. Tawny takes this life seriously."

I hesitate. "Really? Because I got the impression she and Sway fuck around on each other."

Rock sighs. "I don't get into their personal shit anymore. But Sway never had an ounce of self-control."

"So what's with all the loyalty these guys are always talking about?"

"Loyalty to the *club*, Hope. If Tawny's fuckin' around, she ain't fuckin' brothers."

I take a second to let that sink in.

"Hope? You know that's not who I am, right?"

Guilt for the sliver of doubt I had earlier crawls through me. "Yes."

"Made plenty of mistakes in my life. Losing you won't be one of them."

"Carla thought she was going to shock me by telling me about... stuff. I basically told her to get over herself. You're both different people today."

"That's an understatement." He chuckles and runs his hand over my hair.

After a beat, I ask the question that's been on my mind since she showed up. "What did you see in her when you met?"

The question seems to startle him. "Who the fuck knows?"

Even though I can't see him that well, I draw back so we're sort of nose to nose. "Come on, I'm curious."

Warm, minty breath wafts over my face as he sighs. "She came across as soft and in need of protection. Had a tough situation growing up, and I think the message she got was to take everything she could and glom on to the first guy who could support her."

I think about Axel and Hoot's lowly positions in the club. "Weren't you a prospect when you met?"

"Yeah, but it was still an MC. The danger of it all excited her. When the time came it looked like I would take over as president, she really sank her claws into me. Then it looked like it might be Z, so she went at him."

"Jesus."

"When we first met, Carla had a bit of vulnerability about her that reminded me of my mother."

Oh, wow. Rock's never talked to me about his mother before. "You've never told me about her."

Against my forehead, I feel him smile. "She was fun. I didn't think about it when I was a kid, but she had me really young. Got married right out of high school, so she was almost a kid herself. She read to me every day, and I loved the sound of her voice." He snorts. "I lied and told her they hadn't taught us to read in school yet so she wouldn't stop reading to me."

"Oh, Rock, that's so sweet."

"You know, when I started school, I was the biggest kid in the classroom. I'd fight anyone who picked on me about it too. I don't think she knew what to do with me, so she told me how God made me big so I could protect people who were smaller than me."

Holy hell, my heart hurts for him. "Wow. That's a big burden to place on a little boy."

He's silent for so long I start to worry. I didn't mean to sound so judgmental of his dead mother. Dammit, I can't do anything right.

"I never thought about it like that. But yeah, you're probably right."

ROCK

I don't think about it often, but my mother grew up Catholic. Every Sunday morning, she took me to church with her. My father had no use for that crap, but she wanted me to have the experience, I guess. Once in a while, she'd order me to sit outside one of these little rooms tucked in the back of the church and disappear inside for what she told me was confession. She explained if you confessed your sins, God took them away from you.

I never grasped the concept.

Until this second.

Talking to Hope in the dark this way, after everything that went down tonight, is an unburdening of sorts.

After my mother's funeral, I never set foot inside a church again.

Hope relaxes against me.

"You should get some sleep, baby. We've got a long trip tomorrow."

She nods, her nose brushing against my skin. "I'm so happy we're going home."

I love hearing her say that. I want nothing more than to build a home and a life with her.

"Tawny talked some smack about Trinity and even Wrath today. I had to stop myself from clocking her," she murmurs.

Laughter rumbles out of me. "Oh yeah?"

"Yeah."

Her breathing deepens as she slips into sleep, and I enjoy the feel of her in my arms. All the bad shit from the day keeps running through my head. Z getting shot. The acrid stench of smoke still fills my nose. Despite the violent scrub-down I gave myself in the shower, I swear I still smell death and fire on my skin.

It's a long time before I fall asleep. So I lie there enjoying the feel of Hope in my arms.

I'm so thankful I made it back to my girl.

CHAPTER FOURTEEN

ROCK

I WAKE EARLY TO FIND HOPE STARING AT ME. "WHAT'S WRONG, BABY?"

A smile plays at the corners of her mouth. My girl's up to something. After all the serious shit we've talked about and the tension on this trip, I'm relieved to wake up and find her smiling.

"I want to go for a swim."

Huh. Not what I expected, but okay. Not at the top of my list of things to do this morning, but if that's what my girl wants, I'm down for it.

"Get your scuba suit?"

She chuckles. "No. I did the best I could."

Throwing back the blankets, I trudge into the bathroom and splash some cold water on my face to wake the fuck up. When I return, Hope's already in her suit. It's one piece and nothing special, but on Hope, it's stunning. White and snug in all the right places.

"You look pretty in white," I tell her before kissing her cheek.

"Thank you."

"Gonna be one hell of a pretty bride." Christ that's something I'm looking forward to.

The remark seems to startle her. Her mouth twitches. "I... I didn't think I should wear white again," she stammers out.

I don't give a fuck if she shows up in rags as long as she shows up. "Doll, you'll be beautiful no matter what you're wearing."

Some of the awkwardness seems to melt from her face, and she gestures to the swim shorts she's got laid out for me. They're black camo with skulls, and that amuses me.

I plant a kiss on her forehead. "Thank you."

When I'm ready, I turn and eye her outfit. "Put your patch on."

She seems surprised but does it without question.

I grab my phone and her towel and lead her out the door. I've been here before, but the pool is stashed in some alternate fucking dimension. Of course, any helpful signs the hotel might have once had up have long been taken down and replaced with lewd biker posters.

It doesn't take long before the scent of chlorine confirms we're on the right path. The pool is deserted, but it appears crystal clear. Nothing too disgusting floating in the water.

"Tawny said she does fifty laps every night, so the prospects maintain the pool very well," Hope says as if she'd been reading my mind.

"Fifty, huh? No wonder she never ages."

Hope slants a curious look at me. She can't seriously be jealous. I shake my head at her.

The water is almost too warm for my comfort, like swimming in soup. But Hope seems to enjoy herself. She swims lazy laps back and forth while I watch her from the side. After a while, she swims over to me and throws her arms around my neck. I push away from the wall and she wraps her legs around my waist.

Now this I can get used to.

I twirl and spin her around in the water. She leans back, gliding her hands over the surface. I don't think she realizes that arching her back like that puts her perfect breasts on display, her hard nipples straining against the flimsy white fabric of her suit. Shifting my arms against her back, I pull her up out of the water and lean down to close my mouth over one nipple. Her stunned little gasp gets me even more worked up.

I knew I should have brought condoms down with me.

"Morning, fuckers."

Sway.

Hope wriggles her body under the water, pressing herself tight against me. Shielding her from Sway's pervy gaze, I turn us.

"What up, brother?" I grouch at him. Glancing up, it's clear he's not here for a swim lesson.

"Need your help sorting through shit from last night."

"Yeah, okay. Give me a few minutes."

"No problem. Morning, Hope," Sway calls out with a leer.

Hope chuckles against me and unwraps one of her arms from my waist to wave at Sway. "Morning!"

Once he finally leaves—prick was sticking around a little too long for my taste—I pull Hope away. "Sorry, Baby Doll."

She curls her hands over my shoulder and uses the weightlessness of the water to jump and wrap her legs around my waist. "It's okay."

"You can't stay down here by yourself."

She wraps her arms around my neck and leans in to kiss me. "I know. Take me back to our room."

She's killing me. Growling a lot of unhappy words, I carry her out of the water. Next to our chairs, she unwinds herself and slides down my body, really not helping the situation in my swim trunks. "Hope," I warn.

My flirty girl strokes my dick through my shorts with the palm of her hand. "Oh my," she whispers.

"Keep it up. That ass of yours is begging for my hand."

Flirty girl vanishes, and suddenly, she's all business.

"Morning, guys," Z calls out.

Now I understand why she got so serious all of a sudden.

"Morning, Z," she chirps. She glances up at me, one corner of her mouth turning up, letting me know she's still feeling playful.

I plant a kiss on her forehead before turning to check on Z. "How you feeling today, brother?"

His eyes dart to Hope before he answers. "Good."

"Ready to head home?" Hope asks.

"Fuck, yes."

She giggles and reaches out to pat his arm as she passes, but he flinches.

My girl misses nothing. She cocks her head at him. "You okay?"

"Yeah, eager to get on the road."

"Come on, doll. Time to pack up."

She laces her fingers with mine and we walk back to our room, Z following behind.

When we get to the room, Hope goes in first.

"Sway wants us out back to sort through the shit we brought back—"

"Yeah, yeah, I saw him. Seriously, you okay? Barry fix you up?"

"Yeah, it was nothing. Fucking stings and I'm sore, but I didn't want to take the painkillers he gave me yet. I wanna get on the road."

"Okay. You and Murphy take the van out back. You know which shit is ours. Give me a few minutes and I'll be down."

Z smirks. "Sorry I interrupted."

"Shut up." But my words have no effect because I'm laughing.

Inside, Hope hums to herself as she packs up our stuff. She's got everything laid out on the bed while she folds clothes and stuffs them into our bags.

"I'll get my things, babe. You don't have to—"

"It's okay. I know you need to meet—"

Fuck me, she's still in that white suit, nipples poking against the flimsy, damp fabric. Before I even know what I'm doing, she's in my arms and I'm pinning her up against the wall.

Worried eyes stare up at me. "Rock?"

My mouth brushes against her ear. "What's the matter? Can't finish what you started out there?"

Her body relaxes in my grasp, and she giggles softly.

"You're not going to be laughing in a minute."

"Oh yeah?" she sasses.

"Yes, my pretty little fuckdoll."

I smile down at her, watching my words sink in, her pupils dilate, the feel of her body relaxing even farther into my hold. Grabbing her hands, I pin them over her head. She squirms, arching her back, thrusting her breasts in my face, circling her hips.

Tightening my grasp around her wrists, I touch my forehead to hers. "How much do you like this suit?"

"Why?"

Looking directly into her eyes so I can enjoy every little reaction from her, I press my chest into her breasts. "Let me tell you what's about to happen." I run my fingertip over her collarbone, down between her breasts, tugging the material away from her skin.

"I'm going to rip this skimpy thing off your body." To do so, I need both hands. "Don't move," I growl as I fist the material and yank. A satisfying tearing rips through the air, along with a gasp from Hope.

The knife I always keep stashed in my pocket opens with a soft snick. Hope's eyes widen. "Don't move," I warn her again.

Each strap cuts cleanly, and the bathing suit falls down her body. I raise an eyebrow at her, and she wriggles so the suit falls all the way to the floor. With one toe, she flicks it away.

"Good girl," I whisper.

"Can I move now?" she asks with only a hint of sass this time.

"No."

I set the knife on the nightstand and snag a condom from the drawer.

Her eyelids flutter shut.

"Look at me."

I place one hand over her wrists again, pressing her body against the wall with my hips.

She strains against me. "Rock," she moans.

My mouth crashes against hers, swallowing her words. I slip my tongue in her mouth, stroking and tasting my woman. She struggles a little, but I'm enjoying her at my mercy too much to let her go yet.

My hand squeezes her hip, pulling her to me. She spreads her legs, inviting me to push one finger deep into her pussy.

"Ah! Rock, please."

Love it. Love the way she begs. "I'm going to roll that condom down my dick, then squeeze inside your tight little pussy that I can't ever seem to get enough of and pound you into that wall until you come."

Then I do everything I promised.

My time with Hope wasn't nearly as long as I needed. But I'm eager to get home.

Z, Murphy, Sway, and his guys have the guns and ammo sorted. Sway looks over the stuff my guys have laid out for us to take home.

Clearing my throat, I ask, "Something wrong, brother?"

"No, just a specific order."

I raise an eyebrow.

"Take 'em. Christ, I owe you a hell of a lot more than that after last night," he says, pointing at Z.

"Rock," Tawny calls out from behind me.

Sway doesn't bat an eye as she sashays over. She surveys the guns and ammunition with a bland expression.

Sway nods at his guys to help Murphy load our van.

"Hope's a good woman for you," Tawny says out of nowhere.

Curious, I face her.

A quick smile flickers over her red lips. "Seems to love ya a whole lot. Got pissed when Carla started running her mouth, but put that bitch in her place quick. Being a lawyer, she's more of a *fight with her words* kinda gal. But you never did like us scrappy types," she says with a laugh.

I laugh with her because it's true, and it's an amusing observation coming from Tawny. "I like you fine, Tawny. You're a good woman."

She smirks. "At least someone thinks so," she says, glaring at Sway.

"You two okay?"

This time she shrugs. "He's never kept his dick in his pants. I knew that going in. But he's gotten sloppier. Doesn't bother tryin' to hide— never mind, Rock."

"Sorry, hon."

Her eyes widen in surprise. "You always were a good one. If you'd been a little older when we met, I woulda ditched him for you in a heartbeat."

I try not to shudder visibly at the image that presents.

She gives me a quick hug. "You take good care of her. She's a nice girl."

"I plan to."

HOPE

After he took me hard and fast against the wall of our room, Rock spent a considerable amount of time outside, getting things situated with the guys for the ride back. I have no idea what that meant, and I didn't ask.

Tawny hugged me and told me I was welcome back anytime, which filled me with some pride. I doubt she says that to everyone who passes through her clubhouse.

Still, I've never been so happy to get on the back of Rock's bike.

We make the two-hour trip back with no stops.

Trinity meets us at the door with a happy expression. "I'm so glad you're back!"

Z gives her a peck on the cheek. "Big bastard behave himself?"

"No," Trinity answers without elaborating.

"I heard that," Wrath grumbles from behind the door.

After we tumble inside, I throw my arms around Trinity for a quick hug.

Wrath meets my eyes over her shoulder. "Cinderella, you survived," he says with a happy smirk.

Rock gives Wrath one of their manly bro-hug-handshakes, then smacks him on the back of the head. "Don't be a dick. She was ready to throw down with Tawny in your defense."

"Oh really?" Wrath grins. "Old broad still bitter she couldn't get in my pants?"

The guys all have a good chuckle.

Trinity shakes her head and leads me away from the guys. "You do okay?"

My shoulders lift. "It was an experience. Not one I care to repeat anytime soon."

She nods knowingly.

"I ran into Cookie the first night we were there. She's tight with their VP."

Trinity rolls her eyes at that. "I'm not surprised. Whenever they were up here, if she wasn't with Rock, she'd be all over him."

I ignore that whole "with Rock" part because it makes my stomach roll.

"Met Rock's ex-wife too. She's a treat."

Trinity snorts. "I've never had the pleasure. She was before my time. But I've heard plenty of stories. Anything else exciting?"

"Not really. I tried to remember your advice, and I don't think I made too much of an ass of myself."

"Aw, Hope. I'm sure you did fine." She pulls me in for another quick hug. "Glad you're back, though."

It feels nice to know Trinity missed me. We talk a little longer before, out of the corner of my eye, I see Rock step back outside. Thinking he might need me to grab my stuff from the van, I follow him out. He's busy barking orders at the prospects, though.

The van has a lot more stuff crammed in the back than it did when we left.

For the first time, I wonder what this trip was really about.

And what the hell did Rock do the other night when he was gone so long "handling business?"

Am I supposed to worry about those things? I guess not.

But I can't help it. "Rock, do you want me to grab my stuff and get it out of their way?"

He turns, surprised to find me outside. "No," he answers with a sharpness I'm not used to hearing directed at me. "Go ahead inside. I'll get everything."

"Well, I actually wanted to run home for a little while. Catch up on some things."

His face pulls into a frown, and I honestly don't understand why. I can already tell he'll be consumed with "club business" for the next few hours, so what does it matter if I'm not here?

ROCK

I hate that Hope wants to run "home." Her home should be here, with me. But I don't feel like bringing that up again, so I don't. Besides, I have a lot of shit to take care of and can't spend time with her the way I want to right now.

Leaning over, I brush a kiss on her forehead. "You leaving now?"

"I think so. You look like you're busy here." She gestures to the van.

She's not being bitchy. Just stating the facts. My girl almost never gives me a hard time anymore about anything she thinks relates to club business. While I enjoyed all the closeness we shared on this trip and how easy she made things for me, I miss her busting my balls all the time. At least then I know what she's feeling. Now, I have no idea. She's so locked down it's hard to get a read on her.

It's unfair, but I don't like it.

It's also unfair that I'm relieved she's going. I want to get these guns unloaded, and I'd rather she's not around for it. There's a steel storage room under the garage where we store most of the weapons we keep up here. Hope doesn't know anything about it, nor does she need to.

One of these days, I want Wrath to do some weapons training with her, but today isn't that day.

I'm such a fuckin' dick. Bitchin' about her not moving in with me. Pissed she's going home. Relieved she won't be around to ask any questions.

Part of me needs her to go. Part of me stops breathing at the thought of her leaving.

Fuck.

I get her bags settled in her trunk and close the lid. She gives me one of her sweet smiles and wraps her arms around my middle.

Suddenly, I feel like I can breathe again.

She tips up her head and kisses my chin. "Despite everything, I had a nice time with you this weekend."

Her voice is low, meant for only my ears, and goes through me like a bolt of electricity. Now I can't stand the thought of her leaving again.

"Yo, prez, are we ready to roll these out?"

I turn and glare at Murphy. "Give me two fuckin' seconds, will ya?"

Against me, Hope's body ripples with laughter. "Go easy on him. He saved my bacon yesterday. Don't forget."

Yeah, I won't forget that anytime soon. Another reminder of all the fucked-up shit I drag my girl through. There she goes again, being all sweet. Sticking up for Murphy 'cause she can't stand the thought of me being cross with him for a second.

"Think you can give Axel a night off? He was planning to take Heidi to a movie," she asks me with a sly smile.

Her request makes me laugh. "He ask you to ask me?"

She frowns, offended, I think. "No."

"Yeah, I'll have him head home." That suits me fine. Don't need Axel handling all our new firepower anyway. That shit's above his pay grade.

Turning, I search for him and snap my fingers. "Prospect."

He hustles over. "What do you need, prez?"

Hope releases me, but I put a hand on her shoulder so she doesn't go far.

Tugging out my wallet, I hand Axel some folded-over bills. "Thanks for all your help this weekend and for takin' good care of my woman. Go take your girl out, okay?"

He gets that wide-eyed look prospects get sometimes. "Yeah. No problem. Thanks a lot, prez. Appreciate it."

I nod, dismissing him.

Turning to Hope, I hook my fingers in her pocket and yank her against me. "Happy?"

"Yes. That was very nice."

"Yeah, I'm a regular Ward Cleaver."

Her mouth quirks. "You are, in your scary biker way."

"Hey," I whisper to get her attention. "I had a nice time with you too. Having you there made dealing with all the bullshit a lot easier."

She tilts her head at me, the obvious question written all over her face. *What bullshit?* 'Cause I didn't tell her shit about what really went down.

She rubs her palm over my cheek. "I'm glad. You do so much for me all the time. It's nice to balance the scales a little."

What the fuck is she talking about? I don't feel like I do a damn thing for her, except make her worry and caveman all over her. But I don't want to ruin the sweet moment, so I press a kiss to her forehead and tap her ass with my hand.

"Get going, baby. Get some rest. I'll call you later."

"Okay."

CHAPTER FIFTEEN

HOPE

I'M NOT EVEN AT MY HOUSE FOR TWO HOURS WHEN ROCK CALLS.

"Miss me already?" I answer.

"Yeah, baby, but that's not why I called."

"Oh. Is everything okay?"

There's nothing but silence. "Rock?"

"Uh, Heidi... her grandmother died. Teller brought her up here, and she was asking for you. I know you're probably exhaust—"

"No. I'm leaving right now. Just let me grab some stuff." I rush down the hallway to my bedroom and plow through my closet. "How's Teller? Is he okay?"

"Yeah, I guess. You know what kind of issues they'd been having."

"What happened to her?"

"Heart, I guess."

"Mmm... I knew they shouldn't have let her out when they did."

Over the line, Rock's laughter is warm and rumbly. "I love you, Baby Doll."

"I'll be there soon."

We hang up, and I finish packing some things. As I work my way

223

through my closet, my hand stops on a black dress. I'll need one for the funeral, right?

Crap.

It's the same dress I wore to Clay's funeral. For a moment, I'm stunned with indecision. It's probably too big on me, but that's not why I hesitate.

"Oh, for fuck's sake," I grumble out loud. It's not a wedding dress. It's a plain black fucking dress. I wore it plenty of times before Clay died.

I stuff it into my bag with everything else and head out the door.

At the clubhouse, I run into Teller outside. "Thanks for coming up, Hope."

I give him a tight hug, which he hesitates before accepting. "I'm so sorry." I draw back so I can see his face.

He shrugs. "We were never particularly close. But she pretty much raised Heidi. My mom dumped us there when Heidi was six and never came back for us."

I already know this from helping Teller with the custody dispute between him and his grandmother, but it still breaks my heart a little to hear him talk about it so matter-of-fact.

"Heidi's inside. I'm sorry Rock dragged you up here. You're the only—"

"Teller, it's fine. Of course I want to be here for Heidi. You too."

"Thanks, Hope. There's no danger of them trying to put her in foster care, is there?"

"No. Custody should go to you one hundred percent. I'll start drafting something this week. I can call Charlotte too—"

"That's okay. I have her number. I'll call her."

That gets my attention. Teller's *my* client, so technically, Heidi's lawyer has no business talking to him without my knowledge. I'm surprised because Charlotte seems so earnest. "You really shouldn't be talking to her without me."

His mouth twitches in a short grin. "Yeah, she says the same thing." Before I can question him further, he asks, "Think you can help me with the estate stuff? Grams left the house and everything to Heidi, but it's supposed to go into a trust for her until she's twenty-five. It's a big place to maintain, so I'm thinking of selling it after Heidi graduates and stuffing the money in the trust for her."

From working with Adam, I've seen lots of people who would drain that trust dry contesting the grandmother's wishes. Teller's an honorable guy, and I want to do everything I can to make this easier on him. "Of course. I'll ask Adam to help you with that. It shouldn't be a problem."

Heidi's curled up on the couch when I step inside. Axel and Murphy hover nearby. They both look up when I enter.

Murphy's mouth pulls into a smile when he spots me. "Hey, First Lady, knew you couldn't stay away from us for long." He reaches out and squeezes my hand. "Thanks for coming up for Bug."

Axel scowls at him but seems unsure of what to do.

"I'm guessing you didn't get to your movie?" I ask him.

"No... it was. It was bad. I pulled up the same time the ambulance got there."

I give his shoulder a squeeze and make my way to Heidi. She doesn't move or register my presence until I sit next to her and put my hand on her back. "How are you, Heidi girl?"

Sitting up slowly, she sniffles and wipes her face before focusing on me. "Hi. Did they make you come up here because of me?"

My heart constricts at her words. As if I'm only here because Rock asked me and not because I want to be here for her. "Honey, I'm here for *you*. Do you want to talk?"

She blinks at me and sits up a little straighter. "Not really... Hope, she died right in front of me."

Taking a chance, I wrap her in my arms, and she responds by putting her head on my shoulder. "I'm sorry, honey. That's awful."

"We weren't fighting, though. I got to tell her about this scholarship I got to go to some summer classes, and she was actually happy with me for once. So that's something, right?"

"Yes. That's great. At least you had a nice moment with her before."

"I still feel awful for always being such a brat to her, you know?"

I want to say it's okay, that it's normal to be a brat at her age, but I don't think she'll find that comforting. "That's normal," I tell her instead.

"I wish we could find my mom. She doesn't even know her own mother is…"

"I know." I don't know what else to say to her. I'm not sure how much she knows about any of the time Rock spent helping Teller track down his mother.

Stupid secrets. One of these days I'm going to have to ask Rock to give me a list of what I can and can't say to people around here.

ROCK

As soon as I step out of the garage, I spot Hope's car. No one bothered to tell me she'd arrived. Fuckin' great.

"We're all secure down there, right?" Wrath asks. Since he hates navigating the narrow stairs, he's been patiently waiting in the garage.

Well, patient for him.

"Why didn't anyone tell me Hope was here?"

Wrath glances at the parking lot. "Didn't know."

The door slams behind us. Z works the combination into the keypad for the side door and joins us. "We gonna have a full house for the funeral?" he asks.

I shake my head.

Teller joins us. "Hope's here. She's inside with Heidi. Thanks for calling her."

"Yeah, no problem. You need help making any of the arrangements?"

"No. I guess her lawyer had a set of instructions or some shit. I'll take Bug later to go pick out some stuff."

"I'll start contacting some of the other charters—" Z starts.

Teller cuts him off. "Don't bother. If you guys are there, I appreciate it. But given the way she felt about the club, especially after some of the shit she said at the end of that stuff with Heidi, I don't feel right having—"

"It's not for her. It's for you," I say.

He shakes his head. "I know."

"We'll do whatever you want, bro," Wrath says with a hearty back slap, almost knocking Teller on his ass.

226

Teller shoots him a glare, then focuses on me. "I hate askin', but can I stay up here with Heidi for a few days? She really doesn't want to go back to the house, and—"

"Yeah, of course." And to make that happen, I see who I need to talk to stepping out of the house. "Trinity," I call out. She turns and nods at me, waiting to see what I want.

"We good here?" I ask the guys. I get affirmatives from everyone, so I wave Trinity over and meet her halfway.

"What's up, prez? Hope's inside with Heidi."

"I know. Thanks. Can you do me a favor? Heidi's going to stay up here for a few days. I need you to—"

She gives me a knowing look. "Call the girls and tell them they can't come up?"

"Pretty much."

"Can I at least bring Swan? She won't misbehave, and I could use her help." She lowers her voice a bit. "Besides, she's sorta tight with T, since, you know—"

"Yeah, yeah. I trust your judgment." At the moment, I can't remember which one Swan is, but if Trinity says the girl will behave, I believe her.

While we walk into the clubhouse together, Trinity explains what she plans to do for the wake. I barely hear any of it, though. I reassure her that everything sounds fine, and she thanks me as she heads to the kitchen. My eyes are glued to Hope, who's sitting on the couch with Heidi in her arms, talking softly to the girl who wouldn't respond to any of us an hour ago.

If I were the sort of man who cried, now might be one of those times. All I can think about is the doctor calmly explaining to Hope that she might not be able to have children. It's beyond fuckin' unfair. The woman is already so damn nurturing and maternal. I'm completely slammed and blindsided by the thought of having children with her and then beyond pissed that it might not be an option.

CHAPTER SIXTEEN

HOPE

EVEN THOUGH THE FUNERAL IS FOR SOMEONE WHO WASN'T RELATED TO ME in any way, I feel the pull of the depressing day ahead of us.

This isn't about me, though. I need to be strong for Heidi. I want to be strong for Rock and his club. With those goals in mind, I set aside my own unease.

Rock's already out of bed. The bathroom door is open, so I assume he's downstairs. The funeral isn't until eleven, so I have plenty of time to get ready. I decide to go downstairs and see what everyone is up to first.

The living room is empty. In the dining room, I only find Heidi, Axel, and a very relieved-to-see-me Trinity.

"Morning, Hope."

"Hey, Trin. Where are the guys?"

"War room. Church."

Odd.

Heidi turns around and flashes a quick smile at me.

"How're you doing, Heidi?"

She lifts her shoulders. "Okay, I guess. More nervous about getting there on time and stuff."

Trinity lays a soft hand on my arm. "I'll grab you breakfast, Hope."

"That's fine, Trinity. I'll come help."

Trinity grabs Axel's empty plate, and I follow her into the kitchen.

"Is everything okay?" I ask quietly.

As we're walking, she glances at me over her shoulder. "Yeah. Heads up—Sway and Tawny are on their way up for the funeral."

"Oh. That's nice of them."

She snorts out a soft breath. "More than likely, he's using it as an excuse to come up for something else." Her explanation surprises me since Trinity always advises me to "play dumb" when it comes to club business.

"Are you worried?" I ask her.

She shrugs. "Not really." A nervous smile twitches at the corners of her mouth. "I won't be offended if you want to boss me around in front of Tawny."

A harsh chuckle bursts out of me. "Yeah, that's not happening, Trin."

She pulls another sad shrug. "I'm not an ol' lady, Hope."

"I don't give a fuck. You're my friend."

Her eyes widen, and this time she genuinely laughs. "Wow, look at you with the potty mouth."

"What are you talking about? I swear all the time."

Our silly discussion is interrupted by Rock and Wrath entering the kitchen. "You girls okay?" Rock asks, his gaze dashing between the two of us.

"Yeah, Hope's just cussing like a sailor."

Rock's eyebrow quirks up.

Wrath shakes his head. "Cinderella," he mock-scolds me.

Rock settles his hand on my shoulder. "Eat breakfast yet?"

"No, I just—"

"I got it, Rock," Trinity interrupts.

"Thanks, honey." Rock takes my hand, tugging me toward the door.

"Rock—" I start to protest, but he cuts me off.

"I need to talk to you for a second."

"Oh." I turn to apologize to Trinity, but she's already wrapped up in an intense discussion with Wrath.

I practically have to run to keep up with Rock he's moving so fast. He glances at the champagne room but keeps moving past it. I'm so confused. Does he need to talk to me, or is he looking for a place to have a quickie? It doesn't seem like the right time for the latter. We end up in his office next to the war room.

Z's in there working on the computer. "Need me to leave, prez?"

"No. Stay."

Okay, so not a quickie. "Rock, what's wrong?"

"Nothing, doll." He points to an empty chair across from his desk. After we're both seated, Z turns to face us. Rock runs his hand through his hair before opening his mouth. "Tawny and Sway are coming up for the funeral."

"Okay," I answer slowly. "Trinity mentioned it."

Rock's mouth twists down. "It's normal for other charters to come in for a family funeral. Teller didn't want it for his grandmother."

Thinking over some of the nasty allegations she made about the club during the custody dispute, I understand why.

"But Sway found out." He flashes a look at Z, who remains poker-faced. "And he wanted to come up."

"Okay."

"I know you have your hands full with Heidi—"

"But you need me to entertain Tawny?"

Relief washes over his face. "Yes, she likes you, so it shouldn't be a problem."

That's news to me, but I'm happy to hear it.

Rock squeezes my hand to get my attention. "I don't think they're spending the night—"

"It's fine. I'll do my best."

"I know you will. She'll probably want to mother Heidi a little, so that'll make things easier."

Tawny didn't strike me as the "motherly" type, but she did raise two kids of her own, so who knows?

"Trinity's taking care of setting things up at the grandmother's for after the funeral." Rock continues.

Wow, good thing because that hadn't even crossed my mind. "That reminds me, Rock. You know I told you on the trip Tawny had some… opinions on how I should treat Trinity. And before you guys came in, Trinity… Well, never mind. I'm not saying this to be difficult, but I'm not going to treat Trin like shit just so I can look like a proper ol' lady in front of Tawny." Good grief, that sounded ridiculous.

Z bursts out laughing. Rock takes a deep breath before he lets out his own chuckle.

I feel weird talking about this in front of Z, but I don't know if I'll have another chance. "Rock, you know I don't ever want to do anything that reflects badly on you or *this* club, but I won't—"

"Baby, stop. It's fine. I would never ask you to behave differently. And I love how good you are to Trinity. Thank you."

Z watches me with an intent expression that makes me flush. He probably thinks I'm an idiot.

Rock takes my hand and stands, pulling me up with him. "Z and I may need to take off for a little while after the funeral. Murphy will be sticking with you. I'll catch up with you guys at the grandmother's house or here."

I glance down at Z, but he's got his back to us again. "All right."

My eyes search Rock's face. I know there's about a thousand things he's not telling me, but I can't worry about any of it. Heidi is my priority today—and apparently now Tawny.

"Go get some breakfast. It's going to be a long day," Rock finally says.

"Did you eat?"

He flashes a soft smile. "Yeah, doll, I'm good."

"Z, you need anything?" I ask.

"I'm all set, sugar. Thanks."

Stretching up on tiptoes, I give Rock a quick kiss on the cheek. He holds me still for a longer kiss, and my arms automatically wrap around his waist. Forgetting where we are for a moment, I let out a soft moan.

"Seriously, guys?" Z grumbles.

ROCK

"That's some fuckin' woman you got there, prez," Z says after the door closes behind Hope.

Scrubbing my hands over my face, I answer. "I know." I can't help but respect that as much as Hope wants to please me and fit into my world, she won't sacrifice what's important to her to do it. Her loyalty to me, to my club—her refusal to betray Trinity to impress someone else? Yet another example of why I love her so much.

"That *other* situation needs to resolve itself soon," Z points out.

"I know," I say again. "It will. Give him time." Honestly, I don't think even ol' lady status will make Tawny treat Trinity any better.

Z shakes his head.

"Let's worry about one thing at a time. You find anything?"

"Yeah. I got a hit. Small shop in New Hampshire. Brother's telling the truth."

That's nice for a change. "Well, thank fuck."

Sway needs some of the guns returned that we helped ourselves to on his little adventure.

Wrath's vote was for Sway to go fuck himself.

That's why he's not the president.

Not that I like the situation either. It makes us look weak. Sway apologized profusely and has promised to reimburse us with a cash amount. I suppose he expects me to turn it down.

If so, he's going to be disappointed.

Z stands up and stretches. "I'll go give Murphy a hand."

"Thanks. If you want to punch him a few times for me, I won't complain."

Z snickers on his way out the door.

HOPE

My stomach rumbles as I leave Rock's office. Classical music wafts out of the champagne room and piques my curiosity. It's not every day you hear Tchaikovsky played in the clubhouse. The door stands slightly ajar; otherwise, I'd never peek inside.

I recognize the girl dancing, and now I understand how she got her nickname. Saying Swan's graceful is trite and doesn't quite express her movements. As she spins, she spots me watching her and stops.

"I'm so sorry… I heard the music… and the door…" I stammer out. "You're amazing."

She cocks her head to the side. "Thanks, Hope," she answers softly. I've never noticed the faint trace of an accent before.

"Were you a ballet dancer?"

"Yes. My whole family danced."

"Wow. Well, you're really good."

Her cheeks turn pink, and she looks away. "Thank you. I try to practice when I can. Rock gave me the okay to dance at Crystal Ball too, but it's not quite the same."

I can't help laughing at that. "No. I imagine it's not."

She snaps off the radio and throws on a T-shirt over her leotard. "I'm sorry. I like to use the space here because of the mirrors, but with everything—"

"No, Swan, I'm sure it's fine."

Her face twists. "I want to be there for Teller, but he told me not to come, so—"

"Oh." I had no idea they were… whatever, so I'm not sticking my nose in *that*. "I, uh, don't think it's just you. I heard he asked Rock not to have the other clubs come or anything," I say lamely.

She looks very hopeful. "Oh. Okay."

"I know Trinity has to get a lot of stuff together. I'm sure she'd appreciate the help," I suggest.

"Yeah, I can do that."

"Well, I need to eat. I'm sorry I interrupted you."

She stares at me with surprise. "No problem. Thanks."

Heidi and Axel are gone when I return to the dining room. Wrath's sitting by himself, finishing breakfast.

"Why are you out here alone?" I ask when I get closer.

He flicks his blue eyes my way and shrugs.

"I just talked to Swan. She's going to give Trinity a hand."

He raises an eyebrow at me. "That's good."

A well-behaved Wrath is unsettling. "Are you okay?"

This time I get his regular devious smirk. "Yes, sugar."

"Need anything?"

"Nope."

Whatever's bothering him isn't my problem, so I continue into the kitchen. Trinity has platters of food and boxes with paper plates, napkins, and utensils laid out all over the place.

"Damn, you work fast. I wasn't even gone twenty minutes."

She glances up and smiles. "Prepped most of it last night."

"Swan said she's coming in to help."

"Good."

Feeling pretty useless, I grab what I want for breakfast and eat it standing up while talking to Trinity. As I'm finishing, Swan wanders in and asks where she should start.

"We've got this, Hope. You should check on Heidi," Trinity says.

I take that as my cue to leave.

ROCK

Getting the girls in the car was like herding a bunch of otters. Hope's indecisive and running late on a good day. A day like today? It's not her family, but I still don't think a funeral is on her list of things to do—ever. Not on mine either. Already been to far too many in my life.

Heidi is, well, a teenage girl. She burst into tears because she couldn't find the right color lip-gloss or some shit.

I like to think I'm an understanding guy, but *goddamn*.

I didn't feel guilty at all about waiting downstairs and letting Hope deal with that shit. And thank God for her, because Trinity looked as baffled as I felt.

Murphy seems to have set a goal of working my last nerve today. Assigning him to watch Hope finally shut him the fuck up—because he knows Hope will be attached to Heidi.

I swear to fuck, some days managing these guys is as drama-ridden as managing the strippers at Crystal Ball.

Lucky me, I've finally got Hope, Murphy, Heidi, and Axel in my SUV on the way to the funeral. I'm amused as fuck watching Murphy in my rearview. Hope breaks the tension by turning around in her seat to engage him in conversation. A few times, she has to reach out and tap him on the leg when he's a little too focused on Heidi and Axel snuggled up together.

It's gonna be a long afternoon.

CHAPTER SEVENTEEN

HOPE

THE GRAVESIDE SERVICE IS BRIEF AND TO THE POINT. TAWNY AND SWAY MET us halfway and followed Rock's truck up to the private cemetery. The guests are definitely divided in half. On one side sits Heidi with her biker family—a sea of black leather Lost Kings MC cuts. The other side appears to be made up of Mrs. Whelan's friends. Elderly women and a few gentlemen in shades of blue and black polyester. Their side seems to have clear opinions about our side.

Although I'm offended, I can't dwell on it. Heidi hasn't stopped crying since we all got out of Rock's SUV. She turned away from Axel, buried her head in my shoulder, and hasn't left my side since.

We're seated in the front row. Teller's on Heidi's other side. Rock's next to me. He squeezes my free hand and whispers, "Thank you," in my ear.

When the service is over, we stand. Axel hands Heidi some flowers, which she places on her grandmother's casket. Teller ventures to the other side to speak to one of his grandmother's friends.

"Hope?"

Glancing up, I see Charlotte Clark, the attorney assigned to Heidi during the custody case. "Hi, Charlotte."

She turns her attention to Heidi, who lifted her head at the mention of Charlotte's name. A bright smile flashes across her face and she straightens up. "Thank you for coming, Miss Clark," she says softly.

Charlotte's mouth curves into a gentle smile. "Of course. I'm so sorry, Heidi." She glances at me. "If you, ah, need anything, you have my number."

"Thank you."

It's awkward trying to have a conversation here, so I invite her back to the house. As she's leaving, Teller spots her and catches up, walking her to her car. I glance at Rock, and he shrugs.

When we get to the house, Heidi's so reluctant to go inside Axel takes her for a walk.

Murphy stares after them until I nudge him with my elbow. "You okay, Murphy?"

He turns and hesitates before answering. "Yeah, just wish I could do more for her."

I think it's obvious there's more to it than that. Taking his arm, I say, "You're a good guy, Blake."

His face lights up in a playful smirk and he pats my hand. "Are you sure about that? Don't get too carried away, First Lady."

Pulling him away from the others, I say what's been bothering me for a while. "Now that you mention it, Heidi did share something with me that I found a little disturbing."

To say he's shocked is an understatement, but he recovers and puts on his disinterested face quick. "Really?"

"Yes." I lower my voice. "She's a kid. Leave her alone."

"I don't know about that. Sometimes I think she's older than me."

"Yeah, she's a *smart* kid, but she's also an emotional teenage girl. Don't mess with her head."

Finally, a guilty look crosses his face. "You told me yourself the age of consent is seventeen—"

"That's not the point," I hiss at him. "She's still a kid, and you're a grown man."

Murphy glares down at me, but I glare right back. Finally, he says what he's clearly been thinking over. "That girl's needed someone to mother her for as long as I've known her, and I can't tell you how much I respect you for steppin' up and takin' on that job. It's the only reason I'm not tellin' you to fuck off and mind your own business right now."

I raise an eyebrow at him and turn my head slightly in Rock's direction.

"Well, that and Rock would fuckin' kill me." He glances at Rock. "You haven't told him, have you?"

Uh-oh. "No. I don't see any reason to cause trouble. Heidi asked me not to."

"Go ahead. It'll earn me a beatdown from Teller or Wrath. I probably deserve it."

Confused about why Wrath would get involved, I shake my head. "Just leave her alone. She's with Axel. He treats her well—"

His expression hardens at the mention of Axel's name. "Axel's a non-issue once she's eighteen."

"Murphy—what about that girl, Serena? She really likes you."

"She's a way to pass the time when I'm visiting downstate." He flashes me a cheeky grin that I want to smack off his face. "I'll set her up with Axel. Does that make you feel better?"

"Dammit—"

All humor disappears from his face. "Look, I get where you're coming from. I learned my lesson after her birthday. Whether you think so or not, I want what's best for her. She needs to concentrate on school, and I know she's got that college course she's taking over the summer. I'm not plannin' to interfere with any of that stuff."

I think that's as good as I'm going to get from him at the moment. "Okay. Can I ask you something, though?"

"Shoot."

"What if she chooses Axel? You have to realize what she felt for you was a girlish crush."

His mouth opens and closes. Then he lifts his shoulders in a careless shrug. "I love her. That won't change. I ain't gonna kill Axel if that's what you're worried about."

Before I have a chance to respond to *that*, Rock breaks away from his conversation with Sway. A slight frown crosses his face as he takes in Murphy and me. I frown right back at him.

Murphy untangles himself from me. "I'm going to see if T needs anything." He squeezes my hand before bounding up the front steps of the old Victorian.

"What were you two talking about?" Rock asks.

"Nothing. We're both worried about Heidi, that's all." I hate lying to him, but I'm not really sure what to do at the moment.

Rock's gaze sweeps up and down the quiet street. "Where'd they go?"

"For a walk. I can't really blame her for not wanting to hang out inside the house."

He grunts, "Yeah, guess not," while rubbing his hand over the back of his neck. Obviously, something is bothering him.

"Are you and Z taking off now?"

He glances at Sway. "In a bit. Tawny's gonna ride back with you."

"Okay."

All of a sudden, he yanks me closer. Settling his big hands on my hips, he stares down at me with a serious expression. "Two things, Baby Doll."

I raise an eyebrow, curious to find out what he means.

"Thank you for everything you're doing for Heidi today. It means a lot to me."

"Of course."

"Second thing, you look really beautiful."

My heart jumps. I did end up wearing the black dress I brought from home. It *is* too big on me, so I cinched it with a belt, and because it's chilly, I tossed a cardigan over it. Combined with the sensible black shoes I chose because of the uneven ground I expected at the cemetery, I feel like a dowdy nun. That Rock thinks otherwise—enough to stop and tell me—is nice.

"Thank you."

Inside, the house is organized chaos. Trinity's hiding out in the kitchen with Wrath standing guard. Not only did our Lost Kings family follow us back, but some of the grandmother's friends found their way to the house as well. It's an awkward comingling.

Turns out Wrath is just as unfriendly to the elderly as he is to everyone else.

Especially if he thinks one of them is indirectly insulting Trinity.

This is where I think my people skills might come in handy. "Thank you so much for coming, Mrs. Brown. Can I help you find a seat in the living room?" I ask as I take the old woman's plate, offer her my arm, and lead her out of the kitchen.

"That girl shouldn't be in there touching Sue Anne's things," she grumbles at me.

"She's just trying to help out. Sue Anne wouldn't want guests going hungry in her house, right?" I have no idea if this is true or not. Heidi's grandmother didn't strike me as the hostess type, but we didn't exactly meet under friendly circumstances. The woman was more likely to throw a cup of coffee in my face than offer me one to drink.

"That's true, I guess. Are you Heidi's mother?" She leans in and stage-whispers at me, "I thought you were a prostitute?"

Oh dear.

"No. No. I'm a friend of the family."

"Oh. You look nice. Not like the rest of those barbarians her grandson associates with."

My mouth twitches, but I manage to keep it together, find the woman a place to sit, someone else to talk to, and escape into the kitchen myself.

Tense voices reach my ears right outside the kitchen doorway. I can't make out what Trinity said, but Tawny comes through loud and clear. "Where's Hope? She should be taking care of this stuff, not you," she bitches.

Jeez, is it too late to escape out the front door?

But no, I can't leave Trinity. Not when it seems Wrath has disappeared. "Hi, Tawny."

She turns and gives *me* a warm smile. "There you are. *The* old lady of the upstate charter."

Good grief.

Trinity rolls her eyes and sticks out her tongue at Tawny's back, and I do my best not to giggle.

Tawny gives me a tight embrace. "Bet you didn't think you were going to see me again so soon, did you?" she asks.

"No, but it's a pleasure, even under the terrible circumstances. I know Teller and Heidi appreciate you guys being here for them."

She beams at me, and I mentally give myself a pat on the back. Over Tawny's shoulder, I spot Trinity giving me a thumbs-up.

Squelching down my laughter, I focus on Tawny. "Did the guys take off?" I ask.

She waves her hand in the air. "You know the men. Club business can't wait—not even for death. Now where's Heidi? I haven't seen her in a few years." She steers me into the living room and onto the front porch.

We find Heidi and Axel sitting on the front steps together. Tawny fusses over her, which surprisingly seems to cheer her up. Heidi introduces Axel, and Tawny rakes her gaze over him like he's a prime rib.

"You're a prospect, Axel?"

"Yes, ma'am." I've never seen Axel nervous, but Tawny seems to freak him out. I can't blame the kid.

Murphy ambles up and observes the scene. For once, he seems to take mercy on Axel. "Prospect, drinks are gettin' thin. Go grab some sodas," he says, tossing him a set of keys.

Axel catches them midair and nods. "Nice meetin' you, Tawny."

"I'm sure I'll see you again later," she coos.

Disturbing.

Murphy sits next to Heidi on the step and slips an arm around her shoulders. I'm trying to keep an eye on them and keep up with Tawny's chatter. Eventually, I give up. They're in broad daylight. Murphy promised me he'd behave. So when Tawny pulls me inside, I follow.

ROCK

"So this guy whose stash we jacked is legit?" Z asks as we drive back to the clubhouse in Sway's SUV.

Sway chuckles. "Yeah, it's an embarrassing situation. He and his partners run a shop out in New Hampshire. Don't need permits or anything out there."

"So who jacked them?"

"Fucking little gangsters from the city tryin' to move in on our turf. Gonna get ugly before it gets better, I'm afraid."

I'm familiar with the dilemma Sway's facing. "I hear that."

"You still got that snake problem up here?"

"Yup."

Sway just grunts in response.

"So I didn't bring cash to replace what I'm takin' back, but I think you'll be pleased." He gestures for Z to pull one of the bags in the cargo area up front.

A black POF P-415 rests inside. I don't take it out since, you know, we're driving around in broad daylight and all.

"There's two of 'em," Sway explains.

"Yeah, all right. Can definitely use those," I say as I pass the bag back to Z.

"These will be fun to put on paper," Z says, getting all giddy at the thought of blowing holes through shit. "These are supposed to run cooler and be more accurate."

"Good deer gun," Sway comments.

Yeah, I don't really picture Sway stalking through timber with those.

Z taps my shoulder. "Call Wrath, see if they're wrapping up soon."

Wrath answers on the first ring. "What?"

"You with the girls?"

"Not at the moment. All those old biddies were givin' me a headache. Why?"

"Nothing. Wanted an ETA."

"Christ, can't be away from your woman for more than five seconds?" he snarks. Even though he's giving me a hard time, by the sound of things, he's on his way to where the girls are.

"Why don't you have Trin start wrappin' stuff up" I suggest.

"Gladly."

I listen while he barks out orders to Murphy.

"See you in a bit, prez," he says and hangs up.

When we arrive, the clubhouse is empty. Z takes the weapons Sway brought and stashes them in our locker. He brings up the ones we're handing over, and we help Sway get things packed down in the back of his SUV for the trip home.

After that, there's not much else to do besides wait for the girls. Z wanders inside while Sway and I sit outside.

"So this woman, she's it for you?" he asks after a while.

"Yeah."

"'Bout time. Need to have a son to leave the club to."

Well, fuck if that's not a punch in the balls. "Nah. I ain't worried about that. Teller or Z would make fine presidents. Murphy, if he quits his bitching."

Sway chuckles. "Notice you ain't mentioning Wrath."

"Fuck, no. He's got no interest. Need him right where he is anyway."

His mouth twists into a smirk. "Where? Looked like all he was doin' was hovering 'round Trinity back at the wake."

Yeah, I don't even think Wrath saw Sway. Not that we were there very long. I don't feel like gossiping about my brother, though, so I ignore Sway's comment.

For a while, we reminisce about old times. Sway's impressed with our setup. We talk about some of the other changes we want to make so we're more self-sufficient.

"You got some green I can take back?" he asks.

I shake my head. "Man, we're tapped. Sparky's got a sick crop he's tending to. I got this gangster asshole breathin' down my neck for larger shipments."

"That sucks."

"Yes, it does, my friend."

"You need help with the gangster?"

I snort out a humorless laugh. "Not yet. His crew is our largest customer, and they still pay cash."

"Cash *is* king," he jokes. I roll my eyes skyward, and Sway gives me a friendly punch in the arm. "No, seriously, I might be able to hook you up with a crew down my way, if you're interested."

"Maybe." While I appreciate the offer—and I do—I also know

Sway will want a percentage of our sales. I also don't like the idea of needing his help to take care of my club. Might as well just hand him my president patch now if I can't figure this out on my own.

We're interrupted by the return of both cars, and I walk over to meet Hope. Murphy's the first one out and rushes around the car to open the door for Tawny, who pats him on the cheek like he's a kid. She barely throws a glance her husband's way.

Hope flings the back door open, and my breath catches when I see her smiling up at me. She grasps my hand and hops down from the SUV. For a moment, everyone else in the yard disappears. As she wraps her arms around my middle, all the unease from the day evaporates.

"Hey, you," she whispers up at me.

After I press a kiss against her forehead, I ask, "Everything go okay?"

"I think so." She loosens her grip and turns toward Wrath. "Well, except for Wrath scaring all the old ladies out of the house," she explains with a chuckle.

Wrath shrugs. "What? They didn't take any of *your* hints. Had to do somethin'," he explains without a trace of remorse. His gaze falls on Sway, and he lifts his chin. "What up, brother? Long time."

"Yeah." Sway marches over so they can catch up.

"Heidi stay out there?" I ask.

Murphy joins us. "Yeah, she's got school tomorrow. Teller helped her pack up some stuff to bring to his place."

"Good."

Seeing how irritated Tawny is, Hope kisses my cheek and joins her. What they still have to talk about after spending the day together I have no idea, but I appreciate Hope making the effort. I admire my girl for stepping up yet again. It means a lot to me that she tries so hard to make sense of the club's culture—something so foreign to her—and help where she can. She's always so sensitive to other's feelings—something a lot of us around here lack.

Wrath's still catching up with Sway. Trinity looks a little lost as she watches everyone.

"Need help, sweetheart?" I ask as I wander in her direction.

A nervous smile flickers over her face. "Nah, I got it, prez. Thanks."

"Murph," I call out.

"Yeah, prez."

"Help Trin unload, please."

"Yup." He turns and snags the keys out of her pocket, making her laugh.

Satisfied that's taken care of, I'm antsy to be alone with Hope. Seems like we're all outside yapping forever when Sway finally declares it's time to get on the road.

"You sure you don't want to stay?" I ask out of respect.

"Nah, got a meetin' later."

After we send them off, everyone's still standing around bullshittin'. I've been as patient as I can be. Wrapping my hand around Hope's elbow, I tug her away from Trinity. "Need to have a word with my First Lady."

At first, she startles, like she's afraid I'm mad at her. With a tilt of my head and a raised eyebrow, she gets the picture quick.

Her lips curve into a flirty smile. "Yes, Mr. President."

HOPE

I'm exhausted when we finally get back to the clubhouse. Entertaining Tawny used up all my reserves. I struggled not to show my joy when they headed home.

Rock is clearly agitated about something. When he finally gets me alone, he wastes no time leading me upstairs. Once we're in our room, he sits on the side of the bed to take off his boots while I wander into my closet to deposit my shoes and sweater.

"Hope?" His voice pulls me out of the closet, to his side.

As I'm standing in front of him, he tugs me between his legs and drops his head against my stomach. "Thank you for all you did today," he mumbles against me.

I run my hands through his hair, and he hums in pleasure, fisting his hands in the material of my dress. "I need you, baby."

"I'm right here, Rock."

"Don't know what I'd do without you."

I skim my hand along the side of his face. "You won't ever have to find out."

Finally, he looks up at me. "I hope not."

That sounds ominous, and I wonder what exactly went on today.

But he obviously doesn't want to talk about it, so I drop it for now.

His hands are busy working my belt loose. It drops to the floor with a muted clink. Then he tugs up my dress until I pull it up over my head and toss it next to the belt. Underneath, I'm wearing my blue garter skirt and stockings. Not for sexy reasons, just because it was all I had here that would work with the dress. My stockpile of tights seems to have diminished.

I settle my hands on his shoulders for balance, enjoying the feel of his solid muscles beneath my fingers.

"Fuck," Rock breathes out. "You were wearing this all day and I had no idea?"

"I guess."

He runs a finger under one of the garter straps, tickling my thigh. "That's unacceptable, Hope. I need to pay better attention to you." The words themselves are teasing, but his voice is so serious, as if he's upset with himself.

"I'm fine, Rock. What happened today? Why was Sway really here?"

Neither of us says anything—or even breathes—for a moment. It's the most direct question I've asked him about "club business" in a long time.

He tips his head up at me, but his dark eyes and expression are unreadable. "Stupid bullshit, Hope," he finally answers.

It's not much information, but he did answer me, so I push for more. "Did something happen on our trip?"

"Yes."

"They don't have a grow house, do they?"

"No."

My mind is spinning. "Brother charter, though. You have to help them out when they ask, don't you?"

His mouth turns down, and his hands tighten where they're

holding on to my upper thighs. "I don't *have* to do anything, Hope. It's a brotherhood. We're loyal to each other."

He's explained that before. And when he says it about *his* clubhouse—the ones *I* consider his brothers: Wrath, Z, Teller, Murphy and the rest of them—I believe him. The sincerity in his voice at those times is clear.

Now, the words come out like he's reciting a script. "They help us when I need it. Whenever we've had shit with the Vipers, I only had to pick up the phone for Sway and his guys to be here."

"Okay. I understand."

He pins me with one of his presidential stares. "Do you?"

"I'm trying."

He sighs and loosens his hold on me. "I know you are, baby. I appreciate it. How did things go with Tawny? She behave?"

"I caught her giving Trinity a hard time, but I distracted her."

Rock makes a low, growly sound of irritation.

"Can I ask you something?"

The corner of his mouth lifts, but I ask anyway. "Is her dislike for Trinity a general club girl thing or more specific?"

He snorts. "Who knows with her?" His hands slide from my hips down my thighs, tickling behind my knees, and back up, stopping just under my breasts. "Can we talk about something else now?"

It's my turn to smirk. "Somehow I don't think talking is what you have in mind."

"You're absolutely right, Baby Doll."

CHAPTER EIGHTEEN

HOPE

I SHOULD NEVER TAKE TRINITY'S PLANNING SKILLS FOR GRANTED. SHE'S
been after me about organizing some sort of an engagement party for
weeks. Now that the downstate trip is over and things have settled
down with Heidi, she's right back in party-planning mode.

Since I have a bit of an aversion to this sort of thing, it's honestly a
relief to have her help. Rock surprises me by being game for anything.
I don't suspect there's a lot of gruff bikers into wedding stuff, but he
seems charmed by every idea Trinity presents.

The contradiction between the scary biker and loving fiancé make
me love him even more.

Trinity has a folder of magazine clippings and menus in front of
her. "I know usually the parents of the bride are supposed to—"

I have to stop her. "Trinity, it's fine. Trust me. You don't want my
mother involved."

Her smile falters. "I'm sorry, I didn't—"

"Don't apologize. It's not like I need my mom to pay for it. Rock
and I—"

"I'll take care of whatever comes up, Trinny," Rock interrupts.

"Some of them will be my guests, Rock."

He makes that face I always suspect means he's counting to ten in his head before saying anything. Instead of answering me, he addresses Trinity. "Whatever you need, let me know."

"Rock, I have my own money."

"Making it worse, Hope," Trinity mumbles under her breath with a sly smile.

Exasperated, I give Rock a small shove. "This is women's work. Don't you have scary biker business to attend to?"

He bursts out laughing. "Fuck, I love you," he says, planting a kiss on my cheek as he stands.

Trinity nods at him in a way that suggests they just had some sort of silent conversation over my head.

Once he leaves, she turns her attention to me. "So where do you want to have it?"

"We can do it at my house. Just low key."

"Not Rock's?"

I think it over. The last time I hosted anyone else at my house, it was after Clay's funeral. I like the idea of something a little happier being held there. It helps cement my feeling that I'm moving forward. The guilt I expected doesn't come either, which is a relief. Of course, the next logical thing is getting rid of the damn house, but I can't think about that right now.

"Yeah, it's a little closer for some of my friends."

"Okay." Trinity's busy making notes. She stops and taps her pen against her chin. "Low key. Not too simple, though. Something more than a backyard cookout. But we don't want to scare the guys away with anything too fancy either." She seems to be thinking out loud more than looking for any actual input from me.

"Oh! How about some sort of chicken wing tasting thing? There's the restaurant downtown that does like twenty different kinds of wings. You could have little tasting stations."

"That sounds like fun. Messy, though."

"They can do boneless. And then, so it's not too much man food, we can have like really girly gourmet ice cream sandwiches for desert. I just read this whole article and have a bunch of recipes—"

She grabs her folder and starts scattering pages all over the coffee table again.

"Okay. I trust you, Trinity. That actually sounds kind of awesome."

She flashes me a bright grin and jots down more notes. "Open bar of course."

"Can you hire a bartender, though? I don't want you serving drinks. I'll need you to help me survive my psycho mother."

She glances up, surprise clearly written on her face. "Of course, Hope."

"I mean. You're a guest. I want you to enjoy the party too." Hell, I don't know what I mean.

Since Trinity isn't an overly affectionate person, she shocks me by throwing her arms around me and squeezing tight. "I'm so happy for you two."

For some reason, I'm sniffling. "Thanks."

She jumps up off the couch, yanking me along. "Let's go down to Wing Fling and see what they can do."

"Right now?"

"Sure, why not?" she says over her shoulder as she walks over and taps on Rock's office door. Inside, Rock, Wrath, and Z seem to be conducting a meeting of their own. Trinity leans on the door frame. "Hope and I are going to run downtown and check out a restaurant."

She gives the guys a rundown of her chicken wing idea, and they all seem to approve. Rock catches my eye, and I smile and shrug back at him.

"You need one of us to go with?" Wrath asks.

"Nah, we'll be fine."

"Making any other stops?" he persists.

"We're not going to the pinup store," she answers with a giggle.

Wrath feigns outrage, but he's laughing too hard to be convincing.

Z has no idea what's so funny.

The restaurant is smack in the middle of Empire, so of course it's impossible to find parking. We end up walking quite a way.

"Are any of your friends vegetarians?" She's chattering and firing so many questions at me that the walk doesn't seem so long.

Once we're inside, I feel good about the selection. The owners are friendly and more than willing to sit down with us without an appointment.

I end up having to text Rock with a few dates, and we agree on one two months out. Trinity says it's more than enough time to put this together, and I trust her.

We're standing at the register as the owner puts the information into his computer. "Kendall-North. Engagement party."

"Hope?" someone shrieks behind me.

I recognize that voice and stand stock-still, praying the ground will swallow me whole.

"Hope?" Trinity questions.

"Can you finish up here?" I ask her softly.

"Sure."

Pasting on my patient lawyer smile, I turn and greet my former sister-in-law.

ROCK

"Think the girls are okay?" Wrath asks maybe an hour after they left.

"Yeah. Already got a text from Hope looking for a date for the party."

"That's good, right? You said she's been hard to nail down."

I nod, not completely comfortable discussing this with him at the moment.

"Will Lilly come to the party?" Z asks.

"I assume she will. Why?"

Z shrugs.

"What's wrong, brother? She still dodging you?" Wrath asks with a dickish smile.

"You're one to talk."

That's an effective way to shut Wrath up. I'll have to remember it. "Can we focus and get this shit done?" I ask.

There's a bunch of new security stuff Wrath wants added to our compound. Since this crosses into all of our job functions, it makes sense for the three of us to sit down together to order the hardware and work out some of the other details. So far, it's been fine, but I'm well aware these two can only sit down and concentrate on something other than bikes or sex for so long.

Before we clear out of the office, I try to get an update on Wrath's cast. Something he's intensely pissed off about, according to Trinity.

"Another fuckin' week at least."

"You gonna do the physical therapy the doc suggested?" Z asks.

Wrath snorts. "I'll go and get the exercises, then do them myself."

"Good. Well, when you're up to it, I'd like you to take Hope out to the gun range and give her some training."

Wrath's eyebrows lift. "Yeah? You don't want to teach your girl yourself?"

"I'll join you, but no, you can do the training. That's your area."

"Okay. Cool. I got no problem doin' it now. Someone's just gotta drive me out in the side-by-side."

"It's not urgent. I'd just like her to be more comfortable. You remember what happened when we got run off the road."

The corner of Wrath's mouth lifts. "Yeah, but she did okay."

Z and I both cock our heads at him.

"What?"

"Nothing. What kind of gun you thinkin' of having her start with?" I ask Wrath.

He shrugs. "Glock three-eighty? Your little pussy-ass nine mil might be fine too."

"We'll see how pussy it is when I put a few holes through your obnoxious ass," I grumble.

Not at all threatened, Wrath grins. "She can't handle my Glock twenty, but maybe a revolver if she's uncomfortable loading the magazine in an emergency. I dunno. I'll let her test out what we got and see what she likes."

Z shakes his head. "Carrying that cannon around just makes everyone think you have a small dick."

Wrath snorts.

Z turns to me. "Should be real easy for her to get a permit."

"Yeah, I don't need to get involved in that." I agree. I have a connection at the sheriff's office for those of us with less-than-clean records. But being a lawyer should make it easy for Hope to get a pistol permit, so no need for me to call in any favors. The less connection she has to me the better. "Weather is supposed to be nice this week, so let me know when you're feelin' up to it."

"Anytime, brother." Wrath gives me a fist-bump as I walk out of the office.

HOPE

"You're getting married again? Already?" Lynn asks in an extremely loud voice, sending shame spiraling through my body. My cheeks heat up. "How could you? My brother's barely cold in his grave. What's wrong—"

"Stop talking before I slap the shit out of you, lady," Trinity snarls as she steps up beside me.

My entire body trembles. I'm hot all over. Mortified doesn't begin to cover it. Thankfully, Lynn's mouth snaps shut and she takes a step back as she gets a good look at Trinity. While I find Trinity to be sweet and almost shy at times, I'm reminded she can be pretty damn fierce when she needs to be.

Trinity grabs my arm. "We're all set here, Hope."

Lynn's like a cobra I can't take my eyes off in case she strikes again. "Okay."

"Let's go." She steers me around Lynn. As Trinity's hand brushes the door, Lynn grumbles something under her breath at me.

"Hang on, Trin." Feeling a little more in charge of myself, I whirl around. "What did I ever do to you, Lynn?"

"You trapped my brother into marrying—"

Something inside me breaks when it registers what she's about to accuse me of. Before I know what's happening, my palm connects with her cheek. A satisfying pop fills the air, and Lynn's head snaps back.

Through clenched teeth, I manage to get out a few final words. "I loved Clay. You, not so much. Don't *ever* speak to me again, Lynn."

Trinity's mouth is hanging open, but she takes my hand and pulls me out onto the street. "Holy shit, Hope. Nice job."

My lips twitch into an uncertain smile. "I can't believe I did that. Oh my God."

Now that the moment is over, I'm absolutely shaking with rage. Hurt and humiliation are also present in my mind. I can't believe Trinity witnessed me so out of control. I can't believe the lovely couple I spent an hour going over my engagement party menu with heard the awful things Lynn said to me. I can't believe Lynn had the nerve to suggest—

"Hope? Are you okay?"

We're standing in front of the Jeep. Somehow we walked all the way here and I didn't notice.

Trinity opens my door and I slide in. All I can do is stare out the window.

Next to me, she taps out a text, then sets her phone down on the console. "Buckle up, Hope. We're going straight to the clubhouse. We've had enough fun for one day."

ROCK

Are you at the clubhouse?

The text from Trinity surprises me.

Yes, I answer back.

Bringing Hope back now. Something happened. She needs you.

What the fuck?

"What's wrong?" Wrath asks.

"Yo, I'm heading down to CB," Z announces, coming out of the office. He stops when he spots us. "What's wrong, prez?"

"Got a weird text from Trinity." I answer without looking up.

"They okay?"

"I think so. She says they're on their way back now."

"Okay. Let me know if you need anything."

Wrath pulls my phone out of my hand to review the texts. "Wanna call her?"

"Nah, if she's driving, I don't want to distract her."

"I meant Hope."

I shake my head. "They'll be here soon."

When they get here, everything seems fine at first. Trinity laughs and jokes around with Hope. But I've known Trinity a long time; her laughter is forced.

The girls give me a rundown of their meeting with the restaurant before Trinity takes off.

"Everything okay?" I ask Hope.

She glances at me with watery eyes. "Yeah. Can we go upstairs?"

"Sure."

In our room, she moves like a robot while she changes into a pair of sweatpants and an old T-shirt of mine.

Finally, she comes and sits next to me on the bed. Wrapping my arm around her shoulders, I hug her tight to me. "What's wrong, baby?"

"We ran into Lynn at the restaurant."

It takes me a second to remember who the hell that is. "Aw, shit, baby. I remember what a selfish bitch she was."

"Yeah, she overheard we were planning an engagement party and flipped out in front of the entire place. It was so embarrassing."

I'd love to find that bitch and fucking choke the life out of her. "What'd she say?"

"Just that she couldn't believe I was getting married again so soon. Stuff like that."

Shit. "I'm sorry."

"I slapped her, Rock. She got me so mad I actually slapped her across the face." Hope whispers the last words while she stares down at her hand.

I'm not at all sorry about the feeling of pride that surges through me.

"Good. Sounds like she fucking deserved it."

Her mouth finally turns up a bit. "Yeah. I can't tell you how many times over the years I wanted to smack her. Guess it was pent-up aggression."

"I can imagine."

She giggles a little and leans against me. "It was just so awful. Why'd she…? Ugh."

"I don't know why. Sounds like she's been a miserable person for years. Probably just wanted someone to take it out on."

She's silent for a while.

"Baby, you can tell me the truth. Do you feel like it's too soon?"

Hope sucks in a deep breath before answering. "No, Rock."

Thank fuck. I don't know what I'd do if she said yes. "It's done. I'm glad you stood up to her."

"Me too. I think I shocked the hell out of Trinity too."

"Probably."

That's it. We don't discuss Lynn again. Hope moves forward... sort of.

Club business pulls me away from my girl more than I care for. Loco from the Green Street Crew calls another one of his bullshit meet-and-greets. They're our biggest customer, but they're starting to wear on all our nerves.

"He does this shit again, prez, I say we take a vote to put his ass down," Wrath suggests at church the day after.

"Simmer down."

Z pipes up. "He might be right, prez. Something stinks about this. He's way too up in our business."

"I'll take it under advisement."

As much as I dislike it, I need to spend some time at Crystal Ball, cleaning house, too. The phone call I had with Inga prompted me to have *all* the employees—not just the dancers—take a surprise drug test. Should have done this a long time ago. The results were discouraging, and in the end, a lot of people had to be cut loose, which means I need to spend time there filling in for Z and Dex. I plan to leave the hiring to them, though.

I don't *think* Hope's mad about all the time I'm away from her, but it's hard to tell because it feels like we barely talk anymore.

What I do know is every fuckin' night we've spent together since she ran into that fuckin' ex-sister-in-law of hers, Hope's been cryin' in her sleep. At some point, she'll turn and cling to me as if she's trying to keep me anchored to the bed.

Once the sun comes up, though, that invisible space between us comes right back. It's so fucking thick I can't cut my way through it.

Hope's polite but distant when we cross paths. My body's in knots whenever I see her.

I gotta fix this before we get married.

If she ever sets a fuckin' date.

Lately, I'm feeling like the chick in this relationship. I keep pushing her to set a date, but she keeps making excuses.

Is she having second thoughts? Has the reality of what it means to be married to me—married to the club—finally settled in? Has she decided it's not for her, and she doesn't know how to tell me?

I'm too fuckin chicken to ask, because if she confirms my worst fears, I don't know what I'll do.

No. There will be a fuckin' wedding. Even if I have to wait another two years for her.

Or a lifetime.

I convince myself it's not the club. She gets along with all my brothers. They fuckin' adore her. Even Wrath, although he'll never admit it and he still loves pickin' on her.

It's not the club. Unless she's still worried about all the illegal shit we're into. Especially after that fuckery with Sway's club. Shit. I know how ballistic she went when she got called into the ethics board. Let's face it. My activities endanger her career all the time. One arrest could easily get tied to her and bring all the shit right back up.

Has that finally dawned on her the way it's dawning on me?

HOPE

"Babe, have you told your mother about us gettin' married yet?" Rock asks me not long after the incident with Lynn.

My entire body goes rigid at the thought. "No. After she *wasn't* worried about me when I was in the hospital, I don't see the point."

"She's still your mother. Maybe she didn't understand. I probably should have done more and called her back. It was just so—"

"Rock, trust me. It's not your fault. She's always been like this. But if it makes you feel better, I'll call her."

He nods, and I can tell he won't be happy until I make the call. I know how stressed out he's been lately, so I'll just have to set aside my discomfort.

My hands are shaking as I pick up the phone and dial the number. "Hello, Mother."

"Hope! Why haven't I heard from you in so long? You have no idea what I've been through at work..."

And as usual, my mother can't stop talking about her favorite topic —herself. No motherly concern about my recent hospital visit. Not even a simple "how are you."

I flick my gaze to Rock, who quirks an eyebrow at me. A small part of me is embarrassed he's about to find out how little my own mother cares about me. I long to crawl under the bed and hide.

My mother continues for a good five minutes before taking a breath. "Hope, are you listening? Can you believe that?"

"No, I can't. Um, I actually called because I have some news. I'm getting married."

"What are you talking about?" Her screechy voice makes me pull the phone away from my ear. "How can you get married again already? What's the matter with you?"

This is why I hadn't told my mother yet.

ROCK

Lead settles in my gut as I watch Hope on the phone with her mother. Why the fuck did I insist she do this? Even from that brief conversation we had while Hope was in the hospital, I could tell her mother is a piece of shit.

I guess I have some guilt about yanking Hope so deep into my world. I don't want her to feel cut off from her only remaining family.

And maybe a small, selfish part of me thought talking to her mother might get her out of this funk she's been in so she can plan our wedding.

"Mother, it's been almost two—yes. I remember. After Dad. Yes. You waited. I know—"

This is a train wreck. A fuckin' mess I caused. "Give me the phone, Hope."

She shakes her head and walks over to the corner of the room so I can barely hear her.

"No, Mother. No, I'm not pregnant again. That's not—no. He's very good to me." She turns and half smiles at me. "He's a businessman. … A couple different things. … No, I still have my legal practice. It's fine. … No, we're going to have a low-key wedding. … Outside. I don't know yet. … I don't think so. Maybe."

She flashes uncertain eyes at me, and I'm not sure what's causing that panic-stricken face. "Sure, I'll try to set something up."

I can't take any more. She's in the same room, but it feels like we're miles apart. Crossing the short distance, I take her hand because I can't not touch her for another second. Turning it over in my hand, playing with her fingers, stroking my thumb over her soft skin. Her hands always seem so delicate, small compared to mine. She glances up and flashes a nervous smile while listening to whatever her bitch of a mother says on the other end. It's the same smile that always makes my heart stumble and want to do anything I can to protect her.

"Give me the phone, Hope," I whisper.

"Okay, Mom. I need to go. We'll talk about things soon." She ends the call and then hands me the phone.

"What was that about, baby?"

She shakes her head. "Just my mother." She breathes out an exasperated sigh.

"I'm sorry. I shouldn't have made you call her."

"It's fine. I'd be a terrible daughter if I didn't tell her about my own wedding, right?"

I'm not sure how to answer that. She seems to be searching for an answer, not just being sarcastic. "If you guys had a normal relationship, then yeah. But if you don't, then no. Not if it's going to upset you, baby."

She opens her mouth, then closes it.

"What?"

"Nothing, Rock. Can we—I just need to lie down for a while. I don't feel well." Her hand drifts to her stomach, rubbing in circles.

Fuck. Why couldn't I just mind my own business? "What's wrong?"

"I don't know," she mumbles as she walks over to the bed and crawls under the covers.

Now I'm fuckin' scared. I walk over and sit on the edge of the bed next to her. After almost losing her, anytime she so much as sneezes, I'm on alert. "Do you need to go to the hospital?"

She turns over and takes my hand. A ghost of a smile plays on her lips. "No, it's nothing like that. My stomach is just upset."

"Okay." Unsure, I let her be. But I can't help thinking there's something more I need to do for her.

HOPE

Talking to my mother brought up many bad feelings. Planning my first wedding with her had been a nightmare for a lot of reasons.

Reasons she so kindly reminded me of during our brief conversation.

It's probably all in my head, but I'm sick for a couple days after that call. I run a pretty high fever for a day or two and generally feel miserable. Rock's sweet and understanding.

At first.

He's out pretty much night and day. Between Crystal Ball and club business, he's gone a lot. I try not to be clingy and whiny. I don't ask him where he's going or when he'll be back. It kills me, but I sense he's under some strain and I don't want to add to his worries. I've done enough to distract him lately.

I wonder if the time he spent away from the club while caring for me in the hospital and after has caused problems. When I try to ask, he brushes off my concern with a quick smile.

While I'm getting over this stomach bug, I stick to his room. I'd almost rather go home. The clubhouse is so big, and I feel so awful that walking to the kitchen for tea or toast is too much effort. Trinity says she'll bring me whatever I want, but I hate doing that to her.

Rock sets me up with water and breakfast before he leaves in the mornings.

On the third day, I finally feel well enough to spend the afternoon downstairs with Trinity, watching a movie.

Even though Rock's not back from wherever he had to go, I still head to bed earlier than normal. I'm almost asleep when his heavy footsteps enter the bedroom.

He flips on the light, startling me. "Sorry," he mumbles before shutting off the overhead light and turning on a softer lamp. "Christ, Hope. Did you even get out of bed today?"

I bolt upright at his words and tone. Rock's never spoken to me like that.

CHAPTER NINETEEN

ROCK

Yet another bullshit meeting with Loco. I tried to do the right thing and warn the little fuck we might not be able to meet his increased demands. We can rally our regular delivery, but the extra amounts he squeezed me for at our last two meetings might be an issue.

"You call off your western run?" Loco asks me with a straight face.

This *motherfucker* up in my business again. I swear to fuck I want to kill him.

I should have kept my mouth shut. My mistake for trying to treat a gangster with the respect of a normal businessman. This aspect of outlaw life is the same as working a fucking retail job. Even when my customers irritate the fuck out of me, I'm still under an obligation to maintain a certain level of friendliness.

"Yeah, man, they're aware of the situation. Sparky's working his magic to pull the *additional* amount together in time for your drop." My emphasis on additional doesn't make any impression that I can detect.

"I'll allow you an extra two weeks, Rock. That's the best I can do."

Allow? I'm not gonna allow *you to walk out of here without a few holes in your lungs if you keep that shit up.*

"Thanks, man. We shouldn't need it. Appreciate it, though." I *don't* appreciate any of this. Loco has been a constant pain in my ass. But until I can get some other things in place, I gotta pretend I don't want to gut him and toss his body in the Hudson River.

The Hudson River. Mere feet from where we're standing. Fuck, it's tempting.

Although it's galling me to no end—and Wrath almost lost his shit when we took a vote on it—I hand over one of the short barrel rifles Sway gave us. It's a high-end piece for a street thug, but Loco expressed some interest in obtaining one for his personal collection the last time we met.

He looks through the bag. Probably searching for ammunition to go with the weapon. Fucker won't find any. I'm not completely suicidal. "Daaamn, brotha. Where'd you come up with this?"

He knows full well I don't appreciate being called "brother" by anyone who isn't a Lost King.

"Sort of fell in our lap. But you said you were looking for something along those lines."

He cocks his head and stares at me. "Thought your crew was outta guns?" He persists.

"We are. That's a one-time gift. Thanks for your business and all." I hate every fucking second of this little game.

Loco nods and runs his hand over his chin. I just know whatever he's going to say next will piss me off. "Rock, be straight with me. Shit like this don't fall outta trees. Word on the street is your charter down south handles this kind of merchandise."

I shrug.

He smirks in response. "I also hear they got a problem with Shadow Nation pushing up out of NYC into his territory."

Sway never mentioned the name of the crew he's having trouble with. "I don't have details."

"Listen, I know your boys down there ain't as... colorblind as you are," he says. This is true. While I don't care about the color of anyone's skin as long as they deal with me fairly, I can't say that's true of everyone in my world. "Introduce me."

Like fuck. "Can't."

"I ain't askin' you to get involved. Just make the introduction." Yeah, except I know what'll happen. I'm the one in the area, so when problems come up, one of them will be contacting *me*. It's a slippery slope I don't want to set foot on.

"We got a long history, Rock. Your word will have some *sway* down there." His smirk tells me he's done his research.

While he annoys me no end, Loco and his crew have been loyal customers for years. He's never overtly threatened me. He *is* pissing me off lately wanting to dominate my entire supply. Although, the more I think about it, in Loco's twisted, gangster brain, he probably thinks he's doing me a favor.

"I'll take it to the table."

One eyebrow shoots up. *Yes, asshole, that's how our brotherhood works. Gotta put shit like this to a vote.* I keep the thought to myself. He wouldn't understand.

We shake hands and go our separate ways. Thankfully, he left his entourage behind this time.

Z and I meet up at Crystal Ball and head back to the clubhouse. After I fill him in on the meeting, he groans. "Jesus Christ, we can't get involved in that, prez. Wrath might be right."

"Yeah, I'd like to avoid it too. I'm gonna put some feelers out to Ulfric and Stump, but they've never been able to move that much product. Sway mentioned he might have a connection down his way."

Z shakes his head. "You know what that'll mean."

Yes. What's worse? Possibly getting involved in Loco's gun dealing with Sway from time to time, or having Sway involved in every single transaction I make with his contact?

Neither option appeals to me.

I don't have to say anything. Z knows what I'm thinking.

His hand smacks against the dashboard. "Fuck. Empire's stable right now. We go messing with GSC, that's gonna leave their turf vulnerable, and who the fuck knows who ends up taking their place?"

I'd like to say, "They can all kill each other for all I care." But what I actually say is, "My concern is losing our largest income stream. We don't have the manpower and we don't need the exposure of taking on the distribution end of things."

"Be a lot more money in it, though."

He's right.

"A lot more risk," I remind him. "Besides, you feel like standing around weighing out nickel and dime bags all day? I sure as fuck don't."

He chuckles, then turns serious. "Prez, we've been managing our money well for years now. We could take the hit and wait out any shakeup."

This is true. Teller's done a good job since he took over as our treasurer. Our former president became intoxicated with the large amounts of cash rolling in off his brothers' backs and spent it recklessly. Managing our money properly and for the benefit for the *whole* club was our first priority when Wrath, Z, and I took over.

Still, there are a lot of us to support.

"I know. I'd rather not if we can help it."

"CB still brings in a shit ton of cash," he reminds me.

"Yeah, okay."

"I'm just sayin' we'll get through this. Don't stress so much."

One corner of my mouth lifts. "Someone has to worry about big picture stuff, pretty boy."

"Fuck you," he jokes back.

When we get to the clubhouse, I call a meeting. It's informal since not all the brothers are on the property. I have to physically go downstairs and bring Sparky up to the war room where Wrath, Z, and Murphy are waiting. Stash is miraculously out.

"Prez, the plants are doin' better," he assures me as soon as we're all seated.

"Thank fuck."

I give everyone a rundown of my meet with Loco.

Wrath shakes his head, then turns to Sparky. "The plants gonna be affected by this?"

"You mean their potency? It's possible."

"We can't get a rep for selling shitty ditch weed, prez," Wrath grumbles as if I don't know this. "Probably shouldn't have even told the little fuck we were having issues."

"Yeah. That's on me," I answer. "We'll take a vote closer to the drop date. What's worse: not delivering top product, or not delivering at all?"

Murphy pipes up. "We really gotta vote on that, prez? No product at all will fuck us royally."

"Yeah, but a shitty product could fuck us long term," Wrath says.

Sparky bristles at the way Wrath refers to his plants.

I stand, signaling the meeting is over. "We're not going to solve this tonight. Just wanted to keep everyone informed." I point at Murphy. "Fill Teller in?"

"Yeah, of course."

Now that business is taken care of, I'm eager to get upstairs. Hope's been sick, and I've been neglecting her. She's had me worried for days but refuses to see the doctor, saying it's nothing.

Without thinking, I flip on the overhead light when I walk in the bedroom. Hope shakes herself, blinking at me with bleary eyes.

It's no excuse, but I'm so irritated from the other shit going on that I end up snapping at her.

"Christ, Hope. Did you even get out of bed today?"

She sits up, the hurt and shock written clearly on her face.

"What?" she snaps back at me.

"You're asleep when I leave. You're asleep when I get back—" Why am I doing this to her? Why can't I keep my fucking mouth shut?

Fury turns her cheeks red. She tosses back the covers and scrambles out of bed to face me. Arms crossed over her chest, eyes flashing fire. "How the fuck would you know what I did today? You've been gone sunrise to fucking midnight, Rock."

Good. Fight me. Do something. This is the most animated I've seen her in days.

"I've got shit to handle."

"I know. And I've been trying not to bother you, but don't you dare come in here and speak to me—"

I started it, but I'm too much of a pussy to finish it, so I storm into the bathroom, slamming the door behind me. Part of me wants her to barge in and yell at me some more. I fuckin' deserve it.

When I get out of the shower, the lights in the bedroom are all off. I make out Hope's form curled over on her side, facing away from me. Crawling into bed with her is awkward. I know she's not asleep.

Her breath hitches.

I made her fuckin' cry.

Pulling her to me sets everything she'd been trying to hold in loose. In my arms, she shakes and sobs. I bury my nose in her hair, kissing her. "Baby, I'm sorry I'm bein' such a dick. I didn't mean to take it out on you. Please don't cry."

Every tear she's ever shed has cut me. I can't stand hearing my girl upset over anything. But the tears she's crying *because* of me? Because of pain I've caused her by being an asshole? Those stick in my throat like shards of glass.

"Hope." I manage a hoarse whisper. She turns, her soft body sliding against me, and wraps her arms around me tight.

I don't deserve her forgiveness, but I'm grateful for it. Her cheek is still damp against my chest, searing my skin.

"What's happening?" she finally asks, sounding very small and broken.

The words "I don't know" roll around in my mouth, but I hold them in because they're a lie.

After a while, she shifts a little but keeps her arms around me.

"You feeling any better, Baby Doll?"

She nods, the soft skin of her cheek brushing against my chest. "Yeah. I went downstairs to hang out with Trinity for a while. I tried to stay up and wait for you, but I was tired."

Fuck, I'm an asshole. "I'm sorry."

"Do you want to talk about it?"

Do I? It's club business. I've already told Hope more about the club than I think any guy I've known in this life has told his ol' lady. Christ, in another MC, I'd probably get shot for all the shit I've shared with her.

When it takes me so long to answer, Hope sighs and attempts to turn over.

"Stop, Baby Doll. I'm just thinking how to explain—"

"I know I'm not clever at the criminal stuff like you guys are, but I'm not stupid. Maybe I can help."

I know she didn't mean it as a dig, but hearing my girl so casually refer to me as a criminal—even though I know damn well that's what I am—fuckin' stings.

But I've already made her cry once tonight. Picking another fight over something so stupid isn't what I want to do, so I simmer the fuck down and take a breath.

"Remember Sparky's sick plants?"

She sort of gasps and struggles to sit up. "Oh my gosh. I'm such an idiot."

I grab her hand and tug her back down. "What are you talking about?"

"Logically, I understood you're not growing all that for personal consumption."

I snort. "No, babe."

"But I didn't think beyond what the sick plants meant."

Of course she understands what's going on right away. "Yes. Our buyer increased the amount he wants, and if that crop isn't ready, it'll cause problems."

"Oh." She's quiet for a moment, thinking through the implication of my words. "It's not just a matter of lost money, is it?

"No."

"Is this person dangerous?"

"Yes and no. He's a gangster with ambition."

She snorts. "Sounds dangerous to me."

"Yeah. The guys and I had a short meeting when I got back. Sparky says the plants are getting better. He wants to stretch their flowering stage to give us more yield, but we don't have the time."

"Wow, I was wrong. I don't have any useful advice."

I huff out a laugh and kiss the top of her head. "I appreciate you tryin'."

"Is this... person your only customer?"

"No. That's the other problem. I've had to pull a delivery I promised to a new customer. I'm trying to broaden our customer base, and the gangster wants to keep us dependent on his crew."

"So you're basically trying to diversify your portfolio?"

Okay, how can I not laugh at that? She's so fuckin' cute.

She thumps my chest to get my attention. "You can't expand too much, though. You only have so much room down there."

"True."

"Even if Sparky says the plants are recovering... will they still be as, I don't know, good?"

My smile is wasted in the dark. But yeah, my girl catches on quick. "There's some concern about that. We have a certain reputation."

"Oh, I imagine Sparky only wants to produce the best. That's why the gangster wants you all to himself."

It's not a question. She definitely has a grasp of the situation now.

"Why not set up some sort of blind test and have some of your regular hang-arounds or whatever give you an opinion?"

I open my mouth, then reconsider. It's actually not a bad idea. Sparky likes getting opinions on his new strains. This wouldn't be much different.

"It wouldn't be scientific," Hope says in a rush, like she's worried I'm going to dismiss her idea.

"No. It's a good idea. We don't have a ton to spare for something like that." I can think of at least two guys who would be perfect for the task. "I'll bring it up in church."

We're quiet for a while. Her hand keeps restlessly brushing against my chest, so she hasn't fallen asleep.

"Hope?"

"Yes," she whispers so soft I feel the word more than hear it.

"I'm sorry about before."

"I know you are."

"Forgive me?"

She doesn't hesitate. "Always."

Shit, that one fucking word tears me up inside.

It takes me a second to notice, but her hand keeps drifting lower.

"Hope," I warn, halting her exploration. "Don't start something you can't finish."

"Oh, I plan to finish."

HOPE

The nightmares I started having after the run-in with my sister-in-law ease up after Rock confides in me. But for some reason, I'm still paralyzed. Rock's even noticed I'm not into planning our wedding, and now that I know the extent of what he's dealing with, I feel even worse.

There's no way I can explain to him *why* I'm having so much anxiety about the wedding. Not when he's involved in such a delicate dilemma with some... gangster. Compared to the pressure he's under, my angst seems insignificant and stupid. I can't waste his energy or distract him with my nonsense. I just need a little time to work things through on my own. Hopefully, by then, the club's situation will have improved, and I'll tell him everything.

Lately, all the guys seem to be on edge. The lazy, easygoing atmosphere that usually permeates the clubhouse is thick with tension.

When I get a call from Empire Canvassing asking me to come in for an interview, I jump at the chance to get away from the clubhouse. Lilly's friend explained how the lobbying firm he works for represents a lot of the groups pushing for New York to legalize marijuana. That he decided to call me now strikes me as perversely funny.

Given Rock's...business, I feel compelled to explore this job opportunity. Of course, I don't think my interviewers will take "my husband-to-be is a marijuana trafficker" as an appropriate response to the standard "why do you want to work here" question, but I have a few days to figure it out.

Rock doesn't exactly share my enthusiasm about this new career path. Something he makes abundantly clear during dinner one night.

"Remember that lobbyist I told you Lilly and I had lunch with?"

Rock stares at me, so I explain in a rush. "The one who said his firm represents those tech companies trying to get marijuana legalized in New York?"

Understanding flares in Rock's eyes and he nods. Wrath pins me with one of his icy glares. Flustered, it dawns on me a little too late that

I should have had this conversation with Rock when we were alone. "Well, his company wants to interview me for a position. They need an attorney…"

No one speaks.

It's awkward. I realize I might be treading into territory the club won't approve of, and I'm not sure how I feel about that.

Stupid.

Yes, I understand they voted me in and they seem to accept me. That doesn't mean bringing women into the inner business dealings is something the MC embraces.

"That's great, Baby Doll. You'd be good at it. Sounds like it would be full time, though. Are you sure that's what you want to do?" Rock finally says.

Is this his way of telling me he doesn't want me to take the job?

ROCK

I have to give Wrath credit—he manages to wait until the girls leave the table before tearing into me. Trinity seemed to sense we were about to have a blowout, so I think that's why she had a sudden need to take Hope outside to look at some stuff for the garden.

"Prez, you need to shut that shit down."

Ignoring him, I finish my dinner and sit back, crossing my arms over my chest.

"Why? I think it's funny as fuck."

Z's keepin' an eye on both of us. I don't think he's decided which side to land on.

"Listen, it's one thing to let her know what we're into so she can make an informed decision about spending so much time here. And I *do* trust her."

I let out a deep breath.

"But we barely have the county sheriff and Empire PD out of our business. You really think having your wife running around out there advocating for reform is a good way to stay under the radar?"

As much as I hate to admit it, he has a point.

Z finally weighs in. "You're going worst-case scenario, bro. It's so close to being legalized. No one's gonna come knocking on our door because of where she works." Z glances at me, and I nod to encourage him since he seems to be on my side. "Cops have seen us doing a lot of good down in Empire for years. The MC keeps the really bad shit out, which makes their jobs easier, and they look the other way. Lotta charities quietly supported by us, too." He sits back but keeps his eyes on Wrath. "Besides, Hope's as wholesome and respectable as it gets. Having someone like her advocating for reform can only be a good thing."

He turns toward me, and this time I know whatever he's about to say I *won't* like. "Besides, you hooked up with a lawyer only looks good for us." He shrugs and glances at Wrath. "She wouldn't be with him if he was some big-time drug dealer, right?"

"Thanks, asshole."

His face remains neutral. "Calm down. I'm not saying I think that. I'm saying that's what it might suggest to outsiders."

Wrath jerks his chin at me. "Why you encouraging this anyway? You know damn well you don't want her away from you for forty-some hours a week."

At first I was amused, but this entire situation quickly got out of hand. Deep down in a place I'd rather not acknowledge, I'm annoyed with Hope for sticking me in this position.

CHAPTER TWENTY

ROCK

Between our compromised crop, GSC taking up residence in my lower colon, and Hope's despondency, I'm close to my breaking point.

As if all that shit isn't giving me enough of an ulcer, I get a call from the president of the Wolf Knights MC. Their territory borders ours, and we enjoy a friendly, respectful relationship. We've definitely teamed up to handle our other rival—the Vipers—a lot in the last few years.

Other than that, we don't generally do social calls. Except Wrath, who has a working relationship with the sergeant-at-arms of their club, through his gym. Maybe once or twice a year, I'll close down Crystal Ball and host a party where the two clubs mix, just to keep things friendly.

Ulfric isn't looking for a party invitation tonight.

The daughter of one of his members disappeared. Right off the street in downtown Slater—his territory.

"She's twenty, and you fuckin' know how they are. Nose always buried in their cell phones, not payin' fuckin' attention." Ulfric's worked up, and I can't blame him.

"You sure it's Viper? That's pretty fuckin' bold pullin' that shit right in your territory."

"No, I don't fuckin' know for sure," he snaps. "Someone saw her get pulled into one of those pedo vans with the blacked-out windows. Who the fuck else would it be?"

A lotta people, but I keep that thought to myself for now. "Gimmie her description. I know a guy with an in. I'll see what I can find out."

"That gonna cost you?"

It'll fuckin' cost me all right, 'cause my "in" is fuckin' Loco, who's already such a pain in my goddamn ass the thought of askin' the gangsterfuck for a favor is making me see red. "Yeah. Give me a day at least."

"Fuck, Rock. I appreciate it. Cops won't do a motherfuckin' thing. Told us she probably ran off with a boyfriend and we should handle it 'in house.'"

That's a bad sign that Ulfric doesn't have *any* friends in the Slater PD willing to appease him in this matter. Especially since they're known to be one of the shadiest police departments in the area, and I know Ulfric drops a lot of cash to them on a regular basis. "That's a problem, my friend."

"Yeah, no shit. Let me know what you find out."

As soon as I'm off the phone with him, I put in my call to Loco. He's naturally a dick, as I suspected.

"Rock, this is a pretty big favor. You ready to do that thing we talked about?"

"I'm working on it," I grit out through clenched teeth. While I mentioned the introduction Loco wants me to make, we didn't take an official vote on it yet. Thank fuck all I need is a majority, 'cause I know for sure Wrath's vote will be a big, fat, fucking no.

"Okay. Stay close to your phone. I'll see what I can find out," he promises.

It's so late, there's not much chance I'll hear from him tonight. I'm very relieved to end my day and go upstairs to see my girl. Things have been tense between us ever since she announced her job interview. She seems to think I'm more upset about it than I actually am. Other than the brief discussion Z, Wrath, and I had, I haven't had time to give it a lot of thought. Ultimately, if it will make her happy, I want her to do it.

Unfortunately, my bullshit day isn't over.

Motherfuckin' Loco gets back to me quicker than I expected and wants to meet. Tonight. *Now.*

Another fuckin' night away from my girl when we're already on shaky ground.

"I think you'll be pleased. This time *I* got a delivery for *you*."

Oh yeah, I'm fuckin' thrilled.

I round up my guys and give Ulfric a heads up.

There's no fuckin' way he's coming with us to meet Loco, but I do want him close by if this is what I think it is. "Don't know it's your girl. Hang at CB for a bit. I'll come to you when I'm done."

"Yeah. Sorry to be draggin' you into my bullshit, Rock. Having you and your crew out in the goddamn middle of the night like this ain't right. I owe you."

And I know he'll repay his debt. Ulfric's an honorable guy, and he's helped us out in the past when we've needed it.

Teller needs to be reminded of this when he starts bitching about the drive down to Empire.

"Two hours tops. Small price to pay for a club that's had our back more than once. Quit fuckin' whining," Z grumbles.

Murphy has no opinions, which is surprising. Usually he's full of them.

Wrath insists on joining us since we're taking the van.

I gotta run up to my room and grab some stuff before we can leave.

So wrapped up in whatever she's looking at, Hope doesn't hear me enter the room. Ulfric's words rattle in my memory. My girl's never aware of her surroundings either.

Except she should feel safe and secure enough to lose herself in a book or whatever the fuck she's doing when she's in *my* clubhouse.

I'm just on fuckin' edge because of this shit goin' on tonight. Edgy and irritable. "What you looking at, babe?"

She startles and glances up, slamming the book shut and tucking it under the blanket at the foot of her lounge chair. Odd.

"Nothing. Is everything okay?"

No. Everything is not okay. But I can't talk about this with Hope because I don't even know what *this* is yet. Besides, I can't shake the sense she's hiding something from me lately, and I'm determined to figure out what it is.

"I'm fine. What was that?"

"Nothing." She gets up and walks toward me, but the worry lines etched in her face have me on alert.

"What's wrong?"

"Nothing."

She's infuriating. "Stop saying nothing, Hope."

She glares at me and crosses her arms over her chest. But her posture is to cover up something else. The anguish in her eyes is clear. Panic blazes through me because somehow I'm failing her, and I don't know how to fix it.

It's obvious she's been crying, but she's trying to hide it from me for some reason.

"Hope, I'm tired of you not talking to me. Something's bothering you, and you need to tell me."

Her lips part, but she stops herself and rolls her eyes. "This again? I'm fine. Stop making shit up. Are you still mad about the interview? Fine, I won't go. Does that make you happy?"

"It's not about the interview. Fuckin' go or don't. I don't give a shit."

Her lower lip trembles.

I should have said it a little nicer, but it really isn't about the interview or even the past few days. Whatever this is has been brewing since her run-in with that fuckin' sister-in-law of hers and the following conversation with her sorry excuse for a mother that I pushed her into. Somehow I just *know* I didn't get the full story about either event.

"Why do you keep trying to pick a fight with me, Rock?"

"That what you think?"

"I know it. You're mad at me all the time lately."

"I'm not."

She shakes her head, hugging her arms tighter to her chest.

"You call Wing Fling or whatever the place is back yet?" I don't even know why I'm asking. At the moment, I couldn't give two fucks about it. But I know by the way she flinches what her answer will be.

"Not yet."

"Why are you stalling?"

That fuckin' flinch again. Fuck, now she *is* pissing me off.

"Rock! We gotta go!" Murphy shouts from the hallway.

Her gaze skips to the door, then back to me. "You're going out?"

"I gotta handle something."

She nods. I swear to fuck Hope is the only woman I've ever known who can nod sarcastically.

My club bullshit has to be wearing her down. I knew it would eventually. I can't be some nine-to-five drone for her. I've never lied to her about that, and I think she's finally starting to get it. She seemed okay when I opened up to her about our business, but maybe it forced her to rethink our situation. Maybe she's rethinking *us.*

"Look. Maybe we need to slow down. Take a break from everything. You don't seem like you're into gettin' married." The words tumble out of my mouth like garbage. What the fuck is wrong with me? Why did I even say that? I don't mean a word of it.

Yet I don't take back the words.

She gasps and tears fill her eyes. I didn't mean to make her cry, again, but I don't know what else to do to get through to her. I can't fix this if she won't tell me what's wrong.

"You don't..." She trails off and stands there staring at her hand.

At her ring.

Fuck.

My girl's got a fuck ton of pride. I should know better by now. What I'm doing is *not* the way to handle her. From experience, I know she copes with stress by running.

She stiffens her spine and jerks her chin up. "Okay. If that's what you want."

No, that's not what I fucking want at all. But we're locked into some sort of game of relationship chicken, both of us too proud to call it off.

Both of us about to lose.

In a trance, I watch as she slips off her ring and sets it on my dresser. "I'll, uh, go home and—"

There's one big fuckin' problem. If we lived together, she wouldn't be able to run away every time shit gets uncomfortable for her.

"Yeah, *whatever*. I'm done. I gotta go."

I have to get out of here. I'm a fuckin' coward for daring her to leave like that. With my head all fucked up, I have to go take care of business. I despise this feeling of being torn in two. I should stay and tell her I'm sorry, I don't mean it, and shake the truth out of her.

But I don't.

HOPE

Leaving the clubhouse is easy. Stunned, I wait in Rock's room until I hear the last of the guys leave.

Before I go, I pluck a piece of paper and a pen out of my purse and scratch out a quick note. If I leave it under his pillow, I know he'll see it.

It's too risky to pack up all my crap. I can't chance Trinity trying to stop me. I can't tell her what just happened, because I'm not even sure what to say. I grab a few things I need and leave.

Head held high.

No tears.

This is for the best. That's all that goes through my head on the way home. Rock's under a lot of stress. If I keep adding to it, he's going to get distracted and end up getting hurt.

This is for the best.

But it still hurts so fucking much.

CHAPTER TWENTY-ONE

ROCK

WHEN I GET BACK THREE HOURS LATER, I'M NOT SURPRISED HOPE'S GONE.

We successfully delivered the girl into Ulfric's hands, and I washed my hands of the whole thing. Turns out she was shacked up with one of Loco's guys. I explained the ridiculous situation to Ulfric—which included the words 'kidnap fantasy,' mind you—right in front of the girl. Her mortification didn't lessen my irritation in the slightest. I feel for Ulfric, though. He cashed in a big favor—or rather had me cash in one—on what amounted to childish bullshit. He's pretty fuckin' embarrassed.

I'm as gracious as can be for a guy who just torched his engagement.

Yeah, I basically dared Hope to leave, and if anything, my stubborn girl never backs down from a challenge. Her fucking ring sits on the dresser, mocking me.

I shove it in a box and stuff it in the back of one of my dresser drawers.

She left a note tucked under my pillow. Too numb, I fold it up without reading it and stash it in my nightstand.

After the shit I pulled, there's no way she's coming back tonight.

If she comes back at all.

Why did I have to go and fuck up everything with the only woman I've ever given a shit about?

I should call her.

My gaze catches on her bookshelf, everything still in its place. A glance in her closet helps the knot in my chest loosen. My messy girl's clothes are thrown everywhere. Like always.

Maybe we're not doomed after all.

As I drop onto her lounge chair, her scent wraps around me. Somehow it makes me more miserable. Something digs into the side of my thigh, and I yank it out. The book she'd been flipping through when I barged in and acted like such an asshole.

Except it's not a book.

It's her wedding album.

Fuck. Do I… should I… open it?

It's heavy in my hands. White with scrolling gold designs on the front.

The first shots are all Hope. So fuckin' young. All wrapped up in white lace and satin, she made a beautiful bride—no surprise there. Her face is fuller, but I recognize a lot of the same expressions she makes now. There's an older woman who looks a lot like Hope that I assume is her mother. In every picture of them together, the tension in Hope's face is clear.

Sophie doesn't look much different than she does now. She's in most of the shots, helping Hope get ready. I recognize Lilly by her rack. Mara's there too. Clay's sister looked like a bitch even back then.

It's hard to look at the photos of Clay, knowing what's comin' for the poor bastard in a few short years. Knowing I'm in the shadows waitin' to steal his wife.

Fuck.

Through all the chaos of the day, they seem happy together.

The last photo is the newlyweds standing nose to nose, staring into each other's eyes

That one's the hardest.

Something slips out of the back of the album, fluttering to the floor. Snatching it up and turning it over, I freeze.

Even a guy like me knows what a fuckin' sonogram picture looks like.

Kendall, Hope in unmistakable black and white, right next to a very clear date. I flip to the front of the wedding album.

She was pregnant when they got married.

Did they get married because *she was pregnant?*

Obviously *something* happened. I try to think back to when we first met. I'd wondered if she'd been with her husband for so long, why didn't they have any kids?

I remember when I proposed, how anxious she was about the possibility of not being able to have children. She worried I'd end up hating her.

Has she suspected all along she might have some problem? I don't think so, because she seemed surprised in the hospital. Why wouldn't she confide in me about this? I've tried telling her how much I don't care. She's all that matters to me.

I stare at the picture again and a spark of anger lights in my chest. After what we went through together—she almost *died*—why the fuck didn't she tell me about this? Did she think I wouldn't want to hear about something that involved Clay? Does she think I'm really that much of a jealous dick?

Christ, I think of all the times she's busted my ass over being honest with her.

But she's been hiding this from me since day one.

HOPE

Over the last week, I've picked up the phone to call Rock dozens of times.

But I never follow through.

I leave the tracking app installed on my phone. He knows where to find me.

After spending so much time at the clubhouse, being back in my house again is quiet and lonely.

Work suddenly picks back up. Adam has some cases he needs me to help him with, and it feels good to have something else to focus on.

Coming home every night is dismal. It doesn't feel like home anymore. Any happy memories have been tainted by all the sadness I've gone through since Clay died. I know it's time to let it go because it just feels empty. I've never been so alone. Even after Clay died, I was wallowing in so much grief at least I didn't know how alone I was.

Now that I've had Rock in my life, a taste of what it's like to be part of a family, the loneliness is prominent.

Every day, when I come home from the office, I expect to find Rock waiting in my driveway. He never is, so I spend the rest of my nights convincing myself I'm not disappointed. I'm scared I might have finally irrevocably pushed him away.

I struggle to keep moving forward. I don't know what to do. Should I call Rock? I can't bear the thought of him rebuffing my attempt to make things better.

What does he want from me?

Even worse, does he want me anymore?

"Jeez, Hope. Would it kill you to answer your damn phone once in a while?" Mara scolds me Friday night.

Crap. "Sorry, Mara. I'm a bad friend. I don't know why you put up with me." And I don't. Calling people, maintaining friendships, has never come naturally to me. I hate to bother people or burden them with my problems.

Mara has a beautiful baby girl to take care of. She doesn't need to hear me whine about my broken engagement.

Besides, I hate needing people. You get used to it, and then suddenly they're gone.

Rock was different. He needed me to need him, so after getting over my initial awkwardness, it didn't seem so odd.

Then I screwed it up, so once again, I have no one.

"Hope, are you there?" Mara snaps me back to the present.

"I'm here."

"Good. I need some adult girl time. You up for it?"

There's no sense in isolating myself further. "I guess. What did you have in mind?"

"Gee, don't sound so enthusiastic." Her aggrieved voice makes me laugh for the first time in days.

"Sorry. Yes, Mara, that sounds awesome! There, is that better?"

"Not really. What's Sophie up to? Maybe we need her to spice things up."

"I don't know. I spoke to her a little while ago, told her what happened, but haven't heard from her since." I just assumed Sophie was sick of dealing with my drama, so I hadn't wanted to bug her anymore, but I keep that to myself.

Mara's soft chuckle is comforting. I've missed her. While Sophie was my wild friend in law school, the one I went to concerts and barhopping with, Mara was my study buddy. There are definitely some classes I wouldn't have made it through if it hadn't been for her. All those late-night sessions in the library forged a pretty strong friendship, even if we don't always keep in regular contact. When we do get together, it's always as if no time has gone by.

"Anyway," she says, breaking into my thoughts again. "Damon is taking Cora to visit his mother this weekend. How about a girls' night?"

"Why aren't you going?"

"Because I've been a good girl and my reward is *not* having to visit Mrs. Oak," she says without any laughter, but I envision her biting her lip not to giggle on the other end. I forgot how much Mara doesn't care for her socialite mother-in-law. I imagine that makes life difficult for Damon, but he always seems to put Mara's needs first.

Saturday night, we dress up and go to the movies of all things. It's fine because I'm so inside my head, I don't have the energy to keep up a conversation. I should know better, though. Mara is a master at interrogation when she wants to be. She should have been in the military.

We're back at her house and on our second glass of red wine when she pounces.

"So did you call Rock yet?"

"No. He knows where to find me."

She gives me a withering look. "It's not like you to play games, Hope."

"I'm not. He ended it. I'm not going to grovel for him to take me back." That's a lie, though. I'd do anything to be back in his arms.

"*Did* he end it? Or did you shut him out until he didn't know what else to do?"

That feels uncomfortably close to the truth, so I ignore it.

Her two French bulldogs, Bing and Macy, jump up on the couch. Bing snorts as he makes his way into my lap. I can't help scratching behind his big bat ears, making him snort even louder.

"He loves you," Mara says with a chuckle.

"I missed these little guys." Bing curls into a ball and falls asleep in my lap. I keep petting him absently as he snores. "How do they feel about Cora?"

"Oh my God, they love her. They follow her everywhere. Mostly because she leaves a trail of food in her wake." She rubs Macy's plump tummy affectionately. "But I think they're enjoying the peace and quiet."

"I can imagine. What about you?"

"I never thought I'd like being a mother so much, Hope. But even so, I need some peace and quiet too every now and then."

"Think you'll have another one?"

Her mouth twists into a smirk. "If Damon has his way, yes."

I'm happy for my friend. I can't help feeling a little sad about my own defects in the baby-making department, though.

"Please don't take this the wrong way, Hope. I know you think you're strong and independent. And you are. But you of all people aren't meant to be alone. You're so sweet and so full of love. You need someone to share it with. Beyond that, you need someone to anchor you and push you when you need a push." She says it all in a rush, but each word reaches me like a pinprick in my heart. At the word "anchor," my hand automatically reaches up and my fingers trace the pendant Rock gave me. An image of the tattoo with my name inked on his hip flashes in my mind, and I almost choke on my wine.

I snort to cover up how vulnerable her words make me feel. "Yeah, he pushed me right out the door."

Mara flings a *don't bullshit me* scowl at me. "I've known you a long time now. Clay never challenged you. Rock seems like he's good at that. Even more so, he seems to understand the real you. What you *need*."

"You don't think Clay did, do you?"

Mara sighs and looks away. "Honey, I'm not going to speak ill of Clay. I liked him. He was always nice. I'm sure he cared about you. But I don't know. You two always seemed so independent of each other."

"We had demanding careers."

"I have no right to judge. I don't know what you had behind closed doors. No one does but you. You pretend to be hard. To be a lawyer, you have to be as tough as the boys are. Believe me, I understand that. But you're so soft under that tough exterior. You should be with someone who gets that about you."

I *pfft* into my wine glass. "Rock says that's what he likes about me. His friend Wrath says Rock needs my softness."

"See? And you need his hardness."

I burst out laughing.

Mara holds up her hand. "Let it pass, Hope," she demands with a regal but teasing expression. Once we have the giggles under control, she continues. "He's *hard* and demanding. But from what you've told me, and what I've seen, he takes care of you. There's nothing wrong with that. You're soft, but you're not weak."

"I feel pretty damn weak."

"I understand that. I do. But it's not weak to need someone. It's okay to let him take care of you. He needs to be needed, and you need to feel wanted. Together you're—"

If she says "complete," I'll burst into tears. "Is this some sort of strength through submission lecture?"

From her doleful eyes, even my alcohol-addled brain recognizes that was a pretty rude thing to say.

"I'm sorry," I whisper.

"It's okay. A couple years ago, I probably would have felt the same way." Her downcast voice shames me even more.

"It just feels very one-sided."

Mara shakes her head, red-gold curls bouncing from side to side. I'm relieved she has a more cheerful expression back in place. "It's not, though. Those kinds of men are enriched by having someone to take care of. Besides, I bet there are a lot of things you do for Rock that you don't even realize."

My mouth quirks up.

"Besides the obvious."

"I don't know about that."

But I remember our trip to Sway's clubhouse. Besides the scorching sex, he said I made things better for him just by being there. "Maybe."

"Hell, I'm pretty much talking out of my ass here. Feel free to blame it on the wine."

I reach over and squeeze her hand. "No, you're not."

"You gave the ring back, huh?"

"Of course."

"How much of your stuff had you moved into his place?"

"I don't know. Just clothes. Some books. I keep waiting to find everything dumped on my doorstep."

She arches a brow at me. "You left stuff behind?"

"Yeah."

She makes a happy humming noise.

"What?"

"Nothing." She pins me with her courtroom stare. Thank God we've never been on opposite sides of a case before. "You ever going to get rid of your house?"

"What?"

She shrugs. "I don't know. Just seemed like you were half in, half out with Rock. Probably drove him nuts."

"What are you talking about?"

"Were you planning to have him move into your house?"

"No. That would probably be uncomfortable for him. We never— no." Thinking over the last few months, one thing pops in my head. "He did ask me about it a while ago, but I said I wasn't ready."

"Let me guess." She sighs knowingly. "He never mentioned it again?"

"No."

"You probably hurt his feelings."

"What? I doubt it." I shake my head. No. That's not possible.

"Goddamn, you're dense. Just because he's a hard ass doesn't mean he doesn't have feelings."

I want to snap at her, except she's right and I know it. "When he proposed, he brought me to a site he picked out on the club's property to build a house on," I whisper.

"Wow. That's awfully romantic. You're an idiot. He wants to build you a friggin' house. Build a life with you." She shakes her head and finishes her wine.

I wave my free hand in the air. "You moved into Damon's house," I point out like a whiny child.

Mara of course calls me on it. "Nice try. But he'd only lived here a few months and never with another woman."

Bing lifts his head and snorts at me. Jeez, even Mara's dogs are judgmental.

"You remember how excited Clay and I were when we finally were able to afford our own house?"

She nods. "I remember, honey."

"Both of us moved around so much when we were kids. We so badly wanted to put down roots somewhere."

"I know." Suddenly, she sits up and takes my hand. "Your memories of Clay aren't in that house, honey. They're in here"—she taps my chest—"and here." Then she taps the side of my head. "Selling the house won't take away those memories."

"I keep telling myself it's a bad market."

"It's a terrible market," she agrees.

"I finally gave away Clay's clothes and stuff a few months ago. I felt like a real bitch."

She rolls her eyes, lightening the mood a bit. "Why? Were you planning to wear them?"

CHAPTER TWENTY-TWO

HOPE

"Come on, Hope. This is a great criminal case. Guy got caught selling dime bags out of an ice cream truck. How can you say no to that?"

Adam called me in to help him out today, but by "help" he meant "take this crappy case someone referred to me." I'm not falling for it.

"I'm done being the pot lawyer."

He shakes his head, but the corners of his mouth twitch, so I know he's not really mad about my refusal.

"What about some estate planning stuff? I'm drowning here." Adam isn't begging. Not yet anyway.

"I guess I wouldn't mind giving that a try. I barely remember anything from Trusts and Estates, though."

"I know. I'll walk you through it. Don't worry."

"Fine."

I should have known the little bugger was up to something, because the first client he "needs help" with is Teller.

Dammit.

Sweet as always, Teller gives me a quick hug. "How you doin'?"

"Good."

Adam saunters into the waiting room with a big, welcoming smile. "Good afternoon, Mr. Whelan." The guys shake hands, and Adam gestures to me. "If you don't mind, I'd like to have my associate, Ms. Kendall, sit in on our consultation. She's going to be assisting with some of my estate matters."

I make an *I-hope-you-choke* face at Adam.

Teller's mouth lifts in a half smirk. "That's fine. I know *Ms. Kendall* well."

"Oh, that's right," Adam says in an obnoxious, fake-surprised voice. "She represented you in a family matter. I remember now."

How unprofessional would it be if I gave Adam the finger in front of a client?

The three of us take seats around the conference room table. I fight back memories of a time when Rock sat across from me at this table, and I try to focus on the problems Teller's having with the trust his grandmother set up for Heidi.

Adam is far better at time management than I am. The consultation is over in exactly fifty-five minutes. Teller didn't like some of what Adam explained, but I assure him it's standard and we'll work it out.

I walk Teller out and he pauses at the door. I'm afraid to ask about anything related to Rock or the club, but I'm worried about Heidi and want to know if she's okay.

"How's Heidi?"

He grins from ear to ear. "A pain in my ass. Other than that, she's good. I know you're busy, but she'd really like to see you."

Busy has nothing to do with it. "I'd love to see her. Is that...? Can I...?" *Crap.*

"Heidi can have friends outside the club, Hope. I just figured if you weren't with Rock, you didn't want to be bothered with her."

I kind of want to smack him. Yes, the "outside the club" part hurt, but what I'm mad about is he assumes Heidi was some sort of obligation I'm happy to be rid of now that Rock and I are... whatever we are.

"Of course not. Gosh, you better not have said that to her. I don't want her thinking that."

Teller seems surprised, and I try not to hold it against him. He's still young. Plus, he's a guy. He doesn't know he's being a nitwit.

"Have her call me."

"Okay. I, uh, have to go out of town Friday. She gets out of school early, and I usually pick her up and take her to lunch..." He shrugs.

"I'd love to. Fridays are good for me. Are you going to be gone long?"

"Nah. I'll be back Friday night. Quick run."

Club business. I want to ask so bad if Rock's going. But what does it matter?

None of *my* business.

After he promises to have Heidi call, he takes off. The rumbling sound of his bike as he starts it up almost makes me cry.

"You okay, counselor?" Adam asks from behind me.

I count to five before turning around. "Yeah, I'm good."

ROCK

Without Hope here in the mornings, Trinity doesn't join us for breakfast anymore, something I suspect annoys the shit out of Wrath, because he's in a fouler mood than usual.

No one knew what to say when I announced Hope and I were taking a break. Or no one dared voice an opinion on the subject.

"You sure you won't fuck this up, little man?" Wrath sneers at Teller.

"Fuck you, dick. You act like I've never done a drop before," Teller snips back.

Time to interrupt this nonsense. I point at both of them. "You two are givin' me a fuckin' headache. Stump won't be at this drop. It's his RC and a prospect. It's not a lot of product. Should be quick and easy. Plain car, though. No bikes. I'm gettin' tired of Loco knowing every fuckin' step we take."

Teller makes a what-the-fuck face. "I know. We're gonna stop and see Grinder, so we're not flyin' colors either."

"Fine. Good. See if he has an update on his transfer request."

"You want me to ride out separate, maybe lead any GSC tails in the opposite direction?" Z asks.

I actually like that idea a lot. "Yeah. But not alone. Take Dex or Ravage with you."

Murphy slides his gaze to Teller, and my radar goes up. These two sneaky fucks have a way of communicating without words. "You let Bug know you can't pick her up Friday?" Murphy asks.

"Yeah, Hope's taking her out to lunch," Teller answers without looking at me.

Wrath turns his head from the table to cough-snicker, and he's lucky he's still recovering from his broken leg or I'd kick him. Everyone else remains silent. Waiting for my head to explode, I guess.

"How'd that come about?" I ask.

"She sat in on the meeting I had with her lawyer friend about Heidi's trust. I guess she's doing estate planning stuff with him."

"Why? She hates that stuff."

Teller shrugs. "I dunno. Probably needs the money."

My hands are fisted so tight my knuckles ache. Wrath notices but doesn't comment on it.

"I'm sure Heidi will like that," I say as calmly as possible.

When a respectable amount of time passes and the guys go back to bullshitting, I make my exit.

Of course, I can't leave without someone tagging along to annoy the shit out of me. Today it's Z.

I push my way into the office, but he's right behind me.

"Prez, this break thing is killing you. Go talk to her," Z says, slamming his fist into my desk.

"There's nothing to say right now." Which is a total lie.

"The fuck there isn't. Why you being so hard on her?"

Am I? I'm not. I want her to get her shit sorted out. "She won't talk to me about what's bothering her, and we need some space."

"You're such a dick. She probably doesn't want to hurt your feelings. I've never met a woman who's more worried about everyone else's feelings than her own."

Hurt my feelings? I'm her fucking man. Or I was. I can take anything she wants to put on me.

Z cocks his head. "You mad she's still upset about her husband?"

"No. Fuck no. They were together a long time. She wouldn't be the woman I love if she just fuckin' forgot about him."

"You want her to mourn you like that," he states.

I've never thought about it in such blunt terms. "Probably."

He glances out the window and seems to be considering what he wants to say. "Fuck, man—that ride we went on, she practically begged me to make sure nothing happened to you. She fuckin' loves you. Why you punishing her?"

"Shut your fuckin' mouth. You don't even know what the fuck you're talking about."

"Fine. Keep being a dick. But don't you fuckin' forget I lived through the shit Carla pulled. Whether you want to admit it or not, she cut you deep. Anyone who knows you knows you don't just love Hope for her hot little ass."

"For someone who claims to know me so well, you're dangerously close to getting your own ass kicked for speakin' about her that way."

Z shrugs off my threat. "I saw the way you fell for her the day you met, Rock. We all did."

"Shut up."

"We watched you clean up your act after her husband died too."

Surprised, I stare at him.

He shakes his head at me, like I'm one dumb motherfucker. "You weren't foolin' no one."

My fists clench and unclench as I consider how much to say. "It's not only her husband. It's other stuff, too. And she won't... she wouldn't talk to me about it. I can't fix shit if she won't tell me."

"Brother, it's not on you to fix everything in the goddamn world. I know you think it is for some reason. It makes you a good president, but you gotta cut yourself a break." He stops but keeps staring at me. Hell only knows what he's gonna come up with next.

"I know we never talked about it, but I was there in the hospital with you two. Losing a baby is rough. Especially on a girl like her. She's already been through so much."

I can't fucking breathe. In my life, I've been stabbed exactly twice. The pain in my chest right now is worse than either of those times.

"That's part of it." I can't talk to him about the picture I found because I don't even know what it all means yet. Won't know unless I talk to Hope.

Fuck.

HOPE

Mara's not-so-friendly advice has been eating at me all week.

It also gives me the kick in the ass I need.

Every afternoon when I come home, I click on the radio and work for a couple hours, packing things up. When I want to give up and crawl under the covers, I just keep pushing.

"You hated skiing. You're never going to ski," I grumble at myself. Into the donation pile go the skis Clay insisted we buy for a trip we took to Vermont one Christmas. I have plenty of nice memories from that trip. None of them involve the skis.

Clay read spy thrillers. Stuff I can't stand. They fill up three cardboard boxes.

I sniffle a little thinking of the bookshelf in Rock's bedroom. Mostly nonfiction history books. I push it out of my mind before I start crying.

By the end of the week, I almost have everything boxed up or tagged. I'm so close I stay up way past midnight to finish. Over the radio, I catch a news report about a body found in the Hudson River. My brain catches on the phrase *gang related,* and I jump up, racing over to the radio to turn it up.

It's a club. Not a gang. I know Rock takes exception to people referring to the Lost Kings as a gang. But does the media care?

Would anyone tell me if something happened to Rock?

I'm standing there frozen with fear when another report comes on. This time I hear the story from the beginning.

Hispanic male. Late twenties.

Not Rock.

I let out a deep breath.

Convinced more than ever I need to hurry up, I finish packing and don't get to bed until almost four in the morning.

As much as I hate to admit it, I need help getting rid of everything. Goodwill says it will take two to three weeks to schedule a pickup.

I can't wait that long.

Sophie is still hard to get ahold of. I could probably call her brother Ben and he'd help me out. But I know he works odd hours, so I feel weird bothering him.

Lilly and I have been getting together more regularly on our own. When I explain my dilemma, she immediately offers up her brother Alex and his truck.

"I've only met him once or twice. I can't ask him—"

"Trust me. He won't mind. Besides, *I'll* ask him. He can't say no to his baby sister."

"Lilly—"

"Stop. I'm so proud of you for finally doing this. Let me help you finish it."

Crap. I feel like such a pathetic charity case. "Thanks, Lilly. I appreciate it."

I'd forgotten how big Lilly's brother is. Except for the more awkward-to-carry things, he waves off most of our offers to help him load in the furniture.

"Everything, Hope? Are you sure?" Lilly asks.

I'm a little sad to see the couch and dining table go. "Yeah. Everything with a green tag goes. Red tags stay. I'll put them out in the storage container when it gets here. Except the bedroom set. That stays too." I need someplace to sleep. At least for one more night.

The guilt I'd been expecting doesn't come.

What does show up is the personal storage container I ordered. As we're finishing loading things into Alex's truck, the company drops it off. The driver hands me the information for how to schedule the move when I'm ready. I walk around the box a few times. Whatever doesn't fit in it doesn't get to come into the next phase of my life.

Whatever that may be.

CHAPTER TWENTY-THREE

ROCK

"WHAT DO YOU MEAN? WHAT GUY?" I SHOUT INTO MY PHONE. I'M AT THE building site for the house I planned to share with my *wife*, so my mental state is already pretty much shot. This news is *not* what I needed.

Hoot's strained voice through the phone makes it clear how thankful he is not to be standing in front of me while giving this report. "I don't know. Her friend with the big tits is with her too."

Fucking Lilly. What is it with her trying to set Hope up?

"What are they doing?"

Hoot sighs. Poor fucker's been on Hope detail for more days than I care to count. Under threat of an ass kicking, he hasn't mentioned it to anyone else. If he wants to drop his prospect rocker and earn his three-piece patch, he'll keep doing what I ask without complaint.

Yeah, I know I'm a dick. I've made my peace with it.

"Dropping a bunch of shit off at Goodwill."

"What kind of stuff?"

The exasperation in his voice is clear, but he still answers with respect. "I don't know, prez. Some furniture. Boxes. I can't get closer without them seeing me."

"That's good. Stay on her." I'm out of my fucking goddamn mind.

The guy Z hired to help with the construction stuff that was beyond his expertise stands there staring at me, waiting for instructions.

Z finally got his wish. The club bought a subcompact tractor—not just for this project; Z has lots of plans for it—and together, we did a lot of the site preparation. When we hit bedrock and needed heavier equipment, Z called in some of his contacts.

"We're ready to pour the concrete," Jasper informs me.

"It's not too cold?"

"No."

"Good. Do it."

Storming into the clubhouse office, I throw open the door so hard it bounces off the wall, startling Z.

"What the fuck, man?" he grouches.

I don't have patience for his bullshit today. "You still talk to Lilly?"

"Yeah, every now and then. Why?"

"Will she think it's weird if you text her right now?"

Z's already pulling out his phone. "No. Give me a sec."

"Just ask what she's up to."

"Yeah, okay."

The wait for a response seems to take forever. While we wait, he asks me if I'm going ahead with the construction.

"Yes," I spit out through clenched teeth.

Z doesn't say anything. For once, he keeps his smirk and opinions to himself.

Of course, when his phone pings back, a look of recognition settles on Z's face. Great, now my brother knows how fucking insane I am. "She says she's out with her brother and Hope." A sly grin twitches at the corner of his mouth, but he holds it back. "What's going on?"

I relax at the news that it's Lilly's brother. "Nothing."

"Hang on. She says they needed her brother's truck because they're getting rid of a bunch of Hope's stuff."

A spark lights in my chest.

What's my girl up to?

HOPE

"You'll never believe who just texted me," Lilly says with a giggle as she slides her phone into her pocket.

"Who?"

"Z."

My heart seizes. After a deep breath, I grab the next box with renewed purpose. "Oh yeah. How's he doing?"

"Okay, I guess." She grabs another box and follows me inside the back of the Goodwill store where we drop our loads. Alex is busy carrying two of my end tables inside. I don't even know how I'm going to repay these two for all their help. I've only met Alex maybe two or three times, yet he's been so kind all day. Drove his truck down here to help me load all my crap and cart it to Goodwill. He hasn't complained once.

He's also driving me nuts because so far, he's refused my offer to fuel up the truck or feed him dinner. Not that I have anything left at the house to make dinner with.

That thought actually makes me laugh. I'm losing my mind.

When Lilly and I have a moment alone, I tap her arm. "What can I do for your brother? I have to at least pay him for gas."

Lilly shrugs. "Alex won't take your money."

Great.

Out of nowhere, Lilly chuckles. When she pulls her phone out again, I understand why. "He must want to get lucky," Lilly mutters.

She scrolls through the message. "Z wants to know how you're doing."

"Aw, that's so sweet. I miss him." I'm beside myself broken up over Rock. But beyond my broken heart, I miss Trinity and the guys. My lunch with Heidi was nice, but it also reminded me of how much I'd lost. Especially Z, who has always been sweet to me. All of them really became family.

Until I screwed it all up. In hindsight, Rock only asked if we should slow things down. Take a break from planning the wedding. I'm the one who heard "break up." I'm the one who left my ring. Left the clubhouse.

It's not like anyone in the club will still be friends with me if I'm not with Rock.

After more discussion, Alex finally lets me fill his truck at the station near my house.

While we're standing outside, filling the tank, he catches my eye. "What do you say to dinner one night, Hope?"

"Oh sure, you and Lilly should—"

He shakes his head. "No. I mean I want to take *you* out to dinner."

Oh. *Oh shit.* "I... I... Are you...? You mean a date?"

His full lips curl into a smile. "Yeah, if you need to label it. A date."

My heart pitters and my cheeks heat up. "I'm flattered. I like you a lot and appreciate all your help today. But I can't. I'm really not ready. I just got out of a serious..." Oh my God, I can't even finish the sentence. My eyes blink rapidly to clear the forming tears.

"Hey, hey. It's okay. I'm sorry, Hope. Shit. Lilly told me." He shakes his head. "I have the worst timing."

"It's not you. It's me. I'm a mess."

"I don't know about that."

The truck has a huge gas tank. It's taking forever to fill it, but I feel awkward walking away after rejecting him.

"Do you have any place to stay?" he asks.

"I have some leads."

He nods once. "That's good. Go ahead and get in the truck. You're starting to shiver."

After the awkward moment at the station, I'm not sure how to act around Alex. He's a classy guy, though, and doesn't make me feel bad about it. Of course, Lilly knows something's up. As they're getting ready to leave, she pulls me aside.

"What's wrong? You've been weird since we stopped for fuel."

Crap. I don't know what to tell her. My lips curve into a sad smile. "Alex asked me out."

"Oh shit. You want me to punch him?"

"No! Jeez. It was really sweet. I just feel bad. He's so nice. But—"

"You're not over Rock. I understand."

I glance down at my wringing hands. "I don't think I'll ever be over him, Lilly."

She gives me a wicked smile. "Can't blame you there."

"Thanks a lot."

Her mouth turns down, but her eyes still glitter with amusement. "Sorry."

"You're not mad at me for turning him down?"

"Fuck no. He's a big boy. He'll live. He's always liked you, though, so I'm not surprised." Her shoulders pull up in a quick shrug.

"Really? He barely knows me."

She tosses a pointed yet playful look my way. "You're hot and smart, his two favorite qualities in a woman."

I snort, then full-out laugh. "I don't know about either of those."

Lilly grins and pulls me in for a hug. "Take care of yourself. Call me if you need a place to stay. I have a guest room and wouldn't mind the company."

"Thank you. For everything."

Walking into my house feels weird. I can't believe how much better I feel letting go of all that *stuff* that had been weighing me down.

Still brimming with nervous energy, I decide to load up the storage pod.

The rumble of Harley pipes steals my attention as I'm carting boxes into the trailer. My heart thumps wildly at the sound.

Rock. *Oh my God.* I look like shit.

But it's not Rock. I almost cry from disappointment.

"Hi, Z—what are you doing here?" I shouldn't be surprised. He probably hoped to catch Lilly. "Lilly left about an hour ago."

His eyebrows draw down. "I didn't come to see Lilly." He shocks me by enveloping me in a warm hug, then pulls away, still holding my shoulders. "How you been, girl?"

"Okay. Did Rock send you?" I hate the pitiful hopeful note in my voice. Especially when Z's gaze darts away.

"No, sugar. I wanted to make sure *you* were doin' okay. See if you needed anything."

I can't swallow over the lump in my throat. "Thank you."

He lifts his chin toward the storage unit. "What's that?"

I shake my head, not quite sure how to explain. "Just getting rid of some stuff."

He nods but doesn't press me further.

I tilt my head at the house. "Do you want to come in? Want something to drink?"

"Nah, I can't stay, sweetheart. Thanks, though."

"How's Rock?" I blurt out before I lose my nerve.

He pins me with a fierce stare. "He's a miserable prick without you."

For some reason, laughter spills out of me. "I'm sorry," I say.

Z shakes his head. "Don't be sorry. Sometimes shit doesn't work out." He inclines his head as if he knows I'm on the verge of crying. "Sometimes you just need time to sort stuff out."

"Yeah."

"Everything will work out in the end."

I'm too choked up to get any words out, so I just nod even though I'm not sure if I agree with him.

ROCK

Some fucker has the nerve to knock on my door a little past midnight.

I came up here to get away from the party going on downstairs. I should have gone for a ride instead, because all I can see in this room is Hope. *Every-fucking-where.*

Opening my door, I find Teller. For some reason, he decided to bring the party to me, in the form of two club girls who can't be much older than eighteen. At least they better fuckin' be eighteen.

"What?" I bark at him.

"I wanted to introduce you to—"

Fucker doesn't finish because I grab him by his collar and yank him closer.

"Get lost," I growl at the girls. They take off running down the hall. "Are you fuckin' shittin' me?"

He wraps his hands around my arm, but I'm not done throttling his nosy ass yet.

"You've been so miserable. We thought you might benefit from some company."

The "we" is not lost on me, and I'm looking forward to cracking skulls tomorrow morning. "It's not your job to worry about who warms my bed." Disgusted, I toss him backward.

He staggers a bit before catching himself. "She's not coming back, prez. You had to know eventually she'd get tired of this."

I never knew Teller had such a fierce death wish. This time, I wrap my hand around his throat to make sure my message sticks. "What goes on between me and my ol' lady is *not* your business."

"Fuck. Fine," he gasps out while trying to pry my hand off his neck. I let him go and he braces his hands on his knees, gasping for air.

"After all the shit Hope's done for you and Heidi, *this* is how you fuckin' repay her?"

Finally, he has the decency to look embarrassed. "That's got nothin' to do with this."

"Like fuck it doesn't."

He shakes his head and stands up.

"By the way, why are you here in my business when you got a sister to be lookin' after?"

Teller's mouth opens and closes before he answers. "She's at a friend's house tonight."

"Fine. Go before I change my mind and choke you some more."

He slinks off down the hall, and I slam my door shut. When I was younger, I would have put my fists through the wall, kicked stuff, broken everything in sight.

Tomorrow. Tomorrow, I'll go down to the gym and work off some of my aggression.

Tonight? Tonight, I sit down on the bed and finally pull out the note Hope tucked under my pillow the night she left.

I'm sorry.

I love you.

Fuck. That's my girl. Sweet, simple, direct, and to the point. Z's right. I have been an asshole. I need to figure out how to fix this, and soon.

I can't sleep for shit and finally give up trying around four thirty. All my degenerate brothers should be asleep. Downstairs is a fucking mess.

Not my problem.

Flipping on the lights in the gym, I decide to start with some cardio before hitting the weights.

Maybe twenty minutes into my workout, Trinity's door across the hall opens and she wanders in.

"Morning, prez."

"Hey." She seems uncertain, and it dawns on me she's probably used to having the gym to herself this early in the morning.

"Am I in your way?"

Her eyes widen, and she shakes her head. After a bit, she hops on the treadmill next to me.

"You always up this early?"

"Yup," she answers.

She's quiet for a while after that.

"I miss having Hope here," she says after I get off the elliptical.

Fuck. "I know."

"You guys are good for each other."

Are we? She's good for *me*. She's what *I* need. I'm not so sure it works the other way around.

"You and Wrath getting along?" I'm such a dick for going there.

Trin's not mad, though. She grins at me. "Good deflecting, prez."

"I'm headin' upstairs. You gonna join us for breakfast today?"

"No. I have some stuff I need to take care of."

Shaking my head, I wave at her and head back upstairs.

Teller is absent at breakfast. Lucky for him. My hands still itch to wrap around his throat. Murphy's also conveniently missing. No surprise there.

Pointing my fork at Z and Wrath, I fix both of them with a glare. "Were you two in on Teller's plan last night?"

Wrath snorts and Z shakes his head.

"Please. We're more subtle than those two asshats," Wrath answers with a smirk that I want to plant my fist in.

"I don't think you'd know subtle if it kicked you in your thick head."

"Look who's talkin' about havin' a thick head," Z mouths off.

"You have some more fuckin' advice for me, brother?" I spread my arms wide. "I'm all fuckin' ears. You're such a relationship expert. Lay it on me."

His mouth twists and his eyes narrow. Z is pretty mellow most of the time. But he's one of the most lethal motherfuckers I know. It takes a lot to piss him off. I seem to be working him to the brink. "Yeah, I got advice for you," he snaps.

"Good. I'm dying to hear it. Let me warn you—get it all out of your system now. We're running an MC here, not some fucking circle-jerk relationship counseling service."

Wrath snorts.

Turning my head, I pin him with a stare. "You got something you need to get off your chest too?"

"Yeah, here's some advice. You're being an asshole. Maybe Cinderella's better off without you after all."

"Fuck you. We'll work our shit out when we're good and ready."

Wrath turns to Z. "Tell him."

Z gives Wrath a weary look. "Thanks, fucker."

"Spill it," I spit at Z.

He shrugs. "I wouldn't keep waiting for whatever the fuck you're waiting for. Girl like her ain't gonna stay single long."

"What the fuck?" I swear if he gives me another smirky shrug, I'm gonna kick his ass.

"She won't. You know it, and I know it. No disrespect to her, but she's not the kind of woman who does well without a man. Hell, Lilly's brother already tried to push up on her."

"What the fuck you talkin' about?"

"Yesterday, when he helped her move all her shit, guess he asked her out. But Hope said no because she ain't over you."

Thank fuck. My heart's in my stomach, thinking about Hope with someone else. "Why are you waiting until now to tell me?"

He holds up his hands in surrender. "I just found out myself."

Wrath jumps in, surprised, I think, to find himself giving a fuck about any of this. "It's true. He got a text from Lilly a little while ago."

"Motherfuckin—"

Z interrupts the rant I'm about to go on. "As far as he knew, she's *single*. Beautiful woman. Ain't got no ring. No patch. Had to call another man with a truck to come help her out… Any dude's gonna see her as fair game. He won't be the last."

Z knows every one of my buttons to push.

Every. Single. One.

CHAPTER TWENTY-FOUR

HOPE

"It's a great starting price, Ms. Kendall. I'm sure you'll have a number of offers right away."

I honestly don't care. "Do what you have to."

Sheila pauses and gives all the empty space a sour look. "I wish you'd left furniture in the bedrooms."

I shrug because I don't care about that either. Let her work to earn her five percent commission. "Sorry, it couldn't be helped."

She sighs and slips her notes into her handbag. "Leo should have the sign in the ground in a few minutes. I'll put a lockbox on the door if that's okay? I'll call you before showing it to anyone, though."

"That's not necessary." One way or another, I won't be spending another night in this house.

After the realtor leaves, I wander outside. There's a white pickup truck full of lumber and signs at the end of my driveway. My "For Sale" sign looks pretty damn good right in the middle of the grass that borders the quiet, dead-end street.

The truck does a lazy circle in the cul-de-sac and leaves. After watching it disappear down the street, I pull out my cell phone. Blood thunders through my ears, drowning out the sounds in my quiet neighborhood. My stomach twists, but before I can chicken out, I send Rock a text.

I need to speak with you

I don't know what the hell I'll do if he doesn't answer.

Thankfully, I don't have to figure it out, because my phone vibrates almost immediately.

Where are you?

My house.

Give me 20.

Air rushes out of my lungs as relief washes through me. He's coming. I can do this. I *need* to do it now. Before someone else tells him.

It's another beautiful spring day. Warmer than yesterday, but not too warm. With the unpredictable weather we get in upstate New York, it could be like this until mid-June or it could be ninety degrees next week. So I sit down in the grass beside the *for sale* sign and soak up the pretty day while I wait.

I'm not waiting long until I hear the rumble of his bike. The sound sends a thrill through me.

He's here.

ROCK

Hope's ring burns a fucking hole in my pocket the entire way to her house. I can't describe the relief that went through me seeing her name pop up on my phone. The text she sent is so perfectly Hope. I'm a little ashamed she reached out to me first when I know damn well how hard that is for her.

There's not a thing in this world that could have stopped me from going to her. I don't know what she wants to talk about. It doesn't matter. I'm not leaving without her on the back of my bike. At least I know that much.

As always, her narrow road is quiet. I'm reminded of before we were together. All the times I drove by her house, dying to catch a glimpse of her. Then I finally had her, but I let her go. Pushed her away instead of helping her.

I'm lucky she wants to talk to me.

As I approach, I catch her sitting in the grass next to a big white for sale sign. My heart speeds up at the sight. Of her. Of the sign. What I pray like fuck she's brought me here to tell me. Her head tips up, her lips curving into the sweetest smile. I've missed that smile.

At the curb, I shut down the bike and take a moment to fill my lungs with air.

Hope unfolds herself from the ground. "Hi," she says softly.

I'm fighting every urge inside me to wrap her in my arms and kiss the ever-loving fuck out of her. I lift my chin at the sign. "What's this?"

Her hands flutter nervously in front of her. "I wanted you to... I wanted to tell you... for you to see. I put it up for sale today."

My heart constricts and I swallow hard. "You didn't have to do that."

"Yes. I did."

Her head drops and she stares at the grass for a few seconds before finally looking up and meeting my eyes.

"Will you come inside?"

It takes a minute to loosen my tongue. "Yeah. Sure, doll."

Her eyes widen in shock, but she nods, turns, and walks up the driveway. I catch up to her easily. Our arms brush, but her hands are stuffed in her pockets, so I do the same. With measured calm, I take in the storage container next to her garage. This could be something else. She might tell me she's decided to move to the other side of the country. I wouldn't put an impulsive move like that past my girl.

And then what the fuck would I do?

Follow her wherever the fuck she goes and drag her back home with me.

She holds the door open for me to follow her inside. As usual, Hope's a contradiction of shy and sexy. So sweet I want to lick her all over. So sexy I want to take her to the floor and fuck the hell out of her.

Without words, she walks me to her bedroom.

I stop dead when we cross the threshold.

It's bare. Empty.

Everything gone.

I don't know what to think, so I blurt out the first thing that pops in my thick skull. "Your whole bedroom set didn't fit in that little box outside?" I ask, jerking my thumb in the direction of her driveway.

"No. I sold it. To a nice young married couple. They came and got it this morning."

"Oh," I say lamely. "What are you going to do?"

Instead of answering, she walks over and opens her closet door. No more explosion of clothes inside. It's as empty as the rest of the room. Except for two big blue suitcases she rolls out. My heart skips. I can't fit those on the back of my bike.

"Well, I was hoping I could come home with you."

"No. You can't."

She reels back as if I slapped her, and I rush to correct myself. "I mean, Bricks and Winter moved into my house. I'm up at the clubhouse full time now."

Shiny tears threaten to fall, her cheeks reddening. "Oh. Sure. Okay. I, uh… My plan B was a hotel. It's—"

My girl's so nervous. Even all teary-eyed, she's beautiful, and I want to stop time just to take her in, but I can't stand another second of her hurting. Pulling her into my arms and running my hands over her back, I kiss the top of her head. "Baby doll, it's okay. Of course you're coming home with me. Did you honestly think I was leaving here without you?"

She pulls away and stares up at me, tears rolling down her cheeks. I swipe them away with my thumbs. "Please don't cry. Everything's going to be okay."

HOPE

I can't stop the tears. I hate that I've hurt him. "Rock. I'm so sorry. I don't ever want you to think you don't come first for me. You do."

"Baby, you've never made me feel that way."

I grasp his hand, kissing his scarred knuckles. "I love you. So much. More than anything. Please tell me you know that."

He hugs me tight against him, and I soak up all the comforting warmth his body offers. "I know you do. I'm not stupid. I know it hasn't been that long."

It surprises me that the first thing he mentions is Clay. "It's been more than two years."

"Doll, you spent most of your adult life with him. Two years is nothin'."

Have I ever known a more understanding and forgiving person? No, and I don't know what I did to deserve him. He needs to hear the full truth from me. I owe him that. "It's not just Clay. It's losing the baby. Not sure if I can give you any—"

"Hope. You have to talk to me. You can't keep shit like that from me."

"You have so much on your shoulders already. I'm so afraid if I distract you with my silly stuff or add to your stress—"

"Stop. I'm sorry I made you feel like you couldn't talk to me. You can—about anything. You had a life before me. I know that. Your loyalty, your devotion, it's why I fell in love with you in the first place. All those prior experiences made you who you are." He hesitates and runs his hand through his hair. "I think I've got my own fucking guilt, doll. I used to wish so fucking bad you could be mine. Knowing if he was still alive, I'd never have you, I feel like—"

I cry even harder at that. "I don't even know if that's true anymore."

Rock freezes and pins me with a shocked stare. "What?"

One of the painful things I'd been hiding comes out of me in a rush. "I don't. I love you so much. I know I told you Clay and I had a good marriage, and we did. But it wasn't anything near what you and I have."

I can't believe I said that out loud. I have to finish, though.

"Once that thought formed, I couldn't shake it. I started having these dreams where Clay and I divorced so I could be with you, and he was happy with someone else too. And then I'd wake up with such crushing guilt."

"Baby, why didn't you tell me—"

"Then that scene with Lynn made me feel so much worse... about everything."

"I could kill that fucking bitch," he growls.

"Not if I get to her first."

Laughter rumbles out of him and he shakes his head. "You are my little spitfire. Still proud of you for slapping her."

Nervous laughter bubbles out of me. Especially the way he's staring down at me with a more serious expression settling over his features. "I want you to talk to me about *whatever* is on your mind. It's okay to tell me about your first wedding. You won't hurt my feelings."

My breath catches when I remember my wedding album that I left up at the clubhouse. Did he look at it? Did he see?

Rock must sense my mind wandered, because he squeezes me a little harder. "Don't think you have to hide those stories from me. I'm sorry if I tried to push you into marriage too fast." He stops and runs a hand over my cheek. "You took my patch, which was so important to me, Baby Doll. I didn't need to be greedy. I know you're mine no matter what. As long as I have you, the rest doesn't matter."

"You have me. I don't know why you want me, but you have me."

He shoves his hand in his pocket, uncurling his fingers. "Good, then put this back on."

My engagement ring rests in his palm, and my face breaks into a grin. "You want me to have it back?"

"Of course. We don't have to get married now. Or next week. Next month. Whenever you're ready."

I hold out my hand, and he slides it back on my finger. "I'm getting there."

"I know you are."

We're silent for a moment while I stand there and absorb the feeling of belonging again. Rock's leather and woods scent comforts my racing heart. After a bit, I step back and make a show out of patting down his leather cut, searching his many pockets.

His forehead crinkles. "What are you doing?"

"You brought my ring. Where's my patch? I want that back too."

His shoulders shake with laughter.

"It's waitin' for you."

ROCK

I can't process all the things Hope just admitted to me, so I focus on the things I can deal with.

Getting her ring on her finger.

Getting her on the back of my bike.

Bringing her home.

It wasn't anything near what you and I have.

Here I'm always worried I'm not good enough for her. That she deserves some nice citizen husband.

And then she goes and admits that.

Holy fuck.

Because there are so many things I *can't* give her, I try damn hard to give her everything else in my power.

Every fight we've had, every frustrating moment, has been worth it to hear those words.

CHAPTER TWENTY-FIVE

HOPE

Rock ends up calling one of the prospects to bring the van down and collect the few things I want to take up to the clubhouse.

"Leave it unlocked. You can trust them."

"Of course I trust them."

A warm smile turns up his lips and he curls his hand around the back of my neck, pulling me in for a deep kiss. He pulls away slowly and taps his bike. "Get on, baby."

He doesn't have to ask twice.

I hop on the back and wrap my arms around him, squeezing him tight with my legs as the bike roars to life. At the stop sign, he reaches back and pats my knee. Gentle reassurance that I'm still there. I hug him tighter and we take off.

I'm surprised by the hugs I get from everyone when we walk in the clubhouse together.

"First lady!" Murphy shouts as he runs over and picks me up. "You're back," he says, setting me down.

"I am."

"For good," Rock clarifies from behind me.

"For good," I agree.

Wrath drops a kiss on the top of my head. "Missed you, sugar."

He seems so sincere. I run my gaze over him and gasp. "Your cast is finally off!"

"Yup."

I give him a hug, which after a second of hesitation, he returns.

Teller pipes up. "Glad to see you, Hope. Prez has been miserable without you."

"Fuck off," Rock growls.

"Hey, sweetheart," Z calls as he steps out of the office. I get a quick hug from him too. "Told you everything would work out," he whispers in my ear. "Glad you're back." He winks at me as he pulls away.

"Me too."

"Where's Trinity?" I ask.

"She ran out for some supplies. She was hoping she'd be back before you got here," Wrath answers.

I quirk an eyebrow at Rock.

"I wasn't fucking around. You were coming back with me one way or another."

"I guess so."

He leans down and whispers in my ear, "I mean everything I say to you."

A shiver works through me.

"For fuck's sake, take her upstairs already. We don't need to see this," Z groans.

Wrath flashes a dirty grin at me.

"Prospects should be back with her stuff soon. Tell them to leave it outside our door."

Wrath's eyebrows shoot up, but he nods. "Got it."

I can't believe how happy I am to see everyone. "Thanks, guys."

Rock sweeps me into his arms and takes me upstairs. My throat closes when I see my things where I left them. "I figured you'd have my stuff packed in boxes down in the basement or something," I say in a hoarse voice.

"Fuck no, baby. I knew we'd work through it eventually."

"But what if I'd fallen into another eight-month depression or something? I missed you so much it physically hurt."

He sets me down and cups my face with his hands. "I wouldn't have let that happen."

"You had eyes on me?"

"Here and there."

Awareness flares in my love-soaked brain. "You had Z text Lilly when we were at Goodwill, didn't you?"

One corner of his mouth lifts in a sly smirk. "Maybe. Can't say I was happy you needed another man to help you do something I should've been doing for you."

"You mean Alex? He's a nice guy. And it's okay. I think I needed to do that without you. Having you help me get rid of our things… of Clay's things, would have felt weird."

"Fair enough. He didn't have to ask you out, though."

It's *not* fair, but the peeved look on his face sends me into a fit of giggles. "You heard about that too, huh? God, Lilly has a big mouth."

Rock's grumble sends heat streaking through my belly.

"You know I turned him down, right?"

"I heard," he says, a little less cocky. "Why?"

I can't stop fiddling with my hands and I can't meet his eyes. "You know why."

"I need to hear you say it." His low, gravelly voice flows through me like water.

"Because I love you and there's no one else for me."

ROCK

I don't think I'll ever get tired of hearing Hope say she loves me.

Still, there're things we need to talk about.

I'm not sure how to bring up the one topic that's been eating away at me most. But all of a sudden, I don't have to.

Hope's gasp lifts me out of my thoughts. She's standing by her lounge chair, staring down at the wedding album I left sitting there. The sonogram picture is tucked inside but still poking out enough to be obvious.

Now she knows I know.

Her eyes skip to me and she shakes her head. "Rock?"

Closing the distance between us, I take her hands in mine and pull her down on the chair. She picks up the album and sets it in her lap.

"You left it here, doll. I—"

"No, it's okay."

Her hand runs back and forth over the cover, but she doesn't open it. Her teeth sink into her lower lip. Finally, her fingers pluck out the little black-and-white picture. She stares at it for a while before opening her mouth. "You saw this?"

"Yes."

She taps the album. "You looked through this?"

I'm not sure where she's going with her questions, but I plan to be one hundred percent honest. "Yes. You were a beautiful bride."

Her face hardens into an expression I've never seen on Hope before. My girl is always so soft and sweet, but now... she's downright tormented.

"I was miserable."

Holy. Fuck.

The shock must be written all over my face. "Not about Clay." She taps the album. "We weren't ready to get married. I'd just finished law school. I wasn't sure if I'd passed the bar yet—there's a few months between when you take the exam and—well, it's not important. I couldn't find a job. If you don't have something lined up after graduation, it's pretty much impossible to find a job until after you get admitted."

She's babbling, stalling probably, but I've got enough patience to wait and let her get it all out.

I'll wait forever for this woman.

"Clay was waiting to sit for his licensing exams. He had a job but wasn't making a lot of money yet. We lived in this shitty one-bedroom apartment over in Ironworks. Anyway. I was on the pill, and even though I know I can be flighty, I never missed it." She looks me in the eye.

Obviously, someone challenged her on this at some point.

"Okay."

"There was a problem. My doctor switched me, and the new one made me so sick. I was either bleeding, cramping, or throwing up for like a month until they switched me to something else. Then I had this nasty kidney infection. Everyone knows if you're on antibiotics, you have to use a backup. It's like *Being a Woman 101* or something. Crap, I think the pharmacist reminded me." She shakes her head. "I forgot. I started getting sick again, but I thought it was from the new prescription. Turned out I was pregnant."

She stops, and I wrap my arm around her waist, hugging her tight. "It's okay, doll. I'm right here." She sniffles a little and I get up to bring her a box of tissues.

"I told you how useless my mother was after my dad died?"

"Yeah, I remember."

"Well, around my third year of law school is when she got remarried. All of a sudden, she wanted to play mom again. So I humored her. Clay encouraged me to try and fix our relationship. He grew up in foster care and kept reminding me I was lucky to have a mother. I felt guilty and I tried, even though I knew it was a mistake."

I have a hard time swallowing because I almost feel like I did something similar to her.

"So besides Clay, my mother was the first person I told. I was twenty-fucking-five years old. Not exactly the end of the world for me to be pregnant, other than the fact that Clay and I had no idea how we were going to afford a kid. I thought she'd be happy."

"She wasn't?"

"No. She went berserk. Everything has always been about her, and this was no different. She was 'too young' to be a grandmother. She was *so* embarrassed to have such a 'slut' for a daughter. Mind you, Clay and I had been together for more than five years by this point. But she acted like I needed to have a fucking paternity test to know who the father was."

Seeing Hope so angry pisses me off. It's unnatural on her.

"She *insisted* I have an abortion. She wouldn't let it drop."

Christ, I don't even know what to say to that. "What did Clay say about it?"

Hope looks at me like I'm nuts. "I *never* told him that. He would have lost his shit. As freaked out as we were about the financial aspect of it, we were excited about the baby. He was thrilled to have a family of his own.

"When my mother finally understood I was keeping the baby, she insisted we had to get married right away. She went behind my back and got Clay on board with her plan. He thought it would be a good mother-daughter thing to bond over wedding stuff. I knew we were eventually going to get married, so I had no good reason to say no or back out of it without hurting his feelings." She stops and takes a deep breath.

"But it couldn't just be a quickie courthouse ceremony. Oh no. She drove me nuts." She slaps her hand on the photo album, then flips it open to the first page. "I can't look at any of these pictures without remembering how unhappy I was that day."

Jesus Christ. "I'm so sorry."

"I was so stressed out. So sick all day. I kept throwing up. My mother had me so ashamed. I didn't tell anyone else I was pregnant. Clay must have told his sister at some point. I don't know. But Sophie, Mara, Lilly—I never told them."

"Baby, you had nothing to be ashamed of."

"I know. I knew it then too, but I couldn't help it. Mara was going through her own stuff with her ex. They were close to getting a divorce. So I felt really bad about all the wedding stuff I threw at her all of a sudden. I'm sure one of them suspected, since I had to run in the bathroom to puke every five minutes."

Goddamn, Z had her pegged. This story makes it clear just how much she worries about everyone else's feelings but her own. As her man, I need to do a better job protecting her. "What happened after the wedding?"

Her mouth turns up and her eyes go distant. "We scraped together some money and went to Montreal for four days. It was actually a really nice honeymoon." The smile fades to something I can only describe as anguish. "I lost the baby two days after we got back."

Motherfuck. I can't stand hearing all the bad shit my girl's been through. Never said a word to me, either. I feel so fucking useless, like I should have done something for her even though I didn't even know her at the time. I can't help but notice how she hid important shit from Clay too. Maybe if she'd shared this with him, he might have stood up to Hope's mother. Saved my girl from so much misery.

I need Hope to understand there won't be any more secrets between us.

She's quiet for a while but keeps staring at the sonogram picture. "My mother didn't come to the hospital that time either. All she said was it was a shame she wasted so much money on the wedding when it turned out not to be necessary after all."

I've never hurt a woman in my life, but Hope's mother? I want to hunt this bitch down and kill her.

"I cut ties with her after that. Told Clay it wasn't going to work, without giving him too many awful details. We spoke on the phone here and there, she came to Clay's funeral, but other than that, I kept away from her."

"Until I made you call her?"

She looks up at me finally, a sad smile stretched across her face. Her hand reaches up and rubs my cheek. "You didn't know."

Everything falls into place in that moment. Her running away when she can't cope. Her lack of confidence. How hard it is for her to open up and trust. She's basically been rejected by her own mother her whole life.

"I wish you had told me."

She shrugs. "I'm not good at sharing my feelings, Rock. It's really hard for me to let people in. You're the first person to ever know so much of me. You're unstoppable."

I'm probably a complete asshole, but I really like the way she says that.

"You still should have told me. No more, Hope. If something bothers you—no matter how small you think it is—I want to hear about it. There won't be secrets between us."

"It was so far in the past. Female trouble. No man wants to hear about—"

I cut that shit off quick. "I'm *your* man. I want to know anything and everything about you."

Her lips quirk into a brief smile. "When we met, I told you how much you freaked me out. Even then, I felt like you knew too much about me. I made such a big deal out of how I had a good marriage and would never cheat on my husband. I didn't want you to think we had some shotgun wedding... I don't know."

"Honey, I never would have thought that about you. I just wish you had told me so I hadn't pushed you into calling that bitch."

"It was too painful. I'd get sick every time I remembered that whole time period. I was so mad at myself for not standing up to her sooner. I thought I'd dealt with it and put it behind me." Her bright-green eyes, shiny with unshed tears, meet mine. "Then losing *our* baby the way I did? Rock, something must be really *wrong* with me. I feel so defective."

"Hope, you're the closest to perfection I've ever known. You heard the doctor. We can try when you're ready. They'll watch you like a hawk."

She shifts closer to me so our thighs are touching, and I wrap my arm around her. "I just know you'd be such a good father," she murmurs. "And I want to be able to give you that."

My chest tightens with the feeling that I'm meant to take care of this wonderfully strong yet fragile woman. Beyond that, I admire her. Even though she's had so many awful things happen in her life, it hasn't turned her into a bitter person. She's one of the kindest people I've ever known. "We'll figure it out together. I promise."

She pulls away. "Thank you for always being so patient and understanding with me."

The sweet, earnest way she expresses herself twists me. Cupping her chin, I stare into her green eyes and explain how things will be from now on. "Love you. And I *do* understand, but no more running away when you're overwhelmed. No more pushing each other away. This is it. I need you—all of you—and you're going to give yourself to me completely."

Tears tumble down her cheeks, but I keep going. "We have no choice but to take what life throws at us. Good and bad. You've had so much bad, Baby Doll. More than your share. But what we have is good, and I'll do whatever it takes to give you the best for as long as I'm alive."

"I need you too."

I'm so happy to hear her admit it. "We need each other," I clarify because it's the absolute truth. "Every part of me is yours, Hope. There isn't another person in this world who owns me the way you do."

Her arms band around my middle so tight she knocks me into the arm of the chair, but I hold on to her just as hard.

I'm never letting her go again.

CHAPTER TWENTY-SIX

ROCK

HOPE'S EMOTIONALLY DRAINED AFTER OUR TALK, SO I TUCK HER IN EARLY. Having her back in my bed, in my arms... I can't ever take this for granted again. With my girl right where she belongs, I sleep like the dead.

Before the sunlight even curls around the curtains, I'm awakened by Hope pressing her ass into my dick. Beside me, she stretches, and my sleepy arms wrap around her, my hand immediately groping and fondling. My face nuzzles into her hair until I find her neck. "Do that again, Baby Doll."

She mumbles out a sleepy question, so I brush my thumb over her nipples, teasing her awake. She stretches hard, her body shuddering, her ass pressing into me again.

"Morning," I whisper against her ear.

Her hand reaches back, pats my head, and she makes another contented sound.

I should let her sleep. But it's been way too fucking long. My hands work their way to her sleep pants and tug them down her legs. Above me, she lets out a soft giggle, letting me know she's been awake and messing with me.

That's okay. I can be sneaky too.

Not done teasing me, she rolls over on her stomach and lets out a few fake snores. Reaching over to my nightstand, I quietly grab a condom and roll it on. My hands rub and stroke up the backs of her legs to her ass.

I place kisses along her spine, brush her hair aside, and continue kissing along her shoulder. "Good morning, my beautiful girl."

She sleep mumbles something that sounds like, "Morning."

"Baby doll, you can keep pretending you're asleep, but I need to be inside you."

Playful, sleepy Hope vanishes. Eager-for-my-cock Hope arches her back, lifting her ass to me. The curves of her hips fit my palms nicely as I pull her up and back.

"That's my girl. I'll go as slow as I can, but I've been waiting way too long. Just the sight of your sexy ass in the air has me ready to explode."

"Mmm," she answers.

Slowly, I work my cock inside her and have to pause—feels so fucking good to be home again. She whimpers and wriggles to get me moving.

Over and over I slide in and out, setting a relentless pace.

Her hands curl into the sheets, the sight driving me into her hard and fast. But she keeps up, thrusting back against me just as hard. Sitting back on my heels, I pull her into my lap.

"Work me, Baby Doll."

This way, I can hold her. Run my hands over every inch of her and enjoy her gliding up and down my cock. She loops her arms back around my neck and turns her head. Leaning in, I take her lips in a long, lingering kiss.

With my hands gripping her hips, I lift her off me. She stretches out. Spreading her legs, she curls her finger at me in a "come here" gesture.

"I'm right here," I rasp as I fall down over her and slide back into her tight heat.

Her hands glide up and down my arms, over my shoulders, into my hair. "You should wake me up like this every day," she whispers.

"You started it, pressing your hot little ass into my dick."

An indignant expression crosses her face. "I did not."

My hands roam over every inch of her. My mouth finds one nipple, sucking it in, flicking my tongue over the hard peak. Her breathy cries only ramp me up more. My nose follows the curve of her neck, nipping and licking. She squirms, and that's my cue to speed up. Leaning back, I hook my arms under her knees, dropping her legs over my shoulders, pounding in and out of her until she screams.

"Take it."

She takes everything, crying out as she comes apart underneath me.

Shortly after, I follow and collapse on top of her. "You're so fucking perfect, Baby Doll."

"You're pretty fucking fantastic yourself, stud."

Shaking with laughter, I roll over and get rid of the condom. I give her a quick slap on her ass and she yelps. "Come here, sass-mouth."

She rolls over and lays her head on my chest. Her fingers trail the outline of my tattoos, down to the anchor on my hip.

We lie there in silence, running our hands over each other. At some point, she falls asleep, and I enjoy the feeling of having her back in my arms.

HOPE

After my morning wakeup call, it's hard to get out of bed. Even harder when Rock wraps himself around me for round two.

When we finally pull ourselves out of bed and downstairs for breakfast, I'm starving.

"Gotta feed my girl. Need to keep your energy up," Rock teases me with a smug grin.

"I think I kept up just fine."

He plants a kiss on my mouth. "Yeah, you did."

We're not the only ones getting a late start this morning. Trinity, Wrath, and Murphy are sitting around one of the tables in an awkward sort of silence. Wrath jerks his chin at us when we come in, and Trinity turns, smiling broadly.

Z joins us as we're finishing breakfast.

"Mornin'," he calls out as he walks past us into the kitchen.

I lift an eyebrow at Trinity, and she shrugs. The guys are busy discussing business in a cryptic sort of way, as if Trinity and I care enough to pay attention.

Z returns with a plate and joins their conversation.

"So don't get mad, but are you going to set a date now?" Trinity asks.

Well, that's a conversation stopper.

Rock squeezes my hand. Wrath shoots Trinity a dirty look.

I glance at Rock. "Fall?"

"Sounds good," Rock agrees.

Trinity claps her hands together. "Ooo! That will be perfect. It's so pretty up here, and the weather will still be nice so you won't freeze your ass off."

Trinity's off in wedding-planning mode. This time, I feel really good about it.

Actually, I can't wait.

Trinity taps my arm. "I know I'm not a professional, but I've been practicing. Can I make the cake?"

"Please say no, Hope. We're all gonna get fat with her making us taste-test everything," Z grumbles.

Murphy laughs and slaps his hand over his stomach. "Speak for yourself, old man. My metabolism's still in high throttle."

Wrath snorts.

Ignoring the guys, I grin at Trinity. "Of course you can. I trust you."

"Awesome. Now what about the engagement party?"

My cheeks heat up. The party should be in a few weeks. If I hadn't screwed everything up.

Everyone at the table must know—

"I never canceled anything, Hope," Trinity says soft enough that only I can hear her.

"What?"

"I had faith you two would work it out. I think we just need to change the location. We can do it here or at Rock's house."

"Trinity—I don't know what to say." Tears prick behind my eyes, and I take a deep breath so I won't make a fool of myself in front of everyone.

"You're going to need four-wheel drive in the winter up here, babe," Rock informs me, probably to stop me from getting all weepy on Trinity. He points at Murphy. "He'll help you figure it out."

Next to me, Trinity bumps me with her elbow.

"What do you like, Hope?" Murphy asks.

Confused to find myself in the middle of *this* conversation, I mumble out, "Wait, what?"

"You remember how bad it gets in the winter. Your little sedan is never going to make it up the mountain and definitely not up our driveway," Murphy explains. "You want a Jeep like Trin's?" he asks with a nod at her.

I turn to Rock, hoping he'll explain. "Uh?"

He jabs a finger toward Murphy. "Road captain. Vehicles are his job. But if you'd rather have me go with you, we can do that," he says, squeezing my hand under the table.

"Rock just terrorizes the salesmen, Hope. He's got no finesse. You're better off with me," Murphy jokes.

Rock shrugs. "Don't have time for bullshit."

"You don't seem like a truck kinda girl," Murphy persists.

Shaking myself into this bizarre conversation, I answer, "Winter is way off. Why are we talking about this now?"

Rock just shakes his head. Murphy shrugs. "Don't want to put it off to the last minute."

I huff out an irritated breath. "Okay, I don't really care. Something that gets me from point A to B, has a decent radio, and is good on fuel, because I'm terrible about remembering to fill up my tank."

Rock waves his hand in the air. "Prospects will take care of that."

"There's always enough vehicles around, Hope, if you need to borrow one," Wrath adds.

Huh. My mouth pulls into a cheeky grin. "Good to know. I wouldn't mind borrowing your bike."

His surprise is impossible to conceal, but then his eyebrows lower and his mouth curves into a smirk. "You're right. She does have a good sense of humor," he says to Rock.

When everyone stops chuckling at the idea of me taking Wrath's motorcycle for a joyride, Rock lifts his chin at Murphy. "Whatever she wants. Just let me know, and I'll move it from my account."

"Yup."

My hand settles on Rock's arm to get his attention. "Wait. I can buy my own car."

Everyone at the table falls silent. Rock's lips twitch. "Babe, you wouldn't need it if you weren't moving up here. I'll take care of it," he answers slowly.

Trinity leans over and mock whispers in my ear, "It will be easier if you just say *yes, Rock*."

Wrath snorts with laughter.

I turn and glare at Rock. "Yes, Rock," I mimic.

"Good girl," he says with a smirk.

I kinda want to kick his ass.

But it's also kind of sweet—in a bossy, overbearing, caveman sort of way.

Murphy's jazzed about going shopping for a new vehicle. He's obviously well suited to his job. "What do you think? SUV? Minivan?"

"Gosh no." I gasp, which gets a laugh out of everyone. I think about it a little more. "Nothing too big. I still need to parallel park downtown."

He nods. "Normally, I prefer American made, but I'm thinking one of those little Subaru wagons would be perfect for you. All-wheel drive. We'll put some studded snow tires on in the winter, and you'll rip through anything."

Rock rubs his hand over my back and leans over to whisper in my ear, "You won't be leaving the bedroom much next winter. I'm looking forward to being snowed in with my *wife*—a lot."

I shiver from the raw desire in his voice. I can't wait to be Rock's *wife*. Blushing, I glance down at the table. The guys chuckle at my unease.

Eventually, they turn their attention to other topics, and I sit back and enjoy the feeling of being *home*.

CHAPTER TWENTY-SEVEN

ROCK

"I noticed you steered the conversation away from the engagement party this morning," Hope says as I take her hand and lead her outside.

Stopping, I turn and grab her other hand. Our eyes meet, and her mouth turns up. Her pretty green eyes blink up at me, and I swear I could stare into them forever.

"I didn't want you to get overwhelmed," I explain. "Besides, we really do need to get you a better car for winter."

She rolls her eyes, then tugs on my hands. I take the hint and lean down. She touches her forehead to mine. "I'm not overwhelmed. I'm actually really excited." Her mouth curves into a dreamy smile. "I can't wait for you to be my husband."

There are no words to describe the pleasure I feel from hearing her say that.

I press a kiss to her forehead and tilt my head toward the woods. "Let's go for a walk."

She's quiet as we hike. Every time I turn my head to check on her, she's watching her feet. "You okay?"

"Yeah," she answers a little breathlessly.

When we reach our destination, I squeeze her hand, and she looks up.

"Rock, you kept building the house?" She gasps in her beautiful, awed way.

Circling behind her, I wrap my arms around her waist and pull her tight. "*Our* house. Of course I did. I told you—one way or another, you were always mine. Will always be mine," I add to make sure there are no misunderstandings.

"Thank you. I can't believe how much work you've gotten done."

It's true. A lot of trees have been cleared out from the spot. Foundation and walls have been poured. We're essentially looking at our basement.

Curling myself around her, I lean my chin on her shoulder and point. "That's where I'm going to set up our sex room."

Hope gasps and struggles to turn around. "What?"

I can't keep the corners of my mouth down. The expression on her face—outrage and arousal—is both funny and sexy.

"Yeah, you told me about your friend's dungeon room. *Loved* the idea."

Her jaw drops. Christ, this is fun. "Not the entire basement." I wave my hand at the foundation. "Only half of it."

While I am enjoying messing with Hope, I'm also dead serious, and I think she knows it.

After teasing her until she's giggling uncontrollably, she hiccups and can't stop. Holding in my laughter is impossible. "I'm sorry, Baby Doll."

"Jerk-hic-why-hic—" She sucks in a deep breath and holds it until they go away.

"Better?"

She nods. "Rock? I'm sorry."

All the joking has gone right out of her. "'Bout what?"

"Leaving the way I did. You said slow things down, and all I heard was rejection. And I'm sorry."

Aw, fuck. I pull her close and wrap her in my arms. "My fault, baby. I knew better than to push you like that."

"I'm glad you gave me some space to sort through things, but it scared me too."

"I wanted you to figure it out without me complicating things for you. Together or not, you were always mine."

"That's true," she whispers.

I point in the direction of the clubhouse. "You don't know how much shit they gave me."

She tips up her head and laughs. "Even Wrath?"

"Hell yes. Z nagged me every fuckin' day. Teller tried to be helpful by bringing girls up to our room."

Her hands push me back. "That little fucker!" she shrieks. "I'm *so* gonna kick his ass."

The outrage on her face is funny as fuck. Before she storms back to the clubhouse and attempts to carry out her threat, I yank her to me. "Don't worry. I gave him a solid choking."

"Good."

The fact that she doesn't scold me for hurting Teller reveals how pissed she is.

"Mmm… so bloodthirsty, Baby Doll."

"When it comes to my man, damn right," she grumbles, wrapping her arms around my middle and burying her face against my chest.

We stand like that for a few minutes. She never questions whether I took Teller up on his offer.

An almost feathery touch lifts the back of my T-shirt, and Hope's fingers stroke over my back. My cock twitches, and I squeeze her a little tighter.

She tips up her head. "Rock?"

"Yes, Baby Doll."

"Show me the basement."

HOPE

Rock's face is priceless. I'm stunned that he kept working on our house. But so happy. Now that I see the actual foundation and it seems so much more real, I don't know if I can wait another day to make it our home.

"How much longer do you think until it's finished?"

Rock takes my hand as he leads me through the doorway. "I think fall is doable if they keep at it. The hardest part was the foundation."

I'm bursting with happiness as we stroll through the empty space. There isn't much to look at yet, but it's ours.

As we walk back to the doorway, Rock turns and wraps his arms around me. "Won't be long and you can start picking out the finish stuff you want."

I tilt my head so he'll explain.

"Doors, knobs, appliances, paint... that kind of stuff."

"Oh. You don't have any opinions on paint and knobs?"

He sort of half smirks at me. "No, Baby Doll. Paint it fucking orange. As long as you're here with me, I don't care."

"You don't want some sort of man cave?"

He rolls his eyes skyward. "Babe, I've been living in one giant man cave for years. Besides, I'll have my sex dungeon."

"I'm scared to ask what *you* plan on doing in *your* sex dungeon."

"I *plan* to fuck you in it. A lot."

"You might want to stop calling it a dungeon, then."

I expected a laugh for that one—and he is smiling—but he's also got a devious gleam in his eye as he yanks me tight against him. "We can call it whatever you want," he says in a low voice that makes my insides quiver.

His hands roam down and squeeze my butt while he leans down and kisses my cheek. "We can break it in now," he whispers against my ear.

"Um, no doors." I point at the sky. "No roof."

"So? No one has a reason to come out here."

"Yeah, which is why you know the minute you get my pants off, one of the guys will decide to go on a nature walk."

Mentioning "pants" and "off" was a bad idea. Rock's all growly and fiddling with my jeans. "You need a hiking *skirt*," he mutters.

"I don't think—oh!" Talking isn't possible with his fingers stroking me like that.

He walks me backward until I bump into a wall. Then it's game on.

Or rather, pants off and cock out.

Big hands supporting my thighs, lifting me gently while keeping me pinned.

"Oh, oh, Rock!" I yelp as he pushes inside.

He tenses and cups my chin, turning me to meet his ardent stare. "Are you okay? Do you hurt from this morning?"

My hands clamp down harder on his shoulders for leverage so I can move, since he's momentarily stopped.

"I'm feeling *well loved*," I answer breathlessly. "But don't you dare stop," I add.

He nuzzles my cheek and finally starts moving again. Lazily sliding in and out. "Fuckin' love you, Baby Doll. So damn happy you're mine."

His voice is low and husky, so sexy. I clench tight around him. My hips roll with him, and he thrusts faster.

The wet sounds of sex fill the open air, increasing my excitement.

"So good." His warm breath puffs against my ear, and I whine in agreement.

Buzzing bounces through the woods, and it takes me a second to realize the noise is one of the club's ATVs.

In an effort to distract me from the fact that we're about to be caught by someone, Rock moves faster. His hand reaches between us to rub circles over my throbbing clit.

"Better come quick for me, Baby Doll," he rumbles against my lips.

My mouth opens to say, "I can't," but my body blazes with excitement as he shifts his hips enough to hit the spot that sends me over the edge.

I'm not aware of anything for the next few seconds—except how good he feels. Rock's slamming into me faster until he finds his own release. He sets me down slowly, and my legs can barely hold me up.

"Yo, prez?" Someone—Z, I think—calls out.

"Shit!" I squeak, bending over to grab my jeans so fast I get dizzy.

Rock—jerk that he is—laughs at my embarrassment.

"I told you this would happen," I hiss at him.

"Go away. We're busy," he yells back.

My pants are almost in place. "Jeez, that's as good as inviting him in," I grumble.

Of course, I'm right. Barely a second later, Z's in the doorway, laughing at us. "Hey, nymphos."

Rock keeps his back to Z. "Does 'go away' mean 'come join us' where you were raised?"

Z winks at me, and my cheeks heat up even more. I mean, we're dressed now, but it's pretty obvious what we've been up to.

"Oh, sorry, didn't hear that," he answers with a smirk, not looking one bit sorry.

Very slowly, I scratch the side of my nose with my middle finger, and Z cracks up. Rock catches me, and his mouth twists into a grin. "Don't give him any ideas."

We join Z outside. "Guys are ready for church," he tells Rock.

"Yeah, okay. We were on our way back. Didn't need to come track me down."

Z ignores him. "You want a ride back, Hope?"

Linking my arm through Rock's, I answer, "No, I'm okay. Thanks."

Rock smiles down at me. "Fun's over, Baby Doll."

ROCK

Fuckin' Z. As if I've ever missed church. And I'm not late. I'm the president. Not like they can start without me.

Next to me, Hope's somewhere between flustered and amused. "Thanks for bringing me out here," she says.

I reach down and squeeze her ass. "My pleasure."

She giggles and skips ahead out of my reach. "That too. But I mean thanks for the house... for everything."

Her fluttering hands catch my attention, and I grab them. "There's nothing I wouldn't do for you, Baby Doll."

"I know," she whispers.

"Good. Want to give you everything."

"As long as I have you, nothing else matters, Rock."

A feeling of peace settles over me hearing those words from her mouth. I wrap my arms around her. "Knew you were special the moment I saw you in that courtroom."

Mentioning that time in our lives when she was married and I couldn't have her usually brings sadness to her eyes, and I wish I'd kept the thought to myself. But today, the corners of her mouth tilt up and her eyes sparkle with amusement.

"And I knew *you* were trouble," she teases.

"Damn right."

Her grin gets bigger. "The best kind of trouble."

As we step out of the woods, I see the parking lot is full. The ATV Z used to come find us is parked next to the clubhouse, so I assume he's inside giving the guys all sorts of lurid details.

I shake my head. "Sorry our time got cut short."

"It's okay. I knew you had church. Trinity and I have a project we're working on anyway."

"Oh yeah?"

"Yup."

"Do I want to know?"

"Probably," she says with a smirk.

Fuck, I love her.

I stop her before she takes the first step up to the door. "Love you, Baby Doll."

She turns and throws her arms around my neck. "Love you too."

"For fuck's sake, you two," Wrath grumbles from the doorway. "We're all waitin' on you, prez."

Hope giggles and pulls away. "Sorry, sorry. He's all yours."

Wrath grins and holds the door open for her. "You can have him back in about an hour. Then we'll have a big bonfire later tonight."

Hope claps her hands. "Can we do s'mores?"

Wrath chuckles. "Whatever you want, sugar."

She flits around the room, saying hello to Bricks, Dex, and the others.

My brother ignores my death glare and instead quirks an eyebrow at me.

"Simmer down." I give him a more serious assessment. "You ready?"

He swings his arms and cracks his knuckles as if he's getting ready for a fight instead of a club meeting. "Yeah, I'm good," he answers.

Hope returns to my side and stretches up on tiptoes to press a kiss to my cheek. All the guys waiting outside the war room whistle and generally hassle us. Her cheeks turn red and she draws back. "Have a good meeting," she calls out as she heads down the hall toward Trinity's room.

I don't know about *good*, but our situation is more optimistic than it was a few weeks ago.

"Plants are healing, boss. Yield's lookin' plentiful," Sparky informs me once everyone gets their ass in a chair. He's grinning from ear to ear. "I think having your woman down there helped turn things around early enough."

I'm not seeing the connection, which seems to annoy Sparky. "You should send her down again. Plants liked her."

No one even blinks because Sparky says weird shit like this all the time.

"Yeah. Okay. I'll let her know." I can picture that conversation now. Hope will think it's adorable and probably run right downstairs.

Shaking my head, I turn to Teller.

"Things are good. CB's strong."

I nod at Z. "Yeah, we replaced the ones we had to let go. No shortage of college girls coming in looking to make tuition," he jokes and gets a fist-bump from Dex.

My gaze lands on Wrath next. His hands are clasped in front of him on the table, and he's coiled tight with tension. I raise an eyebrow at him, and he nods once before speaking. "Gym's good. Thinking of keeping the kid on." He pauses, and the corner of his mouth lifts into a smirk. "Supposedly, Ulfric's all freaked thinkin' you're pissed with him. Might wanna give him a call."

"Jesus Christ, what the fuck is going on with him lately?"

Wrath shakes his head. "No clue. But that little discovery was a major fuck-up. He keeps that up, you know they're gonna vote him out."

"Whatever, not our problem," I say, turning to the rest of the guys.

Murphy's got details on a run he's trying to organize over the Fourth of July. It will include the whole club, and I'm looking forward to having Hope join us for that trip.

Now that Wrath's cast is off, he's eager to jump back into club business and agrees to join Z on the next Demon drop.

I finally take the vote on introducing Loco to Sway. Surprisingly, everyone—even Wrath—agrees, with the understanding we'll make the introduction but won't have any further involvement.

Once club business concludes, I glance at Wrath. I catch his eye, and he gives me a slight nod.

"Hang tight, everyone. Wrath has an announcement."

Once that fuckery's over with and I'm confident Wrath won't dismember anyone, I run upstairs and grab Hope's property patch. Can't get the image of the cute way she patted me down looking for it yesterday out of my head. With the heavy conversation we had last night and then getting... distracted this morning, I never got to give it back to her.

I need to see it on her. *Now.*

She said she was working on a *project* with Trinity. Hell only knows what that meant.

Trinity's door is open, which is unusual. Giggling reaches me before I raise my hand to knock. Pushing the door open, I find the two of them sitting in front of Trinity's computer.

"Hey," I call out. They both jump. Trinity flicks the monitor off while Hope spins around. Her mouth turns up, and my mind blanks.

"Done so soon?" Hope asks.

Church had never seemed so long. "Yup. Come here. Got something for you."

Trinity snickers and mutters something to Hope, who turns pink. "Wrath's been a terrible influence on you," she teasingly scolds Trinity.

"Trin, you need help setting up the bonfire tonight, have the prospects do it, okay?" I tell her.

"Sure, prez."

I'm getting impatient and raise an eyebrow at Hope.

She turns to Trinity. "Later?"

"Yup."

When she gets close enough, I reach out and pull her to my side. She latches onto the door and closes it as I drag her with me.

"What's gotten into you, caveman?"

"Just missed my woman. We have some time to make up for." I didn't mean for that to come out so serious, but Hope doesn't seem bothered.

"Yes, we do. What's with the bonfire?"

My shoulders lift. "Got lots to celebrate."

She quirks an eyebrow at me. "Oh yeah?"

"Yup." I pull her vest out from behind my back. "Also, I need to see you in this tonight."

"With or without additional clothes?" she sasses.

"Now that you mention—"

She snatches it out of my hands. "Give me that."

I end up helping her into it. She humors me by turning and modeling it for me, then plants a kiss on my cheek.

My fingers trace along her jaw. "Gotta celebrate you being back home. Well, back at the clubhouse. Our home won't—"

"Rock?" she interrupts.

"Yeah, Baby Doll?"

She settles her hand over my heart. "My home is wherever *you* are."

NOTES FROM THE AUTHOR

I NEED TO ADMIT SOMETHING TO YOU—I'VE HAD A TWINGE OF GUILT EVERY
time a reader wrote to tell me they wanted to see Hope and Rock have
a baby. I've known from the beginning that was not going to happen
(there are hints in *Slow Burn* and *Corrupting Cinderella*). I also knew I
planned to have a wedding novella for them at a later point. Although,
as Cara Connelly recently pointed out to me when I sketched out the
story arc for her, it's a wedding *book*. I think her words were something
like "Uh, Autumn, that's not a novella, that's a book, and a long one at
that." All I can say is it will be different, complex, and told from four
points of view. I hope I can pull it off.

Something unexpected happened during the early reading process
for this book. My early readers had an intense emotional reaction to
Hope's ectopic pregnancy. I originally wrote it more from Rock's
perspective and his reaction to it (guilt, because Rock takes on
responsibility for everything). Diving into Hope's feelings was a much
more difficult and painful process than I expected for many reasons.

Over and over, my early readers messaged me and told me how
much the scenes when Hope is in the hospital made them cry. Now
normally when a reader tells me my work made them cry, I say thank
you, as I think it's a compliment that I've managed to put words
together that evoke such a strong emotional reaction (as a reader I feel
the same way, if a book makes me cry it's an auto 5 star for me). But
this time, readers were telling me the scenes made them cry because it
brought back memories of their own experiences of losing a baby. This
time my words were bringing people to a deeply personal and painful
place and I felt *horrible* about it.

I almost considered scrapping that entire storyline, except it had
been Rock and Hope's story all along and it felt wrong to change it. I
also knew Hope had a previous experience that she had suppressed
and this was what would be part of what triggered those memories. I
was encouraged to stick with that storyline because it was actually
cathartic. Unfortunately losing a baby isn't an uncommon experience,
but very often the painful feelings go unacknowledged. Having Hope

acknowledge and talk about it gave her an opportunity to pull everything up from her past that she'd stuffed down out of shame, so she could grieve and process it all.

I struggled to finish Strength from Loyalty. I think I really didn't want to say goodbye to Hope and Rock. Each book has started and ended in a similar place (Slow Burn starts and ends near a courthouse, Cinderella started and ended with a birthday party) and they have always started and ended in Rock's point of view. The original beta version of Strength from Loyalty ended with Hope, which if this was their very last book, would have been nice. For some reason it just didn't feel right. I kept coming back to the beginning church scene where Rock is all tense and jazzed up about the guys voting on Hope. I wanted to end it in church, but didn't want to give anything from the next book away. The second beta version ended with Wrath's announcement. But I knew if I left it that way the screams of "cliffhanger" would haunt me in my sleep. And this book was about Hope and Rock, so it should end with them. Thank you Cassie, Kari, and Virginia for nudging me in that direction.

I hope you liked my version of the property patch. The research on this, I found is limited and almost seems fictional in nature. So, I took great liberties with it, and added the details about each officer adding his patch, because it seemed like something the Lost Kings MC family would do. Having Hope accept something so foreign was a delicate process. By the way, I've been mildly amused with people who complained about Hope not turning into some badass, brawling biker-chick. That was *never* going to happen. It just isn't in her nature. Never mind the fact that Rock has said repeatedly that's not what he wants. Every time I've read that complaint, I've chuckled and said "well, you're not gonna like Book 3 then either!"

It's not as if I've hidden the fact that my series is a romanticized version of an MC. If you need the grit, gore, guts, violence, abusive treatment, and catfights, then there are hundreds of other MC books for you to choose from. I'm not your author. I am in no way dismissing those books. I read and love plenty of them myself. I just don't have it in me to write one at this point. Besides, to me there is nothing more "alpha" than a man who protects and respects the ones he cares about.

One of the core values of MC culture is respect, and I find it incredibly disrespectful to assume every club is the same. Since MC culture is a real thing and so complex, it makes sense that no two clubs are alike. As Rock observes several times throughout the last three books, each club he interacts with has a slightly different culture, and what's acceptable in one might not be in another.

With Strength from Loyalty, Hope and Rock's story now tops out at over 252,000 words. So people who didn't understand why their story was being told over three books—I don't know, that would have been one very long book. As I've said before, I am also setting up the entire series. Those who said they could have told the story in two books, well—I look forward to reading them.

Thank you everyone who has written and told me how much you love Rock. He's been hanging out in my head for over a year now and shows no signs of leaving. So those of you who have written and said you could read about Rock forever—you may get your wish.

BUT, you know who else is hanging out in my head? WRATH. He will not be denied any longer and I am so excited to finally dive into his story. Trinity is a very damaged character, but I am looking forward to getting to know her better. About 55,000 words of their story is written and I think it's a drop in the bucket. At this point I have no plans to break their story into multiple books. We'll see what happens. After the 120 hour marathon that was Three Kings, One Night, I am also looking forward to Murphy, Heidi and Axel's story (you're going to hate me) and of course, Z. Teller also has some issues that need to be explored.

My original plan was to release Wrath's book in May. With all the problems that seem to arise when planning these things out, that may be pushed back. Just know that when I do actually set a date, I hate to change it. I may not be "under contract" with a publisher, but I feel that I'm under contract with my readers, and I take that commitment seriously. If I tell you a book is coming out on a certain day, I will all but kill myself to make sure that happens. But I also want it to be the absolute best it can be.

If I left you with unanswered questions, it was probably intentional. Every scene I write goes through a "what's this scene's purpose?" checklist. My crit partners are also very hard on me in this department. Even if something didn't seem to serve a purpose in this book, I most likely plan to address it in a future book. For example, Sophie's transgressions will come to light in the beginning of Book #5.

In case you're wondering, I write these author notes last. They are unedited. At the moment, I'm on my couch with my Pug snoring next to me. I'm thinking about how amazing it is and how incredibly lucky I am that so many people have connected with my stories and want me to keep writing them.

Thank you!

Autumn

ALSO BY AUTUMN JONES LAKE

THE LOST KINGS MC SERIES

SLOW BURN (LOST KINGS MC #1)

PRESIDENT OF THE LOST KINGS MC, ROCHLAN "ROCK" NORTH, HASN'T managed to find a woman capable of making him want to curb his wild ways—until he meets sweet, innocent, married lawyer Hope Kendall.

Forced to represent the outlaw biker, Hope is rattled by her immediate attraction to Rock. Hope is a good girl in a good marriage. Rock thrills her, but she's not going to throw away everything she's built on a fling with her criminal client.

Rock respects Hope enough to leave her alone, even as he realizes he's become a little obsessed with her. When their connection endangers her life, he'll have to destroy her in order to save her.

After tragedy strikes, Rock is determined to earn Hope's forgiveness and convince her that even with their staggering differences, they're meant to be together.

CORRUPTING CINDERELLA

(LOST KINGS MC #2)

Although widowed attorney Hope Kendall cares deeply for President of the Lost Kings MC, Rochlan "Rock" North, the truth is they come from completely different worlds. Add to that the fact that they are also both headstrong people, and they have a very rough road ahead of them.

Real love isn't a fairy tale.

For Rock that means introducing Hope to what it really means to be part of his brutal and shady world, where the Lost Kings Motorcycle Club is his main focus. For Hope it means accepting the things she can't change, and understanding that Rock is a man who will do anything to keep her safe.

Love doesn't follow any rules.

As Rock continues to draw Hope deeper into his world, painful misunderstandings, past relationships, and opposition from the members of his club will threaten to drive them apart.

How do a lawyer and a badass biker with a heart of gold keep their love alive while their opposing worlds collide?

THREE KINGS, ONE NIGHT
(LOST KINGS MC #2.5)

Three short holiday stories featuring Murphy, Wrath, and Zero.

STRENGTH FROM LOYALTY
(LOST KINGS MC #3)

As a dark cloud descends over Hope and Rock's already precarious future, will a long-hidden secret push them both past the point of no return?

Struggling attorney Hope Kendall loves her outlaw biker boyfriend Rochlan "Rock" North with all her heart, but the questionable activities his motorcycle club is involved in threaten her legal career.

But does she even want this career anymore?

As a near-death situation makes their professional differences seem insignificant, a cloud descends over their personal relationship's already unsteady future.

Even though Hope seems to have finally found her niche in the club as Rock's ol' lady, can she mingle in politics with neighboring clubs as well? A trip to the Lost Kings MC downstate charter will put her to the test.

While Rock works hard to give Hope the honesty she craves without betraying his loyalty to his brothers, tension from outside forces threatens to push him to the brink. But it's the one secret Hope has hidden all along that may finally drive them apart for good.

TATTERED ON MY SLEEVE
(LOST KINGS MC #4)

Tattered on my Sleeve isn't a "typical" romance. It's not even a typical MC Romance. Prepare yourself for Wrath and Trinity's long, tattered tale of lust, fury, and ultimately forgiveness.

Lust.

Eight years ago, the Lost Kings, MC was recovering from turmoil within the club Wrath and Trinity met. Their connection was instant and explosive.

Fury.

After three perfect nights, Wrath knew she was the one. But Trinity's dark past was about to catch up to her and the Lost Kings MC was her only hope for protection. One misunderstanding leads to a mistake that locks both of them into a war to see who can hurt who the most.

Forgiveness.

Once Wrath learns the dark secret that's been fueling Trinity all this time, he'll stop at nothing to prove they're meant to be together and that she's worthy of the love she keeps denying. Can they move past their horrible pasts to become better people and ultimately forgive each other?

WHITE HEAT (LOST KINGS MC #5)

THE QUEEN ALWAYS PROTECTS HER KING.

For straight-laced attorney, Hope Kendall, loving an outlaw has never been easy. New challenges test her loyalty as she discovers how far she's willing to go to protect her man.

IF YOU HAVE HOPE, YOU HAVE EVERYTHING.

MC President, Rochlan "Rock" North finally has everything he's ever wanted. Hope as his ol' lady and his MC earning money while staying out of trouble. The only thing left is to make Hope his wife. But as their wedding day nears, an old adversary threatens Rock's freedom, the wedding, and throws the Lost Kings MC into chaos.

LOVE MAKES THE RIDE WORTHWHILE.

While the club waits for Rock's fate to be decided, Wrath has to balance solidifying his new relationship with Trinity and fulfilling his president's orders.

LOYALTY GIVES AN OUTLAW STRENGTH.

Threats from unexpected places will challenge every member, but in the Lost Kings MC, brotherhood isn't about the blood you share. It's about those who are willing to bleed for you.

BETWEEN EMBERS (LOST KINGS MC #5.5)

A companion to White Heat. Three short stories featuring Murphy, Teller, and Zero.

MORE THAN MILES (LOST KINGS MC #6)

Forbidden love is the hardest to forget...

Blake "Murphy" O'Callaghan, Road Captain of the Lost Kings MC, has the world by the balls. Money. Women. The wide-open road. It's all his, everything he wants...except the one girl he loves, the one girl who's off limits. His best friend's little sister, Heidi.

Abandoned by her mother when she was little, Heidi Whelan's familiar with heartbreak. Especially the heartbreak of falling in love with her big brother's best friend. When Murphy pushed her away, it broke her heart. Now, on her eighteenth birthday, he claims he loves her? Growing up around the Lost Kings MC, Heidi's witnessed his manwhoring ways. He'll never give that up for her. Besides, he's too late: Heidi's in love with her high-school boyfriend Axel.

Axel Ryan loves two things—motorcycles and Heidi. He signed up to be a prospect for the Lost Kings MC because it seemed like a fun way to get closer to her. Now that he's gotten a taste of MC life, he's not so sure this is where he belongs. He's confident Heidi shares his dreams for the future, so even if he chooses another road, their relationship will survive the detour.

With more than miles between them, will the deceptions they've lived with for so long be too much to overcome? Can Murphy convince Heidi that the hard roads they've traveled will lead to the most beautiful destination of all, or is he destined to ride the open road alone?

WHITE KNUCKLES (LOST KINGS MC #7)

TWO TATTERED SOULS

After countless detours, Wrath and Trinity's wedding is only ten days away. Together they've battled their demons and are ready to declare their commitment to each other in front of their entire Lost Kings MC family.

ONE BITTER ENEMY

No one is prepared for the threat that crawls out of the shadows and issues an evil ultimatum. One that places Trinity's future in danger and jeopardizes the entire club. Trinity's more than ready to put her life on the line to save the club. For her it's not a question.

AN IMPOSSIBLE CHOICE

Wrath's role as protector of the club forces him to choose between the safety of his angel or the future of the Lost Kings MC and all they've built together. But Trinity won't relent. A queen always fights for her king. She'll risk everything to hold on to the peace she shares with Wrath.

FAITH IS STRONGER THAN FEAR

When evil takes her for a ride, will Trinity's faith in Wrath and her faith in the Lost Kings MC be stronger than her fear?

BEYOND RECKLESS:
TELLER'S STORY, PART ONE
(LOST KINGS MC #8)

Blood doesn't make you family, loyalty does.

Marcel "Teller" Whelan, Treasurer of the Lost Kings MC, has always been two things—honest and responsible. At ten years old, he was already taking care of his baby sister. At eighteen, he patched into the Lost Kings MC and took a major role in shaping the club's future.

Three years ago, he thought he'd met the perfect woman, only to have her reject everything he is—a Lost King.

One bullet is a lifetime supply.

Now, after an accident that left a girl dead and Teller almost crippled, he's struggling through the darkest time in his life. His niece, sister, and Lost Kings MC family are the only things holding him together, but his reckless actions are bound to drive everyone away.

Then, in the most unlikely place, he crosses paths with her again. The woman he once thought might be his perfect match.

Love soothes our inner demons.

Sparks fly for both of them. She's the ride-or-die woman he needs, able to calm his many demons, and bring the light back into his life. But she has a secret—one that forces him to lie to his brothers.

In chaos we trust.

When Teller's brothers find out who he's falling in love with, it will create a storm of chaos for the Lost Kings MC. But if there's one thing Teller's turbulent life has taught him, it's that sometimes love is worth the chaos.

BEYOND REASON:
TELLER'S STORY, PART TWO
(LOST KINGS MC #9)

When the most toxic people come disguised as family, who can you trust?

BETRAYAL BY BLOOD *cuts the deepest.*

Teller's found his ride or die girl. The light Charlotte brings to his life has touched the darkest parts of his soul. But a devastating secret from her past resurfaces to threaten their future.

Every truth can be erased with one lie.

When a sinister truth is exposed, it forces Charlotte to question everything about herself. Even whether she's worthy of Teller's love.

The darkest betrayals never come from your enemies.

With Teller's love roaring louder than the lies, Charlotte can finally put her demons to rest. But has too much damage been done for her to prove her loyalty to the Lost Kings?

One Empire Night (Lost Kings MC #9.5)

Holiday novella featuring your favorite Lost Kings MC couples.

AFTER BURN (LOST KINGS MC #10)

One spilled secret shines a light on the throne of lies I've been sitting on for years.

A revelation with the power to test the bonds of brotherhood like never before.

Promises I've made to my brothers I burn to keep.

Vows made to my wife I swear to honor.

Through the web of tangled loyalties, one thing remains clear.

Hope is embedded in my soul.

A love so rare I've spilled blood to protect it.

Each painful piece of our pasts brought us to this moment.

Together, we've built something beautiful, significant, and ours.

And one uncovered truth could burn it all to the ground.

STAND ALONES
BULLETS & BONFIRES
Set in the same world as the Lost Kings MC
Murphy and Teller appear here.

The one man she's always wanted is now the sexy sheriff of their hometown.

Battered but not broken, grad student Brianna Avery returns to the childhood home she abandoned four years ago. With her abusive ex behind bars, Bree needs the summer to relax and recover before returning to school. But her overprotective brother decides she needs someone to babysit her in his absence, and he picks the one person guaranteed to drive her nuts.

She's the one woman he can't have.

Telling Bree no has never been easy. Four years ago, Liam Hollister did it to preserve his friendship with his best friend--Brianna's brother. Now, no matter how she tempts him, he's determined to do the right thing. As deputy sheriff of their rural area, Liam is torn between protecting Brianna and wanting her for himself.

Take a risk or lose the chance.

Spending so much time alone together challenges them both. Old feelings and hurts resurface immediately. With each hot, sweaty day, it's harder to deny their attraction.

It's going to be a long, hot summer.

WARNINGS & WILDFIRES
Wrath and Murphy appear here.

It's a hot summer morning and I'm already running late.

I'm no one's white knight, but when I see a damsel in distress, I have to rescue her.

I didn't know it would be Aubrey Dorado, the girl I swore was off-limits.

Now she's under my skin and I can't get her out of my head.

So, I did the worst thing possible and hired her to work in my gym.

Lusting after my new employee breaks my number one rule.

But each day she tempts me with her sweet personality and clever mind.

I've been burned by love before.

Romance is a risk I can't afford.

But how much longer can I resist the attraction simmering between us?

LOST KINGS MC COMING SOON
Zero Tolerance (Lost Kings MC #11)
White Lies (Lost Kings MC #12)

SOCIAL MEDIA

FIND ME ON:
BookBub
Goodreads
Instagram
Facebook
Pinterest
Spotify
Book & Main Bites
Website: autumnjoneslake.com
AutumnJLake@gmail.com
If you loved spending time with the Lost Kings MC, please, do me a favor and leave a review at your favorite retailer, Goodreads, or on BookBub. As a independent author, I rely on reviews to help get the word out about my books. A few quick words can mean so much!
Thank you!

The End

www.ingramcontent.com/pod-product-compliance
Lightning Source LLC
Chambersburg PA
CBHW071246250626

47163CB00002B/355